ONLY IN AMERICA

LUCIANO CANNUCCI

 FriesenPress

Suite 300 - 990 Fort St
Victoria, BC, V8V 3K2
Canada

www.friesenpress.com

ISBN
978-1-03-910463-1 (Hardcover)
978-1-03-910462-4 (Paperback)
978-1-03-910464-8 (eBook)

1. FICTION, THRILLERS, POLITICAL

Distributed to the trade by The Ingram Book Company

DAY ONE — BANG, BANG, OUT GO THE LIGHTS

The mosquito hovers above the desk lamp before rising to the ceiling. The slight movement catches the attention of Larry Evans, sitting uncomfortably on a hard wooden chair. He follows its flight to the ceiling, across to the far wall, and down again toward the illuminated desk lamp. The light source draws it back. It lands on a small clearing on the desk. Without hesitation, Larry slams his open hand on the desk, crushing the mosquito and swiping it off the edge. *Success!*

"What the hell are you doing?" yells the startled Robert Decker, the head of security at the Springvale Starline Hotel, sitting directly across from him.

"What? What do you mean?"

"What the hell was that about?" he says, pointing to where Larry slammed his hand down.

"Mosquito! I killed it. It was bothering me," Larry responds innocently.

"Really?"

"Yes, really! It was bugging me. I hate mosquitos. They serve no useful purpose except to annoy us with their buzzing and their itchy, scratchy bites. There's nothing good about them."

"You are wrong, Mr. Evans. Mosquitos, like most insects, have an important place in our ecosystem."

"No, they don't. They're just freaking mosquitos."

Waving his index finger, the man leans forward. "A little-known fun fact, Mr. Evans. Did you know that mosquitos help to pollinate an assortment of flowers?"

"No."

"Did you know they also help filter out waste and debris so plants can thrive?"

"Again, no."

"Did you know they also sacrifice themselves as food for many other species in our environment and, furthermore, studies suggest they affect the herding paths of caribou in the northern tundra? I think that's pretty cool, myself," the man responds with raised eyebrows and a slight smirk.

"Are you freaking kidding me? Do you know all this stuff, or are you pulling this out of your ass?"

"It is called entomology. The study of insects. A hobby of mine for many years. Now, can you please just sit there and not move or say anything?"

"Well, this is ridiculous! This whole freaking situation is ridiculous!" Larry blurts. He wipes the beads of sweat on his forehead with the back of his hand and rubs them off on his pant leg.

"Be quiet, Mr. Evans," responds the equally annoyed Decker. His assistant, standing in front of the office door all this time, shifts his stance in anticipation of any possible trouble.

Larry adjusts his sitting position on his chair to get more comfortable. The ceiling air vent directly above Decker draws his attention. Angling his head upwards he listens attentively for any sound of it functioning; none can be heard. *That explains the perspiration and the taste of stale air in my mouth.*

"Can you at least do something about the air in this room? It really is bad." Larry raises his hands to the air vent on the ceiling.

"I spend many hours in this office every day, and I don't complain about it. I suggest you do the same, sit there, and be quiet," Decker responds.

Having sat on the hard metal chair for the last few hours, Larry stands up. "I will not be quiet. I want to know why I am still here in this room." He says glancing at his watch, "it's been three fricking hours."

Decker, sitting back in his chair, gives him a stern glare. "Sit the hell down, Mr. Evans, and be quiet. I really hate having to repeat myself."

"Really, and what are you going to do? Rough me up?" Larry goads him. From what he observed during his first encounter with Decker back at the restaurant bar, he seems a little lanky and not too intimidating, given that he is head of security for the hotel. Looks can be deceiving.

"Me, rough you up?" Decker smirks in response. "Not a chance in hell! I do the verbal threats. I leave the physical stuff to the experts." He nods to his assistant.

Standing at the door is a tall middle-aged man dressed in a tightly fitted, buttoned-up blue suit. He is slightly taller than Larry and has easily fifty pounds on him, all of it muscle. He has an intimidating military-style haircut, the back and sides short and getting gradually thicker up top.

Larry hasn't paid much attention to the man in the last few hours. The man has no facial expressions to discern his current intentions.

The name on the hotel badge pinned smartly on his jacket, inches below his neckline has him as one "Reid Beckett."

"Mr. Beckett has many skills. One of them being the ability to physically intimidate a person without leaving any visible evidence." Decker smiles at Evans. "I have seen his handiwork, and I am a fan."

"Thanks, boss," Beckett says.

"Even if you do file a complaint about any alleged physical altercations, it would be your word against ours," Decker states. "Pretty sure with your current situation, your complaint will be dismissed based on the source of the said complaint."

Larry, no longer mesmerized by Reid Beckett, turns to face Decker, annoyed. "My situation? What is my situation? I have been in this fucking office for the last three hours, and I don't know why!"

"I've already told you once to shut up," Decker pushes back.

"No!"

"No?" Decker gives him a stern look. "No, what? No, you will not be quiet?"

"Why the hell should I? Nobody is answering my questions. I want an answer as to why I am in this freaking office with Mr. Rent-a-Cop," he says, glaring at Decker, "and Odd-Job here, ready to 'intimidate me,'" glancing at Beckett.

Decker, edging forward a little more, points his finger at Larry. "I said, shut the fuck up. Do you understand?"

"Fuck you," Larry yells, stands up, and swats all the objects on Decker's desk onto the floor.

Decker glances over to Beckett and nods. Beckett steps forward, grabs Larry's arms, and pushes him hard into a filing cabinet behind him. Larry, unprepared, crashes into the cabinet and collapses to the floor. The force of the hit is powerful enough that several standing file folders topple onto his head.

"That fucking hurt!" Pushing the file folders aside, Larry leans his head back slowly, looks up at Beckett, who is now standing directly over him, a menacing stare on his face. "Are you nuts?"

Larry says, softly rubbing the top of head where the file folders hit him.

Beckett does not respond.

"I did tell you to shut up, but you just wouldn't listen," Decker declares. "Every action has an equal and opposite reaction. Physics 101."

Larry, still reeling from the assault, glares back at Decker. "You are going to pay for this, you asshole."

Beckett glances quickly over to Decker, who nods. Beckett, seemly knowing the drill, inches toward Larry, propped up against the filing cabinet. He slams the side of his right calf against Larry's face. Larry yells out in pain before crashing to the ground again. Beckett steps back and turns to face Decker.

"Too hard?" Beckett asks with a hint of apology.

"Not hard enough, if you want my opinion," Decker says. "You might as well get some wet paper towels and some aspirin. He is going to wake up with one hell of a headache." Decker stands and looks up at the air vent above him. Sniffs the air. "He's right, the air is bad in this office. I'm going for a walk. I might as well pick up the aspirin. Buzz me if he snaps out of it before I get back." Decker opens his office door and exits.

Beckett shuts the door behind him.

DAY ONE — ARRIVAL IN NEWARK

Ten hours earlier

Larry looks out his window as the plane flies over Newark during its descent towards the airport. The flight has been "uneventful," as most flight captains prefer to state when asked. The Delta Air Lines Airbus A321-200 makes a final turn to line up its approach into Newark Liberty International Airport.

The Newark tower operator announces over the captain and co-pilot's headphones.

"You are cleared to land on runway two-two-right. Approach is final."

The Captain responds, "Roger. Cleared to land on two-two-right." She glances over to her co-pilot. "Bob, let's take her in."

The co-pilot acknowledges the request, "Roger that, Captain. Taking her down."

"Ladies and Gentlemen, this is your captain speaking. We have received clearance for final approach into Newark Liberty International Airport after that brief delay. Local time is 7:35 p.m. The current temperature is a respectable eighty degrees Fahrenheit, but with a humidity level of eighty, it will feel closer to ninety degrees. The weather forecasts a 60 percent chance of rain this evening. The flight crew would like to extend our thanks for choosing Delta Air Lines. Flight attendants, prepare for landing, please. Cabin crew, please take your seats."

Following the captain's announcement, the lead flight attendant jumps onto the intercom. "Ladies and gentlemen, as we start our descent, please make sure your seat backs and tray tables are in their full, upright positions. Please make sure your seat belts are securely fastened and all carry-on luggage is stowed underneath the seat in front of you or in the overhead bins. Thank you."

The flight attendants hustle to their designated sections to verify all passengers have followed the broadcasted instructions. With all that done, they take up their positions at the back of the plane beside the wall of food refrigeration and heating terminals.

The lead attendant looks over to the others and asks, "So! What's the verdict, ladies?"

The attendant closest to her crouches over. "Definitely seat 12A," she giggles.

"I wholeheartedly agree with that," the lead attendant responds.

The third attendant nods also. They check their respective seat belts and wait for the flight to end.

Larry Evans, the object of their admiration, occupies seat 12A. Unbeknownst to him, the flight attendants have taken an informal survey on the cutest guy on the flight. The one time he got up from his seat, the attendants got a clear view of his ass in his tailored casual pants along with his height: a tall man at just over six feet, two inches. He is slender in build with wide shoulders, but he does not carry himself as the athletic type. He has brown eyes and dark hair with the specks of grey above his ears being the only indication of his being in his early forties. His clean-shaven look does not help with figuring out his age. Apparently, it was sufficient to his taking first place in today's flight's survey.

The airplane makes a perfect landing with no skipping on the tarmac or any sideways movements. The air flaps on the wings kick in, and the plane slows down, causing some of the passengers to inch forward in their seats while grasping their armrests for comfort.

While the plane turns off the runway and taxis toward the gate, the lead flight attendant's voice comes back on the intercom. "Ladies and gentlemen, welcome to Newark Liberty International Airport. For your safety and comfort, please remain seated with your seat belts fastened until the captain turns off the fasten seat belt sign. This will indicate we have parked at the gate and it is safe for you to move about. At this time, you may use your cellular phones if you wish. Please check around your seat for any personal belongings you may have brought on board with you, and please use caution when opening the overhead bins, as heavy articles may have shifted around during the flight.

"If you require assistance in disembarking the plane, please remain seated until all other passengers have deplaned. One of our crew members will then be pleased to assist you. On behalf of Captain Baldwin, Delta Airlines and the entire crew, I would like to thank you for joining us on this trip and we are looking forward to seeing you on board again soon. Have a nice evening."

Larry, waiting for his turn to get up from seat and proceed done the narrow isle and out, pulls out his cell phone to check for any new messages. Several pop up but only one grabs his attention. He clicks a button to open the body of the message and starts reading it. His eyes narrow as he takes in the content of the message, oblivious to the person who stops in front of him.

"You getting up buddy?" A passenger asks Larry. Larry nods, pockets his phone, gets up quickly, grabs his laptop case from the overhead bin and hurries down the aisle.

DAY ONE — NEWARK

Eight hours earlier

The city of Newark, New Jersey, is home to over a quarter million people. It is the most populous city in the state of New Jersey and one of the oldest in the USA. Arriving from New Haven Colony, Puritan colonists settled it in 1666.

Today, it is the home of the Newark Liberty International Airport, one of the busiest airports on the East Coast. It is also one of the oldest airports. Built originally in 1928, it expanded during World War II and several more times as the population grew. Currently handling over forty million passengers a year and over four hundred thousand flights, it is also one of the hardest to navigate in and out of.

Tens of thousands of people stream in and out of the gates, rushing to connecting flights or navigating to exits. Keeping the whole operation running smoothly is a mammoth undertaking, handled by several thousand employees. Every detail, be it a delayed flight, broken passenger carousel, or even a power failure, can have a ripple effect across the whole airport—not to mention flight schedules across the country.

This afternoon, a flight from Orlando encountered a front tire blow-out on landing, and the plane needed to be pulled back to the arrival bay by the emergency ground crews, thus delaying about a dozen or more flights queued up behind it.

The delay, even for the twenty minutes it took to clear out the plane from the runaway, was enough to crimp the departure of numerous other flights waiting on connecting passengers.

For others, whose destination was Newark, the delay was only a minor inconvenience and not something worth complaining about.

Larry Evans was not inconvenienced by the delay. As a senior sales manager for a software company called Commlink Services, he always makes sure to arrive at his destinations a day ahead of any scheduled meetings. Planning is the key to his success in his dealings.

For the next four days, Larry will be staying in Springvale, New Jersey, a small city on the outskirts of Newark. A large multinational company is looking to implement two-tier authentication into their internal systems for outside vendors—much-needed network security that will protect corporate computers from increasingly sophisticated hackers. They often hold a company's network and data hostage via crypto locking, demanding a ransom before releasing the system back to the company. The solution that Larry's company provides is state of the art, and to date, impregnable.

Larry picks up his travel baggage that he was asked to check in; the flight was overbooked, and the overhead storage was at a premium. He wrestles his way out of the overcrowded baggage terminal where parents and their overtired kids annoy each other. He heads outdoors to the taxi stand and comes to an immediate stop.

The heat and humidity hits him before he sees the lineup. From a quick eyeball count, easily a hundred like-minded passengers are lined up ahead of him like cattle being led to a slaughterhouse.

He peers up at the cloudy dark sky and contemplates the possibility that rain will start soon. He will still be stuck in the slow-moving taxi line. Frustrated, he steps out of line, pulls out his cell phone, and launches his Uber app. Within minutes of launching the app and reviewing multiple pickup options and their fare price, his ride is confirmed and ready to pick him up within five minutes at the designated Uber pickup area. He confirms with the Uber contact that the ride is equipped with air conditioning.

Why did I even bother lining up? He wonders. *I guess old habits are hard to break.* He surveys the area and notices the Uber pickup area. He smiles at the people he passes in the slow-moving cattle roundup.

As the Uber driver pulls away and they pass the taxi stand and the still ever-growing line, Larry shrugs his shoulders. It's a shame that the taxi business has not kept up with the times. Either you adapt to the changing times or you go the way of the dinosaurs.

The traffic is surprisingly light, he thinks to himself. He leans up and glances over the driver's shoulder to the speedometer. Fifty miles an hour. Being a child of the British measuring system and only learning the metric system during high school, he has adapted quickly. A quick mental conversion to metric gives him a speed of about eighty to eighty-five kilometres per hour. *Not bad.*

Larry pulls out his cell phone again, selects a number, and puts the phone to his ear. Waits for the dial tone and the pickup.

"Yeah, it's Larry. I got your text message. I just arrived in town. Running a little late due to flight issues in front of us, but everything is OK. Is everything ready for our meetings this week?" He pauses for an answer.

A reassured smile crosses his face. "Good. See you then." Larry turns off the phone and sits back. Then he leans forward to address the driver. "Excuse me, but how much time before we get to the hotel?"

The driver gives him a glance via the rear-view mirror. "Sir that will be about another twenty minutes. Traffic is very good today."

"Thanks."

"Do you have an appointment to get to? I can speed up."

"No, not today. I am good. No rush." He closes his eyes, not caring so much for the Newark scenery.

DAY ONE — CHECK IN AT THE SPRINGVALE HOTEL

―――

Seven hours earlier

The ride to the hotel is quiet and uneventful, but Larry, being a light sleeper from years of travelling all over North America along with parts of Europe had to constantly remain focused while in transit to avoid any missed connections or other travel arrangement, snaps awake when the Uber driver hits a small bump on the road. His senses kicked in to quickly take in his surroundings. He peers outside the car window to take in the sights; they're still on the highway, headed toward Springvale.

He gives up on napping and pulls out his cell phone again. He scans through his apps. Not really wanting to read from any of the dozen newspaper apps he has installed, he settles for one of the several weather mobile applications instead. Next, he scans through the daily and hourly forecasts for this region and marvels at the discrepancies between what he sees outside the car window and what the application is predicting. Being a weather forecaster is the only job where you can be wrong easily 90 percent of the time and never be fired. *I would love to have that job*, he thinks to himself.

Thirty minutes later, Larry Evans arrives at the Starline Hotel in Springvale, New Jersey. Even though the ride took ten extra minutes than what the driver estimated, Larry still gives him a generous tip and a good review on the Uber app. He can expense the charge when he submits his travel receipts.

He steps out of the Uber and gives the sky a quick glance; the dark clouds have changed to puffy white. Forecasted rain not happening. *What a great job to have.*

Larry stands in front of a simple three-storey hotel. No balcony views, just sealed windows. With three floors at about thirty to forty rooms per floor, he figures that there are just over a hundred rooms of different configurations. Springvale is not famous for its tourism, so the rooms are probably geared toward business accommodations. His chances of getting a room with a single king-sized bed are good tonight. Analyze the situation, compile the data and come up with a conclusion. He prided himself on being right on most occasions.

He grabs a hold of his luggage, a wheeled bag with his laptop bag strapped onto the extended handle. He walks through a double set of automatic sliding doors, leaving the heat and humidity behind him.

As he approaches the front desk, the night front desk manager looks up from his screen monitor. "Good evening, sir. How can I help?"

Larry nods and reaches into the inside pocket of his suit. He quickly pulls out his wallet and passport—Canadian. He pulls out his credit card from the wallet and places both items on the counter. A veteran of hotel stays, he knows the routine.

He glances at the gold-plated name tag pinned right above the manager's shirt pocket. Howard. Always somebody who goes the extra inch when dealing with the service industry, Larry addresses him politely. "Good evening, Howard. I have a reservation for four nights under the name Evans. First name, Larry."

"Thank you, Mr. Evans," Howard says in an equally pleasant manner. "It will be just one moment as I bring up the details of your reservation." He returns his focus to his monitor.

"No worries. I'm just glad to be indoors again. The humidity outside is nasty," Larry exclaims.

Howard glances quickly in response before returning attention to his screen. "Yes, unfortunately, we are expecting it to stay with us all week long."

"We all have to make do." Larry says.

"Mr. Evans, we seem to have a small issue with your reservation. It seems like all the rooms with a single king bed are taken, we only have rooms with double beds remaining. We will honor the lower price. Will that do?" Howard asks.

"Not the end of the world. That will be fine." Larry responds.

He types a few keystrokes on the keyboard and grins in satisfaction, looking back up. "Everything is in order, sir." He pulls out a blank electronic key card from a desk drawer below the keyboard and taps it against a card reader to the side of the screen. All done. He places the key card on the elevated counter between them.

"Here you go. You are in room 213. The air conditioning controls are to your immediate right against the wall as soon as you enter your room. You might want to adjust those right away. The elevators are to the right and down the corridor. Is there anything else you need, sir?"

Larry pauses. He stares at Howard, nods in acknowledgement and then shifts his attention to the right of the reception area where he spots the snack bar stand with an assortment of overpriced chips, chocolate bars, and drinks ranging from water to bottled iced coffees and bottles of domestic beer. *No foreign beers at all.* Switching his survey of the reception area to the left, he spots across the floor, a dozen small dining tables with surrounding chairs, mostly empty, and a polished, dark wood-framed glass wall behind them with a bar and a dozen stools. A man and woman are huddled in what seems to be a deep discussion.

A woman in a tight dark blue dress is seated several stools to the right of them. *Enough distance to avoid hearing any of their nasty whispers*, he thinks to himself. Her dark red hair covers the open back area of her dress.

"Anything else sir?" the front desk manager asks.

He snaps out of his momentary trance. "Eh, yes. The bar. How long does it stay open tonight?" Larry inquires.

"The bar is open till eleven every night. We have a generous assortment of liquor and domestic beers."

He glances quickly over to at the bar scene and then back to Howard. "You don't have any imported beer?"

"Not enough demand."

"Not even Canadian beer?"

"No, sir."

"Labatt?"

"Nope."

"Molson?"

"Nope."

"Alexander Keith's?"

"Sir, no imports!" the front desk manager exclaims in polite frustration. "We can, however, have one of our staff members deliver some tomorrow. There will be a charge, but if you order enough for your stay, it might be worth your while."

"Nah, our accounting department goes through our claims line by line with a surgical knife. Not worth the hassle and headaches."

"Very good, sir."

"Well, then, I will need to make do. Thanks. I might come down later."

"An additional note. The bar closes at eleven, but the kitchen closes at ten thirty, in case you are looking for a light meal."

"Thanks for the tip. I'll keep that in mind. Good evening." Larry reaches over the counter and retrieves his passport and credit card along with his room key. He pockets them, turns around, grabs his wheeled suitcase with the strapped-on laptop bag, and takes off down the corridor toward the elevator bank.

Howard watches Larry as he rounds the corner and disappears. He shifts his focus toward the bar area across the floor and towards the bartender, in particular. The bartender, in turn, had also been tracking Larry's progress towards the bank of elevators before glancing over to Howard. He nods his head in acknowledgement. Howard returns the gesture.

DAY ONE — THE HOTEL ROOM

Six hours earlier

Larry exits the elevator and spots the room direction signs on the opposite wall. Rooms 201–212 to the left. Rooms 213–224 to the right. He proceeds down the right corridor. The carpets have seen better days from the constant traffic of the hotel guests over the years. The lighting along the walls is bright, and the door numbers are easy to spot.

He finds his room and opens the door. He drags his suitcase inside and closes the door behind him. He spots the air conditioning control panel and has no hesitation adjusting the setting to lower the current temperature in the room from seventy-eight degrees down to cool sixty-eight. In his head, doing a quick calculation to figure out what twenty degrees Celsius converted to in Fahrenheit. The ventilation system kicked immediately as cool air could be felt from the air vents overhead.

He takes his jacket off and hangs it on one of a dozen available hooks. He pulls out his phone from the inner jacket pocket and places it on the counter along with the electronic door key. Unstraps the laptop bag from his suitcase handle and lies it flat on the desk. He picks up his suitcase and places it on one of the beds.

He removes the combination lock, pulls the zipper all around, and flips over the top of the suitcase.

Inside, neatly packed and sorted are four dress shirts, two pairs of folded pants, four pairs of dress socks, underwear, and a small assortment of T-shirts and other items. All planned out for the duration of his trip.

He transfers each item to the three empty drawers across the room until they're all neatly unpacked and sorted. He walks over to the window, pulls open the dark, heavy cloth curtains, and peers out the window. The second floor provides a spectacular view of the dining room roof, three vents, and air conditioning units. In the distance is one of the giant mega malls that dot the country. A consolidated shopping experience under one roof, making it more efficient for the average person with limited time on their hands.

Only the best view for a senior sales manager. *Man! I need to talk to our travel booking agent when I get back to the office,* he thinks to himself. Since nobody is around to listen to him rant, Larry turns, faces the room, and shrugs.

He picks up his phone from the counter, punches in a number, and puts it up to his left ear. He waits for the connection to go through. "Hi, it's me. Can we meet?" A pause. "See you then." He hangs up, tosses his phone onto the spare bed. Satisfied.

DAY ONE — THE HOTEL BAR

———

Four hours earlier

Larry Evans, after spending the better part of the day travelling to Springvale, is in a clean set of clothes and refreshed after having a hot shower. He tucks his laptop case in his now-empty suitcase and places it near the edge of the table between an armchair and desk chair. He pockets his passport, wallet, room key, and exits his room.

Arriving downstairs to the main floor, he makes his way out of the elevator and heads toward the main exit. He passes the front desk and nods to Howard, who is still managing things. Howard nods back.

Larry stops short of the automatic doors and looks outside. *Do I want to search for a local restaurant, or should I stay in the hotel and grab something at the bar?* He peeks over at the bar. There are only two people being served by the bartender. *Service should be quick,* he thinks to himself, *and it's stifling hot and humid outside. Easy decision.*

Larry turns and makes his way to the bar. He crosses the mostly empty dining area. A couple eating a light meal or appetizer occupy a table near the window overlooking the front entrance. They seemed to have been at it for a while, as the shared dish between them is almost empty. Good choice; it is too late, in his opinion, for a three-course meal. Anyways, the kitchen probably has a shortened menu at this time. Not a big problem. He's down here for a relaxing drink and to see if there are any hockey games on the TVs behind the bar.

The other couple, at the end of bar, that he had noticed earlier when he checked in are still in deep conversation. The single woman with the exposed back is nowhere in sight.

Larry grabs a stool centred along the length of the bar to distance himself from the couple; he doesn't want to be intrusive, but he will still be within hearing distance of their conversation in case he gets bored. He glances over towards the wall that is behind the bar to catch what is playing on the three screens. The two on each end display a basketball game. On the centre one is some CNN report showing the current president talking nonsense again.

Politics have become so partisan that the politicians are losing sight of the endgame, taking care of the entire country. So glad I do not live here.

Not that my country is immune. It is not, but to a much lesser extent, or maybe it is not sensationalized as much in the mainstream media or the some of the lesser known social media outlets with questionable agendas. Polarized agendas has taken over the political climate resulting in few bipartisan interests as most of the players are driven by their own self-preservations. Anybody with a large bank account and wealthy donors who are willing to bankroll their candidacy can run to become the most powerful person in the world. Something is wrong with this system, but nobody is willing to change it.

In the end, there are no hockey games tonight for Larry's viewing pleasure. At least basketball is a half-decent alternative.

Baseball isn't really a sport, Larry thinks for himself, but this is not something that he will utter in the USA.

Larry looks over to the man behind the bar, trying to grab his attention with a subtle wave. The bartender: middle age in appearance, slim with good hair and a flair of confidence as he expertly puts together exotic drinks for the couple at the end of bar finally spots Larry and nods at him. He casually slides over on the opposite side of the bar.

"Hey. How are doing?" The bartender asks.

"Good, thanks."

"First night at the hotel?"

"Yes, just got in," Larry says, gazing at his nametag, "Barney," he responds.

"Well, what can I get for you tonight?"

"Do you have any imported beer?"

"Sorry, we only carry domestic beer."

"Really, none whatsoever? I noticed the front desk concession stand didn't have any, but I had high hopes you guys at the bar would come through and save the day," Larry states, disappointed.

"Don't have much demand for them."

"Not even Canadian beer . . . Molson, Labatt?"

"Sorry, sir, only domestic beer."

"OK, OK. I get it. Kind of disappointing, but I get it. Laws of supply and demand takes precedence. Give me the strongest beer you have."

"Corona coming up," Barney exclaims with a grin. He turns around and walks over to one of the many under-the-counter fridges to grab one. He gently places the bottle onto a beer coaster that he expertly places on the bar milliseconds before the beer hitting it. An exercise he's probably done thousands of times.

"Thanks." Larry smiles at him.

Barney smiles back. "Anything else, sir? Perhaps a quick review of our evening menu? You said you just arrived. So you must be famished or did you eat some of that airline food they serve these days?"

"Definitely famished and I skipped on the airline food, so, yes, I think I will grab a bite. Thanks."

"Not much else to do on a quiet night like tonight."

"You got any hockey on those, by chance?" Larry asks, pointing to the overhead screens.

Barney gives the screens a quick glance and then turns back. "Sorry, but management directives. One sport event and one news event. For sports, basketball trumps hockey these days, especially late in the season."

"That's a shame."

"Tell me about it. I am a New Jersey Devils fan. They might have a chance this year in the playoffs, and the game is on right now." Barney shakes his head in disappointment.

"So, why don't you just change the channel?" Larry asks.

"Nope, the ass at the reception will rat me out. He's been trying to score some brownie points with upper management ever since he got here."

"OK, forget about it. I don't want you to get in trouble. Thanks," Larry says, surprised by his openness.

The bartender reaches under the counter and pulls out a menu. "Here you go."

"Thanks, Barney."

"You are welcome."

"By the way, I couldn't help noticing the tattoo on your arm."

Barney rotates his arm instinctively. "Yeah. Wasn't thinking too much when I made that decision."

"Pretty cool. What does it signify, if I may ask?"

"Sure, no worries. It was rather an impulse decision on my part. The rose and the dagger signify the balance between love and death. Beauty and destruction and all that stuff."

"Interesting," Larry exclaims.

"Actually, not really. I was pretty drunk when I got it done with a group of buddies, and it was cheapest tattoo I could afford."

Larry chuckles. "Well, I'll keep your secret, Barney." Larry picks up the menu—simple with a dozen or so options. A club sandwich and fries, some burgers, and several healthy salads. Not for him tonight. You don't mix beer and salad. A beer and burger, absolutely. A beer and club sandwich, maybe. But adding in greasy fries seals the deal.

"Excuse me," Larry says, getting the bartender's attention again. Barney returns.

"That couple sitting outside in the dining area," Larry says, turning slightly to indicate the woman and man just getting up to leave. "What did they order? It looked interesting."

Barney pauses for a moment. "I think it was a nacho platter. Straight vegetarian."

"Really, what's the fun in that?"

"Exactly, I agree. I would toss in some beef or sausage, or for a slightly healthier option, I'd add some sliced BBQ chicken strips."

Larry smiles and scans the menu quickly. He inches back slightly, snaps the menu closed, and places it firmly on the bar counter. "I'll take the burger. Are the fries greasy, or are they those plain oven-baked ones?"

"Sir, in New Jersey, we pride ourselves in only the greasiest of fries that put a protective coating around our arteries."

"Good, I need a bit of that. So, I will go with the burger, all dressed, extra pickle on the side, and fries."

"Ketchup for the fries?"

Larry thinks for a second. "Do you have any spicy mayo?"

"Spicy mayo? For the fries?" Barney frowns.

"Absolutely," Larry chuckles. "Have you never had spicy mayo with your fries?"

"Can't say I have."

"Picked it up in Belgium several years ago. They have an assortment of mayo flavours over there. You should try it some time," Larry advises.

"OK. Food for thought." He smiles and departs with the order.

Larry watches as the bartender rings in the order on the smart console that communicates with the kitchen. No more little white slips of paper to pin on a revolving wheel.

With his attention focused on the bartender, Larry senses a feeling as a hand gently caress his right forearm. Startled at first but quickly regaining his composure, he alters his attention to the attractive woman with a tight blue dress and long dark hair who has silently slipped into the seat beside him. He gazes her over slowly. Taking in every detail of her face and figure.

"So, do you want some company? You seem to be here alone."

"What gives you that idea?"

"Earlier tonight when you arrived, I saw you in the reflection over the bar. It extends over the dining room to a great view of the front desk."

Larry examines the reflection off mirror and is able easily see an almost panoramic view of the reception area passed the dining room. She's right. The view is clear. "Good observation."

She smiles.

"I gather you are here alone also. I saw you earlier tonight when I arrived. At least, I saw your back. You were sitting on the stool I am currently occupying."

"Very observant of you, Mr.?"

Larry pauses. What is she doing? What's her angle? He looks her over again. Her right hand is still resting on his arm. He peers down at it. He leans over slightly toward her, not too much. "The name is Evans. Larry Evans."

"Well . . . nice to meet you Evans. Larry Evans." She smiles at him and straightens up. "So, Larry, why don't you buy me a drink, and we can talk some more?"

"Sure! What do you like?"

"Martini. Two olives."

Larry turns to Barney, raises his hand slightly to get his attention. "Yes, sir?"

"Martini. Two olives for the lady. Another one," he says, indicating the beer, "for me."

Barney walks away to attend to the order.

"So, Larry." She pauses as she looks into Larry's eyes. "What are you doing in our lovely city of Springvale?"

"Just came in from Montreal on business," he says.

"Oh. Canadian?" she asks.

"Been living in Montreal for a good part of my adult life, but I was born in a smaller city out West in Canada. A place most people have probably never heard of unless you are a fellow Canadian. Saskatoon." He smiles.

"Sassoon?" she replies with a confused stare.

"Saskatoon. I was born in Saskatoon."

"OK. I would stick to Montreal. People know that place."

"I'll take that advice."

"So, what does Larry from Montreal do?"

"The woman asks a lot of questions." He grins, but continues. "I work for a software company that provides end-to-end communication solutions and internal security protocols for Tier-1 clients."

"Tier-1?" she asks.

"Companies with a lot of money to spend." He chuckles. "And I am very good at it."

"Very good! How good?" she asks.

"I have only been with the company for the last six months, but I have already closed four big deals, all in mid-eight figures."

"That is most impressive, Mr. Evans," she exclaims.

"The company is very happy," he acknowledges.

Barney delivers the martini to the woman.

She gives him a wink and smile. "Thanks, Barney." Picking up the glass, she turns to face Larry and rewards him with the same smile. "Thank you, Mr. Evans. Cheers."

Larry raises his beer bottle in acknowledgement. They both take small sips from their drinks. "OK. Enough about me," he says. "You don't strike me as a local of Springvale. You look more like a big city girl."

She smiles. "Should I take that as a compliment?"

"No reason to insult a lady I just met, especially one as lovely as you." It's his turn to smile.

"Well, thank you, Larry, but what gave it away?"

"Let's start with the fine stylish dress you are wearing. Definitely not off the rack."

"Definitely," she states. "Continue."

He looks down to her hand still resting on his arm. "Finely manicured nails, expertly painted, professionally done."

"Good, continue."

"Your hair."

"What about my hair? You don't like it?"

"I do. I enjoy the look of a woman with long hair," he says.

"So, only women with long hair are big city girls?"

"Not at all, I am not finished yet. Your figure-fitting dress is the result of a disciplined exercise regime, possibly from a personal trainer. Something that you don't readily find in a small town like Springvale."

"His name is Raymond." She says, winking. "Go on!"

"Your accent."

"What about it?"

"You don't have a noticeable one," he states.

27

"Go ahead. I am intrigued by your keen observations."

"Finally, your natural beauty. The little makeup you use only enhances your looks and does not distract from them. You're a person in control of your image."

"Well done, Mr. Evans." She looks straight into Larry's eyes. "Charlotte!"

"Charlotte?"

"That is my hometown. Charlotte, North Carolina."

"OK, I was leaning toward the suburbs of Washington, DC."

"Not too far away. I spent some time in DC during my younger days."

"I guess not too long ago!" He smiles mischievously.

She leans toward him, with her right hand slowly inching up his arm. She places her other hand on the upper part of his leg for support. She whispers into his right ear, "Why, Mr. Evans, are you trying to seduce me?"

This time, Larry pulls back slightly, triggering her to do the same. They face each other. A silent moment passes. Larry pulls back even farther as she removes her hand from his leg. He pushes back his stool to rise, surprising her.

Confused, she states, "Did I do something wrong?"

"No," he blurts, realizing that he doesn't even know her name. "Ms. . . . ?"

"Amanda," she quickly responds.

"I am sorry, but I do not make it a habit of doing this," he says, confused.

Amanda is taken aback. "What exactly do you mean by that, Mr. Evans?"

"Well . . . I mean," he hesitates. "Well, clearly you are not here in this hotel on business matters. I mean, just look at your outfit." He waves his hand up and down in her direction.

"A minute ago, you found my outfit radiant." Her voice is slightly elevated. "Did you not?"

"It was a simple, innocent compliment."

"Your compliment," she states, "and keen observations are far from innocent and definitely not simple."

Larry is taken aback. "Why are you getting so upset, Amanda?"

"I am getting upset because you are accusing me of being someone of few moral values."

"Well, you did accuse me of trying to seduce you—"

Amanda's hand slaps his right cheek. Larry's face stings. He falls back but grabs the edge of the bar counter before losing his balance. He gets up and puts his hand to his cheek. Amanda stands up from the bar stool and is looking at him in anger.

"What the hell was that?" Larry says.

"I will not be insulted by you!"

She picks up the martini glass off the bar and tosses its contents at Larry. Most of the liquid hits him just below his chin and onto his shirt.

This time, it is Larry's turn to raise his voice. "Again, what the hell are you doing?" Larry blurts as he tries to brush some of the drink off his clothes. "Clearly, you're insulted because you did not get the results you were looking for tonight."

The couple at the edge of the bar stop their hushed, intimate huddle to look in Amanda and Larry's direction. Barney approaches the centre of the bar.

Amanda swings with her left hand to strike Larry again, but she misses as Larry quickly sidesteps it. Surprised, but not totally, she swings with her right hand. She misses Larry again by mere inches.

"Are you done?" Larry says. Frustration and restraint are setting in at the same time.

"What's going on here?" Barney calls from behind the bar.

"This man—" Amanda says, pointing at Larry.

"This woman is batshit crazy," Larry says. "She slapped me in the face and tried to do it several more times. Didn't you see her?"

"I am not batshit crazy as you stated," Amanda claims, inching toward Larry, preparing to strike again. "He accused me of being a slut."

"I did no such thing!" Larry replies as he repositions himself in anticipation of another attack.

"Lying bastard!" she yells, takes another step forward again, and swings at him again. Larry backs up to avoid the flying fist.

Amanda advances, swings furiously again in frustration without success. Larry, having had enough, steps forward and raises his arms in surrender, trying to calm her down.

Surprised by his sudden forward movement, she steps back, catches the raised border along the bar with one of her high heels, loses her balance, and stumbles back. With her hands extended forward, she is not quick enough to grab anything as she falls backwards. She hits her head on the bar floor runner and lies motionless.

Larry, stunned by the sudden turn of events, stares at Amanda's body on the floor.

Barney, equally surprised, by what just happened, rounds the edge of the bar and hurries over to Amanda. The couple at the end of the bar also approach.

Barney leans over to examine her. "Call 911 for an ambulance, and call the police," he shouts to the front desk.

Without hesitation, the front desk manager picks up the phone and places the call.

"The police?" Larry asks. "What for?"

The bartender turns to Larry. "You assaulted her. I saw it. I am pretty sure the couple behind you witnessed the same thing."

Larry turns to face them. They both nod their heads in unison.

"What the hell is going on here?" he asks, exasperated. "This is a joke. She clearly struck me first and repeatedly swung her fists at me." Pointing at Amanda, Larry proclaims, "She should be the one who should be arrested."

"The only place she is going is the hospital," Barney responds as the front desk manager, followed by two other staff members, approach.

"Well, I am not sticking around," Larry says. He starts to move away, but the front desk manager blocks him. The other two staff members take up position immediately behind him.

"Sir, please step back and sit down until the police arrive," The front desk manager asks.

"I didn't do anything! Are you blind? I did not touch her," Larry proclaims in frustration.

"Sir, please step back and sit down until the police arrive," Barney repeats as the front desk manager and the staff cut him off from any exits.

Larry, clearly outnumbered, decides that a retreat is his best option. He steps back and collapses on the stool.

DAYS ONE TO TWO — THE BACK ROOM WAITING GAME

——

Three AM

Many people never get to see what goes on behind the scenes of a hotel. The staff area, laundry areas, kitchen, heating and ventilation rooms, security guard room. Why would they? They only come for a comfortable stay in a clean room on a comfortable bed with air conditioning in the summer and heating in the winter. They come for the free Wi-Fi and a good selection of cable channels along with happy hour drinks and hot breakfast buffets.

Unfortunately for Larry Evans, he is now sitting on a hard wooden chair with no armrests in the hotel's security office. A room he did not plan to see during his trip. It is one in the morning, and he has been in this room for almost three hours.

Larry gently rubs the side of his face with a damp cloth Reid Beckett, a security guard for the hotel, has given him. His cheek is swollen, and every touch is mildly painful.

Sitting across from him behind the desk is Robert Decker, the head of security for the Springvale Starline Hotel. Decker, a strong name for the head of any department. He stares at Larry in silence.

Decker's assistant stands in front of the closed office door. The name on his hotel tag has him as one "Reid Beckett," another strong name. It must be a prerequisite to get a job in the security department of this hotel. A Waldo or a Todd wouldn't have a chance.

Larry finally breaks the silence by attempting to get up from his chair, clutching the towel in his right hand. "Well, what's going on?"

"What are you doing?" snaps Decker.

"I am getting up!" Larry declares.

"Please sit down now, Mr. Evans. I will not tell you again." Decker stiffens, ready to step forward again at a moment's notice. "Or do you want a repeat of what just happened?"

Larry glances between the two of them and decides to remain sitting. "Yeah, about that. You said your henchman wouldn't leave any physical marks!" Larry points to his red cheek.

"Beckett got carried away. It happens on rare occasions. Very rare occasions. But in his defence, you did show signs of an impending physical attack."

"Impending physical attack! Really?" Larry pauses. "I'd hate to see what would happen with an actual attack."

"Easy enough. I'd call in his older brother, who is just outside the office." Decker smiles.

"I'm the baby brother," Beckett adds with a smirk.

"Can you at least tell me what is going on?" Larry shrugs, giving up on that line of conversation.

Decker looks at him, slightly annoyed at being in his office so late at night rather than in the comfort of his bed.

Decker decides to answer before Larry can annoy him further, but first, he quickly glances at his watch on his right hand.

Unusual for a person to wear a watch on their right hand, Larry observes. *He's probably left-handed.* Of more interest is that the watch has a crown on the left side, something that isn't seen very much. Must be either a custom watch or an expensive one. The head of security must pay well.

"At this moment, Mr. Evans, the local police are taking statements from all the witnesses in the bar along with the front desk and any kitchen staff that witnessed the assault—"

"The assault? What assault?" Larry interrupts. "I did not touch her. Never even laid a hand on her."

"The woman you are referring to was taken to the hospital by ambulance several hours ago. She incurred a severe head injury in the fall. As I was saying, the officers out front are taking statements. When they have completed this, they will have some serious questions for you. Right now, it is my honour or punishment—still figuring that out—to sit in this room with Mr. Beckett here," he says, pointing at the guard standing at the door, "and babysit you. No more questions, as I am not in the mood to answer any. Do you understand?"

"But I—"

"What did I just say? No! Wait, do not talk. Just nod your head that you understand."

Larry nods.

Decker pulls out his phone from his jacket pocket, swipes across it, and places it to his left ear.

Curious, It must have vibrated in his jacket pocket because he did not hear any ringtone. Larry strands to catch a snippet of the conversation.

Decker, in a low tone, acknowledges whatever he has been told. He grins slightly, then hangs up and pockets the phone. "Well, Mr. Evans, do you want to hear the good news or the bad news?"

Larry, startled by the statement, blurts, "Oh, I can talk now? Because a moment ago, you basically told me to shut up."

Decker gives him an irritated glance. "Good news, or bad?"

"The good news."

"OK, Mr. Beckett and I are done for the night. We can go home."
He smiles at Beckett. Beckett smiles back and relaxes his stance.

Larry is now totally confused. "How is that good news for me?"

"Oh. Did I say good news for you? Nope, that was wrong. That
was good news for us." Decker points to himself and Beckett.
"There is no good news for you, only bad news. Multiple witness
reports have led the police officers outside to book you for aggravated assault. You are going to jail tonight and most probably will
be in front of a judge tomorrow morning. The police officers will
be here shortly. I need your room card so I can send one of the
staff personnel to pack up your belongings."

"Are you shitting me? I didn't do anything wrong," Larry says.

"First of all, Mr. Evans, you will refrain from doing any shitting here. I just had the floors redone. Secondly, I don't care if you
'did' or 'did not.' That's not my job to decide." Decker then smiles
at Beckett.

Beckett nods and smiles back. "Good one, boss."

Decker puts forward his hand. "Room card, please?"

Grudgingly, Larry reaches into his front pants pocket, pulls out
the room card, and places it in Decker's outstretched hand.

Decker gives him a winning smile. "Thank you."

Just at that moment, there's a knock at the door. A voice calls
out, "Springvale Police. Let us in."

"With pleasure," Decker calls and waves at Beckett to open
the door.

Three police officers step into the office. Decker looks at the
first officer and says, "He's all yours, Mike."

"Thanks," replies Mike, shaking Decker's extended hand.

Larry, observes the interaction between them. *Calling him by
his first name. They must know each other outside of their professional environment. This is only getting better*, he thinks to himself.
"Friends, are we?" questions Larry.

Decker and Mike both turn to face Larry, their happy demeanor quickly fading.

"What?" Larry asks innocently.

"I am done babysitting him," Decker says. "Officer Michael Winters has some questions for you. We're out of here."

Mike and the two officers behind him step aside as Decker and Beckett leave the security office. The officer closest to the door shuts it behind them, and Officer Winters sits down in Decker's old chair behind the desk. The other two officers stand at attention in front of the door.

He places a metal clipboard with a cover on the desk. He opens the cover and pulls out a carbon copy form. With a pen, he starts writing some notes on the document, checking off boxes, and at one point, referencing his watch before jotting down more information. "I will need some information from you," he states without looking up at Larry, who has been staring at him in silence. "Your full name, please."

"Larry Evans."

"Any initials or middle names?"

"None."

"Age?"

"Forty-six."

"Current city of residence?"

"Montreal."

"Canada?"

"Well, Quebec is the province. Canada is the country, but that is correct."

Michael looks up from his document. "Nice town. I've been there once in the summer."

Larry wants to acknowledge his comment but decides not to.

"Current employer?"

"Commlink Services, based out of Montreal. We have offices in several cities in both the USA and Canada."

"The purpose of your visit to New Jersey?"

"Strictly business. I have a full schedule of meetings starting today—now, actually" Larry says as he checks his watch.

Michael continues scribbling notes. "OK, now we will go through, in detail, everything that was said and done that led to the assault in the restaurant bar."

"What! Are you joking?"

"Nope. I am not."

"I didn't do anything!"

"Mr. Evans, it's late. I need your full cooperation so we can call it a night as soon as possible."

"So you're saying that I can go after you question me?"

Michael looks at Larry and shakes his head. "Nope, not at all. You are definitely going to answer all my questions, and then these two fine officers," Michael says, pointing to the officers guarding the door, "will definitely escort you down to the police station where you will definitely be kept for the remainder of the night."

"What!" Larry exclaims.

"In the morning or sometime during the day, you will probably be brought to the local courthouse to be arraigned in front of a judge."

"On what charges?" Larry demands.

"We have eyewitness accounts from multiple people that claim you assaulted Ms. Chase in the hotel bar," Winters says.

"Assault! Are you kidding me?"

"Mr. Evans, the police are not in the business of kidding people."

"It was a rhetorical question! Do you know what a rhetorical question is?" Larry asks.

"Yes, Mr. Evans. I am aware of what rhetorical questions are. Now, can we get down to answering my real ones?"

Larry leans forward in his chair. Tired and agitated, he massages his eyes with the bases of his palms. "Go ahead so we can get this over with. As you said, it is going to be a long night."

"Thank you, Mr. Evans, for your cooperation. The sooner you answer our questions, the sooner we can bring you to the station and pack you away for the night, and the sooner my boys and I can get a few hours of shut eye before we meet the judge."

Officer Winters's questions and detailed notetaking eats up the next ninety minutes. The clock on the wall displays 4:30 a.m. when the door opens.

One of the two police officers standing at the door steps out, his right hand gripping the handle of his pistol in its holster. He looks left and right down the corridor. Content on finding it empty, he steps forward.

Finding the whole reaction over the top, Larry blurts out, "Really? I highly doubt there's a gang of ninja assassins after me."

The officer ignores him and waves him out. Larry walks out, his hands cuffed behind his back. Officer Winters, who has his hand on Larry's right shoulder, guides him from behind.

The second police officer exits the office, closing the door behind him. The group hustles down the corridor towards a utility door with the lead officer calling out into his communication link.

Reaching the utility door, another police officer opens it. The four men step through the doorway and head toward the main doors. Along the way, a scattering of hotel staff and police officers turn to face Larry and his escorts.

Outside the hotel, two police cars are parked in front of the entrance with their engines running, probably having been notified in advance. A waiting police officer opens the rear car door. When Larry reaches the car, he bends his head and slips into the rear seat. One of the escorting police officers gets in besides him and closes the car door. The second police officer and his escort get into the front passenger seat. Once the door is closed, the police car accelerates out the hotel lot and into the general traffic, followed by the second police car.

Larry, arms cuffed in the back, leans forward slightly and stares down at his shoes. He spots a small red mark on the top of his shoe. Blood. 'God, I hope that's not hers!'

DAY TWO — THE POLICE STATION

—

With the early morning traffic being light, the drive to the police station is quick.

The first vehicle, the one containing Larry Evans, pulls up to the security gate. Officer Winters flashes his badge at a video camera. Seconds later, the gate door rolls open, and the two vehicles proceed inside. The cars park side by side near the back entrance to the building. There are about twenty parking spots, about half of them occupied by police cars or vans. The remaining vehicles look like unmarked cars.

Inside the station, they pass through a security door leading to a room where a duty officer is stationed. A ground to ceiling protected glass wall with only a small opening for exchange of items and a speaker system right above it for communication separates him from visitors.

The duty officer presses a button on a desk panel. "Please empty your pockets of all items along with any jewelry, including rings, chains and watch and place them in the tray in front of you," he says.

Larry, still in a state of bewilderment, does not respond at first but is nudged into action by the officer to his right. He nods and empties the contents of his pockets. He then pulls off his gold band on his right ring finger along with his watch and places both items in the tray provided. One of the officers takes the tray from the extended shelf built into the glass partition and holds it in front of Larry as he places everything into it. Larry smacks the side of his pants to indicate that he is done.

The duty officer behind the glass presses his intercom button again. "Please remove your belt and shoes and place them in the tray provided."

"You have got to be kidding me!"

"Please remove your shoes and belt and place them in the tray provided," he repeats.

The officer to his side nudges him again. Larry hesitantly unbuckles his belt, places it in the tray. He then removes both his shoes and does the same with them. The officer holding the tray places it on the elevated shelf.

"Mr. Evans, all your personal belongings will be secured in the property room during the course of your stay at this police station. They will be returned to you only upon which time you are found innocent of any crimes that you have committed. Do you understand, Mr. Evans?"

Larry nods.

"Please verbally respond that you have understood what I have just stated."

"Yes, I understand what you have told me," Larry mumbles.

"What size shoe do you wear?"

"What?"

"I said, what size shoe do you wear? We have taken away your footwear, so it only makes sense to provide you with replacement footwear that does not include laces."

"Size ten and half, wide."

"Is a ten and half regular fine?"

"Do I have a choice?" Larry asks.

"None whatsoever."

"OK, then."

The duty officer pulls out a pair of dark grey loafers from underneath his counter and places them in front of him on the tray. The police officer to Larry's left offers the tray to Larry.

Larry quickly slips them on. He steps up and down on his spot to get a feel of the shoes. "A little tight but I'll get used to them. Thanks," he says to the duty officer behind the glass.

He nods. "Officers, please escort Mr. Evans to Interrogation Room Three. Somebody will be there shortly."

The two officers lead Larry to a door beside the protected glass station. The lead officer waits for a buzzing sound as it unlocks, and they go down a corridor and into the interrogation room. He is left alone as the two police officers disappear.

Moments later, the door opens to the room, and a female officer Larry has not seen before walks in. The woman is not in uniform, but she's definitely a police officer, as Larry spots the small bulge of a pistol holster on her right hip.

She sits across from Larry. One of Larry's police escorts stands at attention in front of the door.

"My name is Detective MaryAnn Lewis. I will be in charge of this case going forward. I have already reviewed your file. An electronic copy was forwarded to me while you were in transit. This is what is going to happen in the next twenty-four hours. It is very important that you listen and understand everything that I am going to tell you."

Larry nods.

"Good," she responds. "Now, let's get some mandatory paperwork out of the way before we proceed with processing." She pulls open a folder that she has carried into the room with her. Then she pulls out a pen from inside her jacket pocket and begins to write some notes on one of the documents.

Larry nods again.

"Are you Larry Evans?"

"I am."

"Do you presently live in Montreal, Canada?"

"Quebec."

"What?"

"I live in the city of Montreal, which is in the province of Quebec. That is equivalent to your states."

"So?"

"Well, when somebody asks you were you live, do you answer Springvale, USA, or Springvale, New Jersey?"

Detective Lewis gives him an unimpressed look. "I get it."

"So, yes, to your question, I presently live in Montreal."

"Can we move on with the questions, Mr. Evans?"

"By all means."

"Are you a Canadian citizen?"

"Yes."

She checks something off on the document in front of her.

"Born in Canada?"

"Yes, in Saskatoon," he replies.

"What? What do you mean by Sassoon?"

"I said Saskatoon. Not Sassoon, or whatever it is you heard me say."

"OK, what is that?" she asks. "Saskatoon?"

"It's the city where I was born."

"Really? That's a city name?"

Larry is baffled by her statement, bordering on ignorance. "If I were you, I wouldn't go there. You people down here have names like Intercourse, Pennsylvania, or Kalamazoo in Michigan, for starters. Do you want me to continue?"

"Point taken. So, you guys have provinces and not states up there. What province is Saskatoon located in?"

"Saskatchewan," he says.

"Oh, for fuck's sake. You're shitting me, right?"

"Never!" Larry takes on a deadpan expression.

Annoyed, the detective asks, "How do you spell it?"

"S-A-S-K-A-T-C-H-E-W-A-N, *Saskatchewan*. Name comes from the Indigenous Cree people, meaning *swift flowing river*."

"You are presently residing in Montreal?"

"I am."

"How long have you been in Montreal?"

"About five years, give or take," Larry responds.

"Prior to Montreal?"

"I lived in Toronto for a few years, then prior to that, I was out West in Vancouver. Before that, I spent a few years in San Francisco on a work visa."

"Reason for all these moves?"

"Work related. I go where there's work. It's easy for me. My skills are in high demand."

Larry's slight air of arrogance does not go unnoticed by the detective. "And what are these so-called skills of yours?"

"Without getting into details, I bring people together to solve problems. I match up clients who have certain needs with people who can fulfill their needs. I am able to identify problems and present solutions in a timely and efficient manner. It is rare that my projects go past deadlines or over budget. I am that good, and I am paid very well for my results."

The detective, clearly annoyed by his arrogance, collects her temper. "Fine! Now, the purpose of your visit to New Jersey?"

"I am here for business."

"Please elaborate."

"I am here to close a multimillion dollar contract with a local company in New Jersey. I am the senior account manager on the project."

"What is the name of the company you work for?"

"Commlink Services. We are based out of Montreal, but we also have offices in several states for sales and product support. Some of our bigger offices are also involved in R&D."

"Just to clarify, R&D?" she asks.

"Research and development. We have some partnerships with universities in Boston and Stanford, California via grants from the local state governments."

"Impressive. University towns."

"Our business uses cutting-edge technology. We collaborate with the brightest minds in both countries. They are usually located in cities with top university talent. Hence, Stanford, Boston in the States, and Montreal and Toronto back in Canada."

"OK. Thanks for the quick lesson! How long was your planned stay in New Jersey?"

"My trip was for four days in town. I was going to make a quick stop back in Newark to visit our office there, and then I was going to fly out to Dallas for another round of negotiations with a different company. Another week there, if you need to know."

The detective nods at this information, "You are a busy man, Mr. Evans."

"Yes, I am. It is a tight schedule," he says, not wanting to exaggerate the importance of his role in the contract negotiations.

"And after that trip is done?"

"Back home for a week of work. Some time off to relax, and then back on the road again."

"Do you have meetings scheduled with this company today?"

"I do. My first appointment is scheduled for today at ten this morning. Based on my current predicament, I gather I will not be attending this meeting."

"That is correct, Mr. Evans," she says without emotion. "I would say this whole week is a write-off, and next week doesn't look any better."

"I need to contact my company to notify them that I can't make it."

"At the moment, you will sit there until I finish asking my questions. I will then go over what will happen in the next twenty-four hours. Do you understand?"

"When will I be able to contact my office?" Larry asks.

"I just finished outlining to you what's going to happen in the next few hours. Do you understand?"

Not getting the answers he is looking for, Larry sighs. "Yes, I do."

"Good," she replies, still without any facial expressions. "Once we are done, you can reach out to your family and employer to bring them up to speed."

"I don't have any family to notify. Parents are deceased, no wife, no girlfriend presently, no pets, and no plants to feed at home. It's easy for me to move around. Relocate to different cities and countries. I have few personal belongings. I'm not a very sentimental person. Whatever I have that I can't take in a pair of travel bags, I keep in a long-term storage site."

The detective pauses her writing. She stares at him for a moment and then returns to the document. "I need the names of your clients and their contact information so I can verify your presence in our state."

"Why do you need that? I just finished telling you what I do."

"Mr. Evans, kindly provide me with your business contacts. I need this information documented to make sure the person accused is who he or she claims to be and is in our town for the reason he or she states. At times, it helps the accused. In your case, it really won't matter too much."

"What do you mean by that?"

The detective pauses her note-taking. "Contact information please?" she asks again.

"I don't have that information on me. All my personal belongings were taken when I was processed. You'll have to ask the guy behind the bulletproof glass for that."

"Thank you, Mr. Evans. I will get the information afterwards."

"Again, what did you mean, 'it really won't matter too much?'"

"OK, here is how it stands. Once we leave this room, you will be placed in a cell for the remainder of the day until somebody comes and gets you. Do you need a court-appointed lawyer, or do you have the means to get your own?"

"I have the means to get my own legal counsel!" he declares, arrogance clearly evident towards the detective.

"That's good. One less guilty person to be a strain on our overworked public defenders."

"Did you call me guilty?" Larry asks. "Isn't that a little presumptuous of you?"

She ignores him again. "Tomorrow morning, you will be brought in front of Judge Clarence Lerno. You are lucky, Mr. Evans. Do you know why?

"No. Why?"

"This town doesn't see a lot of traffic through our courts; therefore, we can accommodate your hearing pretty quickly," Detective Lewis states.

"Oh, goody!"

"The judge will review the charges and decide on the matter. You will state your plea, and the judge will announce the next court date."

"Again, what did you mean by 'one less guilty person?'"

"Mr. Evans, I have been in this line of work for a long time. I have seen many cases like this, many characters like you. And you know what?" she asks, stone-faced.

"Please, do tell."

"It always ends up the same. They deny, deflect at first, and then when the odds and the evidence are irrefutable, the guilty party confesses."

"So, you've already passed judgement?"

"In my mind, and not just mine, you are guilty. I do not need to look further. We have multiple statements from witnesses stating you assaulted the woman in the bar during what seemed to be a lover's quarrel," she responds. This time, her voice is slightly elevated.

"You must be mistaken," Larry says. "I did not touch her. I didn't lay a finger on her. Do you understand what I am saying? You people have it all wrong." He leans across the table in frustration.

The police officer standing at the door inches forward in anticipation.

Detective Lewis, seeing him from her peripheral vision, waves him off, and he steps back with a determined look.

Detective Lewis leans forward also, raises her head a bit, and wrinkles her nose. "How much alcohol did you consume yesterday evening?"

"What?"

"You have a distinct smell of alcohol on you. You were at a hotel bar; I assume you had your fair share of alcohol during the evening."

Larry shakes his head in disbelief. "How much I drank?"

"Yes, Mr. Evans. How much did you drink?"

"If you must know, and I doubt you will believe me, I had one bottle of beer at the bar. I had ordered a second one but never had a chance to start it, as all hell broke loose."

"One bottle of beer only?"

"Yes. I already told you that."

"No hard alcohol? Scotch, whisky, maybe?"

"One bottle of Corona, if I need to be more specific."

"Did you have anything to drink in your room before you came down to the hotel bar? From the mini-bar, for instance?" Lewis inquires.

Larry shakes his head.

"Are you sure? Because from the conversation officers had last night with the front desk manager, he said you inquired about their brands of beer at their concession stand."

"I did ask him, but I didn't pursue it further, because they did not carry the brands I enjoy," Larry replies.

"What are those brands, if I may ask?"

"I am partial to Canadian beers—Labatt, Molson. The hotel only stocked domestic beers. I was told that there was not enough demand for imports. So, to answer your question again, no, I did not have any other alcohol other than that single beer at the hotel bar. No hard stuff. Nothing from mini-bar in my room. Period," Larry claims in defiance. "I don't think I can be clearer than that."

Detective Lewis puts her pen down on the table. "Mr. Evans, how do you explain the distinct smell of alcohol on you?"

"The woman tossed her drink at me before she struck me," Larry states.

"Her drink?"

"Yes. She was drinking a martini, but I think there is more of it on me than what she drank."

"It smells more like you took a bath in it. I don't think one solitary drink would leave that much of a smell on somebody's clothes."

"I've never had a great sense of smell, so I guess I didn't notice it. I don't know what else to tell you. It was the one drink from her."

"The odour on your clothes, the alcohol you supposedly consumed, and the behaviour at the bar just doesn't add up," Lewis states.

"My behaviour? What behaviour? I already told you that I did not touch her!"

"Mr. Evans, we have witnesses that claim you did. Witnesses that say you struck her several times and evidently pushed her backwards, at which point she fell and hit her head against the bar runner!"

"I didn't do it," Larry repeats. "What about the notion of 'innocent until proven guilty?'"

Detective Lewis looks at her watch. "Well, you can tell that to the judge tomorrow morning."

"For God's sake, it's a hotel. There must be video cameras on the main floor, reception, and bar area."

"We have already checked, and the security camera footage for the bar and restaurant area is not available for whatever reason. Anyway, like I said, we have multiple collaborating witness accounts. They are solid, and they paint a disturbing picture of your actions."

Larry sits back in his chair.

The detective looks at her notes for a moment and then gives the officer a nod. She closes her folder, pushes back from her chair, and gets up. She takes two steps toward the door and then turns around. "You know what?"

"What now?" he asks, frustration taking over.

"When I mentioned the victim's fall and how she hit her head against the bar floor runner, you didn't even blink for a second. You didn't show any emotion. You didn't ask what her status was."

Larry collects himself. "You're right. I didn't ask. So?"

"Aren't you a little concerned about her injuries? How she is doing. She was taken away to the local hospital. Did you know that?" she asks.

"Yes, the hotel security dude told me while I was locked up in the security office for hours on end. He questioned me about the incident, accused me of something I didn't do, and now you're asking me why I didn't inquire about her condition?"

"I do want to know why," she says.

"I didn't ask about her condition because I don't really care. I don't know her, never met her before tonight. She pulled up a stool beside me at the restaurant bar and initiated the conversation. We exchanged a few friendly words before she lost it on me and assaulted me."

This statement triggers an emotion from the detective. She steps over to Larry and slaps him before the police officer behind her can react.

Larry jerks back from the slap and raises his arm to protect himself. His face stings. "What the hell is wrong with you? Are you insane?" he yells.

She doesn't respond. Instead, she steps back and looks at the police officer, indicating with her eyes to move aside. When he does, she opens the door and exits.

The police officer follows her out and closes the door behind him.

Larry sits back on the chair, rubbing his face. "Did you see that? Did you see what she did?"

"Don't look for sympathy from me. You won't get any."

DAY TWO — THE SPRINGVALE HOTEL

—

Noon

A man and woman step out of one of the hotel elevators into the lobby. Their luggage in tow, they proceed to the front desk. The man places his room key on the counter.

Howard, the front desk manager, looks up from his screen and smiles.

"We are checking out early today. Not staying another night after the incident at the bar last night. My wife," indicating the woman beside him, "didn't get a good night sleep and was very upset with the event."

She nods in agreement.

"My deepest apologies to you both," Howard says. "We endeavour to avoid any unpleasant events as much as possible, but it is hard to interpret people's attitudes these days whenever alcohol is involved."

"Thank you for the concern, Howard," the man states politely.

"One moment, please, as I close out your account, Mr. Jeffery." Howard taps a few keystrokes on his computer. "The account is settled in full. The hotel management has waived all charges to your room along with any meals charged at the hotel restaurant during your stay."

Mr. Jeffrey raises his eyebrows in surprise. "That is most generous. Thank you."

"Have a pleasant trip home. We hope we will see you back in our city soon."

"Thanks. A good day to you too," Mr. Jeffrey responds. The couple turn, take their luggage, and leave the hotel.

DAY TWO

Afternoon

"Hello, Mr. Evans, my name is Benjamin Dowds, the law firm sent me down to act as your attorney in this case." Benjamin Dowds had walked into the police station earlier. He sat down quickly with the duty officer who filled him on the procedure for meeting with clients behind bars. Once that was done, the duty officer escorted him to the interrogation room where Larry had been waiting for about twenty minutes.

Larry takes in Benjamin Dowds's appearance. Shorter than himself at just under six feet tall, he is slim with short dark hair and a dark complexion. He's packaged in a sharp dark grey suit and a razor-thin tie.

Dowds stops short. "What?" he asks Larry.

"No disrespect to your wardrobe, but didn't those ties go out of fashion in the nineties?

"None taken, and yes, they most probably did, but I consider myself a Renaissance man when it comes to fashion."

"Well, who am I to argue? It seems you'll be doing that for me in front of the judge."

"Good. Now, can we get to work? I've been told we only have a one-hour window. Enough time for you to give me, your attorney, the lowdown on everything I need to know about this case. I need to know how we are going to plead our case in front of the judge."

Larry stands up and extends his hand in greeting.

Dowds waves it off politely, "Sorry, I don't shake hands. Now, we don't have much time. Our appointment in the front of the judge is tomorrow morning. Surprisingly fast."

"Yes, the detective who interviewed me said the court docket is pretty open," Larry confirms. He sits back down on one side of the table while Dowds grabs a seat on the other side. "Go ahead, start asking away. I am an open book," Larry declares.

"Good, a cooperative defendant always makes defending them a lot easier." Dowds pulls out his audio recorder from his briefcase, places it in the centre on the table, and turns it on. "I will be recording this session and any others, as I prefer it over taking notes. I find it more efficient that way. Do you have any objections?"

"None whatsoever."

"Good. Before we get started, do you want something to drink? Water, soda, coffee?"

"Water would be good. It seems the air conditioning in here isn't holding up well against the temperature outside," Larry states.

"That's true. I'll get the guard to bring us some bottles." Dowds stands up, walks to the door, opens it slightly, and asks the officer posted outside.

Dowds resumes his position at the table. "So, from a copy of the police report of their witness interviews and your interview, there seem to be diverging views on the events that transpired last night."

Larry looks at him, trying to figure out his angle or which side he is batting for. *Is he my attorney, or is he working for the prosecution as a plant?* "I am starting to get that impression from the people that I have talked to in the last twenty-four hours," he states calmly. "I don't know why this so-called 'divergence' in the facts surrounding the events exists. I can only talk about what I did, and more importantly, what I did *not* do, which was strike this woman."

"OK, so tomorrow morning, we'll go into court in front of the judge and unequivocally state that you are innocent. Is this what you want?" Dowds asks.

"That is not only what I want as my plea; it also happens to be the truth. I did not touch her. Her injuries were self-inflicted, simple as that." Larry shakes his head.

"What about the eyewitnesses? There are multiple people who claim otherwise. What do you say about them?"

"Simple. They are lying!" Larry blurts out.

Dowds shakes his head in apparent frustration.

Before Larry can continue, there's a knock on the door. An officer steps through and places two water bottles on the table.

"Thank you, officer," Dowds states.

Larry nods in agreement. "Look, Mr. Dowds. I don't know why this is happening like it is, but the simple truth is that I didn't lay a finger on that woman. She approached me, I bought her a drink, and we chatted for a while. She was becoming friendly. She placed her hand on my thigh at one point, but I never touched her—even after she got upset and struck me. Her injuries, unfortunately for her, were caused accidentally as she fell backwards and clipped the side of the bar runner on the ground. That is exactly what happened."

"What did the bartender say to you?" Dowds asks.

"I tried to leave, as the whole situation was ridiculous, but he told me I wasn't going anywhere. He told the front desk manager to call the cops."

"Did you actually try to leave?"

"Well, yes and no. I didn't move; I wanted to. Within seconds of the accident happening, the bartender, front desk manager, and several employees from the kitchen surrounded me."

"So, what did you end up doing?"

"I sat down until hotel security was called over. At that point, they removed me from the area and placed me in the hotel security office with two gentlemen until the police took over."

"What happened afterwards?" Dowds presses.

Larry takes a sip from his bottle of water before continuing. Dowds does likewise.

"Afterwards, the police officers grilled me for several hours into the morning until they took me down to the station," responds Larry.

"Did they at any point read you your rights?" Dowds inquires.

"Rights?" Larry asks.

"Yes, here in the USA, the police read you your Miranda rights before they question you. It's not mandatory, but if they don't, that's when they have an issue."

"What issue, Mr. Dowds?" Larry asks.

"If the police officer or whoever interrogates you fails to read you your Miranda rights beforehand, then the prosecutor cannot use what was discovered during the interrogation as evidence against the suspect at the trial," Dowds explains.

"I see," Larry states. "Well, you will be delighted to know that nobody did. I think one group thought the previous group did, and so on. In the end, nobody did."

"That is fabulous. Absolutely fabulous!" Dowds states ecstatically.

"Well, Mr. Dowds, I'm glad that you're glad."

"Yeah!" Dowds responds. "Another question?"

"Go ahead."

"Any mention of surveillance tapes or videos during any of the interrogations?"

"Nope! Only that there was no footage. I don't know the details," Larry responds. "That's kind of important, right?"

"It's very important. For starters, the prosecution needs to provide hard evidence besides eyewitnesses. Also, you need it as evidence to prove what you said in your interrogations was exactly what happened."

"I see where you are going with that. Then I guess we need to get those videotapes or files or whatever as soon as possible—if ever!"

"Yeah," Dowds agrees.

"Is that it?" Larry asks.

"For the moment, yes," Dowds says. "I will see you at the courthouse in the morning. Get some sleep. It seems like it was a long night for you."

"It was. Adrenaline has kept me going up until now. I need a few hours. Hopefully the bed in the cell is comfortable."

"From experience—not my own, of course—" Dowds says, smiling, "cots in jail are usually not comfortable places to sleep. Regardless, get some rest. It's going to be another long day for you."

"Thanks," Larry states as he gets up to offer his hand, but he pulls back, remembering. *What an odd man*, he thinks to himself.

"Have a restful night, Mr. Evans." Dowds salutes him and knocks on the door.

The guard on the other side opens it and lets Dowds out. He waits for Dowds to put some distance from him before he glances back to Larry and calls out, "OK, pretty boy, back to lock up for you."

DAY THREE — HOW ARE YOU DOING, AMANDA?

Detective MaryAnn Lewis arrives at Summit Oaks Hospital the next morning. Her goal is to get a statement from Amanda Chase, the star witness from this whole ordeal.

She hands over her ID to the attending nurse at the front desk. The nurse on duty confirms her identification before she escorts Lewis to Ms. Chase's room. It is a private room with only one bed. *This will make the interrogation easier*, Lewis thinks to herself.

The nurse approaches Amanda, who turns to face the nurse at the sound of footsteps approaching her bed.

"Amanda, you have a visitor," she says softly. "Detective Lewis is here to take your statement regarding the assault at the Springvale hotel. Are you up to it?"

Amanda glances from the nurse to Detective Lewis. She nods. "Sure."

On cue, Detective Lewis pulls the empty chair up beside the bed. She sits down and takes out her pad and pen.

The nurse steps back to the far corner of the room without having to be told and sits on another empty chair.

"Ms. Chase, I am Detective MaryAnn Lewis from the Springvale Police Department. I would like to ask you a few questions. Is that OK?"

Amanda pushes herself up a bit to try to peek around the detective to locate the nurse. Spotting her puts her at ease, and then she lies back down.

"Don't worry; the nurse will be in the room during the whole interview process."

"OK," Amanda whispers.

"Can you confirm that the man in this picture is the man who assaulted you?" Lewis produces an eight-by-ten picture of Larry Evans from the leather pouch on her lap and holds it up at eye level.

Amanda leans forward. She stares for a moment, focusing. "I'm still a little fuzzy, but it looks like him," she finally says.

Detective Lewis, not completely satisfied, changes her tactic, "OK, let's try a different approach. When you were at the restaurant bar at the Springvale hotel, you sat at the bar. Can you tell me who else was there?"

Amanda turns her attention towards Detective Lewis. "There was a man sitting in the middle of the bar. A couple was sitting at the edge of it," she states.

"That's good! Is that all? Anybody else?" asks Detective Lewis.

"The bartender. That's it," she states.

"OK. That's good," Lewis responds. "Now remove the couple at the end of the bar. Remove the bartender. Now focus just on the man in the middle of the bar. You got that?"

"Yes," she says coolly.

"The man you encountered in the restaurant bar at the Springvale hotel—was he the man in this picture?" Lewis holds up the picture again.

Amanda nods.

"I will take that as a yes," Lewis says. "Prior to the night of the assault, had you ever met this man before?"

"No," she responds quickly.

"So that was your first encounter with him?"

"First, only, and hopefully the last!" Amanda replies nervously.

Detective Lewis puts the picture back in her pouch. "Why were you at the hotel? Your name doesn't show up in the hotel register."

"I was having a drink," Amanda states.

"Yes, I am aware of that fact. What I am asking is why you were having a drink at the hotel if you were not a registered guest."

Shifting slightly in her bed, Amanda peers into Lewis's eyes in with growing annoyance. Slowly, she states, "I like that place." She squints slightly. "What are you trying to say, Detective?"

"I am trying to understand why you were present at the hotel bar."

"As I mentioned, I like the place. It's comfortable. It's a nice place to have a drink—"

"And to pick up men?" Lewis asks.

"Excuse me, are you accusing me of being a hooker?" Amanda raises her voice slightly, just enough to get the supervising nurse's attention, who stands up and comes closer.

"Ms. Chase, I am trying to understand your intentions on the night of the assault. You clearly were not a registered guest of the hotel. There are half a dozen watering holes within a half-mile radius of the hotel. I did my homework before coming over to meet you. So, I ask you again, why didn't you go to any of those places?"

"I like the place. How many times must I repeat myself in order for you to understand what I am saying?" Amanda responds defiantly.

Detective Lewis pauses and gives Amanda a blank stare. "I checked the city's records, Ms. Chase, and you are not a resident of Springvale. Actually, you're not even a resident of New Jersey."

"And . . . is there a question in there somewhere, Detective Lewis?"

"I don't like your tone of voice, Ms. Chase."

"Well, that makes two of us, then." Amanda leans over to the side. "Nurse, I am getting tired," she says.

The nurse moves over to the edge of the bed. "Detective Lewis, that will be all for tonight. You can come back tomorrow during visiting hours."

Detective Lewis flips her notepad closed, pockets both it and her pen in her inner jacket pocket, pushes the pouch under her arm, stands, and nods to Amanda. "Thank you for your time, Ms. Chase. I will be back when you are more rested." Detective Lewis turns away, nods to the nurse, and proceeds out the door.

Amanda watches as Detective Lewis leaves the room and then shifts over to the nurse. "Thank you."

The two of them watch Detective Lewis leave the room.

"She was a little pushy for my taste," the nurse says.

Amanda smiles. "Yes, she was. I do not like pushy people."

"Will you need anything else at the moment?" the nurse inquires.

"Why, yes. Would you push the room phone closer to me? I would like to call my parents to tell them I'm all right."

"My God, for sure. You wouldn't want them to worry," the nurse agrees. She pushes the small night table closer to the bed. The phone is within easy arm's reach.

"There you go. I will leave you with your call. Buzz me if you have any issues or discomforts."

"Thanks again, nurse." Amanda smiles and watches the nurse walk out the door. She picks up the phone to make her call.

DAY THREE — THE COURTROOM

——

Time passes quickly this morning for Larry. He is sitting on a bench in a holding room beside the main courtroom. A courtroom officer hands over a brown bag with food inside. Larry barely has the time to munch down the chicken wrap and a handful of almost-cold fries before he is ushered into the courtroom.

He walks over to a bench and sits between two police officers on the right side of the courtroom. He takes in the surroundings of the room and nods in admiration by the size of it. The judge's bench is bookended by two flagpoles draping American flags. His observations are a little surreal that it resembles a courtroom on TV cop shows and legal dramas. The high ceiling supports half a dozen fans running at maximum speed—not helping, as the hot air is just being circulated around the room. More than half the men sitting in the public area wearing ties have loosened them. Their suit jackets are off and resting on their laps. The women seem to have planned ahead, wearing light, loose-fitting attire.

He peers quickly over his left shoulder to see what is going on behind him. About a dozen people, mostly men, sit on benches. Several of them wear badges on thin cords around their necks. They must be reporters for the local TV station or newspapers. He catches the attention of a woman who stared right back at him.

She is also wearing a badge. He turns back as his neck starts to crimp up.

The court officer stands up. "All stand in the presence of Judge Clarence Lerno," he announces.

Whoa, just like TV, Larry thinks to himself.

Everybody in the courtroom stands as the judge enters the room from a door beside the bench. A short, thin man with thick, grey hair, cut short, military style. His quick steps up the stairs towards his bench bodes well for his fitness. The elevated bench gives him an unobstructed view of the room. "Just before we start, I will ask that all parties in attendance be brief in your opening statements, as this unseasonably hot and humid weather has wreaked havoc on our air-conditioning system. Let's be productive and to the point. I thank all in advance for your cooperation. I am a firm advocate of the Sixth Amendment, so let's get started. I now bring this session to order." Turning to face the court clerk, he asks, "What is the first case of the day?"

With documents in hand, the clerk responds quickly and in a practiced manner. "Your Honour, the first case on the docket is the city of Springvale, New Jersey, vs Larry Evans for assault in the first degree against a woman named Amanda Chase."

"What does the prosecution say in this matter?" The judge looks over to two men dressed in dark blue suits and shiny shoes.

The attorney closest to the centre stands up, adjusts his suit jacket, and addresses the judge, "Your Honour, my name is Thomas Albert Jr., attorney for the plaintiff. We charge the defendant, one Larry Evans of Montreal, Canada, with the crime of aggravated assault with intent to do bodily harm to one Amanda Chase during a verbal exchange at the Springvale Starline Hotel Bar and Restaurant on the night of May 4th. Additionally, we would like to enter a charge of attempting to flee the scene of the crime on the same night."

"Thank you, Mr. Albert." He pauses for a second. "Are you of any relation to Thomas Albert Sr.?"

"Yes, Your Honour. Thomas Albert Sr. was my father. He passed several years ago."

"My condolences to you and your family. Your father was a very spirited attorney. Very passionate about his beliefs and defending his clients. We sparred a few times right here in these four walls," Judge Lerno says. "If you bring half the passion that your late father brought to the courtroom, this will make for an interesting trial."

"Thank you, Your Honour. My father recounted many stories during his retirement about his encounters with you—quite interesting stories," Thomas Albert responds.

"Encounters!" The judge grins. "Interesting choice of words." He turns his attention to the prosecution and then the defendant's table. "What is the plea of the defendant in this matter?"

Benjamin Dowds, Larry's attorney, stands. "Your Honour, the defendant pleads not guilty on all charges against him. He is innocent of these charges."

The judge looks at Larry. "Is that correct, Mr. Evans? You are claiming that you did not assault this woman, this Amanda Chase?"

Larry mumbles under his breath.

"Please stand when you are addressing the court, Mr. Evans. I don't know how you guys do it up North, but in the USA, you show respect by standing when you address the court."

Larry jumps quickly to his feet, straightening his jacket. His reaction is met by chuckles from the public. "Sorry, Your Honour. No disrespect to you or the court. I have never been in a court either here or back in Canada, so I am not familiar with courtroom etiquette."

"Back to the question at hand. Please repeat your earlier response, as I didn't hear you the first time, and I doubt Ms.

Cavendish, our clerk, did either." He gives the clerk a quick glance, and she responds with a shake of her head to confirm.

"Your Honour, I did not assault this woman. I didn't even touch her. She assaulted me, Your Honour."

"Most interesting. Thank you, Mr. Evans. You may be seated." The judge turns his attention back to the prosecution table. "I gather the prosecution has evidence to support their claim?"

The attorney stands again. "Yes, Your Honour, we have testimonies from three witnesses who saw Mr. Evans strike Ms. Chase." The attorney sits down again.

The judge turns back to Larry. "Mr. Evans, are you still sticking to your plea of not guilty?"

Larry stands up again. "Yes, Your Honour, I am still keeping my not guilty plea. I did not do it!"

"Well, the morning is starting to become an interesting one." The judge grins.

Benjamin Dowds stands and announces, "If it pleases Your Honour, may I address the court?"

"Go ahead, Mr. Dowds. You always seem to bring a little spice to your cases." The judge grins again. Larry gives Benjamin a puzzling glance and quickly surmises that this is not the first time these two have crossed paths in the courtroom.

"Your Honour, these charges are false and have no basis in truth. It is a total waste of the court's time and should be dismissed immediately. Additionally, I am filing a countersuit against the Springvale Police Department for wrongful arrest and assault against Mr. Evans and against the Springvale Starline Hotel management and staff for defamation of character and harm to the impeccable reputation of my client. Finally, we are filing a complaint against the Springvale Police Department for failure to advise my client on the nature of his arrest in an acceptable period of time. As you so stated, the Sixth Amendment provides the accused the right to be informed of any pending charges. My client was held for over six hours before he was informed of the pending charges. We are suing for substantial financial damages against all parties."

The prosecution attorney jumps up from his seat and bursts out, "That is totally absurd! This is totally absurd!"

A low mumbling erupts from the people sitting in the public area.

The judge quickly picks up his gavel and slams it against the gavel block twice. "Order in this court," he declares and faces the prosecution table. "Mr. Albert, I will not allow these sudden bursts from either bench. If this continues, I will put the person responsible in contempt of court. Do I make myself clear?"

"Yes, Your Honour," Dowds responds, followed quickly by lead prosecution.

"Good. Now, we will reconvene in three weeks' time to start this trial. The two parties will submit their witness lists and the material discovered to the court as soon as possible. Do you understand?"

Both the prosecution and the defence acknowledge the judge.

"Now, three weeks from now, I am expecting solid cases from both parties." The judge slams his gavel. "This defendant will remain under custody at the local jail until then." Looking at the prosecution table, he announces, "and don't worry, he will not be eligible for bail of any amount. Does anybody have an issue with this?"

Dowds stands up and exclaims, "Your Honour!"

"Go ahead, Mr. Dowds."

"I would like permission from the court to place Mr. Evans under protective custody, as I am concerned for his safety."

The judge gives Dowds a long stare. "What makes you believe your client would be in danger behind the cell at our local police station manned by our highly respected officers who have sworn an oath to protect all our citizens, Mr. Dowds?" The judge glances over to the prosecution table. "Gentlemen, do you agree with my assessment, or do you think Mr. Dowds has a reason to be concerned about the safety of his client?"

The lead prosecutor stands up. "Your Honour, my respective colleague should not be worried about the safety of his client."

The judge acknowledges his response and then glances at the crowd behind the separation banister. He spots a uniformed officer with chevrons cleared stitched on his shirt collar. Not a regular beat cop, but a captain or higher. The judge points at him. "Can you please stand up and state your name and rank?" he calls out to the officer.

The officer, taken aback by the sudden spotlight, hesitates for a moment and then stands. He straightens his uniform jacket. "Yes, Your Honour?"

"Name and rank please?" the judge asks again.

"Yes, Your Honour, sir. Name is Assistant Police Commissioner Albert Burrows, sir."

"Good, we have somebody in the house who can comment on the concerns of the attorney for the defendant."

"Yes, sir," the officer responds.

"Now, Assistant Police Commissioner Burrows, as a representative of the Springvale Police Department, do you think Mr. Dowds should be concerned about the safety of his client while he is residing at the local station for the three weeks?"

"No, sir, the attorney for the defendant should not be concerned at all. Our officers are professionals and are capable of handling any threat internally and externally targeting any person who is being held within our facilities."

"Thank you, Assistant Police Commissioner Burrows," the judge says. Glancing over to Dowds, the judge asks, "Does that address your concern?"

"Yes Judge, it does. Thank you." Dowds smiles at the judge.

"Good. That is all for today. We will see each other in three weeks' time. Hopefully by that time, either the air conditioning system will be repaired or the temperature outside will be more agreeable."

Muted chuckles emanate from the public area.

As the judge stands and exits the courtroom, the members of the prosecution and defendant tables stand in unison along with the people in the public area.

"There will be a fifteen-minute recess before the next case will be heard," announces the court officer.

Larry turns to Dowds, "What was that all about?"

"I just put everybody on notice not to mess with you in any way. A storm's a-coming, as they say down South." Dowds pats Larry on the shoulder just as Larry's escort shows up to take him away.

Benjamin Dowds waves to him before exiting the courtroom via the main doors. Larry is escorted to the backdoor by two police officers. He gazes at a small bronze plated statue of the scales of justice on top of an elevated wooden stand. *'Hopefully justice will be served.'*

The two prosecuting attorneys stay back until everybody except the court officer has vacated the room. The lead attorney glances at the officer. Not worried that he is within earshot to the conversation he is going to have with the other attorney.

"Any news from the hotel security on the video surveillance files yet?" asks the lead attorney apprehensively.

"As it stands, the hotel security manager has not been able to find the video files for that whole evening. Every hour, they roll into a secondary hard disk but according to the manager, everything from five in the evening onwards is nowhere to be found. They have reached out to their vendor for assistance."

"Hmm. Not good," he says, concern crossing his face.

"What's wrong? The case is good."

"There is something that is rubbing me the wrong way. I can't put my finger on it."

"What! We have witnesses, remember? Multiple witnesses. Not just one."

"I know, but I don't think that is enough. There is something about Larry Evans that is bugging me."

"He's just another scumbag preying on defenceless women," the assistant attorney responds.

The lead attorney quickly glances at the court officer again. The officer, too busy with paperwork on his desk does not notice them. Focusing back to his assistant. "He said clearly, 'I didn't do it.'"

"So?"

"He sounded too confident. A little too much for my comfort. Usually, a defendant will claim that the witnesses are lying or that the events have been misconstrued. Mr. Evans, on the other hand, is clearly stating that he did not do it. That he didn't assault her. Big difference."

"We need those surveillance files, or—"

"Or else, the case will be blown and we'll have a huge lawsuit against our clients," the lead attorney concludes. "Send some-body over to the hotel and make them sit with the hotel security manager until you have something."

"Will do." The assistant picks up his suitcase from the desk and they both exit the courtroom, leaving the court officer, alone with his paperwork.

Outside the courtroom, two people stand twenty feet from the main door, a man and the woman Larry spotted in the courtroom earlier. The door to the courtroom opens, and the assistant hurries down the corridor toward the exit.

"That's one of them from the prosecution team," the woman points at the assistant on his way out. The man beside her nods but does not say anything. Seconds later, the lead attorney steps out of the courtroom heads down the same corridor.

The man turns to the woman. "You follow the assistant, and I'll follow the boss. Let's see where they leads us."

DAY THREE — WHERE IN THE WORLD IS AMANDA CHASE?

—

"Yeah, the nurse just left the room," Amanda says on the phone. "She won't make another room check for forty minutes. I'm getting dressed now. Pick me up at the hospital's east exit in ten minutes."

She waits. "OK, thanks, I'll see you then." She hangs up the phone, gets out of bed. She walks over to the closet, picks out the dark blue dress she was wearing the night at the bar along with jacket that she draped over the seat next to her. Kind of them to bring that along.

She quickly changes out of the hospital gown and into the dress. Puts on the jacket and grabs her shoes and walks over to the door of the room. She opens it slightly, looks through. The corridor is empty. Slipping out, she silently walks down to the first door with an illuminated exit sign above it. She opens the door into the staircase steps through. She slips into her matching blue heels and hurries down the stairs. Arriving at the exit to the exterior, she stops to listen for any sounds. '*Good. Job done.*' She opens the door and rushes out into the night.

DAY THREE — FAN SUPPORT

Evening

The main door leading to the holding area opens. The enclosed area, composing of eight, equally sizes jail cells is a mixture of grey painted cinder block walls fronted by thick metal bars evenly spaced out with a cell door equally made out of the same sized thick bars.

Larry stands up from his cot and walks over to the cell bars to investigate.

Two officers walk into the holding area, each one carrying a large standing fan. One officer walks to the end of the hallway and positions the fan in the centre aisle away from anyone's reach within the cells.

The other officer does the same at the front of the hallway. They run the respective extension cords to the nearest wall electrical receptacle and plug them in. When the fans rev up, the wind rustles Larry's hair and face. He stands there for a moment, enjoying the new found breeze before collapsing in relief on the cot behind him.

"There have been some complaints about the oppressive heat and humidity in the detention area," one of the officers shouts, "so the city leaders have decided to provide us with some additional fans to combat the ninety-degree heat and stuffiness in the detention area. Enjoy the breeze, gentlemen. The heat and humidity will be with us for the next week or so."

DAY FOUR — CALLING HOME

Morning

"Mr. Evans," the daytime duty officer calls out. An older gentleman compared to the rest of the officers at the station. A veteran police officer.

Startled, Larry jumps up from his cot and approaches the cell bars where the duty officer is standing. "Yes?"

"We have an interrogation room set aside for you so you can contact your family, friends, and employer if you so wish to do so. You have been granted one hour to notify all parties of your current status and make whatever arrangements you need."

"Arrangements?"

"Personal arrangements—the upkeep of your residence, mail pick-up, stuff like that."

"OK. I understand."

"Please step back while I open the cell door. I will escort you to one of the rooms."

"Thank you, officer."

"Belker. Officer Carl Belker."

"Thank you, Officer Belker. I doubt I will need the whole hour. Don't need to make many calls. Only the hard one to my employer. They will be pissed."

"OK, then maybe order pizza for the station, if you remember your credit card number," Officer Belker responds with a wink.

"Actually, I do," Larry says. "What toppings do you like?"

"All dressed. All the time." Officer Belker opens the cell door and steps aside to let Larry through. "Down the hall, through the doors, and to your right. First room."

Larry advances down the corridor and shouts over his head. "Get me the number to the pizza join so I can put in the order."

DAY FOUR – DAMN GOOD PIZZA

Evening

"How did your calls go?" Officer Belker is sitting across from Larry outside the jail cell, in the corridor separating the four cells on the one side with an equal number on the other side, consuming his second slice of all-dressed pizza.

Larry sits up on his cot with his back to the wall, working on his third slice. "Not good. Not good at all. My manager exploded over the phone. Called me all sorts of names. Told me what an incredible disaster this was."

"Is it?" Officer Belker asks.

"Yes. We'll probably lose the contracts on the two clients I had lined up meetings with this week. Many millions of dollars of work. Upper management is going lose their shit. Screw up the bottom line."

"Really?"

"I think he is more upset at his performance bonus then losing the contracts. I do the leg work; he gets the fat bonuses. No justice in this world sometimes."

"Can't your company reach out to the client and try and rescue the project?"

"They did. The reception was not good when they were told that their primary contact on the projects was in jail on assault charges. Word got around to the clients before I was able to notify my employer. Not too professional."

Belker shakes his head in disappointment.

"They even flew down a few account executives to meet with the clients at the off-site meeting rooms that had been arranged ahead of time. The clients never showed up," Larry says, attacking his slice of pizza with a renewed sense of vigour. "On a separate note, can you do anything about the living arrangements here? For one, the bed is really painful. Are all the cells the same size?

Taking another bite out of his pizza, Officer Belker raises his hand to Larry, indicating that a response is forthcoming. "All the cells are the same size. Ten by twelve feet. The mattresses are all the same. The one you have is actually a new one. You're the first to use it."

"OK. At least that's good to know."

"The best I can do is get you a second pillow. I don't think you want an extra blanket with this heat and humidity going around?"

"I'll pass on the blanket. The fans in the hallway do help, so thanks for that," Larry responds. "Damn good pizza, Officer Belker. Good recommendation."

"Thank you for covering the bill. The boys in the station thank you also." Officer Belker raises his slice of pizza in salute.

Larry does likewise.

DAY FOUR — CALLING RONALD SLATER

——

"Hi, Ronald, this is Owen Fisher over at the *Springvale Journal*. I have something you might be interested in. The name is Larry Evans. Arrested several days ago for aggravated assault at the Springvale Starline Hotel. During his courtroom appearance, he had a unique response to the judge asking him how he pleaded to the charges. Anyway, I'll save that for when you call me back. I've got too much on my plate right now, so it would be great if you could run with it. Will send everything over via email. Thanks again. Call me."

DAY FOUR — OFFICER CARL BELKER

—

As the daytime duty officer, Carl Belker is in charge of managing the workings of the police station in an efficient and orderly manner. One such task is to overlook the current group of inmates in the holding area of the police station.

Belker, an older police officer who has served many years on the street, had requested a desk job to finish off the last few years before he retires with a full pension. His job as duty officer suits him just fine.

When Larry Evans first arrives at the police station, there is a sudden surge of excitement and activity that the station has not seen in months. His unwavering claim of innocence on the assault charge from a man without a criminal record was unusual. Not a single traffic ticket or parking violation was icing on the cake. It breaks the boredom that some police officers had been experiencing, a welcome distraction for some of the staff.

Carl has a good judge of character, developed from twenty years as a street cop, and he sees Larry as an enigma. His disposition of innocence does not fit the crime.

The main door to the holding area opens like clockwork every morning at eight o'clock. Belker walks in and closes the heavy steel door behind him. "Good morning, everybody," he calls out.

Larry stands and walks over to the cell bars. "Officer Belker. A moment of your time, please?"

Belker walks to Larry's cell, standing several feet away from the bars. "Mr. Evans. What can I do for you today?"

"Since it looks like my stay in this cell has been extended for an unforeseeable period of time, what is the possibility of getting some reading material to whittle away the boredom?"

The officer, initially showing indifference, is contemplative. "Your request is not something that is usually asked by an inmate."

"Really? What do they usually ask for?"

"TVs, radios, internet access, other electronic devices."

"Well, then, me asking for a copy of the local newspaper or magazines should be an easy one," Larry replies.

"I guess. The local newspaper sends over a half dozen copies. I don't know why. Don't care, really. Nobody ever reads them. I guess it wouldn't hurt if I dropped one of them by during my daily rounds."

"Thank you, officer," Larry replies with a smile.

"You can call me Carl. Pretty much on a first name basis with the all the inmates," Officer Belker states as he turns to the left. "Right, Jimmy?" he calls.

"You got it, Carl!" a voice yells from down the hallway.

"Well then, thank you, Carl," Larry says.

"I'll bring whatever I find in the reception area to you during the lunch-time rounds. Have a good morning, Mr. Evans."

DAYS FIVE TO SIX — THE NEWS HITS THE PAPERS AND TV

—

Some kind of internal clock tells Larry to open his eyes. He gets up from his cot and walks over to the cell bars, stretching as much as he can to get a quick view of the clock. 8:35 a.m. *Not bad!*

He spots something on the floor, immediately outside of his cell. He walks over to the bars and notices a copy of the local newspaper with several other magazines on top.

I guess if you behave and don't cause a stink, getting some reading material is not an issue. He reaches through the bars and retrieves the stack. He retreats to his cot and starts with the local newspaper. He devours the paper end to end and soon is up to speed on the numerous (non) events of the city of Springvale. He then proceeds with the magazines. This will keep him busy until lunch time.

In the following days, Officer Belker offers Larry a copy of the *Newark Sentinel* after he finishes reviewing it, the only newspaper that he has shown any interest in. Larry, ever the voracious reader, consumes the journal in under an hour.

Larry's meals come in from a local diner about two blocks away. In the morning, the meal is usually eggs with a side order of toast, bacon, and occasionally, some fruit. On the odd days when eggs are not offered, he gets a small box of cereal, an eight-ounce container of milk. and again, fruit on the side. Lunch is more straightforward. Mostly meat or chicken lunches. Light on the vegetables, a bag of chips as a substitute.

Larry, not a big fan of chips, offers them up to Officer Belker as a thank you for the newspapers and magazines.

Supper is pretty much the same as lunch. Not many options available from the diner, it seems.

After several days of sedentary living, Larry takes up exercising in his cell to burn off some of the heavy-calorie meals. With limited mobility due to the confines of the cell, he does a routine of push-ups and sit-ups every few hours. Within days, the exercise routine turns into a mini obsession for himself, admittedly, this is long overdue. His body weight is normal for his six-foot-two inch frame. As a rule, he does not indulge in unhealthy food frequently, but he is not a complete stranger to it either. Maybe he has a high metabolism.

Soon, he incorporates burpees. He discovers how out of shape he is, out of breath after a dozen burpees.

Not one to sound a call of defeat, Larry doubles his efforts, adding plank jacks, jumping jacks, corkscrews, squat jumps, and a few more that he got from a Google search that Carl did for him.

Larry exercises four times a day for about thirty minutes at a time, always stripping down to his briefs to avoid sweating in his clothes. The workouts usually result in a drenched body from head to toe, at which point he stands against the bars of the door to get as much of the circulated fan air as possible. On the fifth day, with the reported temperature at ninety-seven degrees, Larry restricts his exercise routine too early in the morning and late at night.

While reviewing the local newspaper, he finds a small article, about one hundred words, about him and the incident at the hotel. Both his and Amanda's names are mentioned, but his name is incorrectly spelled. *So, the news is spreading*, he thinks to himself.

This town moves slowly. He decides to do a quick workout session before reading the remainder of the paper.

The next day, nothing new is reported in the local newspaper, but the same article is picked up by the *Sentinel*. No opinion piece included—just a straight pick up. The story has now left the borders of Springvale.

DAY SEVEN — THE NEWS HITS THE MEDIA, ACT I

—

"Here you go, Mr. Evans," Officer Belker says as he hands a copy of the *Newark Sentinel* and the local paper to him.

Larry grabs the papers and quickly retreats back to his cot, propping himself up against the cold cement wall. "Thanks, Officer Belker," Larry shouts back.

Larry starts with the article in the Newark paper. It is well over two hundred words in length and goes into greater detail about the events at the hotel and the courtroom.

"Well, at least they got my name right this time," Larry calls to whomever is listening.

Nobody answers.

The mayor of Springvale, not one to miss an opportunity to get into the spotlight, also chimes in about the whole incident: "This was a disgusting act of assault on an innocent woman. This man should be locked up forever."

DAY EIGHT — CARL'S STORY

—

Larry sat in his small cell reading the *Newark Sentinel*. Out of curiosity, Carl Belker visited him every day.

"So, anything interesting in this morning's paper? Are you becoming famous?" Carl asks with a grin.

"More like infamous. The media is getting creative with my whole situation. I think the alien baby narrative is just a few days away."

"Well, I am glad you are taking this well," Carl responds.

"Only way to take it," Larry says. "I'm in here. Except for my lawyer keeping me up to date on the proceedings, I don't have much to do. Don't have any friends, really. Just a few business associates that I hang around with on the odd social occasion. None that I can really place in the 'friends' category. How about you? What keeps you going?"

"Me?" Carl responds, surprised.

"Yeah. You know my story. You've read my deposition, the police reports. The newspaper articles. I think that covers me."

Carl pauses for a second, then walks over to the opposite wall to pick up a folding metal chair leaning against the wall. He carries it back in front of Larry's cell and sits down. Looks across to Larry and nods. "Where do I start?"

"Well, I'm not going anywhere any time soon, so why don't you start with when you joined the police department? Don't leave anything out. I like details. I'm a details man," Larry says.

"OK. I've been with the department for twenty-eight years now. Started out up in Newark for the first ten. Was transferred to Springvale, as they needed the help with street gangs—not that you would notice now. It took a few years, but I led a task force that did a good job of putting the bad players behind bars and making the city a better place to raise a family.

"Met my wife Julia in Springvale shortly after I got here. Met her at a dinner party hosted by a fellow cop on the task force. Quickly discovered that it was a set-up for Julia and me to meet. Well, first impressions were enough. We got married shortly afterwards." Carl pauses.

"Go on! Do you have kids?" Larry asks.

"Nope, unfortunately, we couldn't. It was not to be. But we had each other. That was enough for us."

"How was the work-life balance?"

"It was a little rough when the task force was in full swing, but it got better once we got the upper hand on the gang situation. Personally, I wanted to get out of the task force the day I met Julia, as I wanted to spend as much time with her. It took many years but was finally able to push the commissioner to shift me back to desk duty and minimize my risk of injury or worse on the streets. I wanted regular hours, to be home for supper at night, and to give up my overnight shifts. I know Julia never liked it when I was scheduled on overnights. She kept having dreams of getting a call out of the blue that had something had happened to me and I wouldn't be coming home." Carl sighs.

"Well, it seems like you've been able to live up to your side of the arrangement," Larry states.

"Yeah. Five years ago, I was transferred to this position. Well, that lasted about six months. My wife took ill, and within months, passed away due to misdiagnosed conditions."

"Fuck! I am so sorry to hear that, Carl." Larry shakes his head.

"With only a police officer's salary, I couldn't afford expensive lawyers to go up against the firm representing the hospital. I had to drop the suit as the legal bills piled up."

"The system screwed you. Damn! That's not right!"

"Nope, it is not. But I've learned to live with it, and I've moved on slowly. But I've got my health. I've got two years left for full pension. I'll be good," Carl says.

"You will be, Carl. I have a feeling you will be."

"Thanks, Larry. You're a good listener."

"I have to be," Larry says.

Carl interrupts him. "It's part of the job. Yep." He gives Larry a friendly smile.

DAY NINE — THE NEWS HITS THE MEDIA, ACT II

—

The article about Larry and Amanda has grown to about four hundred words; again, coverage is being handled more by the *Newark Sentinel* than the local paper. This article repeats many of the previous articles but also introduces comments from several hotel staff members and police officers who don't want to be identified.

Now it starts, Larry thinks to himself. *Unidentified persons coming out of the woodwork to provide their commentary on the events.* Some statements bend the truth a little too much. Other statements were completely fabricated. The fake news has started.

During a quiet period at the front desk, Carl comes by to see Larry in his cell. He hands Larry a newspaper through the cell bars. "Did you know that Ms. Chase is now carrying your alien baby? It's all there in the *Global Inquirer*. You know, if it's printed in there, it must be true," Carl says, trying to keep from laughing.

Larry shoots him a dirty look and skims through the pages. He stops. "Did you see the article about Springvale water tests? It's causing penises to be 40 percent smaller than the national average."

Carl turns and starts walking away, raising his middle finger to give Larry a salute.

DAY NINE — THE NEWS
HITS THE MEDIA, ACT III

—

A local TV reporter and cameraman show up at the police station and get as far as the beginning of the corridor leading to his cell before they are intercepted and escorted out. The scuffle and elevated voices grabs Larry's attention at first but quickly decided to not waste any further time on discovering it's source. He returns to his reading.

That evening, one of the police officers on duty tells Larry that he has made it on the local news channel. He is becoming a local celebrity, mostly due to the ever increasing fabricated stories involving Larry and his supposed illicit affair with Amanda Chase,

Surprisingly, as a gesture of goodwill, Officer Belker gives Larry a small used radio so he can listen to music, talk radio, and listen to hockey games. Even though his team, the Montreal Canadians, have a storied history with twenty-four Stanley Cup victories to their name, the last dozen years and more have not been kind to them.

However, being an avid hockey fan, he supports his team through both the good and the bad years.

DAY TEN — THE NEWS
HITS THE MEDIA, ACT IV

Picking up on the statements from the previous day's article, the police chief and local elected officials comment on Larry's predicament. One of these officials is the mayor of Springvale, Jonas Frakes. He has been the mayor for the last twenty-odd years, due mostly to running elections unopposed.

In some circles, there is talk that opposing candidates were influenced and intimidated to not run against him. Frakes also has several local businesses that thrive on city contracts. Again, investigation is highly discouraged by persons of interest.

Frakes is one who enjoys the spotlight, making himself known at local social outings and making sensational statements about current events.

"Mayor Frakes, Mayor Frakes. Any comments about the ongoing trial of Larry Evans?" one eager reporter shouts during another of Mayor Frakes's importune media announcements.

"Thank you, Charlie. Always nice to hear from you." The mayor winks at him. "I have said this before, and I will say it again, I cannot wait until the verdict is announced and Mr. Evans is sent to prison for a long time. We do not like people like this in our city.

We do not want them roaming our streets. We will not tolerate criminals like this in Springvale. We will not tolerate them in the great state of New Jersey, either."

DAY TEN — TWEETING
THE NIGHT AWAY

Claudia Frakes, the devoted, supportive wife of Mayor Jonas Frakes, has had enough of his late-night tweet marathons. Several heated arguments about his obsession have ended with the two of them sleeping in separate beds to cool off. This is not really a problem, as the elegant house they occupy has five bedrooms.

Claudia walks into his study and discovers Jonas sitting back in his dark brown leather chair behind his desk facing away from the door. "Are you on Twitter again?" she asks.

He types away furiously on his phone and doesn't notice her presence until she yells at him. He spins around, annoyed. "What do you want?"

"I am tired of you getting up immediately after dinner and hiding out in your study to bash away at the target of the week on Twitter and Facebook," Claudia exclaims.

"So, your point is?"

"Have you ever stopped to think that everything you type and every comment and personal attack you make might come back to bite you in the ass one day? People find a false sense of security in declaring their opinions on Facebook, Twitter, Instagram, or whatever else is out there. They don't realize that everything they say is recorded, saved on some cloud file up there." She points upwards in defeated frustration.

"I'm not worried. I only comment on the Larry Evans trial these days. He is totally guilty!" Mayor Frakes says confidently.

"This obsession isn't healthy. It isn't healthy for us. For our marriage. Please, Jonas, stop. Come to bed," Claudia pleads.

Jonas rests his hands on the armchair, phone in his right hand. "I'll be up shortly."

Claudia, exhausted, hunches her shoulders. "Don't bother. I'm going to bed. Alone!" She turns and walks out of the study.

DAY ELEVEN – THE MOSQUITO INCIDENT REVISITED

"What are you doing?" Carl inquires with a quizzical look on his face as he watches Larry roaming around in the confined space of his jail cell, clutching rolled up newspapers in both hands, swatting his immediate surrounding, both high and low.

"Eh!" Larry wipes around to face Carl, who is standing out in the hallway. "How long have you been there?"

"Long enough."

"What?"

"It this some kind of new yoga mediation sponsored by the newspaper industry to increase readership?" Carl chuckles in amusement.

"No." Larry responds without hesitation. "It's those damn mosquitos."

"What about them?"

Larry leaps closer to his cot and slams one of the rolled-up newspapers down against the metal post. "Damn. Little shits are too fast."

"Why are you doing that?"

Larry turns to face Carl, his forehead beading with sweat, his eyes burning in intensity in his battle with the mosquito. "You too?"

"Me too! What?" Carl asks.

"You are not going to start lecturing me also about the role of the mosquito in our ecosystem also?"

Carl, squinting his eyes in confusion, "What are you talking Larry?"

"Pollinating. Mosquitos apparently are important in the pollinating process in our eco-system.

"Who the hell told you that shit?"

Larry pauses and takes in a deep breath before answering, "fuggedaboutit!"

"Ok, Tony Soprano." Carl says as he shakes his head in amusement, turns, and walks back out of the holding area.

DAY TEN — THE NEWS HITS THE MEDIA

—

Carl Belker walks into the holding area and up to Larry's cell. "Hey, movie star, you made the local TV news again and the front page of the paper." He hands over the newspaper through the cell bars.

Larry grabs it quickly, unfolds it, and looks at the headlines.

"They even reached out to your company back in Montreal for comment, but they refused to give any," Belker says.

"Thanks, Carl."

Belker turns around and is about to walk out when Larry raises his index finger to stop him.

"What?"

Larry looks up from the paper with a smirk. "Do you want me to autograph the paper for you? It could be worth big bucks someday."

"Jackass!" Belker turns and walks away, shaking his head.

DAY TWELVE — THE NEWS HITS THE MEDIA, ACT V

—

The *Newark Sentinel* articles become increasingly creative as both Larry and Amanda avoid making any statements to the media. One imaginative reporter, coined the whole coverage as LarryGate and within hours it quickly went viral.

The previous day, Benjamin Dowds told Larry that Amanda Chase had left the hospital several days after she was admitted and has not been seen since. The news outlet, surprisingly, has only become aware of this now, so it has fallen on reporters to get creative, referencing unnamed sources about Larry's sudden "erratic" behaviour in his jail cell. According to them, Amanda has admitted to knowing Larry before the events at the hotel bar.

Lovers' quarrel conspiracies come out of the woodwork. The governor of New Jersey is asked to comment about LarryGate, but he politely declines.

The president of the United States, on the other hand, jumps on the LarryGate bandwagon and rides it into town at an outdoor news conference.

The gathering consisted mostly of local and national reporters, out in front and center with a small coward of supporters immediately behind them. Security was tight as it always is for any outdoor event. President Campbell, dressed in a tailored dark blue double breasted suit with a matching vest; unusual for a politician to wear but President Campbell wore it well. The suit complemented his slim six foot frame perfectly. His square shaped face, angular jaw and dark hair with only a hint of grey completed the polished package that made him popular with voters.

Before stepping in front of any crowd to address the media or give a speech to the public, President Campbell always rubbed his presidential pin on his suit jacket collar before stepping on a stage as a sign of good luck.

"Mr. President, what is your stance on the ongoing reports of the Larry Evans and Amanda Chase court case? There has been a lot of commentary by local politicians and mayors," one reporter yells out.

"Oh! You're talking about LarryGate." The President responds, always one who keeps up to date on issues that are grabbing local, regional, and national interests. "As for this one, who hasn't paid attention?" The president looks across the gathered reporters, most of them nodding in agreement. "I think it is disgusting. The attack was disgusting, and I hope he gets to go to jail for a long time."

"So, you believe he did it?" the reporter asks. "Right now, he still claims he did not."

"The facts are there. Multiple witness, from what I understand, have come forward. They all say the same thing. He hit her, and it is disgusting. Not a fan on assault toward women," the president responds.

"So, you think justice will prevail, Mr. President?" the reporter adds.

"Yes. Absolutely. Scum like this should be locked away. There is no space for people like this in our society."

"How about the rumours that he was in town visiting his illegal wife and that he was arranging to bring her back to Canada? Any comment on that, Mr. President?"

"Well, I have not heard about this one in particular, but I will definitely have to look into it. Maybe get Immigration to look into this," the President responds.

"Mr. President, there is also a national security angle here," another reporter says. "Mr. Evans represents a Canadian software company that develops secure communication applications used by many of our larger corporations and even some government agencies. Are you concerned that Mr. Evans was compromised and that he poses a security risk to our country?"

"Well yes, that is an important matter, and I will get the justice department to look into the matter. If it is an issue, then we might need to sanction the company itself. We cannot let our guard down at any time when it comes to protecting our communication infrastructure."

"Mr. President, Mr. President," several more reporters shout, waving their hands.

"That's all for now. I've got to go now to run a country. Thank you all." The President waves at the press corps, turns around, and leaves, followed by several dozen assistants and Secret Service agents.

DAY TWELVE — BAD NEWS

———

Evening

The main door to the holding area opens, and Officer Carl Belker walks up to Larry's cell. "Larry!" he calls.

Surprised by the unexpected visit, Larry quickly gets up and walks over to the cell bars. "What's up, Carl?"

"Just got a note that some person from your company up in Montreal will be here tomorrow to meet with you. Some human resources person."

"Well that just freaking great. HR visits are never good news. If they're coming from Montreal, I really don't think they're coming to give me a raise."

"Sorry, Larry. I just deliver the message."

"No worries, Carl."

"On the bright side, it looks like the heat and humidity is finally breaking, and we will be back to a more seasonal seventy-five degrees." Carl gives him a quick smile and then turns and exits.

Larry sits back on his cot, crunched forward, holding the back of his head with both hands. "Shit!"

DAY THIRTEEN — VISIT
BY HUMAN RESOURCES

—

On the morning of the thirteenth day of his incarceration, Larry is not in his cell, but sitting in an interrogation room on one side of a square metal table. His hair is unkempt, and he's gone nearly a dozen days without shaving.

An empty chair is opposite him. The room, itself, is in a desperate need of a fresh coat of paint as cracks are clearly evident as Larry burns away time examining the room. There are no hanging signs or pictures. Nothing. With no clock on the wall, he doesn't know how long he has been waiting. His personal watch was taken from him when he was arrested and processed.

The door opens, and an unfamiliar police officer walks in. Besides Larry's daily exchanges with Belker, he has dealt with more than a dozen different officers over the two weeks he's been in jail, most of them not very kind.

An elegantly dressed woman in a grey business suit walk in behind him and immediately sits down across the table from Larry. She places her thin leather briefcase on the table, flips it open, and pulls out a file folder. She pushes the briefcase aside and places the file folder in front of her. She looks up to the officer and nods. "Has the room been checked?" she asks.

"Yes, as per your company's request, it was checked yesterday evening and again twenty minutes ago. Nothing was found, and the room has been sealed since then. It's clean."

"Thank you for verifying this, officer. That will be all."

The police officer looks over to Larry, who does not give him the satisfaction of looking back, and then turns and exits the room, closing the door behind him.

"Please confirm that you are one Larry Evans from Montreal, Canada. Also, please confirm that you are employed by Commlink Services as a senior sales manager."

A look of confusion crosses his face. "Who are you?" he inquires.

"Please, answer the question."

"Yes, I am Larry Evans from Montreal, Quebec. That's the province where I live. Canada is a country. Now, who are you?"

"My name is Susan Sanders, the human resources manager for Commlink Services. Your employer," she responds.

"Ah. You came all the way down from Montreal to visit me?"

"This is not a social visit, Mr. Evans. I am here on company business."

"Company business?"

"Yes, I am here to review and advise you on your change of status."

"Change of status! What about my status?" he asks, his interest piqued.

"Mr. Evans, I am here to inform you that as of nine o'clock this morning, you are no longer an employee of Commlink Services. Due to the nature of the events that have transpired here in New Jersey and the code of ethical conduct you signed when you were hired, the company has come to the conclusion that it is of our best interest for you to no longer be associated with our company and the corporate values it stands for."

"Excuse me! Are you firing me?"

"No, we are terminating your contract, as your services are no longer needed."

"No longer needed?" he asks. "I have client projects in progress and am on the verge closing several others. How can I no longer be needed?"

"Your open projects have all been reassigned with little interruption. All your files for prospective clients have equally been re-assigned."

"You can't do that!" Larry exclaims.

"Mr. Evans, there's no need to raise your voice. This decision has been made, and yes, we can do it. It came down from upper management last week. We have been working on the paperwork needed for us to part ways with you."

"On what grounds?"

"Excuse me?"

"On what grounds?" he asks, his hands shaking in frustration. "I mean, why am I being fired?"

"Terminated, Mr. Evans!"

"OK. OK. Fuck. Terminated! Same fucking thing as fired," Larry responds.

"No, Mr. Evans. It is not." She pauses for a moment. Looks down at the paperwork in front of her. She then reaches over to her briefcase, lifts it slightly to check something.

Larry scrutinizes her with curiosity.

She shoots him a brief glance and then returns her focus to the documents in front of her. "This is how it is going to play out, Mr. Evans. Based on the code of conduct outlined in our corporate governance policy, the acts that occurred on May 4th of this year are in direct violation of Sections 2, 7, and 11. These all have to do with conduct unbecoming of an employee—an arrest for assault and an assault on a member of the opposite sex.

"Due to these charges, it has been deemed by our board of governors that you are to be terminated immediately without any financial indemnification.

"Furthermore, all accrued salaries, performance bonuses due, and accrued vacations to date will be withheld in order to cover any liabilities the company might incur if we are called in any way during the trial. All corporate credit cards and cell phones have been cancelled and reclaimed from your personal belongings at the hotel and are now in the possession of the local police."

"What?" he exclaims. "You're leaving me with nothing?"

"Mr. Evans, the incident that transpired on the evening of May 4th was horrendous and unspeakable. The company has suffered much negative publicity because of your actions. Even the President of the United States has condemned you. He has asked the Department of Justice to investigate the company for possible national security violations by you. Continued association with you is poisonous for our company. We are taking a financial hit because of you."

"But I didn't do it!" he exclaims. "You haven't given me a fair chance to explain what really happened. I am being treated like shit!"

Pausing, Susan Sanders' expressionless face changes to one of anger. "Honestly, I don't give a shit. You men are all the same. I do not need to hear more from you. We've heard enough from the police report to make our decisions."

"I did not do—"

Ms. Sanders interrupts Larry as she stands up and points her finger at him. "Listen, the decision is made. You are out. You get no severance pay. No vacation pay. Nothing. Do you understand?" She pauses and looks down intently at Larry. He returns her stare.

The tense moment comes to an end when Susan picks up the folder and hands it over to him. "This is your copy of the termination agreement. Please sign it and return it to us as soon as possible." She looks into her briefcase to make sure everything is in order, flips the clasp closed, and locks it in place. She grabs it off the desk, turns, and heads toward the door. She knocks on the door. It immediately opens. She goes down the corridor without looking back.

The guard's eyes follow her until she is out of sight. He then brings his attention back to Larry. "Come on. Grab your documents, and let's get you back to your cell."

Larry obliges by picking up the documents left by the HR manager, and goes out the door into the corridor. The guard follows him closely.

DAY FOURTEEN — HOTEL DISCOVERY: TAPES, PLEASE!

The door to the security office at the Springvale hotel is closed and locked from the inside.

Three people occupy it. Two men stand behind a third who sits in front of a computer with multiple displays of live video footage from cameras covering the entire hotel.

The earlier arrival of the well-dressed men drew some stares from staff members in the reception and dining area. Everybody remained quiet as they walked by, heading toward the front desk. Moments later, the front desk manager called over one of his assistants to take over as he escorted the two men through a door marked "Staff Only."

The security manager types away on his keyboard, and the manager scrolls through multiple directories of video files.

The taller of the two standing gentlemen says, "So, can you bring us up to speed? Do you have what we need?"

Pablo Sanchez, the hotel security officer who is sitting, nods. "Yes, I found the missing files earlier this afternoon in an incorrectly named subfolder. The daily video backup maintenance job was referencing the incorrect folder."

"Was the maintenance job altered recently?" The taller man asks.

The security officer clicks on one of the open folders and scans through the list of files. "The job was last modified about seven months ago. Probably part of the final fiscal year code changes. We then go into a code freeze for about three months where any software update or patch needs executive corporate approval. Besides that, there is nothing unusual."

"Thanks for checking," the taller man responds.

"I'm reviewing all the video file time-stamps to make sure all the time sequences are accounted for. Give me a few more minutes," the sitting man replies as he types.

"That is good news. Our boss will be very happy to have a copy of these files," the tall man states politely. He gives his associate, standing beside him, a quick glance.

"Normally, it's against the rules of the hotel," the officer states, "but if this will help put that predator away for good, then, yes, I will make a copy for you."

"Have you reviewed the missing video files Mr. Sanchez?" the taller man asks.

"Not really. Too busy right now to waste time watching them. I'm taking off for vacation this afternoon, so you guys are lucky that you came today. Another hour, and you would be waiting for two weeks until I got back," the security guard states.

"Well then, we thank you very much for your cooperation. Have yourself a great vacation," the taller man says.

"I will. Two weeks on a nice quiet beach on a small tropical island. What else can you ask for?" the security officer asks as he fumbles through his desk drawer. He pulls out a thumb drive from his top desk drawer and plugs it into an available port. He types a few commands on the keyboard and waits a few moments as he watches the LED display on the thumb drive flash. He sits there, uncomfortably watching the slow progress of the completion bar as the two men hover over him.

The process is slow, as each video file is fairly large. *I hope there is enough space on the thumb drive*, the security officer thinks. Not a big fan of people looking over his shoulders, the security officer wipes his forehead with the back of his hand.

With the transfer process completed, Pablo hands the thumb drive to the tall man. "All the video files for the missing time are accounted for. The thumb drive is compliments of the house, or hotel, so to speak!"

"Thank you again Mr. Sanchez." The taller man says.

The shorter man, having stayed quiet during the whole meeting, finally speaks. "It would be beneficial for the prosecution that this information is not shared with anybody else who comes calling. We want to slam the defence when we reconvene next week."

Pablo stands up and looks over the two men standing before him. He nods.

The men turn and proceed out the door of the security office and out the hotel toward a waiting car. They quickly jump into the car and race away.

DAY FOURTEEN — WE NEED THE TAPES

—

Roughly ten minutes later, another vehicle pulls up in front of the main entrance of the hotel. A dark blue Lincoln Town Car with tinted windows idles while two smartly dressed men in blue suits, nearly matching the colour of the vehicle, get out from the rear passenger doors. They close the doors from either side and proceed toward the entrance. The car parks in an empty spot for short-term parking.

The front desk manager looks up from his terminal. "Gentlemen, how can I help you today?"

One of the men reaches into his suit pocket and pulls out a leather ID badge. He flips it open to display a picture of himself below an inscription of the FBI logo. "Hi, Howard," he says, taking in the manager's name tag, "my name is Special Agent Marco Shearing, and this is Special Agent Anthony Sutcliff." He indicates the man standing beside him.

Taken aback, Howard reviews the badges and then looks back up to them. These days, fake IDs are becoming harder to spot. "Again, what can I do for you?"

"We need to speak to the person in charge of hotel surveillance right away," asks Agent Shearing.

"Well, I guess that would be Pablo Sanchez," says Howard.

Agent Shearing smiles. "Well, then. Please call him for us. We need to speak to him about a case we are working on. Time is of the essence."

"OK, well, Agent Shearing, that will be a problem."

"And why is that?" Agent Shearing inquires.

"Well, Mr. Sanchez has gone on a vacation. He was actually just here, picking up a few items. He had a meeting with two other men in suits. Gentlemen like you two in his office and then took off. You missed him by about ten minutes."

Agent Shearing frowns at Agent Sutcliff. "Two men in suits, just like us?"

"Yes, that is correct."

"Can you describe them in greater detail?"

"Well, not really, as I was on my break, and it seems like Pablo— that is, Mr. Sanchez—met with them directly. I only saw them on their way out. They were official looking."

"Official looking?" Agent Shearing asks.

"Yeah. You know. Dressed like you two. Nice suits, nice shoes, clean shaven, and they both looked like they were in shape."

"Did you see their faces?"

"Nope, only a side view, as I said, they were walking out the door."

Agent Shearing pauses.

"Well, who is in charge while Mr. Sanchez is off vacationing?" Agent Sutcliff asks clenching his fists.

Howard explains the backup process for security monitoring. "When our in-house personnel are not available for an extended period of time, the whole operation is handled by a sister hotel's personnel."

"OK, then, what is the location of the sister hotel?"

"Colorado Springs, Colorado."

"What? I thought it would be a hotel in the next city over," says Agent Sutcliff.

"Head office wants to expand their reach, not limit their selection of sister hotels to a small geographical region."

"Well, that's very admirable for your operations, but—"

Howard interrupts him. "Yes, not good for your inquiries. You see, when the in-house security manager is off-site, our physical surveillance facilities are locked down, and all access to the surveillance system is transferred to sister hotel personnel."

"What if we break down the door?" demands Agent Sutcliff.

"Nothing is saved locally on the surveillance computers or even on our hotel network. The whole process is heavily encrypted on cloud servers, and I would have to bill you for damages to the door," responds Howard, smirking. *Small victories against government snooping*, he thinks.

"Thank you, Mr. . . . ?" Agent Shearing asks.

"Johnson. Howard Johnson, and no, no relation to the Howard Johnson hotel chain."

The two agents look at each quizzically, then turn and head out the hotel's main entrance.

Howard raises his hand and waves as they walk away. "Please, come again!"

DAY FOURTEEN — AND THE WINNING FILES ARE . . .

The car carrying the tall man and short man pulls in front of the *Springvale Journal*. The short man pulls out his laptop and plugs the thumb drive into the laptop. After launching a secure web portal, he quickly uploads the thumb drive's contents to the cloud.

Next, in an email to the *Springvale Journal*, he attaches the URL to the web-storage site. He titles the email, "Not everything looks as it seems."

Then he hits SEND.

The short man looks over to the tall man. "Call it in; transfer is done."

The tall man pulls out his cell phone, selecting a number from his contacts. He waits a few seconds as the connection is made. "The transfer is done. Email sent." The tall man disconnects the call, not waiting for any acknowledgement.

He turns off his phone, flips it over, and pulls off the cover and the underlining battery pack. He hands the two parts over to the short man and removes the SIM card and cracks the cell phone in half. He hands the remaining parts of the phone to the short man and nods in satisfaction.

"Let's get going." The tall man says to the driver. The driver nods, puts it into gear into drive, pulls away from the curb, and merges into traffic.

DAY FOURTEEN —
REPORTING THE NEWS

———

Maggie Summers, seasoned reporter for the *Springvale Journal,* is in front of her laptop at an open desk; the desks are first come, first served, and nobody except the managers and editors with offices have permanent desks.

Everybody literally packs everything they need on their laptops and stores all their stories and research information on the cloud. For a small local newspaper, this helps with the lease and maintenance costs on the large brick-and-mortar building.

It is a quiet, uneventful morning until an inbox notification flashes. The sender is not someone she knows, therefore a quick virus scan before opening it to make sure it is not hazardous to her laptop is a no brainer. Within seconds, the results come back negative and she proceeds to open the email. The body of the message is empty except for reference to a URL link. She grabs the link and runs it through a URL scanner to make sure it does not contain any malware.

Nothing turns up. She clicks on the link, bringing her to a directory of dozens of video files. *Interesting.* She clicks on the first file and watches the video with passing interest for a moment before cocking her head as she recognizes a man in the video. *Wait.* She stops the video, pulls out her wireless ear buds from her laptop case, directly beside on the ground. The tapered silicone hearing pieces fit in comfortable into her ears. *Damn, should have done this in the beginning.* Maggie leans forward and restarts the video from the beginning with the volume raised. It lasts just over six minutes before she collapses back on to her chair. She stares at the directory of video files. On the bottom ribbon bar of the open window she sees the number of files. Twenty-nine other items.

She closes her laptop screen and looks around the office floor, spotting Emily Stiles, her trusted co-worker. She waves to get her attention and points to the small conference room on the opposite side of the room.

Emily nods. It's not the first time this scenario has occurred.

As Emily gets closer, Maggie whispers, "Get in the room and close the door behind me. Close the blinds."

Emily, intrigued, does what she is told.

Maggie places her laptop on the table. They both grab chairs on the opposite side of the door in case somebody walks in unannounced and they need to minimize the video.

"Watch, but don't say anything. Do you hear me?" Maggie states.

"What's going on?"

"Just watch, and don't speak!" Maggie clicks on the first video file. The video starts playing and the ladies watch in silence. With the first one finish, they look at each other; Maggie face is flushed with excitement whereas Emily's is pale in comparison from a growing sense of fear.

"Play the second one." Emily states with apprehension. Maggie then clicks on the second file.

Several minutes after watching the second video, Emily turns to Maggie, stunned. "What the fuck is this?" she states, hyperventilating.

"Calm down, Emily!" says Maggie, grabbing Emily's arm and staring into her eyes. She pauses. "What we have on this storage site is proof that will exonerate Larry Evans."

What was just said is mind-blogging, as the consistent narrative in the news and on social media is all wrong. The character assassination of Larry Evans has been ruthless, reaching all the way to the President of the United States. The media, the police, and politicians at all levels of government have ridiculed Larry Evans's repeated statements that he did not touch her. Once these videos make the airwaves, the reconciliation process will be immense.

"I smell a story," Emily says after coming to her senses, realizing how much publicity this will generate.

Maggie releases her hold on Emily's arm and pushes back from the table. Glancing at her, digesting her statement and analyzing the situation.

Maggie's continued silence speaks volumes. "What is going on, Maggie?"

No answer.

"Maggie?" Emily calls out.

Maggie, snapping out of her daze, finally responds, "This whole thing is fishy!"

"Fishy! Why?"

"The timing of this reveal. And from what I gather, these files are from a dark email account that we will never be able to find. Emily, have we published any articles related to the Evans case?" Maggie inquires.

"Pro or con?" Emily asks.

"Doesn't matter. Any articles at all?"

Emily ponders for a moment. "I don't think the paper has published any opinion pieces. We might have reprinted a fact-only piece in the beginning, but nothing since."

"Well, it seems we were chosen. Whoever sent the videos wanted a news outlet that has not yet taken a side or published anything on the incident. Interesting!"

"So, what's next—?" Emily starts her statement but then pulls her chair over to the laptop. Clearly, something has clicked in her brain. She takes command of the keyboard and attacks it with the clear determination of a person on a mission. The screen lights up with text-based windows, an area of the internet that is harder to access.

Maggie, having pulled the chair beside Emily, is fascinated by Emily's hidden skills.

For the next few minutes, Emily hacks away at the keyboard, alternating between gleeful excitement and frustration and despair.

"Ah ha!" Emily announces.

"What, what?" Maggie asks.

Emily pushes back from the table. "Nothing. Absolutely nothing. The email trail is cold. Whoever sent the email is clearly very good. I pride myself in my skills in surfing the dark web, but whoever sent the email covered his or her tracks very well. It's a dead end. I am sorry, Maggie!"

"OK, so what do we do next?" Maggie asks.

"We download all the video files and watch them all to get a full understanding of what we have. OK?" Maggie says.

"Gotcha. Then?"

"We definitely get the videos out there as quickly as possible. We will work up a copy. Get the boss to sign off on it. Have the videos authenticated and become famous," Emily says.

"Or infamous, in some people's eyes," Maggie states, shattering Emily's dreams. "Don't worry, Emily. We are a team, and as a team, we will make sure we get our full credit. Fuck whoever gets pissed off. We are doing the right thing in freeing an innocent man."

They stand up in unison and high-five each other.

DAY FOURTEEN —
WORKING OVERTIME TO
GET THE STORY RIGHT

Evening

The meeting with the managing editor is quick and to the point. With a happy grin, he signs off on their plan and offers them any resources they need.

Emily, the computer expert of the two, disappears into a corner of the office with noise-cancelling headphones, a box of jujubes, and a thirty-ounce bottle of Pepsi for caffeine. The work ahead of her will easily be an overnighter.

She reaches out to her contacts, ones she does not share publicly as most of them have dubious backgrounds, for recent chatter on anything related to untraceable emails. Next, she scours the dark web for any email signature or IP trail—any indication of where the email with the attached files came from.

Maggie works on the byline for the news release. The managing editor has given her several assistants to validate the videos. Both experts in the field, they strip apart the recording, looking for any signs of continuity manipulation. After several hours, they look over to Maggie and nod.

The recording is genuine.

James Marsala, the managing editor of the newspaper walks over to Maggie and Emily, sitting close among piles of draft paper copies with scribbles all over, food wrappers and empty food cartons across several desks. He eyeballs the clutter but remains silent before turning his attention to the reporters.

"This is big," he says. "I want no screw-ups. I want an outside expert to validate our video recording. It is not enough with just our in-house people. Emily, use your contacts and get me some-body reliable."

Emily nods.

"Maggie, how is the copy going?"

"Handed over to legal about thirty minutes ago. They'll get back to me on any issues that could blowback on us," Maggie responds.

"Good. Good. Keep going. All eyes on the prize," the manager calls out.

"And what is the prize?" Emily asks.

"To save an innocent man. Now get going and don't forget to clean up all this mess. Everything goes in the recycle bins." He turns around and walks away. "Goddamn! I love days like these," he barks.

At two in the morning, Maggie walks over to Emily to see how she is doing.

Emily, absorbed in her work, doesn't see her approaching and jumps out of her seat when Maggie puts her hand on her shoulder.

Maggie steps back and chuckles.

"What gives?" asks Emily. "You startled me!"

"Sorry," Maggie responds. "You have any updates?"

"Nothing. Nada, zip!" she states.

"At all?"

"Whoever sent the email is good," Emily says. "I mean, really good. Really freaking good. The email trail is clean. Even the GPS point of origin traces back here."

"What! What do you mean, back here?"

"Well, the digital footprint I was able to scrub from the email had GPS coordinates. When I investigated them, they pointed to our building."

Maggie's curiosity is piqued. "Somebody from here sent it?"

"I doubt it very much. The journal's internal network signature would be all over the email. It's more likely that somebody was outside the building within the coordinates' radius. You need to remember that unless you are using military GPS applications, coordinates have a variance of three to four metres. About ten to twelve feet."

"Look at you, Ms. Metric!" Maggie laughs.

"Oh, shut up!" Emily states. "I took a look at the buildings outside camera footage around the time the email was sent, and I didn't see anything."

"So, what next?" Maggie asks.

"I reached out to my associates—serious people in the dark-web community. They're impressed and a little concerned that there's somebody operating at this level of secrecy."

"Why?" Maggie asks.

"What is on the dark web and the people who reside within in it are the best of the best," Emily explains. "There's nowhere on the internet that they can't access. It's been like that since the internet was born. It's a closely guarded secret, and some kind of unholy alliance exists between them and most countries' intelligence services to keep the peace. Sure, every once in a while, a rogue operator goes bad, but that person is either brought back into the fold or disappears and is never heard from again."

"So? I'm still not getting it."

"Well, when somebody tries to hide the origin of a message or piece of communication, the usual way is to bounce it through multiple paths with false IP addresses or to hijack somebody's account to send out the communication. Other times, messages can be broken down in parts, sent from multiple servers, and reassembled at the destination. It's hard, but serious hackers have done it." She pauses to take a sip from her Pepsi bottle. "What we are dealing with here is a totally clean email. Almost to the point that it looks like it was typed directly on your laptop! Whoever has that skill set is way ahead of the game in security communication methods. This means a level of electronic communication exists that we are not even aware of. *That is what's scaring them.* They have no control over it, and these are people who need to live with being in control and respecting a balance between them and intelligence services. To them, somebody is not playing fairly, and major shit is going to happen if this party or individual is not identified soon."

"Whoa! I get it, I think." Maggie says as a sense of enlightenment overcomes her.

Emily smiles at her friend's realization and asks, "Please, tell me you typed the email so we can all relax?"

"You got me. I'm busted. It was me," Maggie declares, smiling.

Emily chuckles. "Thanks, I can rest easily now."

"Everything is done on my side." Maggie looks at her watch. "The story is going out in a few hours."

"And that is when the shit storm comes rolling into town," Emily says.

"Yeah!"

DAY FIFTEEN — MORE TV COMMENTARY

"Breaking news tonight on the attack at the Springvale Starline Hotel," the TV anchor proclaims. "For more details, we go live on-site to the Fourth Precinct where our reporter, Walter Murdock, has the latest on the alleged assault case on Amanda Chase by Larry Evans."

The TV video feed switches to a framed full shot of man standing in from of the Fourth Precinct police station. A subtle nod up front as he acknowledges his cue to commence his report.

"To recap, Canadian citizen Larry Evans was in Springvale on a business trip. On the night of May 4th, Evans, having just checked into the Springvale hotel, was seen conversing with Ms. Amanda Chase at the hotel restaurant bar. Moments later, an intense argument turned violent when Mr. Evans struck Ms. Chase, which witnesses say was unprovoked. What seemed like an open-and-shut case turned into turmoil when Evans claimed in court that he did not strike her at all. This statement contradicts multiple witnesses who have stated that Mr. Evans repeatedly struck Ms. Chase on the night of the assault."

Since the release of this statement, the story has taken on a life of its own. The local police and both local and state politicians have chimed in, most of their commentary based on unsubstantiated information.

To put the icing on the cake, President Campbell has also recently decided to bash Larry Evans, stating behaviour like this "should be met by the highest levels of punishment." He also states that any attempts to extradite Larry Evans back to Canada will be denied.

President Campbell states that he wants the world to take notice; nobody can enter the country and randomly assault good, hard-working Americans and get away with it. This statement itself has brought renewed commentary about the President's role and his influence on the judicial system. Whereas some politicians claim he is stepping over the line between executive and judicial branches, others praise his commitment to protecting the average American citizen. The opinions are drawn clearly along party lines.

Well, tonight comes word that all this political sabre-rattling could be for nothing.

"An unnamed source claims that the previously missing videos from the hotel restaurant bar have been discovered. As of yet, we still do not know if the video will provide the definite evidence to convict Larry Evans or exonerate him from charges. We will continue to pursue this evolving story as more information is made available. This is Walter Murdock reporting from Springvale, New Jersey."

DAY FIFTEEN —
SLEEPING HABITS

———

Benjamin Dowds, Larry's attorney, shows up at the police station early in the morning. He walks right up to the duty officer. "Good morning, Officer Belker. How are you today?"

Carl Belker spotted him when he walked through the door but kept his head down, occupying himself with some paperwork until Dowds's creeping shadow over his desk announced his presence in front of him.

He smiles at Dowds's greeting. "I am fine, thanks Mr. Dowds. Here to see your client, I presume?"

"That is correct," Dowds responds.

"OK. Room Two to your left. I'll bring him over in five minutes."

They both go their separate ways, Dowds to Room Two, Belker to get Larry Evans.

The room is to the right of Belker's desk and halfway down the corridor. Dowds parks himself on one side of the table. He is without his usual briefcase today, as this will be a quick meeting. He crosses his legs and sits back on the chair, waiting.

A minute later, Larry walks in. He acknowledges Officer Belker, who closes the door to the room for privacy. He sits across from Dowds in the empty chair.

"Good guy?" Dowds asks, nodding toward the departed Belker.

"Yes. He treats me well," Larry responds.

"Good to hear. What's with the goatee?" Dowds asks, pointing.

Larry instinctively rubs his chin. "Just trying something different. What do you think?"

"Get rid of it. It makes you look like evil Spock."

"Evil Spock! What are you talking about?"

"I guess you're not a *Star Trek* fan."

"More *Star Wars* than *Star Trek*," Larry replies.

"Well in one of the episodes in the original series, Captain Kirk goes into a parallel universe where everybody is evil. To differentiate between the good Spock and the evil Spock, Evil Spock sports a goatee. Actually, it's more of a Van Dyke beard than a goatee, but a lot of people don't know the difference. Anyways, Evil Spock tries to eliminate good Captain Kirk in the parallel universe, but in the end, Kirk gets away."

"So, what does this have to do with me?" Larry asks.

"Get rid of the goatee before we go in front of the judge again. You look evil," Dowds states firmly.

"Yes, Mr. Image Consultant sir!" Larry salutes him.

"Thanks."

"So, what brings you down here today? I didn't think we had anything scheduled," Larry inquires.

"You are correct. We didn't have anything on the books. Two things to talk about," Dowds states.

"OK, go ahead. Not going anywhere."

"First, I assume you've heard talk of the hotel video files of the night in question being found?" Dowds asks.

"I did. News travels fast in the station."

"Good. If the video files do exist and they prove your innocence, then I will go straight to the judge to get these charges dismissed," Dowds proclaims with a growing sense of confidence.

Larry gives Dowds a reassuring smile. "They will. I will be vindicated." Then he turns serious. "I still don't understand why this is happening to me. I've done nothing wrong. People I don't even know have accused me of a crime I didn't do. I just don't understand it. I've been locked up in this jail for the last fifteen days. I've lost my job. My career is ruined. I'll probably go bankrupt with legal fees."

"We will get through this. I believe in you. Like you said, I don't understand who is behind all of this, but we will get our day in court, and I'm sure justice will prevail."

"Good, glad to hear that. I needed that." Larry says, pausing for a moment before continuing. "So, what is the second item you wanted to talk about?"

"Right! I just need you to be extra vigilant during the next few days. I would assume more at night rather than daytime, as there is more daytime traffic in and out of the police station."

"OK. What's going on, Dowds?"

"My sources at City Hall tell me that the mayor is very upset at you, so I want you to be careful."

A look of concern crosses Larry's face. "Dowds, what are you not telling me?"

Dowds adjusts himself in the chair. "I have researched the mayor. He is a bit of a loose cannon, if you need to know. He will not take the news of the surveillance tapes very well. He might be prone to lashing out at anybody this time—not just on Twitter, but through any other social media. I'm concerned he'll come at you in a physical manner, if you know what I mean."

"I'm in jail. How could he do that?" Larry asks.

"He is the mayor of the city. He has been for almost twenty years. Do you think you get to stay in office for that long without some verbal intimidation and breaking some bones when needed for people who don't believe what he is capable of doing to get his way" Dowds asks. "I am sure the police commissioner would be part of it."

"So, what do you want me to do? Not that there is much I can do!" Larry raises his hands over his head. "Remember, I'm in jail."

"Well, I need you to change your sleeping habits for the next few days. Be more alert at night. Rest during the day. If they come at you, it will be at night. Fewer people, fewer witnesses. You understand?"

Larry nods in agreement.

"I'll see what I can do on my side," Dowds responds.

"What do you mean by that?"

"It means I will do whatever I have to do to make sure you are alive and healthy the next time we go in front of the judge."

"Hopefully that will be the last!" Larry states with a wishful look.

"It will be. Have confidence in me."

"Thanks, Dowds, for everything you have done."

"Thank me when you step out of the courtroom a free man." Dowds stands up, and Larry does likewise.

They shake hands, and Dowds steps out of the room and waves to Officer Belker. Dowds glances back to Larry and then proceeds out.

DAY SIXTEEN — BACK TO THE SPRINGVALE JOURNAL

Emily and Maggie walk into James Marsala's office, the managing editor for *Journal*. They sit down on two old, slightly broken, uncomfortable chairs across the desk from the managing editor. He keeps the chairs in this condition to dissuade visitors from overstaying their welcome. He either gives them approval to run with stories, rejects them outright, or tells them to come back with a different angle.

As managing editor for the *Journal* for the last fifteen years, James is a no-nonsense kind of guy. He is detail-oriented, never one to run a story without double or triple checking a story and its sources. He also has unwavering loyalty toward his staff. At the top of his list are Emily Stiles and Maggie Summers, two very competent journalists. When the Larry Evans exoneration story hits his desk, he knows their work and research is bulletproof.

This morning, the morning after the story broke, the *Journal* was inundated with calls from representatives of major outlets. As the *Journal* owns the videos, any use by others for reprint or airing comes at a cost. This is good for the paper financially. Unsurprisingly, James Marsala is in a very upbeat mood.

"Ladies, today is a good day." He smiles at the two women across from him.

They smile back.

Maggie inquires, "And why is that, Mr. Marsala?"

"Well, until recently, we've been experiencing declining revenue. Most newspapers are actually under the same strain. It's a changing world. Our online presence is not nearly enough to supplement the revenue drops from the printed copy. It isn't common knowledge, but upper management has been in advance discussions about staff reductions."

Looks of concern and confusion cross the women's faces.

James quickly waves his hands at them. "No, no. Don't worry. It's not that at all. Actually, the reverse is true. The Evans story has generated so much republishing revenue that we can cover operating costs for the rest of the year and late into the next year. We are up on both print and online paid membership as well. Management is locking in licensing rights for long-term deals across the nation and across the pond where the news is just starting to peak." Marsala pauses for a moment. "This means that all our jobs are safe for now and will be for some time. I hope that by then, I will be retired. Hence my happy disposition."

The two women, smiling, stand up and walk around the desk to give their editor a hug: a rare event.

DAY SIXTEEN — MORE TV COMMENTARY

—

"Breaking news tonight on the attack at the Springvale Starline Hotel. New revelations in the form of surveillance videos, previously thought to be lost, have surfaced, completely exonerating Larry Evans, the accused.

"The defendant, the subject of numerous media attacks from police department officials, local and state politicians, and even the President himself, has left many people reeling. What will happen after this case is officially dismissed? We have been told that the defendant's attorney has requested an emergency meeting with the judge presiding over this case, along with members of the prosecution. All indications are pointing to a clear dismissal.

"If this is the case, what will Larry Evans and his attorney do to exact justice for his being wrongfully accused? Furthermore, as the details of the case have reached a global audience and the world has reacted and passed their own judgements, how will Evans settle all the wrongs that have been heaved upon him? Remember, the media frenzy for this case has painted Larry Evans in the worst possible light. An evil, angry man prone to attacking women with no justifications.

"Will he go after the hotel management and staff who painted him as a man assaulting an innocent woman, a picture that now seems to be fabricated? Will he go after local police department officials for denying him basic rights for his defence?

"Will he go after the local politicians who jumped on the bandwagon, heaping vicious personal attacks on him without facts?

"Finally, will he go after the President himself for making him a target of personal assault and influencing calls for a very stiff sentence? We have reached out to Larry Evans and his attorney for comments, but they have declined our request."

DAY SEVENTEEN — CITY HALL

——

Jonas Frakes, mayor of Springvale, is in his office, sitting back on his custom-built Timko dark leather executive chair. Not your everyday chair, but then again, Mayor Frakes is not one to settle for Ikea furniture.

He's recently had his office enlarged by taking down the wall to an adjacent office to make space for a dark mahogany polished conference table surrounded by eight matching leather armchairs. His office is decorated with original artwork purchased via Springvale tax dollars.

His expression is usually one of indifferent confidence. But this morning, his features are anything but composed. He quietly sits with his cell phone pressed against his ear. A cigarette dangles from his lips, and he puffs smoke through his nostrils.

Finally, he stands up from his chair, pulls the half-smoked cigarette away from his lips, and crushes it in the crystal ashtray in the middle of his desk, filled with half a dozen crushed cigarettes.

Across from his desk two male executive assistants sit in a state of quiet nervousness, awaiting the verdict. "We're fucked!" The Mayor states as he disconnects his call and looks over at the men. Both are well dressed in custom-fitted dark blue suits.

One of them, clearly having more courage than the other, blurts, "Sir, what is the outcome?"

The mayor shifts in his chair, his face contorted as he glowers at the two men. "The surveillance videos from the hotel are real, and they are damaging in every way. The problem is that they are damaging, but not against him. No, no, no! That would be too much to ask for! They're damaging against us and whoever slighted him in the media. The man is totally innocent. He never touched the woman, as he stated to the police, the public, and the courts. Nobody believed a single man versus multiple collaborating witnesses." He looks utterly defeated, understanding the impending doom that will fall on him and his administration.

"But Mr. Mayor, what about the witnesses? The case seemed airtight," the courageous assistant responds.

"Doesn't really matter now, does it! Those testimonies are useless against the actual video surveillance files. When the prosecution sees them, they will certainly be forced to drop the case. The judge will then render a verdict of 'not guilty' for Larry Evans, and that is when the lawsuits are going to fly all over the place. He is going to destroy me and this administration for all the negative comments that were made against him." He pauses and looks to the silent assistant, waiting for him to speak.

"What makes you think he would do that?" asks the assistant.

The mayor stands up from his chair, rests the palms of his hands firmly on the desk, and gives him an icy stare. "What makes me think that? It's what I would do if I were in his shoes. I would rip new ones from every single person who slighted me. That's what I would do. Revenge is the name of the game."

"Mr. Mayor, what if he just disappears without going after his detractors? He is from Canada, remember!" the assistant points out.

"Yeah, you have a point there. Canadians! They are too fucking nice. I hate Canadians." He looks over to Donald, the courageous one. "As a precaution, if we are in a situation where we are dealing with a Canadian who wants revenge, what is the city's liability insurance coverage for a shit storm like this?"

"Sir, the city has a floating liability coverage of approximately $25 million. We use it in the event where damages are paid out for court cases that place the city in the wrong. It hasn't been touched since we had that drunk city worker plow into those rows of cars last fall," he replies, beads of sweat starting to form on his forehead.

"I remember that one." He settles back on his chair, and a small sense of reassurance crosses his face. "What was our payout on that?"

"I don't have the exact figure on that, but I would say just north of $700,000," Donald says. "He did damage twelve cars. Most of them were complete write-offs. Sir, I must also mention that Mr. Evans and his attorney can, additionally, come after you, the local police officials, the police department, and any other government official that slandered him. Most of these, on a personal level, are not covered by the city's liability fund."

The mayor jumps up from his chair and shouts, "Are you fucking kidding me, Donald?"

"No, sir, this is not a kidding matter," he says, turning away slightly to avoid the mayor's glare. "Sir, if I recall, most of your commentary was in a social or personal setting outside the parameters of City Hall. Therefore, he can come after you on this account, along with the public statement made by the Mayor's Office. It's a double hit."

The other assistant chimes in. "Mr. Mayor, with the videos clearly exonerating him, the chance of an appeal by anyone who Mr. Evans sues will be useless and not worth the paper it's written on. Our best bet is to settle as soon as possible before the damages against the city and to you personally become unaffordable. Make an offer now before they hit us with the suit itself."

The mayor looks at him with a focused gaze. *What a mess! What a fricking mess I got myself into. I should have listened to my wife!*

He turns his attention back at the first assistant and responds, "Get me a number that the city can afford, one that does not insult him. Also, reach out to my accountant and see how much I can absorb personally. I need numbers by the end of day. I want to get ahead of this. That will be all," he dismisses them and sits back on his chair and turns away.

The two assistants stand up, turn, and walk out without a word.

Frakes's dismissals are always the end to any conversation. No other words are needed. Just get up, walk away, and do what you are told to do.

The mayor looks over to his desk phone and reaches over to pick up the handset, but stops. Instead, he reaches into his jacket pocket and pulls out his personal cell phone. He turns it on and punches in a number. The dial tone rings twice. "Police Commissioner Maco!" Frakes announces.

"Yes, sir, Mr. Mayor, what can I do for you?"

"I'm sure by now you have received the details of the Evans hotel security video files?"

"The police force's legal team briefed me first thing this morning. The prospects don't look good for the city, the police force included," Maco says.

"They do not, Police Commissioner. They definitely do not."

"So, what can I do for you, Mr. Mayor?" Maco asks.

"Well, it's more what you can do for us all. I mean, all of us who will possibly be stuck in this predicament."

"Mr. Mayor, what exactly are you talking about?"

"Evans is a problem for all of us. Evans is the thorn that needs to be removed and removed quickly before it infects us all—you just as much as me."

There's a brief pause on the other line. "Mr. Mayor, I don't think I like where we are going with this conversation."

With his voice elevated, Frakes says, "Maco, I need you to put pressure on Evans. Plain and simple."

"Pressure! Pressure to do what?"

"To back off on any thoughts of retribution against us—against you, the police force, against me and the city," declares Frakes.

"You are talking about intimidation, Mr. Mayor."

"Call it what you like. I want him silenced."

"Mr. Mayor—"

"Listen, Maco, and listen well. I brought you in as police commissioner almost fifteen years ago. You have done very well for yourself, and I have made sure you have been protected all these years. You owe me, and I am calling in my favour. Do you understand?"

"Mr. Mayor. I appreciate all that you have done for me. It has worked out well for me, like you said, these last fifteen years, but we need to be careful with how we handle this."

"Maco, all I want is some of the magic that you are famous for. Convince Evans to play ball with us. I don't want the details. I will leave that up to you and your resources to handle."

"Yes, Mr. Mayor. Consider it done," Maco states.

The phone goes dead. Maco hangs up on his end and begins to slowly rotate his chair around, admiring his elegantly furnished office. *Yes, the last fifteen years have been good to him. Will the next fifteen years be just as good? What about the next fifteen days?*

DAY SEVENTEEN — CAREER CHOICES

—

Evening

The police station is quiet the night before Larry Evans's big court session. The night duty officer is Robert Vines, a middle-aged man on a temporary desk assignment, pending review from a charge against him. He has been accused of excessive force during the apprehension of a suspect after a convenience store robbery. His career as a police officer is potentially over, and he is very susceptible to any offer that might save his career.

"Springvale Police Department, Officer Vines speaking. How can I help?" he asks into the phone.

"Officer Vines, this is Police Commissioner Maco."

"Yes, Commissioner. How can I help you?" He narrows his eyes, tense.

"Officer Vines, I am aware of your current situation regarding the alleged assault on a suspect in custody and your temporary desk assignment. How are you handling it?"

Officer Vines hesitates for a moment, trying to formulate an agreeable response that also expresses his frustration. But he doesn't know the reason for the police commissioner's call, so he sides with caution. "Commissioner, thank you for asking. It has been a stressful few weeks with all the back and forth with the Internal Affairs Department, the constant interviews, and write ups. To be honest, I'm not happy with the initial recommendations from the IAD. This isn't who I am. I need my name cleared so I can get back on the streets to what I do best. I'm not made out for desk work."

"I understand. IAD investigations are never good for the career of a police officer," the police commissioner says. "There is always a lingering suspicion and lack of trust even after an officer has been proven innocent."

"Well, that doesn't bode well for me, then!"

"That is why I am calling. I can quickly accelerate the dismissal of these accusations on your record."

"OK. That's good to hear . . ." Vines pauses for a moment, trying to figure out the eventual ask.

"I need you do something for me. Something simple and easy. You do this, and you can consider yourself back on the beat by the end week. No more desk work, shuffling papers."

"What do you want me to do, Commissioner?" Vines responds eagerly but with a hint of reluctance.

"Easy. Since you are on overnight duty this week, I want you to do the following. From one to one thirty in the morning, your presence will not be required at the front desk. Disappear during this time. Go for a walk. Leave all security access keys on the desk in full view."

"That's it?"

"That is all. I know you can do it. It would resolve all your issues. All you need to do is disappear for thirty minutes. What say you?" the police commissioner asks.

"Yes, Commissioner. Consider it done."

"Thank you, Officer Vines." The commissioner hangs up.

DAY SEVENTEEN — THE BOYS PAY A VISIT

Evening

Two minutes to one in the morning, Vines pulls out his security keys from his pocket. He places them on the lower level of the front desk, pushes the chair in, and walks to the men's toilets. There, he is going to stay for the next thirty minutes, no questions asked.

At exactly one o'clock, the station's front glass door opens. Two men dressed in black pants and turtleneck sweaters walk in. Their faces are covered with full-face balaclava masks and both wear black leather gloves.

One of them picks up the security keys from the front desk and follows the other towards the cell area.

The lead man opens the first security door as the other checks the list of cell numbers on the pegboard.

"Cell six. Nobody adjacent to or across from him."

"Good, let's get this over with. I need a beer," replies the second man.

They each pull on a pair of night vision goggles, powering them up as they step through the door. The only light comes from the emergency exit signs on both ends of the corridor.

Their steps are quiet and controlled, making sure to not awaken the two other inmates, but it won't make a difference if they are seen; with their full body coverage, identifying them would be impossible.

They stop in front of the sixth cell. The lead man inserts the security key into the lock and unlocks it silently. The second man pulls open the door wide enough for the first man to rush into the room—straight toward the metal cot where a man is sleeping under a blanket.

The first man strikes him with jackhammer precision. Blow after blow without letting up. The blows come fast and hard.

The lead man stops after thirty seconds of repeated blows to the stiff body. He breathes heavily. "This is a message from all parties concerned. You will not pursue this any further if you value your continued existence in this world."

The man pulls back, looks at the motionless body for a moment, a low moaning sound coming from underneath the blanket. The man grins in satisfaction. *Job done!* He turns and steps quickly out of the cell. The second man closes the door and relocks it.

They exit the corridor, walk back through the secured door, past the front desk, and out the door.

DAY SEVENTEEN —
THE OVAL OFFICE

—

The room is filled with the president's inner group of advisers. All of them handpicked by the president himself, not necessarily for their political experience, but more for their specific areas of knowledge that the president lacks. Most of the picks are old acquaintances from before he ascended into office, but some say those are the best people to surround yourself with. People you trust before you become famous.

Henry Mood, senior adviser to and long-time friend of the president, is standing centre stage in the Oval Office. He has a remote control in hand for the LED screen attached to the wall to his right. He flips the screen off and turns to the president.

Besides Henry Mood, also in the room is Jason Stands, six foot four, heavy framed, and dark haired with a full beard—another long-time friend. Phil Norton, Daniel Esposito, and Mark Deerson round out the group of advisers. None of them match Henry Mood's stature. Strictly a boys' club. This was the president's choice, and nobody who wanted to keep their job questioned him.

"Mr. President, this does not look good. Not good at all," Henry Mood says, referring to the surveillance tapes.

Henry called an emergency meeting with the president thirty minutes ago when the first announcement was made on the news channel. The story is now cycling every fifteen minutes on all major news channels and has gone viral on the internet.

Jason Stands steps forward and interjects, "We can put a spin on this—"

"A spin!" Henry interrupts. "There is no possible spin that we can put on this!"

The president remains silent.

"Henry," Jason blurts out, somewhat upset by being cut off, "there is always a way to get around any scenario. We are in the United States of America. We can fix this problem."

"Fix this how?" Henry asks. "What do you have in mind, and is it legal? Or are you going to bring in one of your guys to do a 'job?'" Henry has seen Jason's handiwork before. It could prove embarrassing for the president if it ever became public.

The president still says nothing.

Jason Stands gives Henry Mood a stern look. He clenches his fists for a moment then relaxes. "What I do is solve problems. How I do it is not any of your goddamn concern. Do you understand?" he asks, giving Mood an icy stare.

The president grins slightly.

"Jason, we are not talking about a two-bit hustler or low-level criminal," Henry says. "We are talking about Larry Evans. The person in the spotlight across the country. A man who was accused of assault by multiple witnesses. A man who has been attacked in the media for his alleged crime with countless false stories and insults on his character without a shred of evidence. He's been attacked by political figures across the country." He pauses for a moment and gives the president a quick glance. "And now we discover that he is not guilty of the crimes that he has been charged with. It is not hearsay at all. There's clear evidence that proves everything that has been said is false."

Henry's face muscles tense as his frustration rises. "All this, and you are still thinking about a way to fix this? Jason, there is no way around this. The only innocent person in this mess is Larry Evans. Everybody who has dragged his name in the mud and attacked his character in the media is guilty."

The president stands up from his chair, straighten his suit jacket, and rubs his presidential pin attached to his jacket collar with the side of his right thumb. Everybody's attention immediately turns to him. He walks around his desk with controlled casualness and stands in front of it for a moment, looking over the group in front of him. "All of you are my advisers. I hand-picked each of you for your raw talents and expertise that I thought would benefit this country. I am not one of those presidents who claim to be an expert on everything there is to know on how to run a country—especially the USA, a country that demands leadership and guidance on navigating these somewhat crazy and exciting times. That would be both foolish and dangerous for this country.

"On the other hand, I think I am a good judge of character. I do not pretend to have a doctorate degree in medicine, and I cannot make expert decisions that would affect the health of our citizens. I have Phil Norton for that." President Campbell points to one of his advisers standing in front of him.

Phil nods his head and smiles in acknowledgement.

"Excuse me, Dr. Phil Norton, graduate of Johns Hopkins University."

Phil chuckles.

"I do not pretend to have all the answers to address our economy. I did graduate from Columbia, a top-ten business school. I did well for myself financially before entering politics over twenty years ago, but that all pales in comparison with Mark Deerson, a graduate of the executive MBA program at Stanford

University. And I guess, because it was not challenging enough, he also completed a graduate program in international economics."

Mark nods his head at the president's recognition.

"I could list out the wealth of experience of the remaining members, Henry, Jason, and Daniel. It is tremendous what we have in this office. You gentlemen have been my go-to team for the last few years, and hopefully it will carry over into our second term in office. You guys are my experts." He sweeps his pointed finger across the room. "I need you to work together to come up with a solution to fix my mistake," President Campbell states, taking in their surprised expressions. "Yes, I made a mistake, but I will never admit it in public."

The group chuckles, and the president turns to Henry. "Henry, we are caught in a crisis here, and we need to get out of it without making the presidency look weak. We need to work together before blowing this off as a no-win scenario. The combined brain trust in this room, as I mentioned earlier, is tremendous. I am sure that you, Henry and Jason, can come up with a solution."

Henry looks at Jason and nods reluctantly.

The president looks at Jason. "The two of you have come through for me before. You have done a great job these last few years. I need you to now fix this in whatever way you can as long it does not trace back to this office."

"Yes, Mr. President," declares Jason with a newfound air of confidence.

Henry stands still.

Looking around the room, the president announces, "I want everybody to get on board with this. Understand?"

All heads nod except Henry's. He looks down.

The president narrows his eyes. "Henry, are you on board?"

Henry looks up at his president but does not say anything.

"I asked you a question!" The president states.

Straightening, Henry says, "Mr. President, serving you in this administration has been a once-in-a lifetime dream for me. We have done a lot of great stuff together, but I need to draw the line here. I cannot in good conscience be a part of any of this. Mr. President, you cannot give this order. An order, knowing Jason that will be along the lines of disposing of Larry Evans."

"Henry, I have given the order. I need you guys to accomplish it in whatever fashion provides me with results!" declares the president, clenching his hands in frustration.

"Then regretfully, I can no longer serve you."

"Henry, get on board, goddammit!" the president yells.

"I am sorry, Mr. President. What you are doing is wrong, and it will come back to haunt you and this administration," says Henry. "Please accept my resignation effective immediately." Without waiting for a response from President Campbell, Henry walks toward the door.

Jason reaches out and grabs his arm. "Wait, Henry, you can't walk out. We need you for this. You're the best spin doctor around."

"You need me to cover up whatever illegal action your thugs are going to do to Larry Evans. That is the only solution that ever comes out of your mouth, Jason. I will not have a hand in this. Now, let go of my arm," demands Henry.

Jason releases his grip, and Henry continues walking.

"Henry be reasonable. You can't go," calls the president.

Henry stops at the door and turns to face him. "Mr. President, I have told you on numerous occasions to not comment on certain public matters, but you have persisted in your attacks and ignored me on multiple occasions. We have been lucky over the years in fixing the situations that you've gotten this office in, but this is a no-win scenario." He raises his index finger. "Actually, the only way out is to do something you never will."

Bewildered, the president asks. "And what is that?"

"Apologize to Larry Evans and accept whatever punishment may fall on you."

"Never! I will never apologize to that scumbag!" the president yells, losing his composure.

"Scumbag! Don't you understand? Don't you get it? He is innocent, and you've attacked him in front of the American public! For what? A three-point bump in your ratings. Don't be a fool and think this will die down. It is only the beginning."

"You don't know what you are talking about. I am the president of the United States. He can't come after me!"

"For your sake, I hope not." Henry opens the door and walks out.

The president turns back to face the group. He looks over to Jason. "You have your orders. Get it done quickly."

DAY SEVENTEEN — CAN I GIVE YOU SOME ADVICE, MR. PRESIDENT?

"Thank you for taking time to meet with me, Chloe," President Campbell says. "Have a seat." The president points to one of the two black and gold trimmed leather chairs across from him. The president leans back on his chair, a sense of reassurance crosses his face. A friendly face, in Chloe Williams, is in the Oval Office. Chloe Williams sits down, drops her leather note book on the empty chair beside her.

"Now, this is strictly a personal chat and will not be registered in any logs. I want to make sure whatever comes out of this discussion does not have any bearing or undue influence on the executive and judicial branches of the government. This is strictly a conversation between friends."

Chloe Williams's eyes go wide, and her eyebrows rise. "A conversation where one friend is the president of the United States and the other is the attorney general. What could go wrong?" She smiles, winking in acknowledgement.

President Campbell sits back on his chair, speechless in words but not in facial expressions. His tight lips, curved upward, say it all.

"Just finished an unpleasant meeting with my advisors on the Larry Evans situation. It did not go well. Not well at all. Henry resigned."

"Henry Mood?" she asks, wide eyed.

"Yes. He and Jason did not see eye to eye on how to deal with this little crisis we have. Actually I have." The president admits.

"Well, Jason's approach to conflict resolution is a little unorthodox Mr. President." Chloe responds.

"Is that your subtle way of saying 'illegal'?" Chloe asks.

The president snickers, "no comment."

"Mr. President, I understand the damage Larry Evans could do to you. I don't want to know your plans, but I suggest you take some precautions against your detractors in case stuff goes sideways and you need to use your get-out-of-jail-free card. Don't go at it alone," she advises.

"Thanks, Chloe. I will take that into consideration," he responds.

"Again, this is harmless advice from one friend to another," she says. "It's plain and simple. It's always best to take full credit when things go right but spread out the damage when they don't."

"I took the liberty of pouring some wine before you got here. I know you are partial to French wines." He states.

"I do. Thank you Mr. President." She reaches over and grabs her glass.

"Here's hoping I never run into you in a dark alley." He raises his glass of wine.

She follows and they salute each other.

"You need not worry on that account," she says. "You brought me into this administration when other people questioned your reasoning. I questioned your reasoning at times also. I thought you were a fool, but you made a strong case as to why I should be the next attorney general. I am behind you 100 percent, Mr. President."

"Thanks, Chloe. That means a lot to me," he replies.

DAY SEVENTEEN — ROAD TRIP

———

Jason hurries back to his little office on the second floor of the West Wing. A devilish, almost childlike grin forms across his face. *President Campbell likes my plan. I will show Henry how things get done.*

He shuts the door behind him and reaches over a panel on the side of the door to activate his personal Faraday anti-surveillance cage. Whereas a typical Faraday cage blocks all incoming and outgoing signals, his model has been adapted to allow only certain signals on secured bandwidths through. He controls all electronic signals in and out of his office.

He walks around his desk and collapses into his chair. He pulls out a key from his jacket pocket, inserts it into one of the locked drawers on the side of the desk, and opens it.

Inside the drawer, he grabs his modified Finney smartphone, a military-grade secure smartphone. Unbreakable.

He turns it on and waits until a small green light on the top right side of the phone flashes, signalling that the automatic virus scan is complete. If the light ever flashes red, Jason will immediately dispose of the phone. This has only happened once in the three years he has had the system in place.

He dials a number he knows by heart, one he has remembered for what seems an eternity.

He waits several seconds before the line picks up. A smile crosses his face; his most loyal contacts always pick up. "Alexandra, I have a job for you. High-value target extraction. Simple. Out of the country. Are you available?"

Not bothering with any social pleasantries herself, she responds, "Yes. Which country?"

"Canada. Montreal in particular. Do you have a crew available, or should I even ask?"

"I always have a crew ready at a moment's notice, and yeah, you shouldn't have asked."

"Understood," Jason responds with reservation in his voice.

"Send me the details, and I will start prepping right away. What is the operation window?"

"Forty-eight, max seventy-two hours starting now. The window is closing fast. Can you get it done?" he asks.

"Again, another question that shouldn't have been asked."

"OK. I am hanging up now. Details to follow in thirty minutes." He hangs up the phone. "Thank God she is on my side," he murmurs.

DAY EIGHTEEN — JUDGEMENT DAY

—

With the video files released to the media, Dowds quickly petitions the court to advance the hearing that is scheduled to take place in five days. He is in a fighting mood and doesn't want to waste another second of Larry Evans's life.

"Larry, just waiting for the next available time slot," Dowds states over the phone. "It will be a quick in-and-out once they see the videos."

"Good. I'm tired of the prison life. Thanks again for all the work you've done," Larry says.

Judge Clarence Lerno easily grants Dowds's petition to move the court date, as the verdict is almost a foregone conclusion. Nonetheless, the judicial process must be followed.

The courtroom is crowded. Reporters from numerous publications and media outlets take up all the public seats.

Sitting near the back of the courtroom is Police Commissioner Maco, along with two fellow officers.

At exactly ten in the morning, two courtroom police officers escort Larry Evans in from one of the side entrances.

Police Commissioner Maco, with his jaw gaping and forehead wrinkles bunched in surprise, leans over to the two officers beside him. "I thought you took care of him," he whispers. "You told me you took care of it! Does he look like somebody who was severely beaten?"

"Police Commissioner, we must have hit him thirty times, and we hit him hard," responds the police officer closest to him. "Really hard! He didn't move at all."

"Did you actually see his face?"

"He was covered with a blanket from head to toe and lying on his stomach," he responds. "And no, we didn't see his face, but he felt the blows. I heard him grunt and moan during the first dozen or so hits. He was quiet after that."

Maco shakes his head at the screw-up. "You guys better pray that the message you gave sank into his brain, or your careers are over."

"Police Commissioner, we passed on the message word for word."

"We will see!" he whispers.

Larry Evans is dressed in a simple light grey suit. As he makes his way around to the defendant's desk, photographers get up and start snapping pictures. Usually, cameras and video-recording equipment are banned, but because of the ramifications of the case's outcome, the judge has allowed their use.

After Larry, his attorney, and the prosecution attorneys settle behind their respective desks, the officer of the court announces the judge's arrival.

Judge Lerno enters from a side door, proceeds up to the bench, and sits down. He bangs his gavel to announce the start of the court session and looks over to the defendant's table. "It has come to my attention that the defendant's attorney has evidence in his possession that will shed new light on this case. Mr. Dowds, do you have anything to say?"

Benjamin Dowds stands up. "Thank you, Your Honour. Yes, indeed, the defence has evidence that will clearly exonerate my client, Mr. Larry Evans, of all charges. We would like to submit to the court video surveillance files of the hotel bar and restaurant on the night of the assault.

"The video files show that Mr. Evans did not, at any point, attack or even touch Ms. Amanda Chase in any violent matter or otherwise. In fact, Ms. Chase repeatedly assaulted my client with strikes to his face.

"Lastly, the video files show that Ms. Chase incurred her head injuries by stepping back and accidentally colliding with the bar floor runner—not from punches by my client." Dowds steps around the table, walks over to the judge's bench, and hands his the thumb drive.

"It's been over two weeks since we last saw each other," the judge says. "When did these videos surface?"

"Your Honour, the videos were brought to my attention yesterday by news media."

"OK, and where did they get the videos, Mr. Dowds?"

"Your Honour, according to my understanding, it seems an email was sent to a reporter with a link to a secure website. The reporter then downloaded and reviewed it."

"Are the recipients at the new outlet aware of who sent the email?"

"They are not, Your Honour," Dowds states. "Apparently, any trace of its source has been erased. The news outlet did an extensive investigation on the properties of the email, but they could not trace anything. The sender's location was covered quite well."

"Have outside experts confirmed the surveillance videos' authenticity?"

"Yes, Your Honour. Third-party experts have reviewed the videos, and they are indeed authentic," Dowds replies. "I have copies of their report. Your Honour, at this time, the defence would like to offer into evidence a thumb drive with the video files of the night in question retrieved from the Springvale Starline Hotel as Exhibit 1 and the video expert's testimony of their authenticity as Exhibit 2."

"Request granted, Mr. Dowds. Please proceed."

Dowds hands the thumb drive to the court clerk and then walks back.

Judge Lerno glances over to the prosecution table. "Any questions or observations from the prosecution before we continue?"

The lead prosecutor, Thomas Albert Jr., stands up. "At this point in time, we do not, Your Honour," he says in a distressed tone.

The judge announces, "OK, then. We will take a one-hour recess for all parties to review the new video evidence." Looking at Dowds and the prosecution table, the judge states, "Gentlemen, please follow me into my chambers for review." The judge picks up his gavel and slams it down. "A one-hour recess is now in order." He stands up, thumb drive in hand, and walks back to his chambers.

The defence and prosecution attorneys follow him into his private quarters with a court officer. Larry turns around to face the public area. He spots Maco and grins in delight knowing that the verdict is now a forgone conclusion. Maco, tight lipped, red face remains silent as he stares back.

DAY EIGHTEEN — THE JUDGE'S PRIVATE QUARTERS

———

The judge walks around the side of his desk, removes his gown, and hangs it on a standing wooden coat rack. Several other gowns are already on the rack for rotation purposes.

He sits down behind his desk and calls out to the court officer closing the door. "Bobby, plug her in, please." The judge tosses him the thumb drive, and the officer expertly catches it.

Bobby walks over to the wooden wall-to-wall cabinet, opens one of the glass doors, plugs in the thumb drive into an available port, and turns on the TV. He has repeated this process numerous times. He picks up the remote control and tosses it back to the judge.

The attorneys in the room are taken aback by the gesture but relax when the judge grabs it without hesitation.

"There you go, Judge, all set," the officer exclaims.

"Thanks, Bobby." The judge smiles at him. Then he turns to face the three attorneys, still standing and looking for direction. "Well," the judge says, pointing to the empty chairs in front of the TV, "are you going to stand throughout the viewing, or are you going to sit down?"

Dowds glances over to the two prosecution attorneys. They all nod and sit down for the viewing.

"Thank you," the judge exclaims. "Now, let's see what all the commotion is about." The attorneys don't see his grin, as they are facing the screen, but Bobby catches it.

He smiles back at the judge.

DAY EIGHTEEN —
THE VERDICT

—

Judge Clarence Lerno is a stickler for keeping his court proceedings on schedule. If anyone before his bench fails to stay on time, he immediately reprimands them on the first occurrence. Second occurrences are more severe; fines and depending on the length of the tardiness, overnight stays at the local police station. On the third occurrence, well, nobody has yet to test that threshold. This was Judge Lerno's castle. He made the rules and expected everybody to abide by them.

Exactly one hour after he calls the recess, Judge Lerno sits behind his bench, glazing over the crowd that has filtered back into the courtroom. The number of spectators has grown as news of the video review has spread.

Judge Lerno bangs his gavel. "Court is back in session." Turning his attention to the defendant's table, he asks, "Mr. Dowds, do you have a statement?"

Dowds stands up. "Thank you, Your Honour. If it pleases the court, I would like to file a motion for the immediate dismissal of all charges against the defendant, Mr. Larry Evans, on the grounds of new evidence provided to the court that completely and undoubtedly proves that Mr. Evans did not, at any point, touch or attack Ms. Amanda Chase.

"Any injury sustained by Ms. Chase was due to her accidental stumble backwards that resulted in her striking the bar floor runner with the right side of her head. Mr. Evans was, in no shape or form, responsible for the awkward fall backwards, as the video clearly shows he was more than an arm's distance away from her.

"The defendant has suffered weeks of abuse and personal attacks from the media and political figures alike. He has been tried unjustly by the Springvale Police Department and has had to put up with fabricated testimonies from witnesses in a coordinated attempt to have him arrested and imprisoned for a crime he did not commit. Numerous members of law enforcement and the media have ignored and rejected Mr. Evans's repeated explanations and claims of innocence. Nobody was willing to accept his explanation, as simple as it was. All they saw was Amanda Chase's bruised head, and he was proclaimed guilty."

Dowds pauses dramatically. "Well, the verdict is 'not guilty.' He is innocent, innocent beyond any reasonable doubt. Innocent as clear as there is light during the day and darkness at night. This is an open-and-shut case. Innocent." Dowds sits down. He looks over to Larry and smiles. Larry nods in agreement.

Judge Lerno shifts his focus to the prosecution table. He doesn't see two eager, hungry lawyers ready to pounce on the defenceless defendant anymore, but two dejected, solemn faces. "Members of the prosecution, do you have a statement?"

Thomas Albert Jr. stands up and clears his throat. "Thank you, Your Honour. In light of the recent video evidence that was provided to the court and the review done within the judge's chambers, it has become clear that the charges laid against Mr. Larry Evans are without merit. As stated by Mr. Dowds, the video shows that Mr. Evans at no point struck Ms. Chase. Furthermore, he was not at all the reason for Ms. Chase's head injury. Therefore, the prosecution asks the court to dismiss this case with prejudice if it so pleases the court."

The prosecuting attorneys fall back in their respective seats, hoping the worst is over.

Instead of responding, the judge glares down at them but remains silent.

"Your Honour?" Thomas Albert Jr. calls out in an anxious voice.

"Yes, yes. I heard you and your statement, but before we continue with the dismissal of this case, I have a few questions for the prosecution."

The two attorneys glance at each other in nervous confusion.

"So, clearly the video evidence is a non-starter for you guys at this point," the judge says. "It has destroyed your case completely. What I want to know, and I am hoping you two will be able to give me clarification on this, is how we have such a huge discrepancy between the multiple eyewitnesses and the victim accounts on the night of the assault, none of which match up with the actual events that transpired and were recorded in the video that we just reviewed."

"Your Honour—" the lead attorney starts.

"Stand up when addressing this court. Do I really need to remind you about basic courtroom etiquette, Mr. Albert?"

Thomas Albert rises out of his chair quickly, and the crowded courtroom is filled with muted chuckles.

"Quiet, everybody!" Judge Lerno says, slamming his gavel down before addressing the attorneys once again. "I'm expecting an answer. An answer that is worthy of your years of experience as prosecution attorneys and even for the memory of your late father, Mr. Albert. So help me, if you say anything that remotely resembles an 'I don't know,' I will hold the two of you in contempt of court for wasting this court's time, resources, and the defendant's undo stress."

The judge pauses for his statement to settle in. "Now, I ask you again. What do you have to say about the discrepancies, about the obvious false statements from the eyewitnesses? Speaking of the eyewitnesses, I want them all taken into custody for uttering false accusations."

Thomas Albert looks at the judge in silence. He clenches his fists behind his back. "Your Honour, we have attempted to contact all the eyewitnesses, but we have been unsuccessful."

"All of them?" The judge clearly agitated by what he is hearing.

"Your Honour . . . yes, Your Honour. All of them," Albert responds. "We have been unable to track them down. I have asked the Springvale Police Department along with state authorities for assistance. Presently, we don't have any idea if they're still in the state—or in the country, for that matter."

"How about the hotel employees? Are they able to provide any information?" the judge asks.

"Your Honour, the hotel management has terminated all the employees who provided the false testimonies. Follow-up to their personal residences was fruitless, as they seem to have left those locations. Our detectives followed up on the last known residences of Amanda Chase, Howard Johnson, the reception manager of the hotel and Barney Willis, the bartender at the hotel have come up empty. All of them have recently been vacated with no forwarding address."

The judge shakes his head in disappointment. "I have been a judge for just over twenty-two years now, and this is first time I have seen such incompetence by state attorneys. Mr. Albert, I will see you in my chambers after this court session is over."

"Yes, Your Honour," he responds.

"You may sit down now."

He does.

The judge gazes over to the defendant's table, smiles, and then turns his attention back at the prosecution table. "It is my duty to bring this circus of a trial to an end. The motion to dismiss all charges against Mr. Larry Evans has been granted. Mr. Evans, you are a free man.

This is one of those bittersweet moments where justice has been served. You may find solace in that the state of New Jersey allows a wrongfully accused person the right to pursue any parties that have contributed to your incarceration and any parties that have damaged your personal character or status in any fashion. Mr. Evans, I leave you to your very capable attorney to pursue whatever avenue you wish. Thank you. This court session is closed." He stands up, raises his gavel, and bangs it on the bench.

He turns and walks out of the courtroom into his chambers, immediately followed by Bobby, the court officer.

Larry turns to Dowds and gives him a big hug. The crowd behind them, separated by a three-foot wooden bannister, inches closer to them. Most of them are reporters wanting statements from the Larry and Dowds, new celebrities.

Dowds spots Police Commissioner Maco at the back of the courtroom, standing with two police officers. He smiles at the police commissioner and winks.

Maco, visibly upset by the verdict, turns to his two officers. They both lean over to listen to him. After a few seconds, they nod their heads in agreement, turn, and head for the courtroom exit. Maco turns back to face Dowds and grins.

Their behaviour triggers alarm bells in Dowds's head. He gets the attention of one of the court officers to come over, and after he does, Dowds leans over, pointing to the media. "Can you get us out of here without them being any the wiser?"

The court officer smiles. "Yes, sir. Come with me."

Dowds motions to Larry to follow him and the court officer. Dowds pulls out his cell phone, and as he walks, starts typing out a text message.

The three of them head to a door on the other side of the judge's bench. The officer opens the door and points inside. "Walk straight down the corridor, turn left, and then go through the door at the end of the corridor. The door opens to an alleyway in the back of the building."

Larry and Dowds nod in appreciation and go down the corridor.

DAY EIGHTEEN —
VERDICT RENDERED

—

"Breaking news this afternoon on a story concerning Larry Evans, the man accused of assaulting Ms. Amanda Chase at the Springvale Starline Hotel. What was once considered an open-and-shut case, with multiple witnesses describing an enraged man assaulting Ms. Chase without provocation, has taken a 180 degree turn.

"New evidence presented in today's court session proves that without a doubt, Larry Evans was not responsible for Ms. Chase's head injury. The video shows Ms. Chase taking a misstep backwards and away from Mr. Evans. Mr. Evans has therefore been exonerated. Surprisingly, the video shows Ms. Chase attacking Mr. Evans, who he did not fight back.

"The video evidence was so clear-cut that the prosecution requested for the court to dismiss all charges against Mr. Evans. Judge Lerno accepted the request, and all charges were dismissed immediately. Larry Evans is a free man this afternoon."

DAY EIGHTEEN — TAKE THE QUICK WAY HOME

The getaway from the alleyway behind the courthouse to the Newark airport is performed with military efficiency. Stepping into the alleyway, Larry Evans and Benjamin Dowds meet two men waiting for them outside with a waiting Lincoln SUV. With communication pieces clearly noticeable in their right ears and gun holsters peeking through from the inside of their open suit jackets, the two men position themselves in a protective stance, ready to intercept any intruders. None are evident.

They rush Dowds and Larry into the back seat and join them in the vehicle, one man in the front and the other sitting in the front passenger seat.

A second vehicle immediately behind them is parked at an angle to block any vehicle from squeezing through. Not even a motorcycle.

As soon as all the doors close, the SUV accelerates down the alleyway and quickly merges into street traffic. The second car blocks a black four-door sedan from racing in. It comes to a screeching halt behind the parked car.

The two officers from the courtroom are in the sedan's front seat. Frustration is evident on their faces.

A few minutes into the drive, after recovering from the excitement of the quick getaway, Dowds leans over to Carson Days, one of his men that he has used over the years. "You got everything set up at the gate?"

"Yes, sir, all paperwork is filed, the flight plan has been submitted, and the plane is prepared for immediate takeoff," replies Days.

"Good," Dowds answers.

Dowds shifts his attention to Larry. "The plane will get you to Montreal in two hours. My contacts will get you out of the airport before anybody suspects anything. I will be back in town some time tomorrow afternoon as I have paperwork to prep and file before I make it up there."

Larry nods.

"Do you have any personal items at the police station that you want us to pick up, or are you good?" Dowds inquires.

"Only thing with any sentimental value is my ring. If you can retrieve it that would be great," Larry says. "Everything I left, I can replace."

"Consider it done" Dowds says.

"Thanks."

"For the next few days, we need to stay under wraps and let the anticipation of your next move grow. Our accusers will continue making dumb, incriminating comments. Once I'm in Montreal, we strike, and we strike hard. They will settle fast to stay out of the public's scrutiny. I have lined up all my resources leading up to what is coming next. They are already hard at work pitting these people against each other."

Larry takes all this in and smiles. "Good job, Ben. On a side note, how are you with malpractice lawsuits? I need a favour."

"Well, I've handled a few, but unlike other lawyers with huge egos, I know my limits. Give me what you need done, and after

I review it, I'll either handle it myself or get my friends to take care of."

"You seem to have a lot of friends," Larry says.

Dowds smiles. "It's always good to have friends—especially friends who owe you favours."

"Thanks. I'll forward you the information when I'm back in Montreal," Larry responds. "Now, let's keep our eyes on the endgame. Payback's going to be a bitch."

Everybody in the back seat laughs. Larry leans back and closes his eyes for the remainder of the drive to the airport.

DAY EIGHTEEN — HOME SWEET HOME

—

"Does Dowds own this aircraft?" Larry asks as he leans into the beige leather chair, rubbing his palms down the length of the armrests. The Beechcraft Super King Air aircraft is jetting toward Montreal. The eight-seater comes with many luxuries not available in most first-class sections of larger planes. He's drinking steaming coffee and eating a toasted bagel with a generous spread of cream cheese, the first sense of comfort he's had in over two weeks. It's a nice change. Not a healthy one, but it's nonetheless better than the diner meals he was subjected to back in Springvale.

"No, sir, he does not," Patrick Malone responds, sitting diagonally from him. "A very appreciative client has loaned it to him."

"Whenever he needs it?"

"Yes, sir. That is my understanding," Patrick replies.

"Nice trade off."

Patrick smiles. "Mr. Dowds's bartering abilities for his services rendered are quite extraordinary."

"I am quickly coming to that happy realization. A man of many trades, from what I'm seeing. A gifted lawyer and a crafty problem solver."

"He is quite a character, sir," Patrick responds.

"This conversation is strictly between you and me, right?" Larry asks. "You won't mention this to him? It might go straight to his head."

Patrick remains silent.

Larry presses his lips together. "You're going to tell him, aren't you?"

"Yes, sir," Patrick answers without a glint of humour.

"Damn! There go my legal fees."

DAY NINETEEN — AND STILL EVEN MORE TV COMMENTARY

"A day has passed since Larry Evans was acquitted from all charges stemming from the alleged assault on Amanda Chase. Mr. Evans seems to have gone underground. His attorney, Benjamin Dowds, has turned down all requests for comments and has declined any and all interviews.

"As for the prosecution, it has been reported that the attorney general has dismissed all members of the legal counsel for this case, and they will face further actions by the state bar association.

"All witnesses that testified have disappeared. It seems they are afraid of possible repercussions from either the prosecution for submitting false statements under oath or potential personal lawsuits from Larry Evans. At this moment, it is a waiting game to find out what Larry Evans's next steps will be. We at the station have also reached out to local police officials, state representatives, and the office of the president for any commentary, but all our requests have been denied.

President Campbell, however, chimed in last night. When asked if he would apologize for his personal attack against Larry Evans, he doubled down, claiming that Larry was guilty and the footage was manipulated. His claim was that Hollywood has the technology to alter footage.

We at our station have reached out to film industry experts to comment. They reviewed the footage made public to all news outlets and confirmed that it was indeed authentic and unaltered. This is just another theory the president has put forward that has now been debunked. Thank you."

DAY NINETEEN — OPERATION SNATCH AND GRAB

—

Montreal Saint-Hubert Longueil Airport is situated roughly twenty kilometres from downtown. The airport can handle general aviation aircraft only with no more than fifteen passengers, which is perfect for the Bombardier Challenger 650.

The one that arrives at Saint-Hubert Airport has no identifying markings except a small American flag on both wings.

Ground crew members direct it into a large hangar at the outer edge of runway 06L/24R, which is the longer of the two runways, one that was originally built for the military in the early thirties.

The hangar doors open as the plane approaches. Standing on either side of the doors are several men in suits, wearing dark sunglasses to block out the afternoon sun. All of them carry HK416 assault rifles with straps over their shoulders. Once the plane clears the doors, they begin to close, and the ground crew departs through a side door.

Meanwhile, the well-dressed security detail have all made their way into the hangar and taken up position around the plane in a square formation. The airplane door opens downwards and turns into a flight of stairs.

The first person off the plane is a woman wearing fatigues, polished boots, and a short jacket with multiple pockets. Four men, similarly dressed, immediately follow her. All of them are carrying fully packed duffle bags. The last members to disembark are the two pilots. They nod to their passengers and depart for the offices at the back of the hangar.

Standing about fifty feet from the airplane, Jason Stands, national security advisor to President Campbell, smiles and greets them as they approach. "Thanks for coming on such short notice," Jason says. He is in front of a hardwood table filled with laptops, maps, and water bottles. "Help yourself quickly to the water before we get down to business."

The woman stands still as the four men walk over to the table. They each grab a water bottle except for the last one, who grabs two, turns around, and tosses one over to the woman in charge. She nods at her second in command.

"The window is short, so let's get going with the briefing," Jason says.

"Sir!" acknowledges the woman.

"The target is one Larry Evans, currently located in Montreal. Any of you not aware of who Larry Evans is? He is the current irritant in our administration's sights. If not contained in the next forty-eight hours, he will become a big problem for the president."

"Do we have a confirmed location, sir?" the woman asks.

"We tracked him to Montreal after he bolted from the Springvale Courthouse two days ago. It wasn't easy, but we found out how he got out of the country quickly. The exact location is documented behind you on the maps on the table. It's in a quiet residential area on the outskirts of downtown Montreal. Security, from our initial intelligence report, is nonexistent, as his location is not common knowledge.

"The parameters of the mission are simple: extraction if possible, termination if not. Whatever the outcome, Larry Evans needs to disappear. If problems arise and any or all of you are detained, then the American government will totally disavow any knowledge of this operation—hence the substantial payout. I gather nobody has any issue with the payout?" He looks at the group.

Silence.

"Good," Jason says.

Once Jason has concluded, the woman turns to her squad. "OK, you heard what the boss said. Break down the gear. We'll have an intel review in twenty minutes."

The group of operators nod and disperse.

"Alexandra!" Jason calls.

The four men continue toward the jet, but Alexandra stops, turns to face Jason.

He approaches her. "I need this mission to go down without a hitch," Jason says. "I don't want to give you lessons on how to run an operation, but we cannot have any blowback on this. Nothing can go wrong. The Canadian government will have a field day if this operation goes south."

"Understood, sir."

"I know you. I know your work. That is why I picked you. You have never failed me before. If this takes a wrong turn, I want you to handle the fallout quickly. I will take care of you. The boys, they are another story. Understood?"

"Yes, sir," she responds. "Anything else, sir?"

"No, that will be all," Jason replies.

She turns and heads toward the jet to regroup with her unit.

Jason follows her progress back to the plane, but he's suddenly knocked backwards by the blast wave when two explosions blow the two front doors off their hinges. There's another explosion at the back door. Smoke canisters are tossed into the hangar, and a SWAT team dressed in body armour, helmets, and full-faced gas masks rush into the hangar.

The immediate targets are the four armed guards around the perimeter of the airplane. Shots are fired from armed men in full military gear and body armor. The rubber bullets, usually non-life threatening can still leave open wounds depending on the area of impact. The men are downed quickly. Alexandra and her team are the next targets to fall. All with well-placed shots.

Jason Stands, standing in disbelief, absorbs the pain of a rubber bullet as it strikes his upper chest. The presence of bullet proof vest saved him from any severe wounds but would still leave him with a noticeable mark for weeks to come. He collapses backwards onto the hard cement floor.

"Don't move and remain on the ground. Arms and legs spread out." Yells a member of the SWAT team.

Several of the SWAT members rush onto the airplane to check for any additional bodies. Seconds later, they come out giving the all clear signal.

A tide of other SWAT members and medical personnel flood the hangar. They check everybody on the receiving end of the rubber bullets to make sure they aren't carrying any weapons, and the medics check them for injuries. Others point their assault rifles at the people on the floor.

Another person goes by each captured target and takes pictures of them. Once the "OK" is given, they are handcuffed and lifted off the ground. Within minutes, they are grouped together, easily sur-rounded by over a dozen armed SWAT members with a secondary circle behind them providing additional coverage.

Several SWAT members pry open the hangar doors. Black SUVs with RCMP logos drive in, followed by two large security trucks. More armed personnel get out of the vehicles.

The leader of the group, a man in uniform, approaches. "Gentlemen, and lady, welcome to Canada! I hope you enjoy the stay." he declares with open arms and a grin on his face.

Jason Stands drops his head in disgrace. *I am so f---.*

DAY NINETEEN
— INTRODUCING
RONALD SLATER

—

Ronald Slater is an investigative reporter from the *Newark Journal*. He has been at his job for fourteen years, and he is very good at it.

What a case this is turning out to be. It seemed ordinary at first. Late at night, a single man in a bar was chatting up a beautiful woman when suddenly, his intentions were misunderstood, and violence erupted. Then, after several weeks of character assassination, the previously lost hotel surveillance videos appeared. All charges were dismissed.

But then Larry Evans and the witnesses all disappeared, sending off massive alerts in Slater's brain; something was definitely not kosher in the state of New Jersey.

The surveillance videos were made available to all media outlets shortly after the case was dismissed. Slater downloaded a copy of all the videos from the *Springvale Journal* website; his managing editor approved the fee.

At first, it was a combination of curiosity and a hint of boredom that made him watch the videos. Newark is not a hotbed of criminal activity or political intrigue, so the week was progressing at a slow pace. That quickly changed after watching the full slate of videos. Slater re-watched them three times.

He gets up from his worn-out wooden chair that he's had since his first day in this job. He's made numerous personal adjustments to it and done repairs over the years, including fixing the worn-out castor wheels and the squeaky springs on the pivot column. It's almost like an old pair of running shoes or a faded and torn concert T-shirt. The original oak stain on the chair has long since disappeared from the armrests. The thought of re-staining it over the years has crossed his mind, but it quickly vanishes, as he would need to use another chair while this one was out of commission. For some, routine is comforting. For Slater, it is his chair.

Slater walks over to his managing editor's office. The office door is closed, but through the glass door, behind the partially drawn blinds, he catches a glimpse Carla Di Rienzo sitting behind her desk.

He knocks gently on the glass. She looks up, smiles, and waves him in.

He sits down on the only free chair in the office, the two others piled with file folders. The chair similar in style, and possibly as old as the one in his office but not as comfortable.

"Mr. Slater, what can I do for you on this totally uneventful day?" she asks, restless. There's been a lack of newsworthy stories to populate the next edition of the paper. No stories equals no paper and no money.

"Ms. Carla Di Rienzo, how the heck are you?" he asks playfully.

She looks up from the document on her desk. "Really, Ronald, what's on your mind? It better be worth my time." She raises her hand to halt him from responding, puckering her lips. "No idle chit chat, Slater. Get to the point. I don't have time today. You waste my time, and it will cost you. Five dollars per stupid remark." She points to a glass jar partially filled with quarters, a few ones, and some five-dollar bills. "I need to put some money aside for my next vacation, and I figured the swear jar and your mouth are easily good for a hundred dollars."

"Well, that sucks!" Slater blurts, not quick enough to stop himself.

Carla points to the jar, grinning.

Slater rifles through his left pocket and pulls out a small handful of bills. He sorts out three one-dollar bills and two twenties.

"I only have three dollars, and I don't want to pay in advance for future discretions. Can I owe you?"

Carla pulls out a slip of paper, scribbles "I owe you two dollars. Ronald Slater," and hands it to him, smiling.

He accepts the paper, bundles it with the three one-dollar bills, and drops it into the jar.

"Now, Mr. Slater, how can I help you?"

"Ms. Di Rienzo . . . Di Rienzo! Is that Italian or Russian? An old buddy of mine in high school was called Vladimir Di Rienzo, and he was Russian. Any relation?"

"Vladimir!" she shouts in jest, playing along. "You knew Vlad?"

Slater, caught off guard, bursts out laughing. "You got me, Ms. Di Rienzo." Getting down to business, he says, "Several weeks ago, I got a call from a colleague of mine from Springvale about the Larry Evans case. He claimed the whole case felt weird. He did some investigating but couldn't really continue, so he sent it my way. I read the material and then reviewed the security footage. I actually watched it several times, and I'm at a loss."

Carla's playful banter turns on a dime. Slater is a jokester and flirt at times, but when it comes down to business, he is dedicated to his job—obsessively so. "At a loss! Why?" she asks.

"We have multiple witnesses claiming unequivocally that Larry Evans not only struck Amanda Chase repeatedly, but also knocked her down. We are talking about multiple witnesses, all with similar depositions. The couple at the end of the bar stated that from their view, Evans struck her. The bartender stated that Evans struck her also, and he had a clearer view than the couple did, but they all made the same statement. The front desk manager, from his vantage point, claims he saw Evans push her. He didn't see Evans's blows. Which is plausible, as his attention was on his work, and he only shifted his attention to the bar when the voices rose in volume."

"OK, I am following so far." Carla motions for him to go on.

"OK, so we have four witnesses who either saw most of the event or got parts of it. Additionally, there were two kitchen staff members who rushed out of the kitchen to see Amanda Chase on the floor and the bartender attending to her. They didn't have direct knowledge of the events, but they placed Larry in close proximity to Amanda. Six people. Four direct witnesses with similar accounts and two indirect witnesses who place Larry at the scene of the crime."

"Correct," Carla says. "We have six solid accounts of the event. But the case was dismissed."

Slater smiles, happy that she's on the same wavelength. "When the prosecution originally asked for the surveillance videos, they were told they were unavailable," he says.

"The prosecution asked, but what about the defence?" Carla asks. "Considering that Larry stated he did not touch her, you would think they would ask for the surveillance tapes also. But from the public court records, that was only done almost a week after his arrest."

Slater points at her in agreement. "Exactly my thought. The more I think about this case, the more I think there is some funky business going on."

"The videos! They weren't originally available, but two weeks later, they suddenly appeared. Are we sure it didn't just take two weeks to manufacture them?" Carla asks.

"Nope, on two accounts. First, it would probably take a lot more than two weeks to produce the almost thirty minutes of video that is on the files. Second, the cost of that work would be in the hundreds of thousands if not millions of dollars. Who would spend that kind of money to alter a court case on an ordinary sales manager making maybe money in the high five figures?"

"Just a thought," she says as glances over to her laptop, hits a few keys. She examines the screen and then returns her gaze back at Slater with a smile. "OK, I like where you're going with this. I just checked our quarterly travel budget, and you're in luck. I have some money in the budget. I want you in Springvale to dig up whatever you can about the witnesses and the local police station. I need a thousand words from you in two days."

"That's doable," Slater says, generating a smile from Carla. "I'll probably get even more for a follow-up article. I'm also going to stop by Summit Oaks Hospital to pay a visit to Amanda Chase's doctors and see what they have to say. There has been very little on her in the media." Slater gets up from his chair and starts walking toward the office door. But then he turns before grabbing the doorknob. "So, what ever happened to Vladimir?"

Carla looks at him with a solemn look. "He died several years ago. Tragic hot air balloon accident. It was messy," she says with a tight-lipped half smile.

Slater smiles in return, nods his head, and walks out of the office. Carla leans back in her chair and shakes her head in amusement.

DAY NINETEEN – LET'S GO FOR A RIDE

———

The Montreal police wasted no time in shutting down both sides of Dorchester Boulevard immediately in front of the large, multi-storey RCMP headquarters to all residential traffic.

Armed officers stand outside their vehicles and redirect traffic down the side streets. A dozen more are spaced every fifty feet along the length of the blocked street.

Three SUVs with RCMP decals pull up to the street blockade on the east end, and several officers carrying assault rifles surround the vehicles. One of the officer's steps toward the lead vehicle with another armed officer in tow. The driver's side window automatically rolls down, and they exchange words and identification badges. Everybody is on high alert. They have all been briefed of the detainees arriving at the RCMP headquarters.

The police officer outside the vehicle hands back the IDs, steps back, and waves to one of the cars blocking the path to back up.

The three SUVs advance past the blockade and stop in front of the RCMP's underground garage entrance. A dozen members in armoured gear exit the vehicles and take up strategic positions, ready for the oncoming vehicles containing the captured American operatives.

Thirty seconds later, another RCMP convoy of SUVs and four armoured vehicles approach. Officers wave them through the blockade. As they approach the building, two heavy metal garage doors roll up, and the whole convoy rolls smoothly inside.

Once the last of the SUVs pull into the garage, the security perimeter collapses inwards as the armed police officer retreat into garage before it shuts its doors.

DAY NINETEEN — YOU'VE GOT A LOT OF EXPLAINING TO DO

———

The basement of the RCMP headquarters houses many secure rooms and corridors for detaining people of interest. Security personnel in full-body armour, carrying assault weapons and sidearms, guard one of these corridors. There is only one entrance, and it is manned by armed guards in front and behind bulletproof glass. Anybody accessing this corridor, which is continuously monitored via overhead cameras, must go through three sets of doors with no handles.

Three officers dressed in dark uniforms and protective vests lead the way. Two additional men dressed in dark blue fitted suits follow them. ID badges are visible on their vests or jacket pockets. The taller of the two has a full head of dark and grey hair with a stubble of a beard but well kept. The other man is slightly shorter and noticeable younger in age and clean shaven.

One by one, they go through the motions of identifying themselves. The bearded man asks the younger man. "Alain, what's the first one's name?" Alain walks to the first cell door. He reads the LED panel beside the door for information on the detained person in the room. "Harlan White," he announces to the group behind him.

The second officer nods and opens the door by typing in the security code onto the panel. The door opens, and the two men in suits walk into the room.

Sitting up on the edge of a metal-framed cot is a young man in his early twenties, clean-shaven and sporting a military-style crew cut.

"Are you ready to talk to us about your visit to our city?" the bearded man asks.

The inmate looks up and shakes his head in defiance.

The two suited men turn around and exit the room without hesitation. The door closes quickly behind them.

The group proceeds to the next cell.

"Rickey Young," Alain announces, and the second officer unlocks the door.

The inmate in this room is also seated on the edge of his metal cot. "What do you want?" he asks.

"Are you ready to talk to us about your visit to our city?" the bearded man asks.

"Hell, no! You can kiss my ass!"

"Thank you, I will pass." He turns and exits, followed by his colleague. The door closes behind them.

They proceed to the next cell.

"Frederick Laforge," Alain announces, getting into a routine.

This time, the bearded man steps forward and asks, "Where was he born?"

Alain looks back at the screen and scrolls through some information. He turns back to the bearded man. "Lafayette, Louisiana, sir."

"Thanks. Let's see if he has any attachment to his roots. Open the door."

Alain types in the code to unlock the door, and they walk in. *"Bonjour, je m'appelle Commissaire Principal André Boucher. Êtes-vous prêt à nous parler de votre visite dans notre ville?"*

The man in the cell gives them a confused look. The bearded man glances over to his colleague and shakes his head, smiling. "I had high hopes for this one." He turns back to the inmate. "Now, are you ready to talk to us about your visit to our city?"

"Go to hell!" the inmate shouts.

Chief Superintendent Boucher looks over to his partner. "I much prefer when they stay silent."

"I agree," Alain says.

Chief Superintendent Boucher returns his attention to the inmate. "Are you sure you don't want to talk? This is your chance before you go to prison forever."

"Fuck off!"

"Much better silent," Chief Superintendent Boucher states.

They turn and exit the room. The door closes quickly behind them.

In the corridor, Chief Superintendent Boucher turns to his partner. "Finish with the remaining operatives. I'll talk to Jason Stands."

"Yes, sir. I'll come by when I'm done. Hopefully one of the others will talk."

"I doubt it, but let's get it out of the way."

The two suited men split up. One uniformed officer follows Chief Superintendent Boucher; the remaining officers take off with his partner.

Jason Stands sits nervously in a small ten-by-ten-foot room with no windows. There's just an uncomfortable metal chair anchored into the cement floor in the centre of the room. He has been handcuffed since he and his whole squad were arrested in the hangar. The handcuffs are attached to a metal chain bolted to the floor.

He tries to raise his hands, but only gets as far as his chest, the place where the rubber bullet hit him. Breathing is uncomfortable. Two other rubber bullets hit him in the upper-left calf and his right shoulder.

Jason does another examination of the room. Not much to take notice of except the four surveillance cameras looking down at him from each corner of the room.

The door opens, and three men walk into the room. Two of them are in RCMP uniforms, and Chief Superintendent Boucher follows them. With their arms folded and expressions stern, the uniformed officers take up position in front of him on opposite sides of the room.

Chief Superintendent Boucher looks Jason over. "Mr. Stands, my name is Chief Superintendent Andre Boucher. We need to talk about why you are in Canada with a group of ex-military personnel, a plane full of restricted firearms, military surveillance equipment, computer equipment, and documentation outlining what looks like a snatch-and-grab on Mr. Larry Evans. We have spoken to your colleagues, but they have not been very forthcoming at the moment. Do you care to comment on what I have just stated?"

Stands raises his head and smiles. "I don't need to talk to you. All I need is for you to uncuff and release me so my crew and I can return to the United States before you get into further trouble, Chief Whatever! Don't go Inspector Clouseau on me!"

Boucher clears his throat. "That's Chief Superintendent Boucher. I am a ranking member of the RCMP detachment here in Montreal."

"Yeah. Whatever! Let's make this easy for everybody, and I'll be on my way," Stands responds with a contemptuous attitude, rolling his eyes at Chief Superintendent Boucher.

Boucher pauses for a moment and turns to face the officer to his left, who gives him a tight-lipped grin. Boucher looks back at Stands. "Can you repeat that? I didn't quite understand."

"I said, uncuff me. Let me go now," Stands demands.

Boucher gives him a quizzical look. "So, are you saying that you refuse to cooperate?"

"I don't have to say shit to you," replies Stands.

Boucher gives him a look of confusion. "Why would you want to say shit to me?"

"What?" Stands responds.

"You said, 'I don't have to say shit to you.' Well, I don't want you to do that. I just want to know why you're here in Canada."

Frustrated, Stands blurts, "That's just a saying people use when they don't have to answer to anybody."

"Yeah, I know. Don't let the French name fool you. I am fully bilingual." Boucher smiles for the first time. "Now, just to clarify, can you repeat your answer so I have it documented?"

"I said, I don't have to say shit to you," replies Stands smugly.

Boucher gives the two other officers a quick glance. "You guys get that?"

The officers nod.

Boucher looks up to one of the four overhead surveillance cameras. "You guys get that?"

"We got it in the recording Chief." A voice in his micro earbud confirms.

Not finished, Stands adds, "I demand that you release me. My boss back in the USA won't be happy that you've detained me. You will pay for this."

"And who would that be?" Boucher inquires.

"Who?"

"Who exactly is your boss back in the USA? You said your boss wouldn't be happy. Who is that? Who is this person that won't be happy with how we have treated you so far?"

"You know who!"

"I know what?"

"My boss!"

"Mr. Stands, as of thirty minutes ago, I didn't know you existed. Why do you think I would know whom you report to? Why don't you enlighten me, Mr. Stands?"

Frustrated, Stands blurts, "The president of the fucking USA. That's who, goddammit. Now, release me!"

Boucher hesitates for a moment while Stands recovers from his outburst. Boucher brushes an imaginary piece of link from his arm sleeve. "Mr. Stands. You are not going anywhere. You are definitely not going to see any part of the United States again. Based on the initial discussions that I just had with my superiors before I entered this room, I have been told that your government has disavowed any knowledge of your actions in Canada. They referred to you as a 'low-level assistant with no direct access to the president.' They are building walls between you and the president as we speak."

"I don't believe you! The president has my back. He signed off on this mission," Stand declares.

"The narrative we are getting from your government is different. My superior has been in touch with your secretary of state, and she has no knowledge of your trip up here."

"You lie. You lie!" Stands responding angrily, raising his hands as far as the limits of the extended chains anchoring him down.

"I can play you both the audio and video tapes. We talked via video chat. The quality was very good, actually. Nice woman. We brought her up to speed on the situation, including the arrest of you and your operatives."

Jason leans back in his chair and hesitates. "I am a senior adviser to the president. You cannot do this to me."

"According to the American government, you are a low-level assistant with no direct contact to the president of the United States. I think you're suffering from delusions of grandeur, Mr. Stands." Boucher pauses. "Again, do you want to see the video? I can get my assistant to fetch a laptop."

Lowering his head, Jason murmurs, "My government wouldn't do this to me. They can't. They just can't." Jason looks down.

"Mr. Stands," Boucher says in a more comforting tone. "Again, do you want to see the video? It's kind of revealing, in my opinion."

"What do you mean?"

"The extent to which your country and your superiors are going to cover up your little trip up North. They are totally disavowing you and your group."

Stands, still looking at the floor, shakes his head. "I want to see a lawyer!"

"That will not happen, Mr. Stands. You are in no position to ask for or receive any legal protection. You see, right now, you and your group of soldiers are being held under the Canadian Anti-terrorism Act, and therefore, you have no access to any legal representation. The Anti-terrorism Act supersedes any legal protection from the Canadian Charter of Rights and Freedoms. There are critiques to some of the provisions of this act, but in the end, it has done a lot to stop and detain criminals like you who enter our country to do it harm."

"Are you kidding me?"

"Mr. Stands, you will not get the time to get to know me, but I don't kid around when it comes to a bunch of yahoos like you and your associates. You think foreign laws do not apply to you and that you have *carte blanche*. By the way, that's French for 'go fuck yourself.' Do you understand?"

"OK. OK. I get it! I'll tell you what you want." Stands raises his head to answer Boucher. "What do I get in return?"

Boucher shakes his head with a tight-lipped grin. "Again, Mr. Stands, you do not seem to grasp the situation at hand. Here's how this is going to work. One, you are going to tell us everything about your trip to our lovely country. You will tell us where you got the equipment, who supplied you with the plane, the intelligence information on the laptops, the restricted weapons, the ammunition, and all the other nasty gadgets we confiscated. You will tell us who gave you the orders. You will tell us who financed this operation. Basically, you are going to tell us everything."

Boucher pauses to catch his breath. "Two, you will go to our Special Handling Unit facility in Quebec for the most dangerous of inmates and become a lifelong member. That's all you get. No pardons from your government, because we will never release you back to the USA. You and your crew will never be offered up in any political negotiations between our two countries. The only positive outcome from your testimony will be that you will put the guilty people behind bars who wanted Mr. Larry Evans to disappear. Besides that, you and your friends will spend the rest of your natural life in jail. Do you understand what I am saying?"

Stands digests Boucher's words. "Get me a paper and pen, and you will have it all."

"What about your pals?" Boucher asks.

"Fuck them, let them rot."

"OK." Boucher turns to one of his officers. "Get him everything he needs." Boucher turns and walks out the door into the corridor, followed by the two officers.

One of them continues down the corridor, but the other huddles with Boucher. "We didn't have any video sessions, did we?" the officer asks. "We haven't even told the Americans about this. How did you know he wouldn't ask to see the video?"

"Because I offered it to him many times. I almost forced it down his throat. You were in the room. You saw me ask him. To him, it had to be true."

"What if he called your bluff?"

"He wasn't going to. I know his type," Boucher responds. "His narcissism got the better of him. They are all high and mighty when they are in control, but they crumble like a house of cards when they are on the receiving end of the law. This one's foundation was a crumbling mess. I bet you'll get a full confession in half an hour."

The officer smiles. "If there is one thing I've learned over the years, it's never to bet against you."

Boucher smiles back. "You will go far if you stick with me." He grabs the officer in a playful headlock as they walk away.

DAY NINETEEN —
MISSION SHUT DOWN

———

A black GMC Yukon XL pulls up in front of a single-story house on Westminster Avenue. The passenger door opens, and Benjamin Dowds steps out. The driver also gets out, walks around the front of the vehicle, and together, they walk up the sidewalk to the door. Dowds's assistant, Randall McGregor, former SAS of the British Army, knocks on the door. He turns and glances down the sidewalk and then surveys the immediate area while waiting for it to open.

Moments later, the door opens, and Dowds and McGregor step in. In the back room, Larry Evans sits at a small table with three empty chairs. A pot of French-press coffee, half full, and several cups are set on the table with an open box of doughnuts from the local Tim Hortons.

"Heads up." Dowds calls out Larry as he flips him his ring across the room. Larry catches it and quickly puts it back on.

"Thanks for that." Larry says with a smile.

Dowds nods and steps up to table to peek into the box to see what's left. Not impressed, he shifts his attention to Larry. "Life treating you all right, Mr. Evans?"

"Life is good, Mr. Dowds," he chuckles. He reaches over and shakes Dowds's hand.

Larry looks over to McGregor, "Nice to see you Randall."

"Thank you, sir," McGregor replies, staying in character.

"They feeding you well? Enough sugar in your diet?" Dowds asks, nodding to the box of doughnuts.

"Can't complain," Larry responds.

"So, do you want the good news or the bad news first, which will turn into good news?" Dowds asks.

Larry frowns. "What do you mean, 'which will turn into good news?'"

"Well, our American friends, and I use that term loosely, have decided to take you out of the picture. Permanently."

"What do you mean, 'permanently?' Who are these people?" demands Larry, tilting his head back with mix of confusion and fear.

Dowds waves his hands, "Oh, don't worry about any of that threat stuff. I've got it already taken care of. Those bozos tried to enter Canada in a private jet at Saint-Hubert Airport with a plane full of arms and ammunition. They've been arrested. Something about importing firearms illegally into our country. An anonymous person led the RCMP there right after they arrived. One of the people arrested was Jason Stands."

"Jason Stands—should I know who that is?"

"Jason Stands is a senior adviser to American President Campbell. Right now, the RCMP is keeping everything under wraps. Not releasing anything to the public. They also recovered laptops and other documents that outlined a snatch-and-grab on you."

Larry recovers from his panic attack. "Tell me, Dowds, what exactly did you do before becoming an attorney? I am very interested."

Dowds pauses for a moment, glances over to McGregor, and then looks back to Larry. Deflecting the question, Dowds says,

"Let's stick to the topic at hand. As I mentioned before, I've got good news and good news. Which do you want first?"

Larry decides to drop it and move on. "Give me the good news," he says.

"I have filed the lawsuit against the Springvale Starline Hotel, its management staff, the Springvale Police Department and the Mayor's office for the following: false arrest and defamatory statements; libel and slander by the hotel staff; deliberately denying your basic rights while you were arrested; and assault from when the police investigator struck you in the interrogation room, not to mention the hotel security officer who smacked you into the office cabinet. The lawsuit is asking for personal damages in the amount $30 million."

"Good, when should we hear something?"

"Oh, very soon. I have given them a twenty-four-hour window before the lawsuit is 'leaked' to the newspapers. I will probably be back in New Jersey tomorrow, or at the latest, the day after to meet with hotel management."

"Very good, Mr. Dowds. Very good."

"As for this Jason Stands fellow, I have notified the American State Department about his arrest, and they are willing to work out something else. If this ever got out, the ramifications would be enormous."

"OK, good. What about the malpractice lawsuit? Any updates?" Larry asks.

"Yeah. All done. Like I said back in New Jersey, I have friends who owe me favours. They took care of it quickly. They have associates on the hospital board in question, and they leaned on them to reopen the investigation. They quickly came to the conclusion that the hospital was at fault. We are finalizing the settlement amount."

"OK, now it's my turn. When can I leave this place and get back to my apartment?" Larry asks, looking over to Patrick Malone and

Arthur MacEvoy, the two guards that have been protecting him since he returned to Montreal. "Not that I don't enjoy the company of these two fine, outstanding gentlemen," he says, grinning.

Patrick and Arthur smile in response.

Dowds cocks his head towards them in a perplexed manner "I would say a couple more days, at most." Returning his gaze slowly towards Larry. "Once the lawsuit against our Springvale friends hits the public airwaves, it will be a good time for you to reappear. Are you good with that?"

"Yeah, as long as Arthur sleeps in the basement. He snores like a screaming steam train going through a tunnel."

Arthur, shocked, blurts, "I do not!"

Larry walks over to Arthur, smiling, and hugs him. "You are right, it isn't your snoring that keeps us awake, it's the constant farting." Larry steps back quickly.

Patrick, laughing out loud, steps between them.

"Mr. Evans, you are not a nice man," Arthur says, pointing a threatening finger at him.

"That is true! However, you still fart a lot." Larry turns, runs out of the room, and quickly goes up the stairs.

Patrick grabs Arthur and whispers something that brings a smile to his face.

Dowds sees this and inquires, "What did you tell him, Patrick?"

"Nothing to worry your little head about. Everything is under control." The two men walk out of the room.

Dowds looks over to MacGregor.

Macgregor responds with a slight grin, "Don't worry, they will not leave any visible marks."

Dowds shakes his head and sighs.

DAY TWENTY — YOU NEED TO MAKE A DECISION, MR. MAYOR

———

The Mayor's Office, Springvale Police department and the management at the Starline hotel in Springvale all receive registered notifications that lawsuits have been filed against them.

Mayor Frakes, who has been expecting the lawsuit and has prepared as much as he can with his legal team and personal lawyer, is floored by the lawsuit's scope. Frakes, his assistant, and his PR staff are named in the suit for character assassination along with numerous individuals who took to the media to attack Larry Evans. The suit references multiple defamatory claims.

The Springvale Police Department is implicated in the suit along with the police chief, the lead investigator, arresting officers, and the detectives who interrogated Larry Evans.

The damages are listed in the tens of millions of dollars. If Frakes settles, it will bankrupt the city and him personally.

In the conference room, the mayor, the city's legal team, his personal lawyer, and numerous senior city officials assemble. All of them sit silently as they review copies of the lawsuit.

Nobody dares speak first for fear of verbal abuse from the mayor, whose political and financial future is collapsing in front of him.

Finally, Jonas Frakes lifting his eyes away from the document and shifts his stare over to this legal team. "So, what is the verdict, guys? How fucked are we?" he asks, not caring to retain any decorum.

The most senior lawyer speaks up. "Sir, the work on the lawsuit is very good; it is tight and leaves us with almost no way to fight for a dismissal or even delay the proceedings. Every attack on Larry Evans is detailed with specific references of who said what and when. He's even provided a DVD with all the audio and video recording for our review. This Dowds fellow is very good at his job. We will need more time to tear it apart."

"Well, if you haven't already noticed, time is something we don't have much of," the mayor states in disgust. "We have forty-eight hours to settle, or the damages go up. Can they even do that?" he asks, unsure about the particulars of the law.

"Mr. Mayor, there are certain aspects of the law where damages can be applied if the defendant tries to delay the process unnecessarily. Clearly, Dowds and Evans have done their research on New Jersey state law and want to put this to bed quickly."

"How about the First Amendment? I have a right to free speech, don't I?"

"You are correct," one of the lawyers says. "The First Amendment does protect our freedom of speech. It is our right to stand up and state what we believe in."

"There! I was just speaking my mind. I can't be liable for that, can I?"

"Not so fast, Mr. Mayor. There are limits to the First Amendment, and you did unfortunately cross them—multiple times. You uttered threats and verbal abuse toward Mr. Evans. These are not protected. Your statements on camera, in radio interviews, and on social media were both slanderous and libellous."

"Well, how about social media outlets? Everyone makes comments on these apps. Is he going after them?"

"Sorry, Mr. Mayor. Legislation that was passed under Section 230 of the Communications Decency Act back in 1996 protects social media providers, including Twitter, Facebook, Instagram, and a slew of others, from liability of materials published by third-party users—in this case, you, Mr. Mayor."

"Well, I don't agree with that."

"You are not alone in that regard, but for the moment, the law exists."

Dejected, Mayor Frakes looks over to his personal lawyer. "Bob, how exposed am I, according to this lawsuit?"

"Sir, as my colleagues mentioned, the lawsuit is structured in such a way that we don't see any sections we can poke holes in. Dowds and company have gone to great lengths to document all your indiscretions towards Larry Evans. It is solid piece of work and fighting it will just run up your legal fees. I will be honest with you, sir. This is a no-win scenario. Settle now; avoid any penalties for delays and my unnecessary legal fees. You will need all the money you have."

"Geez, Bob, you are all heart. I guess keeping you on a fat retainer for all these years hasn't bought me a single hour of free legal advice. I won't forget this" the mayor shakes his finger at him, displeased with his advice. "By the looks of it, I will need to sell the main house, the cottage, and drain my investments to cover the damages. This lawsuit will totally bankrupt me—"

"Sir, it is worse than that," Bob interrupts. "From what I've calculated, all your investments, including $600,000 in stocks and your holdings in the sports bar on Blake Street, total an estimated $1.5 million. The one on Higgins Avenue is worth about $800,000. If we find the right buyer for the property on Rachel Street, it could bring in another $1 million. The two doughnut shops on the

East Side could easily bring in about $300,000 each, and the four automated car washes could be sold for about $2 million in total. Finally, your principal residence and your cottage up North are worth about $3 million, totaling about $9.5 million. It will still not be sufficient to cover the $12 million in personal damages. They will put a continued seizure on your salary until all debts are paid," Bob says, shifting in his chair, not comfortable having to summarize the mayor's dilemma.

"Fuck! Fuck! And more fuck! This can't be happening," the mayor shouts, his face flushed, his emotions taking over, slamming his clenched fist on the hardwood table.

"Sir, I suggest we start negotiations with Evans and company to reduce the damages in exchange for some sort of contrite confession, maybe in a public forum, that can possibly save you from bankruptcy," Bob proposes.

"Are you saying that I should apologize in public?" the mayor stands up and yells.

"Sir, with all due respect, you did publicly attack him with very defamatory statements that were not true," a senior official barks. "It was a clear attack on his character. It was uncalled for, and now the city is libel because you could not control your mouth." The senior official's outburst clearly puts his career in jeopardy, but at the same time, everybody else in the room was thinking it.

The mayor turns to face the senior official. "How dare you talk to me like that? I am the mayor; I will not stand for this."

Having found his courage, the senior official pushes back. "How dare you put the city in jeopardy like this? This lawsuit will bankrupt the city, put hundreds of employees out of work, cancel basic services, and all you care about is how I address you. God damn it! Clearly your priorities are screwed."

"Mr. Arnold, you are walking on a dangerous tightrope. I suggest you back off, or you may find your career in this city in jeopardy," the mayor lashes at him, slamming the palms of his hands down on the table, startling most the participation in the meeting. His domineering control of the city was showing some serious cracks in the foundation. Defiance from his staff was something he rarely encountered.

"Mr. Mayor, it is best for the city and for you personally to not only offer a public apology to Larry Evans, but to offer your resignation as Mayor to save the city from bankruptcy," Mr. Arnold says.

Frakes, infuriated, is about to respond when two other officials stand up in unison.

"I have to agree with Mr. Arnold," says the first. "In order to save the city, it is best that you resign immediately."

"Since we have the whole legal team here, a letter can be quickly drafted, approved, and signed within an hour," adds the second.

The senior legal associate stands. It is his turn to chime in. "Mr. Mayor, as terrible it would be for your legacy, it is important to put the viability of the city ahead of your personal well-being. I also agree with the recommendations of Mr. Arnold and his associates."

"I don't believe what I am hearing; I really don't," Frakes yells. "I have done so much for this city, and this is how you pay me back. By forcing me out!"

"It is the best for the city," Arnold responds.

"Go to hell, Arnold!" yells the mayor.

"Sir, please do not make this more difficult than it has to be," says another official, standing up.

With the tide turning against him, the mayor says. "I will not resign. We will fight this, and we will win."

"Have you not heard a bloody thing?" Arnold yells. "The lawsuit is solid; the city is facing tens of millions of dollars in damages. It is a no-win scenario, and all you think of is saving your own skin." Arnold pauses for a moment. "We can do this now and announce it before the end of day, or we can reconvene with council members to vote on a resolution for you to step down, preferably voluntarily. If not, we will force you out. I don't think we will have an issue getting a majority vote. Whichever way you look at it, by this time tomorrow, you will not be the mayor of this city. We can only pray to God that this will be sufficient for Dowds and company to drop their suit against the city."

The mayor surveys the room for support, and none is offered. He peers over at Arnold. "Draft a letter. I will sign it," he states with a sombre look. He sits back in his chair.

Arnold turns to the legal team. "Draft the letter; the mayor will sign it. Send a copy of it to Dowds and ask if we can negotiate better terms. ... Mr. Mayor, we will send you resources who will help you to clear out your personal belongings by the end of day. We want to send a clear signal to Dowds that we are serious about this lawsuit."

The members of the legal team get up and rush out of the room to draft the letter; not wanting to remain in a room with a mayor in collapse.

He eyes the rest of the group slowly with contempt in his face. Arnold is the first one to get up, "Mr. Mayor." He nods, turns and walks out. Slowly, the remaining members of the group follow suit.

Jonas Frakes remains quiet during the exodus. He peers down at the table, reaches over to grab the crystal ash tray in his hand and in a quick gesture, hurls it at a glass sculpture on the opposite end of his office, obliterating it.

DAY TWENTY — MISSION LOST — UPDATE

Henry Mood, senior adviser to and long-time friend of the president, stands outside the Oval Office, waiting to get in. He glances towards the executive secretary, who tries not to make eye contact, but in the end, Mood's insistence wears her down.

"He is almost done with his meeting," she says.

"Thanks," he responds in frustration. He paces back and forth in front of the secretary and the two armed marines stationed outside the office. A dozen Secret Service agents are within ear shot.

The secretary hangs up from her phone. "The president is free now," she says. "You may go in."

"Thank you Agatha." Mood says he rushes into the Oval Office. He closes the door behind him; his news is classified.

"What is going on, Henry?" the president asks.

"We have a situation, and it isn't good!"

"What is it?"

"Jason Stands and his goons are under arrest in Montreal. Multiple counts of possession with the intent to import illegal arms into Canada."

"Goddammit!" The president stands from his desk and walks toward Henry. "How the fuck did this happen? They are supposed to be professionals—experts in these operations."

"Apparently local and federal officers raided the hangar where the airplane was parked immediately upon its arrival. A SWAT unit was also part of the raiding party. They were caught off-guard and had no time to hide their weapons or any of the mission's materials.

"The RCMP now have all the laptops and maps detailing the plans to snatch Larry Evans. Also, the RCMP knows who Jason is. The operatives themselves can be traced back to the United States. Jason got sloppy in his haste to put the operation in motion. He didn't bring in help from outside the country to minimize the risk and blowback."

The president clenches his jaw, rubbing his neck but remained silent as Henry continues. "Mr. President, I know you don't want to hear this. However, I told you the last time we met that this was a foolish, a very risky plan. And now we have a potential international incident with our friends to the north because that idiot Jason Stands fed you a plan to solve your issue. It backfired spectacularly."

"Listen, Henry," the president says, angrily pointing his finger at him. "I don't need a lecture from you right now. I need your help to solve this."

"You begged me to stay after I stormed out of your office several days ago, and you still went ahead with this stupid plan. Goddammit, Mr. President, when are you going to learn that you can't solve all your problems by sending your hit squads to clean up your messes? This is not a country run by a dictatorship; this is a democracy. You are not above the law."

Getting a dressing down from a subordinate is something that rarely happens. President Campbell did not take it well. In this matter, he remained silent in response choosing to terminate the conversation by heading towards the Oval Office via the secondary door. Just before he grabs the doorknob, he turns and gives

Mood a stern, determined look. "Never forget who you direct your comments to, Mr. Mood. I am the president of the United States, and you work at the pleasure of the president." The president walks out the door.

Henry does the same, though through the entrance he came from.

DAY TWENTY-ONE — DOWDS VS. HOTEL MANAGEMENT

—

The Springvale Starline Hotel, catering to their business demographics, has several small conference rooms, elegantly furnished with all the necessities required for small meetings of two to eight people. Two larger conference rooms, separated by a retractable dividing wall, can each accommodate up to forty people. There are also about a dozen pods with phone and internet access, allowing businesspeople to keep in touch with their respective home offices or clients in a private area.

Today, in one of the small conference rooms, is the hotel manager, Holly Waldon; the hotel's regional director, Ralph Gibson, who arrived early this morning from Albany, New York; and a corporate lawyer named Catie Peters. All present to discuss the lawsuit filed against them by Benjamin Dowds, who is sitting across from them.

"Good morning, all. Thank you for this meeting. My name is Benjamin Dowds. I am the legal representative for Larry Evans, a guest who stayed at your hotel several weeks ago. He is suing your hotel for your staff's false accusations of assault on one Amanda Chase and for his ill treatment during his restraint in your security office. All of this is documented in detail in the lawsuit papers in front of you," Dowds declares.

All of them remain silent during his speech.

"As Mr. Evans's legal representative, I'm here to inform you that we are seeking two items from the hotel's management," Dowds says. "They are both indicated in the lawsuit, but just to make sure everybody is on the same page, I will summarize. Are we good?"

The three individuals nod in silence.

Dowds continues. "Item one: we request that all hotel staff listed in the lawsuit be immediately terminated and never to be rehired by this hotel or any other hotel branch within the corporate umbrella." Dowds glances across the table from him. "Please feel free to stop me whenever you need any clarification or wish to comment."

Ms. Peters breaks the silence. "Thank you Mr. Dowds. We are clear with this item and have already taken steps to meeting this requirement. Most of the names listed in the lawsuit have already been terminated. We are just wrapping up a few problem employees."

"Do you need any help in the matter?" Dowds asks, aware what the answer will be.

"Thank you, but we will handle it internally," she replies, emotionless.

"OK, the second item is financial compensation for my client's lost wages—current and future wages—as Mr. Evans's employer terminated him due to your hotel employees' defamatory statements and actions. Without those false statements, my client would still be gainfully employed. As his reputation has been destroyed, and his future employment is questionable, we are seeking compensatory damages in the amount of $15 million." Dowds pauses to let the number sink in. "I think this is fair, and at the same time, it will be a notice to all future claims of false accusations to be careful before making such inaccurate claims. That is all I have to say," Dowds concludes.

"Mr. Dowds, we understand the situation our staff have put Mr. Evans in and the hardships he has experienced. We have read the court summary and have further reviewed the video files from the hotel. We are at a loss to the actions taken by our staff members who participated in this charade, nor do we condone their actions. We don't understand what their endgame was in making these false accusations. I don't think we ever will. What is more puzzling is that we pride ourselves in vetting all employees within our organization to only hire people who meet our standards in integrity and character." Ms. Peters responds.

"Clearly you will need to review those vetting practices." Dowds says.

"Clearly. The board has already mandated this," she says.

"What about following up with the terminated staff?" Dowds asks.

Peters pauses for a moment, glances over to her two colleagues for some sort of direction. They both nod. "With regards to the staff members we terminated, they have all since left the city, and we have been unsuccessful in following up with them," she states.

"That is most unusual, Ms. Peters. Have you contacted the police in this matter?"

"No, we have not. We are keeping this internal, and anyway, the Springvale police force has their own issues, courtesy of your client, Mr. Evans."

"Issues originating from your staff making false claims, Ms. Peters," Dowds rebukes.

"Point taken, Mr. Dowds," Ralph Gibson speaks up. "Let's move on. The monetary damages you are claiming are rather high, in our opinion. We would like to see the damages reduced."

Dowds, fired up by the challenge, goes into overdrive. "Let's get one thing clear, here. I am not a run-of-the-mill lawyer trying to get my client a big settlement with a figure I pulled out of my ass." Dowds looks over to Ms. Peters. "Pardon the language," he apologizes.

"I've heard worse in the lawyers' pit," she responds.

"OK," Dowds says, "the number is reflective of Mr. Evans current salary, which I can provide to you, his performance reviews, and his career tracking to VP status by the end of the year. He was projected to receive a personal performance bonus and a payout from corporate profit-sharing. Your corporation has the ability to easily absorb this hit, as you are on track to surpassing your quarterly forecast. Occupancy rates are high and expected to remain high. Convention booking are up. You guys are firing on all cylinders so forgive me if I don't believe you can't afford the monetary damages listed in the lawsuit."

Dowds pauses to catch his breath. "I did my homework before putting this number together, so please do not insult me with your pleas for negotiations. You can either settle today while I am still in town or face a court date when I will go for double this amount." Dowds looks at his watch. "It is presently 11:25. I am going for an early lunch and will be back by one o'clock, at which point I will either have a check in front of me for the full amount, or I will submit this lawsuit to the courts." Dowds stands up, picks up his briefcase, and pushes back his chair. "I will see you all in just over an hour." He turns, walks to the door, and exits without another word.

The three hotel individuals remain silently in their seats until Holly Waldon turns to face the two others. "Really! This was the plan you two had? Coming down from the corporate office to piss off the lawyer who is suing us so he will up his demands. Brilliant! Absolutely fucking brilliant." she states in frustration. Then she collapses back in her chair, shaking her head.

DAY TWENTY-ONE — RONALD ASKS QUESTIONS IN SPRINGVALE

———

Reporter Ronald Slater, reporter for the Newark Journal, arrives at Newark Liberty International Airport and chooses to wait in the taxi lineup, forty people deep. Big mistake; after waiting twenty-five minutes, the line moves a dozen feet. He steps out of the line, scans the area for rental signs, spots one to the right, and walks toward it. *Time to rent.*

The drive to Springvale is uneventful. He already reviewed the dozens of questions in his notepad while waiting in the taxi lineup. Crosschecking against his notes and checklists. He was ready for the busy day ahead.

On the previous day, he called ahead to arrange a meeting with a representative from the local police force. He tried to track down the hotel witnesses to get their side of the story.

Well, the witnesses—all of them—have been a bust. None of them are employed at the hotel anymore.

When the surveillance videos became public, the bartender was let go for not providing an accurate picture of the events on the night of the assault.

The front desk manager was terminated for the same reason.

As for Amanda Chase, her last known location was at the local hospital, but she has since left.

He would like to speak to the hospital staff who treated her during her stay. He plans to visit the hospital after his appointment with Detective MaryAnn Lewis. If even one of the two meetings pan out with relevant leads, he is batting .500. Always the cautious optimism, Ronald Slater is determined to get answers to growing fascination of LarryGate.

DAY TWENTY-ONE — RONALD SLATER AND THE DETECTIVE

Slater pulls in front of the Springvale police station early in the morning. He parks across the street, as all other spots in front of the police station are occupied.

He sits in his car, head down, reviewing his notes for the upcoming meeting, oblivious of the car that pulls up beside him. The beep from the driver's horn startles him. He peers over to the car and driver, who motions to ask if he is leaving his spot. Slater narrows his eyes and shakes his head.

Frustrated, the driver pulls away and rejoins traffic. Slater follows the progress of the car as it pulls away, then returns to his notepad momentarily before flipping it closed.

He pockets it inside his jacket, gets out of the car, and looks both ways before dashing across the street. He walks up to the main glass door and goes inside.

The duty officer, just like Slater sees in movies and television cop shows, is behind the desk, facing the main door. He has chevrons on his sleeve, indicating that he is a sergeant.

Ronald Slater steps up to the desk. "I am here for an appointment with a Detective MaryAnn Lewis at ten o'clock. My name is Ronald Slater."

The duty officer peeks at his watch. "Have a seat. I'll page her and tell her you're here, but I need a picture ID."

Slater pulls out his wallet, plucks out his driver's licence, and hands it over.

The sergeant looks at it, back at Slater, and then returns it.

Slater nods and heads to a row of empty metal chairs attached to the wall.

A few minutes pass as Slater reviews his notes. At 10:02, a woman walks over to him.

"Hi, I'm Detective MaryAnn Lewis," she says. "You must be the reporter from Newark."

He stands up to greet her. "Yes, the name is Ronald Slater." He extends his hand, but she nods and points to the corridor where she came from.

"This way, please," she states as they walk into the heart of the police station. She points to a wooden door up ahead. "Right into this room." She opens it, and they step in. She closes the door behind them. They grab chairs on the side of a table in the middle of the room.

Detective Lewis starts first. "Now, Mr. Slater, I will be quick and to the point."

"OK," he responds, slightly startled.

"I assume you're here to talk about the Larry Evans Case. Well, the city, the police station, and even the mayor are the subject of an ongoing lawsuit at the moment. I myself am one of the defendants in this lawsuit, so what I can say or acknowledge will be very limited in scope."

"Actually, that will not be much of a problem, as I'm not here to talk about the lawsuit at all," Slater replies. "However, whatever tidbits you are willing to offer would be of interest for possible future articles."

"No can do on that subject."

"Ok. Doesn't hurt to ask." Ronald says with a slight grin, trying to keep the conversation cordial.

"So, why are you here then?" she asks.

"I am working on a piece strictly about Larry Evans—not the lawsuit."

"What do you want to know about him? That lousy piece of . . ." Detective Lewis stops herself.

"OK, so I guess you're not a big fan of Larry Evans?"

"I am not," she replies.

"When was the last time you saw Mr. Evans?"

"At the courthouse when the case was dismissed. That was not a good day for the city and a lot of others, I can tell you."

"That was the last time?"

"Yes, he disappeared through the rear exit, I guess to avoid the media reporters. Good move. He hasn't been seen since. People are speculating that he is back in Montreal, huddled up with his lawyer."

"What do you think?" Slater asks.

"I think he's either back in Montreal or dead," she says.

"Dead! Are you kidding me?" he bursts out.

Lewis leans slightly forward. "You've got to understand where you are right now. This is Springvale, New Jersey. This is Jonas Frakes's city; he runs it with an iron fist. You don't mess with Frakes if you want to keep all your body parts intact, Mr. Slater."

"Whoa! That is quite an accusation."

"Accusation. I would not call it that. Not much into dealing with accusations."

"Then what would you call it?" Slater is intrigued by this unexpected detour in the conversation.

"Facts, Mr. Slater. Facts. Jonas Frakes is not a nice man. Sure, he looks after the city but he also makes sure that the city's agenda benefits his agenda." Lewis responds.

"And you know this firsthand?" Slater asks.

"It's almost a rite of passage for new police officers to be addressed by Frakes. Mine came almost twelve years ago, three months after I graduated from the police academy. It was not a pleasant experience, one I would rather not talk any further about, thank you."

"OK, that is fine Detective. Back to Larry Evans. What did you see in him when he was being interrogated?"

"A smug, arrogant bastard," she states. "When I mentioned that Amanda was in the hospital, he didn't even ask about her condition. He said he didn't care. That he didn't know her."

"Is it true that you struck him while in the interrogation room?"

"I cannot comment on that. Goes toward the lawsuit," she says, smiling at him.

He nods. *We shall not speak of this again.* "OK, on to a different subject. Amanda Chase—when was the last time you spoke to her?"

"Not too long ago. Over a week, if not longer."

"Whereabouts?"

"The hospital in Springvale, Summit Oaks Hospital."

"Yes, that's what I have in my notes," he says, flipping through his pad to confirm. "How was she?"

"Not very helpful."

"In what way?"

"In all ways. She refused to answer any questions. Surprisingly, she refused to provide any information that could have helped the case. I think we all know why now," she states.

"Yes. That was most unusual. This whole----", Slater pauses, searching for the correct word to describe this event.

"Cluster fudge!" Lewis responds with a bit of levity.

"Cluster fudge. I'll go with that. Myself, I was leaning towards a more colorful metaphor but this is good." Slater states before moving on. "Anything else you can add that would be helpful, Detective Lewis?"

"There is nothing else that I can volunteer at the moment with the lawsuit currently in play. Off the record, from what I hear, it's going to be a bloodbath for the city and everybody named in the suit. Present company included."

"OK, well, in that case, I thank you for your time. I'm sure you have a lot to prepare for." He stands up and offers her his hand.

She stands at the same time and shakes it. "Good luck on your investigation, Mr. Slater."

Slater turns and exits the room. Lewis remains, sitting down silently.

DAY TWENTY-ONE — RONALD SLATER AT THE HOSPITAL

After leaving the police station and getting back into his car, Slater pulls out his notepad to jot down a few notes. Deep in thought, he does not notice a car pull up beside him again. The driver honks. Startled again, Slater gives the driver a stern *no* when the driver asks if Larry is going to give up his parking spot. The driver gives him the one-finger salute and drives away.

What is wrong with these people? Slater thinks to himself. *Can't a person just sit in his car without getting harassed? What a town!*

I need a drink! He peeks over at his center console and notices that his Starbucks coffee that he picked up earlier in the morning is still there. He picks it up, hoping it is still reasonably warm, and takes a sip. He cringes in response — cold. He puts it back down, starts up the car, puts it into gear, and pulls into traffic. His next stop is Summit Oaks Hospital to get an update, if there is one, on Amanda Chase.

Thirty-five minutes and less than ten miles later due to heavy traffic, Slater pulls into an empty parking spot close to the hospital's main doors.

He looks around; the lot is less than half full. *Kind of strange for a hospital parking lot. Is this good? Either not many people are sick in this region, or the hospital is not well regarded. Not up to standards and people don't come here for treatment.*

He gets out of the rental and continues to examine the immediate surrounding. Interesting! Sunny day. *Not too hot. No humidity. Nice day for staff, during their breaks, or even some patients not restricted to their rooms to wander about. You would think, but nobody is outside. I've got to ask when I get in. Got to get to the bottom of this. There might be a story here. Large state funded hospital lies unused. Your tax dollars at work. Or are they? Investigative reporter Ronald Slater brings you all the facts. Boy the mind wanders a little too much when you are looking for the next big story.*

"Focus Ronald. Focus!" he mutters to himself as he steps away from the car.

He walks through the main doors, sprays on some hand sanitizer from a dispenser, and rubs his hands together. He walks over to the information desk.

The lady receptionist in attendance looks up and asks, "How may I help you, sir?"

"Full disclosure, I am a reporter from the *Newark Journal*, and I am doing some background research on the Larry Evans story. Have you heard of him?" he asks.

"I have. It's been an interesting topic of conversation around here. At one point, his assailant spent a few days here recovering."

Slater, taken aback by the statement, asks, "What do you mean by 'spent a few days?'"

"Well, Mr. . . . ?"

"The name is Ronald Slater."

"Well, Mr. Slater, Amanda Chase was indeed treated here. However, she only stayed for a few days and then was released. Actually, if I recall, she left the hospital on her own. She was not discharged by her attending physician. Still under observation from what I heard. Caused quite a bit of excitement that night when it was discovered that she was gone. Staff and security running all over the hospital searching for her." She recounts.

"Were you there that evening?" Ronald asks.

"Goodness no. I just handle the day shift. I heard it from Nurse Shelley the next day. She filled me in. You know, the nurses like to talk a lot about people of interest during lunch time. It breaks up the boredom these days with all the changes happening."

Intriguing! "Do tell?" He smiles.

"I shouldn't really. Not right now anyways, you are here about Amanda. Everything else can wait for another time." She responds.

"You are right. I get sidelined easily." He smiles at the receptionist. "Ok. My understanding is that her injury was not a minor one." Slater pulls out his notepad, jotting down some quick notes about a possible hospital story. "OK, since Amanda Chase is no longer a patient of this hospital, would it be possible to talk to a doctor or nurse who treated her?" he asks.

The receptionist looks him over one more time. Ronald cocks his head, gives her a smile. She winks at him and turns her focus to her screen for a moment. Some mouse movement happens, a few clicks and then turns back to Slater. "Good or bad news—which do you want first?"

"Always start with the bad, and hope for good news to make up for it," he states.

"I like that!" She smiles again.

"You can use it. You have my permission." Slater smiles back, hoping all this innocent foreplay will get him access to somebody who can talk about Amanda.

"Well, the doctor who took care of Ms. Chase is not on call today, but the primary nurse who assisted her is actually working tonight. Given the fact that it's a little slow today, I don't see a problem with you talking to her. Give me a second." She picks up her phone, dials an extension, and waits. "Hi. It's Judy at reception. Is Nurse Pearson available to talk to a visitor?" she asks.

"Thanks, Judy," Slater says quietly.

"OK, thanks." Judy hangs up and turns to Slater. "She's on her way. You can sit right over there." She points to a bench on the wall.

"Thanks again, Judy." He steps away and sits down on the bench and pulls out his notepad to review his notes.

Within minutes, Nurse Pearson arrives. Judy points to Slater. Nurse Pearson smiles, nods, and walks over. A tall woman, as tall at Ronald, slim, wearing a light blue nurse uniform with all the appropriate security badges attached to her shirt pocket.

Slater stands up and offers his hand in greeting. Nurse Pearson shakes it.

"Thanks for finding time for me," he says. "Where can we talk?"

"How about right here?" She points to the bench.

Slater nods and sits back down as Nurse Pearson grabs a space beside him. "Nurse Pearson, I was told that Amanda Chase was under your care when she was admitted."

"That is correct. She was not here for long. Actually, a pretty brief period, if you consider the severity of her head injury."

"How long did she stay?"

"Two days. In total, less than forty-eight hours, and then she was gone."

"But you said it was a serious injury."

"Exactly. Typically, we give patients like this round-the-clock supervision for over a week, checking in on them every hour, on the hour."

"Well, did you not persuade her to stay?" Slater asks.

"Absolutely, but she left late in the evening when supervision in the ward was low. She just slipped out."

"Slipped out. That's strange."

"Yes, it was," Pearson says. "Almost like she timed it between check-ins. That was the same night Detective Lewis was here to talk to her, but Ms. Chase was not very pleasant to her."

"What do you mean?"

"Well, she refused to answer any of her questions even though they would have helped the case at the time."

"Exactly. Who knew at the time it was all a lie with the video evidence released to the public now," Slater responds.

"Yes. I don't get it either. The injury was genuine. Her condition was real. But---"

"But why go through all of this and lie to the cops. To Detective Lewis." Ronald steps in. Sorry for interrupting, please continue."

"No worries. So, right after the detective left, she asked for a phone. I brought her one, and she started making calls. She said she wanted to notify her parents, so I left the room to give her some privacy."

"And what happened afterwards?" Slater asks.

"I left her to her calls, and I continued with my rounds. About an hour later, she was gone. Not in her bed, and all her personal items were gone."

Slater stares at Nurse Pearson for a moment, perplexed. "What happened when you discovered she was gone? That she was not in her room anymore?"

"Well, I notified security immediately, and I did a complete search with the other personnel on the floor. We didn't find her. I called Detective Lewis, and she said she would look into it."

"Is that all Detective Lewis said?" Slater asks.

"Yes, but I got the impression from her tone that it wasn't a priority," Pearson states. "Anyways, I haven't heard back from the detective since."

"That is indeed strange. Come to think of it, when I spoke to the detective this morning, this didn't come up at all. Then again, she also wasn't in the mood to provide me with any real details about Amanda. This whole case is getting weirder and weirder."

"So, what are you going to do?" Pearson asks.

"Well, there isn't much I can really do except report on it and hope people start asking questions."

She smiles. "I guess that's what a good investigative reporter does."

"Thanks. And thanks for your time and for answering my questions. I won't keep you any longer."

They both stand up together, and he offers his hand.

She accepts and shakes it. "Have a good day, Mr. Slater."

"You too, Nurse Pearson." He turns and walks out the door.

DAY TWENTY-ONE — WHAT ABOUT THE MAYOR?

—

"Breaking news from Springvale, New Jersey. The mayor of Springvale has just announced his immediate resignation. He has issued a public apology about the thoughtless and insulting words he has uttered toward Larry Evans.

"All this stems from the lawsuit Larry Evans's attorney filed against the city of Springvale, the Springvale Police Department, numerous public officials, including Mayor Frakes himself. As you will recall, after Larry Evans's arrest, Mayor Frakes immediately set out on a daily campaign of attacking Evans's character. A man who, the mayor has now publicly admitted, he had never met.

"The assumption from his resignation, if this is indeed a resignation and he has not been pushed out, is that senior city officials are attempting to save the city from bankruptcy if the court finds the city guilty on all charges.

"As Mayor Frakes is only one of many officials referenced in the lawsuit, we will most probably see further resignations and terminations as a result of the negative publicity that has painted city administrators as a bunch of hooligans."

DAY TWENTY-TWO — DOWDS VS. COMMLINK SERVICES

Spring time is a great time to visit Montreal. It is reborn every spring with fresh flowers, an abundance of leaves on trees, and is filled with the hopes of a great summer. Week-long festivals, active nightlife, and scenic historical sections of the town put the city's four-hundred-plus years in existence on full display.

Today, Larry Evans is not enjoying the splendors of Old Montreal. Instead, he sits across a table from a group of three attorneys representing his old company, Commlink Services. They are dressed in expensive suits, all slightly different shades of blue—a power colour. All are well groomed with no facial hair. Maybe it is a company policy, but who knows?

The meeting room is spacious, but not overly so, enough for a dozen people to sit comfortably. In the corner of the room, closest to the door, a small cabinet holds several platters of complementary fresh fruit, pastries, and half a dozen of Montreal's famous bagels. Jams and other condiments are to the side with a large pot of coffee, cutlery, and glass coffee cups. No paper cups here; image is everything.

Beside Larry is Benjamin Dowds. The best thing Larry has done so far has been retaining him. When Larry met with Dowds several weeks ago at the jail, he presented his case in detail. It took Dowds less than fifteen minutes to sign up and represent him.

Larry glances over at Dowds, who is sitting beside him. Today, Dowds is dressed in a light grey suit. A statement against the corporate lawyers' dark attire.

Dowds, ever confident in his approach, wastes no time. He pulls out four folders containing copies of the lawsuit out of his briefcase. He passes out the folders to the attorneys and then an additional copy to the lead attorney, one Robert Samuels. A distinguished looking older man compared to the two other younger lawyers sitting beside him.

Robert Samuels gives him a perplexing look. "What is this for?"

"This is for your senior partner who chose not to attend. I'm saving Commlink the exaggerated photocopying costs that your group would have passed on to them if you had to do it yourself."

Larry cracks a small smile and snickers.

The attorneys across from him do not find it amusing.

"Gentlemen, what I present to you today is a civil suit against Commlink Services that I have filed on Mr. Larry Evans's behalf, arguing that his termination was politically motivated and not based on any code-of-conduct infraction. In fact, we have reason to believe that the company recently altered your code of conduct in order to support their case for termination. Furthermore, the withholding of any severance pay or monies owed to cover potential legal costs on the behalf of the company was an abuse of the justice system. This lawsuit has been filed in the state of New Jersey."

"New Jersey! You can't do that!" declares the attorney on the left.

Samuels gives the other attorney a look of contempt. In response, the other attorney backs away slightly, acknowledging his mistake of talking out of turn.

Benjamin Dowds shifts his comments towards Samuels. "Do you want me to tell your inexperienced associate who seems to have acquired his law degree from a Cracker Jacks box as to why we filed in New Jersey and not in Montreal, or should I?" Dowds asks, struggling to hold back smirking in front of everybody.

Robert Samuels stares at Dowds, says, "Mr. Dowds has filed this lawsuit in New Jersey because while Commlink Services' main branch is in Montreal, it has offices in New Jersey and several other states. Therefore, he is eligible to file in any state where Commlink Services has a business presence. Additionally, filing in the United States and in New Jersey, in particular, allows for Mr. Dowds and Mr. Evans to ask the courts for a larger settlement than in any other state—far more than any province in Canada. Apart from personal damages, they can also seek fairly large punitive damages if the employer is found to have acted wrongly in terminating Mr. Evans. In our case, this is exactly what they are doing."

Dowds kept his focus on the younger attorney during Samuels's explanation, watching as younger attorney slowly melted into his chair. "Next time, ask for permission before you make comments so you don't embarrass your boss again."

Samuels, flushed in anger by Dowds comments, blurts, "Fuck you, Dowds. This lawsuit is worthless. We will crush you in court!"

Larry shifts in his chair at the sudden outburst from Samuels, looks over at Dowds.

Dowds does the opposite and leans back, showing the experience of a lawyer who has been in this predicament before. "Now, there's no need for profanity," he says before the lead attorney can continue. "Before you make any more statements that you might regret, I highly suggest you get your two young Padawans to review the details of the lawsuit and get back to us. I have a few items of interest that you might want to ponder before we talk again."

Dowds pauses for dramatic effect, imagining himself on TV before a commercial with the camera zooming in on his face and the other principal characters remaining silent and pensive. "Are we good, or do I need to explain myself again? I'm not the one on the clock, here."

Samuels stands up, straightens his overly priced suit jacket, and adjusts his tie, all while maintaining eye contact with Dowds. He is usually in control, and his confidence has taken a hit today. His response is short and to the point. "You can go now, Mr. Dowds, Mr. Evans."

Dowds pushes back from his chair and stands up. Larry, still quiet, does the same.

"Well, this was quicker than I thought. Good day, gentlemen," Dowds says and walks toward the conference room door. He opens it, steps aside, and offers the passage to Larry. Larry smiles and walks out, Dowds following. The door closes behind them.

The lead attorney gets up and turns to the young attorney. "Next time, before you make a dumbass statement like that, don't!" he says, pointing his finger at him. "Just shut the fuck up and listen!"

The young attorney nods silently, not wanting to risk ending his short career.

The other attorney, who has been quiet the whole time, exclaims, "Sir, what about the statement that Dowds made about the items of interest we should be aware of?"

The lead attorney turns to him, still frustrated. "Look into it right away and get back to my assistant if you flag anything. Better yet, get litigation involved to review it also. She has an excellent eye for stuff like this. Let's cover all our bases."

The second attorney nods, picks up his copy of the lawsuit, and leaves the room quickly.

Under his breath, he exclaims, "Fuck!"

DAY TWENTY-TWO — LET'S GO OUTSIDE TO TALK

—

Larry Evans and Benjamin Dowds remain quiet as they walk to the elevator, ride down, and go out the building as planned.

Once outside, Dowds turns to Larry. "How do you feel?"

"I am impressed," he states. "You pretty much called it as it played out."

Dowds smiles. "This isn't my first rodeo, or more apropos in Canada, my first hockey game." They both chuckle.

Dowds continues. "By now, Samuels's flunkies are huddling over the details of the lawsuit to look for the smoking gun. That is, if Mr. Lead Attorney hasn't already fired Cracker Jack, in which case they'll be bringing in a secondary with experience." Dowds looks at his watch: 3:25 p.m. "Hmmm, I would say it's escalated to Samuels's boss by four thirty with the big reveal and . . ." He pauses.

Larry asks, "What's the problem?"

"You know what? I never got the name of Samuels's boss. It would have been nice to personalize the extra copy for him. Oh well. So, where did I leave off?"

"The big reveal!" Larry smiles.

"Yes, once the big reveal comes out, the shit will hit the fan and Samuel's boss will run to his senior partner. He'll bring him up to speed with the discovery. At that point, a call will be made to your best friend in Human Resources," he chuckles.

"And?" Larry asks.

"At that point, our HR person will make her career-ending announcement to the executive board."

Larry absorbs the narrative and smiles mischievously. "I could live with that! She was not a very nice person. Not a fan."

Dowds extends his hand toward Larry.

Larry takes it.

"Mr. Evans, within a week, this should be settled. You will be one rich son of a bitch, and I will be the recipient of twenty percent of your settlement."

They both shake hands and laugh.

DAY TWENTY-TWO — WE'RE SCREWED! SETTLE!

—

The intercom light flashes followed by a small buzzing sound from Susan Sanders's desk phone. She reaches over and clicks the blinking button. "Yes, Janice?"

"Ms. Strauss just called. Your presence has been requested in the executive boardroom right away."

"Thank you, Janice." Susan clicks off the line. She stands up, straightens her skirt, takes a deep breath, and clenches and unclenches her hands. *Well, the day just keeps getting better and better!*

Susan Sanders, director of Human Resources at Commlink Services, steps outside her office, closes the door behind her, and makes her way to the executive board room three floors up. She has just received a call from the senior partner of the legal department about Larry Evans. The news is not good, not good at all.

She approaches the receptionist behind an expensive-looking mahogany desk.

Joanna Strauss, guardian to the executives, greets her and remarks her apprehension. "Susan, is everything all right?" she asks blandly, conveying neither genuine interest nor lack thereof. A most extraordinary skill if you can master it.

"Everything is not all right. Not all right at all," Susan answers. Then she nods to the boardroom's double-polished wooden door. "Are they in there?" she asks, hoping they're not.

"They are. I've been told to let you straight in when you arrive. Are you sure that everything is all right? You are worrying me, Susan."

Susan walks toward the double doors but stops and turns. She nods in false reassurance. Then she heads into the room. *What a bitch!*

The boardroom is on the higher end of executive boardrooms layouts, sixty feet long by thirty feet wide. All four walls and the ceiling are covered in rich, dark wood paneling. Rows of embedded ceiling fixtures provide enough light to properly illuminate the room. Electrical costs were not a concern during the construction of the executive boardroom. The wall immediately to the right of the door is furnished with numerous wood and glass cabinets displaying pieces of artwork from around the world. The conference table, made of the same richly polished wood, is easily forty feet long. In twelve expensive, top of the line, Aurora executive white leather chairs are the members of the executive board.

Susan closes the door behind her, and all conversations quickly come to a halt.

A well-dressed older gentleman on the far side of the conference table stands up. "What do you have to report, Ms. Sanders?" demands the chairman of the board, Walter M. Redman.

Nobody knows what the *M* stands for. Some people who have come up against him have been very creative in attaching a meaning to the initial.

"Mr. Redman, the news from the legal department after their review of the lawsuit is not good," Susan announces.

"Please elaborate, and do so quickly," he says, showing his characteristic lack of patience.

"Well, it seems—"

"Please do not dwell on the hypothetical, Ms. Sanders, only the facts. Do not provide supposition."

Susan stiffens up, clenching her hands together behind her back, not wanting to display her sweaty palms. "No sir. I will get straight to it. The facts are as follows: a recording device with the conversation between Mr. Evans and myself is in the possession of Mr. Evans's attorney. All discussions about his termination, which we made sure went undocumented, were recorded in full. In the recording, I repeatedly reference the board's wishes that Mr. Evans be terminated without any severance or salaries owed. Additionally, I told him that his fairness of dismissal was not my or the board's issue, and much pressure was coming in from all sides to dismiss him. Also, they seem to be aware that the code of conduct was changed to include his indiscretions to protect us and so we could avoid paying out any large sums for his high severance."

"What would we have been looking at if we had paid him off before we changed everything? If he had gone silently into the night?" Redman asks.

"I would say between $900,000 and $1 million, sir."

"And now with everything out in the open—that the code of conduct was modified after the fact—with the reference to political pressure, the recording, and God knows what else they still haven't released, how much are we on the hook for?"

"Sir—"

"Before you answer, answer something else, if you can." His suggestion is more of a demand.

"Yes, sir. Go ahead."

"This Mr. Evans. What was his performance like? What track was he on?"

"Sir, in the short period he was employed by the company, Mr. Evans was above average in all performance appraisals. He exceeded his budgeted revenue generation, and the clients in his growing pipeline had a potential revenue influx of a $250 million annually. He was on track to attaining VP sales status within the next six months. From the feedback we've received from his fellow employees, it seems he was well liked and eager to assist his peers."

"I think I've heard enough." Redman waves his hand. "So, what is the monetary damage we are looking at, Ms. Sanders?"

"Well, if we settle out of court, we are looking in the neighborhood of $45 to $50 million, a combination of personal and punitive damages. If we fight it in court and lose—and at the moment, our odds of winning are very low to non-existent—we are easily looking at $150 to $200 million. Might be even more, depending on the generosity of the jury."

Redman takes all this in. He looks to the board's financial adviser. "What do you think, Thomas?"

"Walter, we cannot fight this in court from what I am hearing now," he says. "The risk of losing is too high. It would hit our quarter results hard, which would hit our share price even harder. We'd have a 15 to 20 percent share-price drop after this hit the market. Roughly a $2 to $3 billion loss in market capitalization. In addition, any fight with the terminated employee would be highly publicized and would damage our reputations. You must be aware of the lawsuit against the city of Springvale and the Springvale Starline Hotel. My understanding is that Evans's attorney went easy on them, but it was still a disaster for both the city and the hotel."

Redman slams his fist on the table, startling the members closest to him. He turns to face Ms. Sanders. "How the hell was a recording made? Did we not sweep the room beforehand?"

"Yes, sir, the room was swept beforehand. This is the normal procedure in termination proceedings like this. I'm at a loss as to how this recording was made. I'm sorry this happened."

"Yet we have a recording of the whole conversation." He stares at her again. "You have failed us, Ms. Sanders, and it will cost us dearly."

"Yes, sir," she agrees.

"Thomas, what number?" Redman asks the financial adviser.

"Anything more than $65 million would impact our quarterly numbers and share price. We can get around the settlement by booking some future earnings earlier, and hopefully we'll have a new signing to cover this in the following quarter."

Redman takes this in and then turns his attention back to Susan Sanders. "Offer $55 million with a buffer of $5 million to settle out of court."

"Yes, sir," she says. "I will make the offer as soon as I get back to my office, sir."

"Ms. Sanders, as soon as you are back in your office and have a signature on the settlement, I want you to clear out your office and get out of the building. Your employment with this company will no longer be required."

Susan sputters but responds nonetheless. "Yes, sir. I will communicate with you directly when everything is done and notify your assistant when I am done clearing out my office. I assume the second task will not require your immediate notification."

"You are correct on that account." He pauses and then waves his hands in dismissal.

Susan turns and exits the boardroom. She walks by Joanna, avoiding eye contact.

"Susan are you ok?" Joanna calls out.

Susan continues walking without looking back.

DAY TWENTY-THREE
— SETTLED, SEALED,
AND DELIVERED

——

Susan Sanders returns to her office. Closes the door behind her. She walks over to her desk and sits in front of her laptop. She gazes at the clock on the far side of the wall. A genuine Rhythm Woodgrain hanging clock she acquired several years ago is the only personal item in her bland corporate office. A beautiful burl wood frame surrounds the timepiece, with the face accented in gold etching. She enjoys the different melodies that ring out every hour on the hour. It is six o'clock in the evening.

She sits back, crosses her arms, and watches as the clock hands make their way around until it reaches seven o'clock.

That's enough time. She pulls herself closer to her desk and starts up her laptop, as she does not believe in leaving her laptop on and unattended.

She opens up a document with corporate letterhead on the top. She prepared its contents earlier this morning in anticipation of the upcoming news from the attorneys. She scrolls to a blank field beside *Settlement amount* and types in $59,500,000. Saves the document.

She pastes the document as an attachment into an email with the title *Final Offer per Mr. Larry Evans's Settlement*. The email is addressed to Benjamin Dowds. Several other email addresses appear in the CC line, including Arthur Randle, the lead attorney for Commlink, Walter Redman, and Thomas Roundtree, the board's financial adviser.

"Fuck the negotiations," Susan mutters quietly. Nobody will hear unless the office is bugged, but she instinctively looks up from her screen and around the room. Then she shakes her head and relaxes her attention back to the screen in front of her, waiting for confirmation that the email has been received and read. Confirmations come quickly.

She shuts down her laptop, unlocks it from the docking station, picks it up, and tosses it against the office wall. The crash makes a resounding noise, leaving a noticeable dent in the wall.

Within seconds, discerning steps from outside her office get louder followed by the eventual knock on the office door.

She straightens her blouse. "Come in."

The door opens. "Ms. Sanders, is everything all right?" Susan's assistant, asks. Genuine concern crosses her face, unlike Joanna, the boardroom guardian.

"Yes, Janice. I'm just clearing out my desk. I've been asked to leave the company ASAP," she says, a sense of relief take hold over her.

Janice covers her mouth in shock. Tears form in her eyes.

"Janice, don't worry," Susan states, rounding the corner of her desk and giving her assistant a hug. "Everything will be all right." She pulls back and takes hold of her hands. "Now, as my last request as an employee of this company, can you help me take down my clock so I can get out of here?"

"Yes, it would be my pleasure to help, Ms. Sanders."

The two of them get started on the clock. Each positioning themselves on either side of it, slowly lifting it from its wall anchor, pulling it forward and then down.

"Thank you for a job well done for the short time we have worked together. I will miss you." Susan says, her moist eyes taking control of her emotions.

DAY TWENTY-THREE —
NOTICE OF SETTLEMENT
TO DOWDS

———

Benjamin Dowds is with Larry Evans in a smaller conference room.

Dowds glances at his watch again, hoping time speeds up but it still only eight at night.

Meanwhile, Larry has slid down in one of the conference chairs with his feet flopped on to another soaking in the man that is Benjamin Dowds, trying to get a grasp of what makes him tick. His attention to detail in his legal filings that has devastated a town and its leaders, a hotel chain and now putting a dent on the bottom line of his former company. His substantial array of resources that so far have address all his needs. His foresight on the inner working of people minds and behavior that have saved him, personally, from serious beating while he was held at the police station. What else does he have up his sleeves?

I think I can read people pretty well. Been in dozens of sales meetings with clients and clearly figure out their intentions or willingness to do business with him with minutes. But Benjamin Dowds is an enigma. I have met my match in him. But I still need him.

"While we wait for an answer from my former employer and we're both sitting here in anticipation, why don't you tell me more about your other resources?" Larry asks.

"Other resources?" Dowds smiles back.

"Oh, I don't know! Maybe the security guys in New Jersey?" Larry exclaims. "The security team in the safe house on the opposite side of the city? Who even has a safe house, let alone a lawyer? Also, you seem to have an information network that told you about the mayor in New Jersey. One that led to the busted black ops at the airport. Do you want me to go on?"

Dowds sits back in his chair and glances at the clock on the wall instead of his watch this time, stalling.

"Don't worry; I have confidence in your legal skills," Larry says. "She will call. Now, can you answer my questions, Mr. Dowds?"

"Larry, do you really want to go down that rabbit hole? Your life is going to get a lot more complicated if you take that first step," Dowds answers.

"Try me!" Larry says. "I think I'm a grown enough boy, and I doubt my life can get much more complicated than how it is now."

Dowds looks at him, expressionless.

"So?"

Dowds raises his index finger to wait.

Larry, slightly annoyed but perplexed, waits for Dowds.

The silence in the office gives way to a low buzzing sound. Dowds reaches into his suit jacket and pulls out his cell phone. He unlocks the screen and notices a notification.

Larry, not one to be kept in suspense, asks, "So? Is that the email?"

Dowds raises his finger again. Finally, he announces, "I think I can retire now!" A huge grin crosses his face.

Larry stands up. "Show me!"

Dowds hands over the phone. "$59,500,000," Dowds says. "Not bad. Not bad at all."

Larry stops reading and raises his hands over his head.

Both he and Dowds break out in laughter. They shake hands, but it's not enough. They embrace.

The laughter and screaming draws the attention of Dowds's secretary, who agreed to work late tonight. As she approaches the conference room, she spots the two men through the glass wall of the conference in a manly embrace, jumping up and down in unison.

Men are such strange creatures!

Initial decision on her part is to keep her distance out of amusement, waiting to see how long these two adults will behave like children. *Damn! Left my cell phone back at my desk. I could have videotaped this!*

After a few more seconds, they stop jumping. They're either out of breath or out of shape or they realize that somebody might notice them.

Dowds and Larry turn to face his secretary. Their faces, slightly red, turn redder when she smiles at them.

Dowds walks over to the glass door and pulls it open. Smiling, he calls out to her, "Dolores, get the champagne and three glasses. We're celebrating tonight."

"Eh . . . Mr. Dowds, we don't have any champagne," she responds.

Dowds's face falls slightly. Gazes at Larry, who is still smiling from cheek to cheek. Improvising, Dowds says, "OK, then a bottle of wine and three glasses!"

"Sir, we have no more wine."

The horror! "No more wine?" Dowds exclaims. "Who drank it all?"

Dolores, holding her composure, responds, "You did, sir."

"When?"

"Sir, the Bilmore case! Remember?"

"Bilmore?" he asks with a look of confusion.

"Bilmore. Mother and daughter arrested for running a brothel."

A light flashes across his face. "Yes, the Bilmore girls! Yeah, I drank quite a bit that night."

"Sir, you drank it all," she says, ready to burst at the seams.

Trying to downplay the incident, Dowds raises his index finger to his lips in a useless gesture of silence towards his assistant. "Ok. Ok. So, what do we have in the fridge?"

"Two cans of Coke and a 7 Up."

"No Pepsi?"

Dolores gives him an intimidating look.

"OK, bring the two Cokes, the 7 Up, and the glasses."

Dolores doesn't move.

Dowds backtracks in his mind to the night of the Bilmore case celebration. "Oh! Yeah. I had that Greek moment again. I broke all the glasses, right?"

"That's why I only buy plastic cups now," she responds, finally breaking into an annoyed smile, turning and walking away to get the drinks.

"You're the best, Dolores!" Dowds calls.

"I want a raise!" she says in the distance.

Dowds turns back to face Larry, doing his best to refrain from cracking up. "How the mighty have fallen Mr. Dowds."

"She really is the best!" Dowds says.

"Then she really needs a raise!" responds Larry.

"She'll be getting a very generous retirement bonus after this. I'm calling it quits," Dowds proclaims. "Sandy beaches and those tropical drinks with the little umbrellas are the only sure thing in my future."

"You mean, you'll retire after we go after the big one. I need you on this. The payout will be much bigger will be worth it."

"And riskier," Dowds responds.

"I don't doubt that, but people can't get away with behaviour like this," Larry says, sobering. "Especially people in power. Everybody should be accountable for their actions: officers of the law, corporate executives, and government officials like the mayor and the president. Dammit, I've lost my job and my credibility because of some made-up accusation!"

"The president is a formidable opponent. He's a popular president. People like him and will support him. And he's got that little thing called presidential immunity. Hard to beat that!" Dowds says.

"He won't be president forever. Remember term limits!"

"Yep. I hear you."

"Remember, with great power comes great responsibility. Words to think about."

"You know you're quoting a movie, right?" Dowds smirks. "I think it was *Spider-Man*. The version with Tobey Maguire."

"Yeah, yeah! Movie or not, it's very apropos to what we are dealing with. Stick with me, Uncle Ben! We have the financial resources now. That's not a problem. We have the law in our favour. If we have to wait until he's out of office, then we will do that because in the end . . ."

"Nobody is above the law," they both blurt out together.

Dolores returns with a tray with three filled plastic cups. She places them on the small conference room table.

"I don't get the whole can?" Dowds complains playfully.

"You get the whole can when I get my raise."

"Deal!" Dowds declares. He picks up two glasses and hands them to Dolores and Larry. Dowds raises his glass. "To victory!"

Dolores starts drinking.

"And to a $59,500,000 settlement!" Dowds says, and Dolores spits out her drink, barely missing Dowds's shirt.

"The hell with the raise, I want a retirement package," she says, grinning.

DAY TWENTY-FOUR — RONALD SLATER VISITS MONTREAL AND COMMLINK

———

Ronald Slater arrives in Montreal on one of the daily United Airlines flights from Newark. Immigration through Canadian customs was a breeze, unlike entering the United States.

I guess Canadians are a more trusting type, Slater thinks to himself, unsure if that's a good or bad thing.

He crosses a two-lane drop-off street where traffic is almost at a standstill. He sees the signs for National Rent-a-Car, his preferred car rental agency, and heads that way. He enjoys the commercials with the actor Patrick Warburton more than anything else but being a Gold Status member, he is in and out of the rental office and driving a car in under fifteen minutes.

Exiting the airport traffic is easy. Within minutes, Slater is driving on Highway 20 East, heading into downtown Montreal.

His first stop is at the offices of Dowds and Associates. The possibility of getting a sit-down with Benjamin Dowds is low, but he still has to try. A good investigative reporter follows up on all the leads, every trail, no stones left unturned, blah, blah, blah. This is what makes Ronald Slater one of the better ones.

Slater pulls up in front of a two-storey stone office building on the outskirts of Old Montreal. The city itself is over 350 years old. This is a drop in the bucket compared to European cities like Rome and London, but in North America, it constitutes a major tourist attraction.

Slater walks up to the door, knocks, and examines the area. He notices an overhead video camera pointed at him. He smiles.

A female voice on the outside intercom speaks. "Please identify yourself and state the purpose of your visit."

"Er? Name is Ronald Slater, a reporter out of New Jersey. I'm following up on a story on Larry Evans; I'm sure you know who he is. You're the attorney on record representing him. I have some questions for Mr. Benjamin Dowds."

"Please wait," the voice says, expressionless.

Slater continues his survey of the land as he waits. Taking a quick peek into the mailbox. Empty. He turns around and faces the street. The buildings across the street are old, large stone buildings with recessed windows and low overhanging steeped roofs. All the buildings have decorated wooden doors. *Nice area*, he thinks to himself.

"I will buzz you in now," the voice says. "Please proceed inside."

"Thanks." He grips the doorknob and pushes it open when the door buzzes.

He steps into a richly decorated, polished wood reception area. There's expensive-looking marble on the floor. On the opposite side of the room is a woman behind a grand oak desk with no exposed front.

He walks to the desk, and before he utters a word, the woman says, "Please proceed down the corridor and through the first door on the left. Mr. Dowds is awaiting your arrival. He is a busy man, so you have twenty minutes of his time. I would suggest you keep the pleasantries to a minimum and use your time wisely, as I will be escorting you out from our premises in exactly twenty minutes. Your twenty minutes commence now." A distinct British accent highlighting the rules of engagement.

Slater, a little perplexed, quickly walks down the corridor and opens the door to the designated room.

Dowds is sitting across the table from him. "Please sit down, and let's get down to business." He points to the empty chair.

Slater pulls back the chair, sits down, and pulls out his notepad and pen from his inner pocket.

Dowds shakes his hand at him. "There will be none of that. No notes, no recordings, nothing."

"But I mentioned to your receptionist that I was a reporter following up on a story about Larry Evans. Did she not mention this to you?"

"She did, indeed. Ms. Walker is very good at what she does—extremely good. I am fully aware of who you are and your reputation as a reporter. You're one of the good ones, and I'm glad that somebody of your calibre has visited me and not one of those sleazy tabloid hacks."

"Thank you," Slater responds, blinking.

"All the credit goes to Ms. Walker. As I stated, she is very good at what she does." Dowds smiles. "So, let's get down to your questions, as the clock is ticking; I'm sure Ms. Walker has read you the riot act."

"Yes, she did," Slater states. "So, Mr. Dowds, are you still representing Mr. Evans?"

"I am."

"Are you aware of the whereabouts of Mr. Evans?"

"I am."

"Ok. Then are you willing to supply me with his present location so I can approach him for comments about the outcome of the lawsuits that favoured him?"

"I cannot."

"You cannot what Mr. Dowds?"

"I cannot provide you with his whereabouts, as it is a private matter. He has asked for this information to not be shared with anybody."

Quickly discovering that this line of questioning is going nowhere, Slater shifts gears. "I see. Then are you willing to provide him with a series of questions on my behalf that he can review and answer?"

"Mr. Slater, I will get straight to the point so we don't waste anymore of each other's time. Mr. Evans has expressly asked me to represent him on all legal matters pertaining to the lawsuits against the city of Springvale, including the hotel, and his previous employer. He does not want to speak to any reporters or media outlets. Given what transpired in the last few months, it is only reasonable to say that he has no trust in these organizations."

"You said you represent Mr. Evans on all legal matters. Does that also extend to the government?" Slater asks.

Dowds smiles. "As stated, Mr. Evans will not now or in the future communicate with anybody. If anyone prints or publishes anything through social media, rest assured that no media organizations have spoken to him. He wants to disappear into the night and never be heard from again. This is the directive that Mr. Evans has communicated to me. This is the directive that I will be enforcing going forward. Furthermore, we will go after any party that continues to print, publish or post any false and misleading editorial about Mr. Evans with all the legal means available. This has to stop and has to stop now." Dowds concludes.

"I understand. I get it. My reporting on this story and on everything I do is always fair, fact based and devoid of any fictional narrative. I pride myself on the articles I write. My opinions are my own and should not in any way interfere with what I write.

Right or wrong, I prefer to present the facts, all the facts and let the reader make his or her decision." Slater says.

"Well, that is refreshing Mr. Slater. Like I said, you are one of the good one." Dowds says.

"Ok. Let's get back to the subject at hand. Remember, I am on the clock." Slater grins.

"Of course, we would not want to cross paths with Ms. Walker, she is probably listening as we speak." Dowds points around the round room in jest.

"You said Mr. Evans wants to disappear into the night. That is kind of hard to believe for somebody who just brought down a city mayor, half his council, and numerous other public officials. Especially in the connected world that we live in, Mr. Dowds. With the good comes the bad. Pretty sure there are numerous detractors still out there not to happy with what he has done."

"We will deal with these folks through the legal system. As for Mr. Evans, it looks like he's doing a fine job right now. He has not been seen in public since he left the courthouse almost two weeks ago."

"We shall see, like you said, I am a good reporter—one of the better ones. I am always looking for a challenge."

They both smile at each other, and then Slater stands up and offers his hand across the table.

"Sorry, I don't shake hands," Dowds says. "It's a personal thing. I hope you understand."

'Whoa. That is weird.' Slater accepts his statement. He has encountered many eccentric people in his lifetime; he just adds Benjamin Dowds to the pile.

Slater walks out the room, down the corridor, and waves to the receptionist, who only nods. He reaches the front door just as the door buzzes.

She is *good*, he thinks and walks out.

Dowds watches Slater exits the office via a video app on his phone connected to multiple surveillance camera covering the building. Slater gets into the car and drives away. Moments later, a side door opens, and Larry Evans walks in.

Larry sits down across from Dowds. "'I don't shake hands. It's a personal thing.' What was that about?"

"I was just fucking with him. Giving him something to write about—not that he has much," Dowds chuckles.

Larry smiles.

"Nonetheless, we should keep a watch on him. I'll take care of it. Get my boys to keep tabs."

"You seem to have a lot of resources," Larry says. "Illegal resources and people with interesting backgrounds, from what I have seen. So far, Ms. Walker is the scariest and most intimidating of the bunch. Is there a Mr. Walker in the picture?"

Dowds purses his mouth and squints. "You know what? I don't know. I try to keep the personal chatter with her to a minimum," he pauses, chuckling. "She scares me a little too, sometimes."

"Where did you find her?"

"Well, that's quite a story. Unfortunately, I can only tell you part of it."

"What do you mean?"

"Ms. Walker is a former SAS member. Part of the 23 Special Air Service Regiment—the 1st Intelligence, Surveillance, and Reconnaissance Brigade. Little is known about the group. That is, publicly known. She along with several of my boys at the safe house are all former SAS."

"How did you meet her?"

"That's a funny story. She actually found me. I was working and living in Northern England for a few years about ten years ago.

Just north of Liverpool, working for a group providing security for government personnel and their families.

"The work was steady and paid extremely well. During one particular job, my group was tasked to provide security for a British official and his family who, at the time, was stirring up some nationalist sentiments toward a certain visible minority group. I was not a fan of his politics. Nonetheless, the security was still needed.

"Anyway, when the family went on an unplanned outing, one that wasn't cleared by my group, the politician's wife and daughter were taken. Not my finest moment, losing a client. Anyways, my group was getting nowhere tracking them down. No leads, nothing, when Ms. Walker contacted me out of the blue with a potential lead. She was just wrapping up her stint at the SAS and heard from one of my boys who happened to know her.

"She offered to assist in the search using her regional network. That information proved to be very valuable, and, in the end, we caught up with the kidnappers. Everyone returned home safely. I was so impressed with Ms. Walker that I brought her into my group. She also introduced me to several of my current staff. They've been working for me for several years already."

"Nice story," Larry says. "But how did a North American lawyer, and a really good one at that, get involved with a private security group in the UK?"

"Well, to make a long story short, I get bored by the routine work. I've never been one to continue doing the same thing, day in and day out. I got to the point where I could tell within ten minutes of meeting a prospective client if he or she was bullshitting me and whether or not I should cut my losses."

"So, what happened next?" Larry asks. "That doesn't really explain your transition from a North American lawyer to a UK security expert."

"No, it does not. You're right. That phase of my life started with Hendrik Vinke, a Dutch businessperson setting up a wind turbine farm north of Toronto. One night, he ended up in the wrong end of Mississauga, and several bad characters looking for some excitement attacked him. He ended up in the hospital, all battered and bruised. I was working on some cases in Toronto at the time, and a lawyer friend of mine asked me to help represent Mr. Vinke in his assault case."

"Had they already caught the assailants?"

"Yes, the police had no problem catching up with them. But the problem was that one of the assailants had some influential parents in the community. They had enough influence to get the judge to dismiss all charges against the assailants."

"What happened next?"

"Clearly, I was not impressed by the whole outcome. I had a client in serious condition in the hospital and two assailants out free and on the streets. So, instead of trying to reopen the case, which I knew would end up being shut down again, I went after the parents—in particular, one father. He seemed like a legit industrial warehouse provider who controlled a large part of the market, but with a little digging here and there along with a few trusted sources I was able to find he was also running some not-too-legit operations, storing illegal merchandise for short-term purposes and for different crime organizations. I had what I needed to take the next step."

"And what was that?" Larry asks.

"I made him an offer he couldn't refuse, just like in *The Godfather.*"

"So, what was the offer you made him?" Larry asks, his eyes wide open, curious to hear more.

"I told him that either he could give up his son and his friends for full prosecution, as they were all of age and would be tried in adult court, or he would go to prison for a long time. He would lose all his businesses, homes, bank accounts, and any other assets he owned when I forwarded the information over to the police and the newspapers the same day."

"Did he try to threaten you?" Larry asks. "Kill you? Maybe make you disappear in a long-term storage container in one of his warehouses?"

"I didn't give him the chance to make the threat. I told him that his answer was time-sensitive, and if I didn't show up somewhere at a certain time on a certain date, the information would be released. If he handed over his son, I would bury the incriminating evidence, and nobody would be the wiser. I also mentioned that the evidence would remain sealed as long as I remained alive," Dowds states.

"So, how did it end?"

"The son and his friends are serving fifteen years for premeditated assault. My client, Mr. Vinke, recovered, invited me to his country, and introduced me to an interesting circle of friends—along with some people involved in executive security services. It piqued my interest, so I got involved. I learned fast, and the payout was amazing at that time. The rest is history."

"Are you still involved with this group in the UK?" Larry asks.

"Now and then, we share information on cases. They have me on a very decent retainer that helps with the bills and staff when times are lean."

"Are they the only ones who retain your services?" Larry asks.

"Larry, if I told you all my secrets, I would have to kill you, and I would have to subcontract that. I don't do disposals." Dowds grins.

"That's all right, just take it out of my settlement," Larry laughs.

Dowds chuckles and then turns to the conference unit in the middle of the table. He clicks the intercom button.

"I have already started disassembly procedures Mr. Dowds," Ms. Walker says. "Completion ETA, two hours." She disconnects before Dowds has a chance to speak.

Larry flashes a broad smile. "Wow! She is good—scary good. Where can I get somebody like her?"

"Don't know, but you can't have her!" he says with a big grin.

DAY TWENTY-FOUR —
I'LL HAVE FRIES WITH
THAT, PLEASE

———

Slater's next stop that day is across town in the suburbs.

He pulls into the small parking lot of a mom-and-pop hot dog restaurant in Montreal's North End. The lot is not flat and is on a slight incline with enough space for maybe a dozen cars squeezed in. He engages the handbrake as a precaution.

He gets out of the car and walks up the concrete walkway into the restaurant. A local landmark called Chez Mon Oncle, it has been around for ninety years, and the menu hasn't changed much: hot dogs, greasy fries, and an assortment of sodas.

He walks up to the counter and stares at the hanging menu behind the counter.

"*Comment je peux vous aider?* How can I help you?" the woman behind the counter asks in both French and English.

Slater hesitates for a moment. There's no real reason to do so, as the options are pretty clear and very limited. Hot dogs and fries, or just hot dogs and just fries.

"Yes, I will have a steamie, fries, and a Coke please," he replies.

The woman turns around and yells in French, "*Un steamé, des frites, et un Coke.*" She turns back to Slater. "That'll be $4.50."

Slater pulls out some Canadian money and finds a blue five-dollar bill among the green twenties. *Man! Got to remember Canadian money is real and not Monopoly money.* She takes it and hands back two quarters. Slater spots the glass tip jar. He won't be able to use them back in the USA, so he drops them in.

Within thirty seconds, the lady behind the counter hand over a paper carton with a hot dog and an overflowing bag of fries along with an empty disposable cup so he can fill up from the soda machine on the side of the counter.

He grabs everything, nods to the lady, slides over to the soda machine to fill up the cup. There are no tables to sit down; he can either stand along the wall counter and eat standing up or take his food to go. Since his rendezvous is at this location, he decides to eat at the counter facing the parking lot.

Slater munches on his fries. *Pretty good. I hope the hot dog is just as tasty.* He takes a bite. *I'm impressed*, he thinks to himself. *Now I understand why this little hole in the wall has been around for ninety years—simple, well-made food. Nothing special.*

This is definitely a pick-up-and-go place, not a place to loiter around. He'll have to either slow down or order some more food if his contact doesn't show up. He bites down again on his hot dog, but in the corner of his eye, he spots a man walk up to the counter. *Hopefully my contact and not another customer, I can't eat any slower. This food is great!*

The man is short and stocky with a full head of unkempt dark hair. He is wearing a spring jacket, and under his arm is a small white grocery bag with the outline of a book or file folder.

The man picks up his order, pours some vinegar on his fries, fills up his cup with Pepsi, and makes his way toward Slater. He parks his carton of food on the counter about two feet away and places the white grocery bag on the counter in between them.

"I'll get straight to the point," the man says, breathing heavily. "In the bag, there's some information on Larry Evans. Not much, but I've been able to scrape together some history. I'm in the process of getting a copy of his high school yearbook. I've found that people of interest, as Larry Evans obviously is, tend to have a circle of loyal friends and acquaintances from early years that they trust. I'll forward the book to you when the copy comes through."

It is Slater's turn to talk. "I'll dispense with the introductions, as I'm guessing it's in your best interest not to share your name? I'm good with that," Slater says. "Why are you doing this? What do you get out of it?"

"Nothing financial. A friend of mine based out of Springvale ended up on the wrong side of the lawsuit settlement between Larry Evans and the city. He reached out to me, knowing that Evans was a Canadian citizen and living in Montreal. We've been friends since high school, but after he graduated from university, he moved to the States to seek fame and fortune. He asked me to dig up any information about Evans, but it was too late to help my friend. He then told me to reach out to your editor, who told me that you were in Montreal. So, there's the whole story all wrapped up in a white grocery bag." The stocky man picks up his hot dog and takes another big bite out of it. Pauses in between chewing to breathe.

Slater stares at him in amazement. *'Buddy, slow down! You are going to give yourself a heart attack.'* Slater reaches down to his own hot dog and decides to finish the last small bite before laying down the next question. They both take a sip from their drinks.

"So, what have you found so far about Evans?" Slater asks.

"Everything I found is in the bag. I don't have time to go over it now," the stocky man says, taking another bite.

Slater pops some more fries into his mouth.

"I'm on the clock and need to get back to work," the stocky man says, "but give me your contact information so I know where to send the yearbook. I'll pass it on when it arrives."

Slater reaches into his jacket pocket, pulls out his *Newark Sentinel* business card, and slides it over to the stocky man. "My email and cell phone number are on the card."

The stocky man grabs the card and pockets it without wiping his hands. He returns to his food and finishes off the hot dog in one last bite. Grabbing his drink, he slides the food carton with the remaining uneaten fries into the garbage bin at the end of the counter. "If you have a chance before you leave town, try the poutine here. It's awesome!"

"What's a poutine?" Slater asks.

"Google it. I don't have time to explain." The man waves goodbye. He disappears out the door, down the inclined parking lot, and around the office building out of sight.

Slater gazes down for a moment at the bag on the counter the man left for him then turns looks out the window of the restaurant. It's quiet with little traffic moving on the single-lane street. Nobody loitering around. He takes a final pull from his soda, grabs the grocery bag, shoves it under his arm, slides the food carton into the garbage bin, and exits the restaurant.

He enjoyed the greasy food and will keep it in mind the next time he is in Montreal.

DAY TWENTY-FOUR —
WE MIGHT HAVE AN
ISSUE WITH RONALD

———

"Inquiring minds want to know," Dowds states.

"What are you talking about?" Larry asks as he walks into Dowds's office. He's spent the last few hours locked up in a private office, reviewing the pending lawsuit.

"Our buddy Ronald Slater is asking around town about you. He met with a man, we don't have an ID on him yet, in a small restaurant in the North End called Chez Mon Oncle."

"Chez Mon Oncle! I know that place! Spent a few years living in that part of town. Great fries and a pretty good poutine from what I have heard. We've got to go there one day. I haven't been in years."

"What is poutine and more importantly, why have you not sampled one?" Dowds asks.

"Poutine is a combination of French fires and cheese curds covered in a brown gravy. A made in Quebec delicacy that became popular in other parts of Canada from what I heard. Myself, I like fries with gravy but not with cheese curds. I hate the squeaky cheese. It makes a funny noise when you bite down on the cheese." Larry responds, grinning in amusement.

Shaking his head in confusion, Dowds get back on track. "I'll take your word for it. As I said, he met a person who handed him a bag with what my man thinks is full of documents. They chatted for a few minutes, scoffed down their meals, and went their separate ways."

"Interesting," Larry says.

"Is there anything I should be aware of, Larry? Any dark ghosts in your closet? Anything that might be used against us in the upcoming lawsuit?" Dowds asks.

Larry pauses for a moment. "Nope. I have nothing to hide."

"Good!" Dowds states, reassured by the response. "I'll keep my men on him to see where he ends up, just in case."

"That's fine. By the way, I reviewed the contents of the lawsuit. Everything looks good. I'm impressed."

"I'm glad. It's some of my finest work. They'll never know what hit them."

"File it. File it now!" Larry blurts in a really bad impersonation of Arnold Schwarzenegger.

DAY TWENTY-FIVE — NOBODY IS ABOVE THE LAW!

Bernie Andrews, the new senior adviser to the president after the departure of Henry Mood, waits outside the Oval Office. His anxiety rises with every step as he paces in the waiting room. Memories of walking into the principal's office in high school flash through his mind, but in this case, he has done nothing wrong— the president has.

The correspondence in his hands has been pre-screened, like everything else that crosses the president's desk. Bernie is aware of the contents of the registered envelope, and he hopes the president won't blow up. The odds are against this; the president has already heard that the mayor of Springvale has resigned along with a dozen other local officials, some of them settling out of court. The wording of the document has been scrubbed by the president's chief of staff and aides to minimize the bloodbath, figuratively speaking, that took place in Springvale.

The executive secretary gives Andrews the signal that the president is ready to see him. He steps into the office and closes the door.

Surprisingly, the president is not alone. His chief of staff, Jack Sully, and the secretary of state, Jane Philips, are present. In the inner circle of the president's cabinet, they are referred to as Jack and Jane.

Andrews takes this as a good sign that he will survive delivering the news; the president will be able to split his grievances among the three of them.

"Mr. President, I have a document that needs your immediate attention." Andrews approaches the president and hands him the envelope.

The chief of staff is puzzled, as he is the gatekeeper to the president in all aspects. He glares at Bernie Andrews. "Andrews, what's going on? What is that?" he asks, pointing at the document that the president is starting to read. "Why am I not aware of this?"

"Sir, it came through the White House in a bizarre fashion."

"What do you mean?"

Bernie explains how the packaged documents were delivered to the East Gate guard about one hour ago. The courier's identification was verified as belonging to a reputable local company. The package was scanned for any explosive devices at the East Gate station. From there, the package was passed to the internal security for inspection to make sure it did not contain any viral pathogen or other dangerous substances. Once it is cleared for any harmful components, it is passed on to the intended department.

"In this particular instance, the package landed on my desk. I reviewed it. Once the subject matter was identified, the decision was made to bring it directly to the president, as this is a time-sensitive manner," Andrews says, glancing over at the president, who is still deeply engrossed in the document.

"What do you mean, 'time-sensitive?' What are the contents of the document?" Sully, a control freak in all aspects of his life, is irate, giving Andrews a sideways glance while trying to discern the president's response to the document. "I am not happy Andrews. This is a clear violation of his protocols."

"Sir—" Andrews starts, but the president turns to face the three of them.

"This is a lawsuit that has been filed against me by the law firm representing Larry Evans, claiming slander against him—damage to his personal reputation on numerous occasions." He flips through the document to find a specific passage. "According to this lawsuit, I willfully attacked him with malice on fifty-seven separate occasions either in print, the TV media, or on social media." He pauses for a moment. "Fifty-seven times. Hmmm, it must have been a slow news period." He chuckles and hands Jack Sully the document. "Take care of this, Jack. I am the president. Nobody sues the president. I don't want this showing up on the evening news, do you understand?" He looks at the three people standing in front of him.

They all nod in agreement.

The president turns to Andrews with a stern expression. "Never bring something like this to me again. Do you understand?"

Andrews nods. "Yes, Mr. President. It won't happen again."

Jack Sully grins in satisfaction and then exits the Oval Office, followed by Jane, who has been quiet during the whole proceeding.

DAY TWENTY-FIVE — WE NEED
TO TELL THE PRESIDENT

——

Jack Sully and Jane Philips exit the Oval Office and walk down a hallway that leads to the Roosevelt Room. Jack pulls her inside and closes the door.

"What's going on, Jack?" she asks as she straightens her jacket sleeve.

"This isn't good. Not good at all, this lawsuit," Jack replies, his head lowered, rubbing his jaw, avoid eye contact with Jane Philips..

"What do you mean? The president took it pretty well, from what I saw. He saw it as a minor inconvenience."

"Jane, the president doesn't know the full extent of the damage that was done by Larry Evans's lawyer in Springvale. We scrubbed the narrative on this big time. Everything that has been presented to the president is scrutinized before it hits his desk. My people are working double-time to make sure anything about the lawsuit is downplayed in his presence."

"Give me the full details, Jack," Jane demands.

"The mayor and at least twelve city officials are gone—resigned or terminated. At the local police department that handled the case, seven officers, including detectives and the police commissioner himself, were dismissed or re-assigned. The initial financial damages were lowered to a sum that the city could swallow without going into receivership. The exact amount is sealed under court order. And even though the mayor resigned, he took a large personal hit financially.

"As for the Springvale Starline Hotel, it was even worse. All the staff members that came forward as witnesses resigned or were fired, and most of them left the city. Management was gutted out by the head office for failure to handle the situation. Financially, the hotel also paid out substantial damages. Again, the amount is sealed under court order."

"Fuck." Jane's jaw drops.

"And now they're coming after the president," he says.

Jane looks at him hesitantly.

"What's on your mind, Jane?"

"Full disclosure, here."

"What?"

"I got a call from a RCMP contact up in Montreal with some bad news."

"So? What does that have to do with anything?"

"Well . . ."

"Spill it, Jane!" Jacks says, his patience clearly starting to wear thin.

"Jason Stands, you know who he is, right?"

"Yes, Mr. High and Mighty Adviser who can do no wrong in the president's eyes."

"Well, he got himself arrested in Montreal," she says.

"What!" he whispers in surprise. "What was he doing in Montreal?"

Inching closer to Jack, Jane grasps his right arm. "Jason was arrested, along with half a dozen ex-military operatives, after arriving at a local airport outside of Montreal. They were carrying illegal weapons, ammunition, and surveillance equipment. Furthermore, they had a lot of documents on the whereabouts of

Larry Evans. It looks like they were planning a snatch-and-run on Larry Evans."

"Are you fucking kidding me? This is crazy. Absolutely crazy," Jack exclaims, clenching his hands, cringing in disgust.

"Nope, I am not. I wish I were! Apparently, the president sanctioned it several days ago."

"What was he thinking? That was an incredibly stupid thing for him to do! If word gets out, he's screwed," Jack states in utter disbelief.

"Jack, right now, I'm the only one who knows—besides you now, of course. My contact in Montreal says they're keeping everything under wraps, but they also warned me not to try to negotiate a release for any of them. In his words, 'they will never step foot on American soil again.' They're upset about the arrogant insurgence of a bunch of cowboys coming into their country."

"Wouldn't you be if the tables were turned?" Jack asks.

"Yeah! I agree. Probably a good thing they decided to keep it quiet. The president doesn't need another hit to his credibility right now."

Silence. Both tight lipped as they fall into step as they proceed down the corridor away from the Oval Office.

DAY TWENTY-FIVE — TWITTER IS NOT FOR STUPID PEOPLE

—

That evening, President Campbell returns to his private study in the White House. Not one to consume alcohol except at formal state functions, he decides to make an exception.

President picks up one of the house phones and calls the down to the steward on call. "Yes Mr. President. How can I help you tonight sir?" The house steward asks immediately.

"Hi. Would you be able send up a nice bottle of red wine to the residence? I'd like to enjoy a drink tonight." The president states.

"Yes Mr. President. Do you have any presences sir?"

"I will leave that up to your discretion. Thanks."

"Will do Mr. President. Is that all?"

'That's all. Thank you."

The White House itself does not have a large collection of wines in the cellar, only enough for upcoming events. This is unlike the days of Thomas Jefferson, who was a big fan of Italian and French wines. Through his worldly travels, he developed a lifelong passion for wines from all over Europe. To accommodate his collection, he had a large wine cellar built in the West Wing. Some say at its peak, over twenty thousand bottles were stored there. Today, most of the wine cellar has been repurposed for other functions and has only a fraction of the inventory.

The house steward called back the president within minutes recommending a nice Chimney Rock Reserve Cabernet Sauvignon. The standing orders are to only stock and promote American wines.

Not being a connoisseur of wines, the president readily accepts the recommendation.

Within minutes, a knock at his door announces the arrival of a staff member with the wine and two glasses. Again, the standing order is for any alcoholic beverage, be it wine or liquor, to be accompanied with a minimum of two glasses. Campbell has accepted this norm over the years.

He thanks the staff member, who places the tray on a small table.

"Is there anything else, sir?"

"Nope, thank you, and good night."

The staff member leaves the study. The president reaches over to the table, grabs the bottle of wine, and pours himself a full glass. Picks up the glass and smells it, pretending he knows what he's doing, and then takes a big gulp.

Hmmm. Good choice. He immediately takes another gulp and then two more. As the glass is now empty, he refills the glass. *Really good choice Mr. President!*

After downing the second glass, he pulls out his cell phone, launches his Twitter app, and spills his thoughts to his 40-million-plus followers.

DAY TWENTY-FIVE — THE LAWSUIT MAKES THE EVENING NEWS

———

Jack Sully's residence in historic Georgetown Village is a nice two-storey brownstone. It has recently been renovated with modern conveniences while keeping the original flooring and the wood-burning fireplace. With two bedrooms, a study, an expansive dining area, and close to two thousand square feet of living space, it is more than enough for Jack's single life.

He made his wealth at an early age as an investment broker for a firm in New York. He had no issue finding living accommodations in Washington, D.C., when he entered politics. This house provides him comfort that other civil servants only dream about.

Lying in bed, he surfs the twenty-four-hour news channels for anything that might ruin his next day. Always good to get a head start on the next disaster.

Lately, the origins of these disasters have been centred around his boss, President Campbell. It's eleven at night, and there's nothing troubling yet.

Maybe I'll get a sound sleep tonight.

As he scrolls through his favourite channels, he suddenly stops on the National News Channel. The scrolling ribbon bar across the bottom of the screen was flashing "Breaking News—President sued."

"Fuck . . . Fuck . . . Fuck . . ." he curses at the screen. *There goes my evening.*

He raises the volume on the remote.

"Latest breaking news—this is an NNC exclusive. It has been confirmed that President Campbell is now the subject of a personal lawsuit filed in the State of New Jersey by the office of Dowds and Associates, representing Larry Evans. Mr. Evans, a Canadian resident, was accused of assaulting Amanda Chase at the Springvale Starline Hotel. Overwhelming evidence from multiple witnesses stated that Mr. Evans assaulted her on the night of May 4th, now almost one month ago. Ms. Chase was hospitalized from the injuries sustained from the alleged attack.

"The news of the assault went viral on social networks with numerous people expressing their outrage at Mr. Evans. Citizens, local politicians from Springvale including the mayor of Springvale, law enforcement officers, state politicians, and even the president hit the Twitterverse to express their disdain for somebody they didn't know.

"Mr. Evans was pronounced guilty on social media almost immediately, and that was only the beginning. Pretty soon, articles and supposed investigations into Larry Evans's past hit Twitter, painting Mr. Evans as abusive, a degenerate, and a habitual drug user. Articles condemning him were re-tweeted and shared hundreds of thousands of times. #LarryGate tweets toward Larry Evans were trending at number one for six consecutive days at the height of the frenzy.

"During this period, Mr. Evans maintained his claims of innocence, saying, 'I did not touch her.' A rather unusual statement at the time, as defendants usually claim, 'I did not do it.'

"Two weeks later, video surveillance tapes, previously thought missing due to a recording malfunction, surfaced that clearly proved Mr. Evans did not assault Amanda Chase. Within a day of the videos' appearance, the case against Larry Evans was dismissed. The shock hit the media world like a ton of bricks. Within a week after the dismissal, Larry Evans took justice into his own hands and went after all the people of influence who promoted the attacks against him. The first lawsuit was against the city of Springvale, its local police department, the mayor of Springvale, and the Springvale Starline Hotel. Justice was swift and expensive for many people.

"Next came the suit against Mr. Evans's employer, Commlink Services. This lawsuit never made it to the courts, as the company deemed it unwinnable. The settlement amount was sealed and confidential, but our sources place it in the range of $50 million.

"Well, tonight came word that a lawsuit has been filed against President Campbell for character assassination. Our sources claim that the suit outlines fifty-seven separate incidents where the president attacked Larry Evans, either on media outlets or social networks—in particular, President Campbell's favourite, Twitter.

"What is striking about the suit is the amount being asked: $250 million in damages, a public apology to Mr. Evans, and a promise to cease all social media attacks against him or anybody else in the future. Breaking any of these conditions will result in further penalties against the president."

"At this point, we have reached out to the White House for comments, but we have yet to hear from the president or any of his aides. This is a fluid story, and we here at NNC will keep you, the viewers, updated as soon as more information is made public. Thank you."

Jack Sully stares at the screen, silent. There is nothing to say, and even if he did, nobody would hear him, as he lives alone. "He is so fucked," he finally blurts.

The phone beside his bed rings, startling Jack out of his trance. He glances at the caller ID and picks it up. "Yes, I just saw it," he responds.

"Jack, oh my God, Jack. You were right. They're going after the president!"

"Jane, get a grip!" Jack shouts. "First of all, they can't prosecute a president while he's in office. He has immunity to criminal prosecution."

"Jack, according to the settlement conditions, they want to censor the president. Tell me how he's going to take it."

"Not very well. Probably go on Twitter to blast the lawsuit!" He chuckles nervously. "There's one thing for sure; we need to come clean about the Springvale Massacre."

There's silence on the phone for a few seconds. "Yeah, we will."

"Jane, I'm going to hit the sack now. I'm not going to think about it for the next five hours—at least, I'll not try to think about it. We'll speak early tomorrow, put together a plan on how to handle the president, and tell him what exactly happened in Springvale."

"OK, good. I just hope we make it to the morning without getting a wake-up call. See you then." She hangs up.

Jack falls back on his bed, staring at the ceiling.

DAY TWENTY-SIX — THE TRUTH ABOUT THE MAYOR HITS THE PRESIDENT

Jack and Jane stand outside the Oval Office. At seven this morning, they took over the Roosevelt Room to strategize their impending conversation with the president. Half an hour into the session, Jack's phone went off. A text message from the president's executive secretary advising him to attend an urgent meeting with the president at eight.

Thirty seconds later, Jane received the same message.

"Well, here goes nothing," Jack exclaims. As the clock strikes eight, the door to the office opens and a marine guard walks out, motioning for them to enter.

They walk to the centre of the room. Seated on one of the couches is Chloe Williams, the first African American woman to be attorney general. The Rhodes Scholar graduated at the top of her class at Harvard. After twenty years in the legal community, she was asked by President Campbell to take the position of attorney general. A most unusual decision on his part, as she was neither a registered Democrat nor a Republican and never openly discussed her leanings. He claimed that her convictions to serve the justice system should not be influenced by either ideology.

This stance started a trend from up-and-coming candidates in the federal courts.

"Ms. Williams," Jack salutes her, as does Jane.

Chloe does not stand but nods in return. "Mr. Sully, Ms. Philips."

"Jack," the president speaks out.

Jack and Jane turn to face him.

"This will be short and quick. I have asked Attorney General Williams to be present this morning to witness our discussion."

"Discussions about what, Mr. President?" Jack asks, feigning ignorance.

"Well, for one, why is it that I need to get my briefings from the late-night news and not my chief of staff? Briefings that are more detailed than what you have provided. Briefings on the mess in Springvale with the mayor having to resign to start with. For another, what about the possible fallout from the lawsuit brought on by Larry Evans's attorney against me? Will I be facing the same outcome?" the president states with increasing anger.

"Mr. President, I can explain."

"Explain!"

"Sir, we didn't think it would be wise to worry you about the fallout from the Springvale case. We thought it would slowly cycle its way out of the news in a few days," Jack responds.

"Well, that doesn't look like what's happened, does it?" the president exclaims. "I know Mayor Frakes. He is a good man. He helped me and our party during the last election. He helped us big time. We owe him. Can't we do anything?"

Jack peers down at the presidential seal embroidered in the carpet underneath his feet, trying to find a nice way to respond without insulting his friendship with Mayor Frakes. Sometimes the truth hurts, and this will be one of those times.

"Mr. President, Mayor Frakes is not an innocent man. Far from it, actually. I had my sources look into him, and I have to be honest with you. You shouldn't associate with him in any fashion whatsoever. He has kept his mayor ship all these years through intimidation, bribery, and hard-nosed tactics against his enemies. Along the way, he has amassed a small fortune that cannot be explained by his salary." Jack pauses, glances over to Jane for support.

She gives him a strained smile.

"Mr. President don't comment any more about Larry Evans and the lawsuits," Jack says.

"Are you telling the president what he can and cannot do?" declares Campbell.

"Mr. President, we had high hopes that we would be able to get away with it and run it's course under the radar, but then your late-night Twitter sessions put an end to it."

"What are you saying, Mr. Sully?" the president demands.

Jane Philips steps forward. "Mr. President, what we're saying is that you've been unable to keep your mouth shut when it comes to attacking people in the news."

"What!" the president explodes.

"Mr. President, your impulsive behaviour has gotten you in trouble on numerous occasions. Most of which we've been able to clear up before it hits the airwaves or social networks."

"My social commentary is my own. My comments are my own."

"No, sir, that's where you're wrong," Jack says. "Your comments, be it on a presidential letterhead or a tweet on a social website, are comments from the president of the United States, not from the average citizen Franklin Campbell. Your comments shape people's behaviour. In this case, Larry Evans. The lawsuit cites fifty-seven separate occurrences of character attacks against Larry Evans. This is not a random commentary; this is an obsession against one person. A person you have never met."

"Bullshit, Jack. What do you know? Are you a psychiatrist now?"

"No, sir, I am not," Jack retorts. "This is simply common sense, and it seems your common sense is lacking in this matter."

The president shrugs. "I am the president of the United States. I need to be briefed completely on matters that affect the country and, especially, matters that pertain to me. You failed to do so, and now we're in a situation."

Jack, perplexed by the comment momentarily, snaps back. "Pardon me Mr. President! A situation? What situation are we in?" he asks, his voice rising. "Oh, you mean the situation where you can't keep your fucking mouth shut? The situation where you're constantly getting into trouble with foreign officials and members of women's clubs? A situation where your inexperience is clearly evident when you blurt out policies that are never vetted for legality or feasibility? We've cleared up so many of your fuck-ups, Mr. President." Frustrated, Jack pauses to collect his thoughts before he continues. "God Damn Mr. President. You are intelligent person. Highly intelligent I must say. You made a success for yourself even before you took the Office of the Presidency, but this Twitter addiction has gotten the best of you. You are not thinking straight when lashing out at Larry Evans or any other person that you think has done wrong in your eyes. You have to stop this shit---".

"You're out of line, Jack," the president yells.

"No, Frank, you're out of line," Jack fires back.

"That is Mr. President to you."

"Then that's Chief of Staff Sully to you. If I'm here this morning to be fired, and I think I am, given that Ms. Williams is present, then I will save you the trouble and quit right now."

"Jack, what are you doing?" Jane asks.

"Furthermore, any statement coming from the White House about my departure better be truthful. I haven't decided to move back to civilian life or spend more time with my family; I simply quit." Jack walks to the door, opens it, and exits.

The marine guard standing outside closes the door behind him.

Chloe Williams stands up and walks over to Jane. "Jane, we need to get this under control, or else the presidency will never recover," she says in a calming voice.

Jane shakes her head and takes hold of her hands. "Chloe, we are way past the point of getting this under control. If you can't see this now, then we are indeed in trouble. You've always been a person of calm reason in this maddening, mixed up, partisan world, surrounded by people clutching steel knives, ready to attack our colleagues from the other parties and wearing bulletproof vests to cover our backs. You can't trust anybody anymore. But I've always trusted you. I've looked up to you and everything you've stood for, but I question why you're here right now. Whatever the reason, I doubt this is the outcome you were expecting," Jane takes a long pause. "The same-day departure of both the chief of staff and the secretary of state—how are you going to explain this to the public?"

Jane lets go of Chloe's hands and looks over to the president. "I'm pretty sure this is not what you were expecting Mr. President, was it? Or were you expecting us to quietly fall into place and toe the party line?"

"Everybody is replaceable, Ms. Philips," the president utters.

"That's right, Mr. President, everybody is!" Jane replies. She turns and walks out the door of the Oval Office.

Chloe Williams looks at the president. "Mr. President, your actions are not helping matters at the moment. You need to get this under control, or else it will be your undoing. You brought me on board as the voice of reason outside party lines. Please listen to my advice and resolve your grievances with Philips and Sully. Thank you, Mr. President." She turns away and exits the office as well.

Campbell stares at the door where his three most senior members of his staff have just left. Two, possibly for good, in genuine anger toward him, and the third with parting words and advice that he values but is unsure if he will he accept.

DAY TWENTY-SIX — LATE NIGHT TWITTER RANT

Another night, another bottle of wine. President Campbell bangs away at his Twitter account, taking no prisoners.

Jane Philips and Jack Sully were not capable of meeting the increased demands of their jobs. Poor performers, the two of them, and they will be replaced quickly. He has a long line of replacements who will do a better job.

The mayor of Springvale, corrupt and abusive to city staff members, has run the city into the ground. There is a high crime rate in his city. Justice has been served.

Lastly, Larry Evans is a liar and a cheat. The videos were faked. Why did it take two weeks for this evidence to appear? Think about it. He promises to have him arrested if he steps back into the country.

The tweets flow like the wine in his glass.

DAY TWENTY-SEVEN —
LAWSUIT UPDATE

—

"Breaking news. This just in: Larry Evans's attorney, Benjamin Dowds, has just made public a revision to the lawsuit filed against President Campbell after his Twitter blast last night. The personal attacks from President Campbell toward Larry Evans have risen to sixty-three counts, as have the monetary damages. The amount now totals $300 million. White House officials have refused to make any comments on this ongoing lawsuit.

"Furthermore, Benjamin Dowds clearly acknowledges the fact that the president has total immunity against criminal prosecution while he is president; he has made it equally clear that they have the financial resources to wait until President Campbell no longer resides in the White House and is no longer immune.

"Benjamin Dowds stated, and I quote, 'The president cannot continue hiding behind the immunity rules that protect a sitting president. He should address the wrongs that we have documented and are a matter of public record. Mr. Evans has clearly stated that he is ready to weather this lawsuit for as long as it takes, and the continued abuse from the president will only cost him more in the long run.'"

DAY TWENTY-EIGHT — THE AUDIO RECORDING

Bernie Andrews, senior adviser to the president, sits beside Chloe Williams, Dr. Phil Norton, Daniel Esposito, and Mark Deerson, rounding out the group of advisers in the president's personal quarters. Also invited are the president's financial advisers. President Campbell has hastily called this meeting after the latest media record announced the revisions to the lawsuit.

Chloe Williams, the attorney general, stands up, paper in hand. "Gentlemen, the president has asked me to put together this meeting to discuss his personal lawsuit." She surveys the group to get an understanding of what is coming next.

Everybody nods. No comments.

"The situation has escalated to the point where the party is questioning the president's credibility. In corridors of power, there are discussions going on with concerns about the president's state of mind. His continued ability to lead this country. We need to get control over the narrative." She peeps over to the president, who nods his approval.

"Excuse me, Ms. Williams," Daniel Esposito interjects.

"Yes, Mr. Esposito?"

"Do we have a plan in place? Have we reached out to Mr. Evans's attorney to acknowledge that we are reviewing the lawsuit? Have we opened discussions with them to try to mitigate this disaster?"

"We have not done so," Williams answers bluntly.

"Excuse me, but I have been practicing law for twenty-plus years. I have read numerous suits against my clients regarding the abuse of power, personal attacks, and character assassinations. I have seen it all. Most of them are worthless and don't stand up to close scrutiny. I have read this lawsuit filed by Benjamin Dowds. I don't know who else in this room has also done so. I have read it completely, in detail, and I am impressed by it. I now understand why the Springvale Massacre, as they are calling it in the legal circles, occurred.

"Dowds posted an airtight, detailed lawsuit against all the plaintiffs that wronged Mr. Evans. In my opinion, the only error he made was settling with the city of Springvale for a reduced amount so they could escape bankruptcy and not lay off innocent city workers. He punished the guilty, and he punished them hard. So, I ask you again—both you, Ms. Williams, and you, Mr. President—what is the plan? Because I can only see one option to solve this situation."

"We are exploring various options," Williams responds.

"What options? Are you going to share them with us?" demands Daniel.

The president gets up from his chair, straightens his suit jacket, and clasps his hands together. "That's simple. I will apologize to him. He wants an apology, so be it! I will give him one. I will stand up in front of the camera and I will apologize to the country for being a bad, bad person!"

Chloe smiles, and several others chuckle.

The president walks around his desk, raising his hands. "And honestly, the American public will eat it up. They're a bunch of sheep. They need to be led. They need to be defended from the outside world and it is a cruel world. I am their shepherd. A shepherd to three hundred million dumbass, idiotic creatures who can't either think or protect themselves. I'll guide them to prosperity. Just look at the economic numbers, employment numbers. It has never been this good." He smiles at the gathering. "In the end, I don't care what the fuck I tell the American people if it means saving me $300 million in a lawsuit. Afterwards, I'll invite Evans and his attorney down to D.C. to ratify this agreement, and I'll have them arrested for uttering threats against a sitting president. In the end, I'll save myself $300 million. All I have to do is say, 'I'm sorry, and I will never do it again.' Then I'll go on Twitter and shame him to no end. Nobody messes with me. Nobody fuckin' messes with me." Slapping his chest with his open palm, a look of determination in his eyes, Campbell looks around the room to size up their response.

The group nods in agreement. They approach him and shake his hands in congratulations. Chloe leads the line. After shaking his hand, she walks away.

Bernie Andrews follows her to the other side of the room. She puts her hands in her jacket pockets and watches as the line of congratulations continue.

Chloe turns to Bernie. "What do you think?" she whispers.

Bernie faces her. "What do I think? Honestly, I don't know where this is going to end up. I have a feeling nothing good is going to come of this. I hope I'm wrong."

"Yeah! That makes two of us."

DAY TWENTY-NINE —
LAWSUIT #3 SETTLED

—

"Breaking News: President Campbell has settled the lawsuit with Larry Evans. In a rare move by the president, he has offered an apology to Mr. Evans for his malicious comments. He looks forward to meeting with Mr. Evans and his attorney, Benjamin Dowds, to celebrate the settlement and turn the page on social commentary.

"The White House speaker has stated that the president has agreed to all the terms of the lawsuit. In return, Mr. Evans and his attorney have agreed to substantially reduce the monetary damages to $30 million. This is one tenth of the lawsuit's original $300 million.

Once again, the president has avoided a costly lawsuit by simply saying, 'I'm sorry, and I will never do it again.'"

DAY THIRTY —
LET'S WRAP THIS UP

—

Dowds and Larry, hanging out in the glass conference room of Dowds's office, both focusing their attention at the recent news report displayed on the sixty-inch television mounted on the wall. They have just finished watching the primetime apology that aired on all the major networks with feeds to multiple other countries.

"Good performance; I am impressed," Larry says.

"Yes, I agree. Good performance. I feel a little remorseful for doing this," Dowds states.

They turn to each other, and in unison, they yell, "*Not!*" They start laughing.

Dowds gets up and proclaims to Larry, "Let's wrap this up."

"I couldn't agree more."

They both stand up and walk out the door.

DAY THIRTY-TWO —
DID HE JUST SAY THAT?

—

Back at the *Springvale Journal*, the activity within the office floor has kicked up since the surveillance videos surfaced. Reporters, editors, research assistants and manager are all in an upbeat mood as an atmosphere of excitement and cheerfulness has taken over the place in anticipation of what will happen next with the Larry Evans case.

It has been several days since the president's apology when an email appears in Maggie Summers's inbox. She peers at the "from" address and quickly gets excited. She gazes over her partition and spots Emily. She waves her arms over the head to get her attention and nudges her head to the empty conference room across the office floor. Emily nods, gets up, and briskly walks over to the room. Maggie undocks her laptop from the docking station and follows. They close the door behind them.

Emily slips into a chair beside Maggie as she opens her laptop. "Last time we did this, we saved an innocent man," Emily whispers. "What now?"

Maggie grins in delight. "I don't know. I haven't played the attached video yet."

"Ah! You waited for me. You wanted to share," Emily jokes.

"Ah! Shut up and listen." Maggie clicks on the play button.

For the next several minutes, they concentrate on the audio recording emanating from Maggie's laptop speakers. When it ends, Maggie clicks the replay button.

The two of them continue to remain silent during the second go around.

"That's who I think it is, right?" Emily asks.

"Yes, that is our president. That's President Campbell, and he just called over three hundred million Americans a bunch of stupid sheep."

"Whoa," Emily groans.

"More like *boom*." Maggie fans her hands out in front of her, simulating an explosion.

"What do we do now, Maggie?"

Maggie stands up, closes the laptop, and looks at Emily. "What else! We go see a man about a president!" Maggie grins in delight, offering her hand to Emily.

Emily takes it, stands up, and they walk straight to James Marsala's office.

As they approach Marsala's office, they can see through the glass wall that he is there and alone. Maggie knocks on the glass door, and without waiting for an invitation, enters with Emily in tow.

Maggie slips into the chair while Emily closes the door behind her.

Marsala looks up from his stack of paperwork. He discovers two smiling, giddy-looking reporters. "So! Who is Woodward, and who is Bernstein?" Marsala points between them.

"What?" Emily asks.

"He means Bob Woodward and Carl Bernstein. The reporters who broke the news on the Watergate scandal back in the seventies," Maggie answers in amusement.

"Yeah, Yeah! I knew that. I just wasn't expecting that," Emily responds, blushing.

"Liar!" Maggie snaps back.

"Am not!"

"Are too!"

"OK, OK. Enough, you too," Marsala says.

He puts down his pen. "The last time you two walked into my office together, you came with a story that pretty much saved the future of this newspaper. From the looks on your faces, you have either another hit or a home run on your hands." He gazes at the two of them. "Spill it!"

"If we're using baseball analogies, then I would think this story is more like a grand slam!" Maggie says.

Marsala's jaw drops. "What the eff are you talking about?"

Maggie puts her laptop on his desk, spins it around to face him, reaches over, and hits enter.

At first, Marsala doesn't understand what's going on, but then he suddenly snaps his head up. He points at the laptop, at them, and then back at the laptop. The women nod.

The recording ends.

"Yes, that's him," Maggie says before Marsala can respond. "The President of the United States calling us all a bunch of stupid sheep and that he would do anything to save himself $300 million. We listened to the recording twice before coming to see you."

"Where did this come from?" Marsala asks.

"Same source as the Larry Evans video," Emily replies.

"Fuck me," Marsala blurts out in surprise.

"I'm happily married," Emily quickly declares.

"Not my type!" Maggie chimes in, winking at Emily.

"You two . . ." he starts, shaking his head at the two reporters. "What am I going to do with the two of you?"

Emily interjects, "I could use a raise, now that we're financially sound again."

"No raise for me; half of it would go to taxes anyway. I'm thinking of a paid vacation to a nice tropical island where I can lie on the beach sipping on drinks with those little umbrellas," Maggie says.

"I kind of like the beach option myself," Marsala chimes in.

"Get your own island, Marsala!" Maggie responds.

The three of them laugh.

"OK, get a write-up on my desk in the next hour. Get legal involved and inform them of every step. Reach out to our affiliate newspapers to see if they want in at primo pricing. No discounts, do you hear me?" Marsala declares.

The two women exchange smiles which each other, nod and then turn their attention back to face Marsala, and nod again.

"What are you still standing around for? Get going!"

Maggie picks up her laptop, closes it, and races out the door with Emily in tow.

DAY THIRTY-THREE
— BREAKDOWN

—

Many people mistakenly think that the Oval Office is part of the main White House building, but it is in fact located on the front left corner of the West Wing. The West Wing houses the offices of the president along with offices for the vice president, the White House chief of staff, and numerous senior advisers to the president, the press secretary, and a small army of support staff. It's a very active, dynamic environment, and seeing somebody rushing down a corridor is a normal event.

One of the president's aides walks along the corridor leading to the Oval Office. Two other men in dark suits and earpieces quickly follow him: Secret Service agents. Behind them is the president's personal secretary, Bernie Andrews. He waves to the executive secretary and the marine guard on duty as he rushes into the Oval Office.

Bernie, in his mid-forties, clearly doesn't follow a healthy exercise regime. He's out of breath as he leans over and takes hold of one of the two couches in the centre of the office. After a brief pause, he turns to face the president, who is clearly annoyed by this unannounced intrusion.

"Mr. President, you need to see this!" He takes the remote and turns on the wall-mounted television. "Breaking News Alert" flashes across the bottom of the screen. "President Campbell insults American public in secret recording."

The aide turns up the volume.

"As we reported just minutes ago, a recording of President Franklin Campbell has been leaked to multiple news agencies. In the audio recording, you can clearly hear the president in a discussion with a person or persons in his personal residence. The television announcer pauses. "He states, 'They're a bunch of sheep. They need to be led. They need to be defended from the outside world and it is a cruel world. I am their shepherd. A shepherd to three hundred million dumbass, idiotic creatures who can't either think or protect themselves. . ... I don't care what the fuck I tell the American people if it means saving me $300 million in a lawsuit.'"

Startled by the statement, his eyes wide open, the president stands up behind his desk. "What the fuck is this? What the fuck!"

"Mr. President . . . sir."

"Fuck!"

"Mr. President, please, calm down."

The president grabs a small ornamental statue on his desk and throws it at Bernie.

Startled, Bernie doesn't react fast enough; the display hits him on his right shoulder, inches from his face.

"Don't ever tell me to calm down, you fucking idiot! Do you hear me? You fucking idiot, I am the president! Never tell me to do anything, especially to fucking calm down!"

"Yes, Mr. President."

"Where the fuck did that audio come from?"

Pausing in thought, Bernie flashes his gaze around the room. There are two secret service agents by the door, and the president's personal assistant sits at a desk outside the door. Beside her are several office aides who have rushed over to investigate.

Bernie, rubbing his shoulder where the small display hit him, refocuses his attention back to the president. "I have contacted all of our resources to investigate the source. We didn't get any advance warning from the media outlets before they aired it."

"Outlets?" the president yells.

"Yes, Mr. President. It seems all the majors got the audio recording at the same time to do the most damage. It was a coordinated attack, not the result of one rogue network. They probably all aired it to make the story seem more legitimate."

The president shakes his head. "This was not supposed to happen. We had an agreement—"

"An agreement, Mr. President?" Bernie asks.

"What?"

"You said we had an agreement. What are you referring too, Mr. President?"

"Nothing. Nothing."

Bernie stares at the president. He observes a man who is visibly shaken. A man who is used to always being in control of the narrative. Now the narrative is controlling him.

"Mr. President, if this story is true," he says, pointing to the screen, "then we're in big trouble." He pauses, watching the president pace back and forth behind his desk. "Is it true, Mr. President?"

"What?" Coming to his senses, the president shoots Bernie a quick glance.

"Is the story true? Is that your voice on the recording? Did you actually call three hundred million Americans dumb idiots?"

"Excuse me?" The president stops his pacing, straightens and gazes over at Bernie. "What are you trying to say?"

"Mr. President, I am—"

"What the fuck are you saying?" the president asks, raising his voice.

"I'm trying to understand whether those words came out of your mouth or were result of a very sophisticated manipulation of a video or audio recording. I need to know what we're dealing with."

"Manipulation of the recording," the president murmurs.

"Mr. President, are you saying it isn't real?"

"Yes. This has to be a great manipulation by some radical left-wing conspiracy group out to get me."

"Mr. President, if you're saying that the recording is fake, then why did you blurt out earlier that 'we had an agreement?' I need to know what you mean by that."

"Never mind what I said."

"Mr. President, sir?"

"Did you not hear me?" The president waves a menacing finger at Bernie. "You do your job, and I'll do mine!"

"And what is my job, exactly, Mr. President? What do you want me to do? Should I go out there and tell everybody that this is left-wing fake news? Or do I prepare for the fallout that's going to happen in the next twenty-four hours? The opposition party and every other group is going to be hell-bent on getting an answer."

The president stares at him momentarily. "You are going to do what I tell you to do. You are going to take over this story, condemn it as an invasion of privacy, and demand that the person or persons who made this recording turn themselves in to the FBI for immediate prosecution. Apparently, I need to remind you that you work at the pleasure of my presidency. You are going to do and say *what I tell you* to do and say. No questions asked. Understood?"

Clenching his jaw for a moment, uncomfortable by the president's last statement, Bernie speaks up. "Mr. President, given your absence of facts and you're clearly not wanting to explain yourself, I will simply not *do* or *say* what you want me to. Please accept my verbal resignation, effective immediately."

"Are you fucking kidding me?" The president's voice rises again. "Are you really fucking kidding me?"

Bernie turns and walks to the door and the two Secret Service agents.

The president picks up a brass rimmed, glass candy bowl from his desk and throws it at him. One of the Secret Service agents reacts quick enough to bat it down mid-flight before it strikes the back of Bernie's head.

The agent stands between Bernie and the president. "Mr. President, I need you to back up and sit down, sir," he announces in a calm voice.

"Fuck off and get out of my way. I'm going to punch that pussy motherfucker." He starts moving around his desk.

The agent raises his wrist to his mouth. "Code Six in the Oval Office. Lock down the Executive Wing. I repeat Code Six in the Oval Office."

After hearing this, the second agent stands beside the first one as a protective barrier between the president and his aide.

"Code Six! What the fuck is a Code Six?"

"Mr. President, I need you to back up and sit down behind your desk."

"Excuse me, I am the president. Don't fucking tell me what to do!"

"Mr. President, I strongly urge you to back up and calm down."

Code Six, being a single-digit code, signals a high-level threat. Within fifteen seconds, six other agents flood the Oval Office, holding firearms but not drawing them. Bernie, the personal assistant, and the other curious staff are quickly rushed out of the room.

Jerry Garcia, a tall, distinguished older agent, walks into the room and stops beside the agent who called in the alert.

"Sir, we have a situation," Agent Garcia says.

"Jerry, what the fuck is going on? What is a fucking Code Six?" The president advances slightly.

"Mr. President, I need you to back up and sit behind your desk."

"You too? Fuck off, Jerry." The president shifts his stance towards the liquor cabinet and declares, "I want a drink. I need a drink!"

"Mr. President, I would advise against that at the present moment."

"Advising me! Are you kidding me? I asked you what a Code Six is."

"Mr. President, a Code Six is a situation where the president has been incapacitated or is in serious duress. Your behavior right now has been compromised. You will be placed in protective security and his personal physician will be brought in to evaluate you. Until we ascertain the situation, the Code Six protocol will remain in effect."

"No fucking way are you giving me a medical exam! No fucking way!"

"Sir, you have no choice. These procedures are put in place to protect the president and the presidency. You cannot override these rules. Now, I need you to sit down, as the medical specialist will be here in under two minutes."

"You are going to pay for this, Jerry! I am going to have your job and your head! Do you hear me? You fucking bastard!"

"No, sir. You don't have the authority to terminate me under this situation. Now, as you have been asked at least three times to sit down and you have refused, I have the authority to restrain you, Mr. President. Please, let's not get to that point."

"I am the fucking president!" he yells, waving his hand and pointing at everybody in front of him. "Do you hear me? I give the orders around here. Not you! Not you, nor you!"

Agent Garcia, silent for a moment as he listens to something in his right ear, speaks. "Mr. President, the vice president has been notified. A Code Six, designated by a senior Secret Service agent, confirmed by a member of the executive group will automatically relieve the acting president of all powers, temporarily, and assigns them to the next ranking member of the state. In this case, it is the vice president." Agent Garcia's demeanor is calm, one he has built and refined over many years of service.

Upon hearing this, the president explodes and rushes toward Agent Garcia.

The two agents standing beside Agent Garcia intercept him. They expertly grab the president by his arms, holding him just tight enough to restrain him but not to hurt him.

"Let go of me!" the struggling president barks out. "Let me go now! Do you hear me? Let me go!" he screams.

The agents push the president back around the desk and force him to sit down on his leather chair.

Agent Garcia steps toward the desk. Hearing footsteps behind him. He turns and grasps the site of two more agents entering the Oval Office, immediately followed by Vice-President Randolph Chamberland.

Garcia turns back to face the president.

The president faces the vice president. "Randolph, do you see what is going on here? I am the president of the United States, and I'm being treated like a prisoner. Do something about this!"

Chamberland takes in the situation in front of him. He sees the Secret Service agents restraining the president, the medical specialist hovering close by, and other agents at attention around the room.

"Mr. President, I need you to calm down," states Chamberland. "We need you to calm down before we do anything else."

"Are you kidding me? Are you fucking kidding me?" the president yells, struggling. "Get your fucking hands off me. I will have your jobs for this!"

The agents stay silent and professional as they hold the president in his chair.

"Mr. President, we need you to calm down now, and no, you will not terminate them," Agent Garcia says. "They are here to protect you and the presidency. You have no authority over them. They take their orders from me. That is the way it is, and that's the way it has always been."

"Fuck you, Garcia!" yells the president.

Vice President Chamberland clears his throat. "Mr. President, under the authority granted to me by the dictates of Code Six of the Secret Service, I hereby relieve you of duties as the president of these United States, effective immediately until which time you are deemed healthy to resume your duties upon review by a senior medical general." Chamberland steps forward. "I am sorry it has to be this way, Mr. President."

"Fuck you, Randolph," the president blurts.

The vice president turns to the medical aides waiting at the door of the Oval Office. He nods. "Sedate and transfer him to his private quarters."

The two medical aides walk over to the president. Positioning themselves on either side, one of them pulls out a syringe from his medical bag and removes the cap as the second aide gently restrains the president's head. The two Secret Service agents hold his shoulders down to keep him in the chair.

The first medical aide pushes the president's sleeve up past his elbow, and the second aide inserts the syringe into a vein. When he pulls the needle back out, the other medical aide applies surgical gauze to stop any bleeding. Their actions are practiced, as if they have done this many times. The second medical aide waves to another team member standing at the door.

The new person comes in with three other members, dressed identically. Two of them carry a mobile gurney. The medical aides and two agents behind the president's desk clear out as the four technicians take over. Within a minute, the president's motionless body is removed from his chair, strapped to the gurney, and gently carried out of the Oval Office. Four members of the security rush ahead of the medical technicians.

Agent Garcia speaks into his communication link attached to his right wrist. "Clear out all corridors up to the president's private quarters. The president is under a Code Six restraint. Please remove all non-essential personnel from passage."

Like a precise marching band, the Secret Service agents exit the Oval Office. They closely follow the medical technicians carrying the gurney with more agents rushing down the corridor toward the president's residence.

The corridors are empty except for White House police and Secret Service agents, who stand at attention every fifteen feet, making sure nobody is aware of what is transpiring.

In three minutes, the president is in his own bed, still unconscious.

Vice President Chamberland, Agent Garcia, and one of the medical aides stand at his bedroom door. Chamberland turns to face the other men standing beside him. "I want him under constant observation by both medical and Secret Service agents, both inside and outside the room. I don't want him left unattended— even when he's sleeping. I want additional security posted in the main residence. No assistants, advisers, friends, or family are to speak to him. Do not let anybody pull rank on you or threaten you. Anybody who has an issue with this, tell them to see me, but remind them to first consider their complaint, as I will not be generous toward those who do not follow basic instructions. Consider this a quarantine of the president until he has been reviewed by the senior medical specialist. Do I make myself clear?" Chamberland asks.

"Yes, Mr. Vice-President," Agent Garcia responds.

"Yes, sir," the medical specialist says nervously.

"Good. Agent Garcia, keep me posted hourly."

"Yes, Mr. Vice-President."

"Good, I'll be in my office trying to do damage control. Reach out to me directly for anything Thank you, gentlemen. Thank you all for your continued work," he first addresses the two men and then turns to the remaining personnel in the room.

They all nod in acknowledgement.

"Agent Garcia, I would like to have a word with you outside," Chamberland says, nodding in that direction.

The two men walk out of the room, followed by the vice president's security detail. Once in the corridor, the agents take up positions outside the vice president's personal space but still within hearing distance. Whatever is said in their presence remains confidential.

"It goes without saying," the vice-president says, "but it's imperative that your agents and on-call medical staff be reminded that the president's status is not to be discussed or even hinted at. If you have to, put the fear in God into them. There's a real possibility of criminal prosecution if there's anything uttered about the president's condition. Do it! 'One person speaks, and everybody is charged,' or some shit like that. Do you understand?"

Agent Garcia smiles. "Fully understood. I'll take care of it."

"Thanks, I'm off." The vice-president turns and departs with his security detail.

Garcia turns to his agents. "Total fucking lockdown. Now I'm going to scare the living shit out of the medical crew," he states with a sinister smile.

DAY THIRTY-FIVE — WHAT'S NEXT, MR. PRESIDENT?

—

Vice-President Chamberland unofficially takes over the president's responsibilities until President Campbell returns to duty thirty-six hours later.

The lockdown of the president's residence is airtight. Nobody is allowed inside unless Vice-President Chamberland grants permission. A few high-and-mighty advisers and assistants challenge this authority on several occasions, but all fail. The Secret Service physically escorts one assistant to the vice president, where he is given a stern dressing down. When he refuses to heed the vice-president's words, he is fired and then arrested for threats made against a public official. Under the strictest of security, each department initiates internal meetings to explain the assistant's termination.

On the second morning of the president's rest, the vice president walks into his private sitting area.

The president's demeanor has completely changed from when he had his meltdown not thirty-six hours earlier. Dressed in casual pants and shirt with no tie, he sits with a cup of coffee in hand, looking out of one of his bay windows onto the presidential gardens.

"Mr. President, may I sit with you?" Vice-President Chamberland asks as he approaches.

Campbell looks up, smiles, and points to the empty chair. "Please sit down, Randolph. Let's talk."

"How are you feeling this morning, Mr. President?" Chamberland asks.

"Thanks for asking, Randolph. I'm almost back to 100 percent. You should expect me in the Oval Office tomorrow morning."

"Good to hear. Now, we do have a few items to discuss," Randolph says as he sits across from the president.

"Yes, my behaviour the other night was not very presidential, to say the least." He smiles slightly.

Randolph returns the smile awkwardly. "Sir, you need not worry about the incident getting out. I had the whole place locked down as quickly as possible with serious threats to anybody who even whispered something to their uncle. I said they'd suffer the full force of the United States government if they did. I must say, it has worked very well."

"Any issues with staff about my unavailability?" the president asks in a sombre tone.

"The only issue we had was Gerald Connells, assistant to one of your advisers. The young guy was trying to overstep the process."

"Yeah, I met him a few times. Didn't like him very much. Norton loves him. Probably because he's at his beck and call, twenty-four seven."

"Exactly what I figured."

"What did you do with him?" The president leans a little closer.

"I fired his ass. He claimed that I couldn't. That he didn't work for me. So, I had him arrested. I told Norton afterwards about Connells's behaviour and lectured him about his vetting processes for assistants," the vice president responds with a grin.

"That's good. Thanks, Randolph, for doing that, and thank you for deflecting any other inquiries from other officials and people in general."

"You're welcome, Mr. President," the vice president responds. "Now, we still need to fight off this damn audio claim. Then we can be back on sound footing."

"Do you know who recorded the audio? Was it one of the attending members? Did a staff member hide the recording device? Do you have any answers?"

"At the moment, we're going on the assumption that it was hidden before the meeting started and was voice activated, but we can't rule out a traitor in our midst. Somebody who has a plan to ruin you."

"Randolph, I need you to get on top of this. I need to discover this traitor. Who is trying to bring this presidency down?" The president pauses for a moment before continuing. "Do you believe this is still related to Larry Evans? I know it's a little out there, but what do you think?"

"Sir, Evans still being involved is a long-shot, but again, I'm not ruling anybody out. But he's a Canadian citizen. Why he would care about your presidency, I don't know."

"OK. About the audio recording, can we just say that it was a fake, made up via some audio trickery?"

"We can, but with the recording now in the public domain, every news organization will have experts validating it if they have not done so already. So I don't think that's a good option, but you can spin it as a dark conspiracy. It's a long-shot."

"OK, I'll think about that," Campbell says.

"I have my people digging at the source. The reporters who broke the story are the same ones who came out with the lost hotel surveillance videos."

"That's good. A pattern of some kind. Good, good! Thanks, Randolph. Keep me informed."

"Thank you, sir. In the meantime, I have some major paperwork to clear up, so I'll be in my office late, prepping for your return. If that's all, Mr. President, I'll get going," Randolph says, getting up.

"That's all, Mr. President." Campbell smiles at him.

"Sir!" Chamberland returns the smile, turns, and walks out of the room.

DAY THIRTY-FIVE — EVENING IN SPRINGVALE

—

Maggie Summers leaves early that evening from the *Springvale Journal* office. She waves to Emily as she bolts to the staircase doors. "Call me on my cell if you need anything; it's always on."

Emily gives her a smile and a thumbs-up in return, hanging back at her desk to do some additional darknet research on the mysterious emails. She opens a secure chat room on a darknet channel with her closest associates:

Emily: You have my email now. Any news?
Sabre27: Nothing.
Adam&Eve: All my contacts are coming up negative. No-go on my end. Scary.
Destro: I surrender. Yes! Scary.
JackRyan_for_Pres: Can you say Holy Grail, anybody?

Emily sits back in her chair. "Fuck!"

An untraceable email is considered the Holy Grail on the darknet. Ever since the audio recording went viral, both she and Maggie have fielded numerous calls and emails filled with profanity and threats. They've both brushed it off with an it's-all-part-of-being-a-reporter attitude. Some people aren't too happy when they're exposed for their wrongdoings.

After spending a few more unsuccessful hours trying to find the email trail and the clock on the wall creeps toward midnight, she decides to call it a night. The late hour and a sudden rumbling in her stomach are clear indications that she has overstayed her time at the office.

After clearing her desk of all unnecessary Post-it Notes and scraps of paper, shutting down her laptop and slotting it into her backpack, she is ready to go. She scans the office floor and realizes that she's the only one left. Quickly grabbing her coat, she hurries over to the elevator doors. The doors slide open without delay. She steps in and presses the button for the parking garage floor. Going five floors down takes all of ten seconds.

The doors open to a dark parking garage. She hesitates for a second before stepping out. *Got to stop putting in these late-night sessions*, she thinks to herself.

Emily hustles over to her car about sixty feet away, noticing that hers is not the only car in the garage. Maybe some of the out-of-town reporters left their vehicles at the office before Ubering to the Newark airport. It's not unheard of.

Reaching her car, she rests her backpack against the door while she rustles through her purse to find her keys, never remembering to take them out ahead of time.

"Ms. Lewis, can I have a moment of your time?"

Startled, Emily freezes. The fine blonde hairs on her arms stand up straight as her breath hitches. In her peripheral vision, she tries to take in the figure of the man.

No such luck; he's directly behind her.

"Ms. Lewis, we need to talk to you and Ms. Summers."

Trying to buy some time while rummaging in her bag, she says, "Who are you? I don't recognize your voice."

"Please turn around so we can talk," he responds.

Emily pivots on her right toe and pulls her hand out of her bag, clutching a palm-sized canister of pepper spray. She aims it at his face and presses the release lever.

Her aim is perfect; he takes the full hit in the eyes.

He stumbles back, dropping a metal object. He drops to his knees, rubbing his eyes vigorously to fight off the sting.

Emily kicks his head sideways to close the deal. Unaware of what's coming the man takes the full force of the kick and crashes to the cement floor away from Emily.

Not wasting any time checking his condition, she finds her car keys in her purse. After beeping open the car door, she grabs her backpack, jumps in, and shuts the door behind her. She starts the car, puts it into gear, and glances out her side window.

He's rolling on the ground in agony. Her heart skips a beat on seeing the metal object: a military-style knife with a serrated blade—serious business.

She accelerates out of her parking spot and down the centre lane toward the exit sign, arriving at the gated exit. She lowers her side window and presses the button to raise the rolling metal garage doors.

What seems like an eternity passes before the doors start to rise. She checks her rear-view mirror. No sign of the man on the ground. Her heart beats faster. She glances at her side mirror just in time to see the man stumbling toward her. He's clearly been staying outside the mirror's field of view to retain the element of surprise.

The garage door is almost open, but the extended bar is still down, blocking her escape.

"Come on! You fucking door!" she yells.

The rolling garage door comes to a stop, which triggers the bar to start rising.

Gripping her steering wheel and focused, she doesn't notice when the man leans his shoulder against her door. With the knife in his hand, he arches forward, slamming the tip of the knife into the driver's window. The window shatters.

"Shit!" she says. Not waiting any longer, she accelerates, scraping the side of her car roof on the metal bar as it rises.

"Stop!" the man yells from outside the window.

Emily peeks out the side window and notices a bloodied hand clutching a knife wedged on the bottom corner of the window against the remaining pieces of the glass. His jacket sleeve pinned against one of shards.

He's being dragged along as Emily drives up the ramp.

"Fuck you!" Emily yells out the side window. She eases the car over to the left to line him up with the wall beside the garage door.

"No!" he yells, and then there's a blunt thump.

Emily stares straight ahead as she turns sharply onto the street and speeds away.

DAY THIRTY-SIX — EARLY MORNING WAKE-UP CALL

The first vibration isn't enough to wake up Maggie, but the second phone call triggers an additional vibration on her iWatch, startling her awake. She leans over to check the time on her digital alarm clock on her nightstand beside her bed; a necessary backup needed to avoid sleeping in. It takes a few seconds for her to focus in the complete darkness. She's not one to keep the curtains or bedroom door open. Clicking on the display button instantly flashes the time: 3:14 a.m.

"What the freak!" Her iWatch vibrates again. James Marsala's name flashes on her cell phone screen. She picks up. "Mr. Marsala? What's going on? It's three in the morning!" she exclaims, rubbing her eyes with her free hand.

"Are you at home right now?"

"Yes. What's going on?"

"OK, good!"

"What is going on?" Maggie yells.

"OK. Don't freak out, but Emily was attacked by some man in our office garage. She is all right, physically. Emotionally, she's a wreck."

"Oh my God! Attacked?" Maggie grasps her chest in shock.

"Maggie! Emily isn't hurt. She's at my house. She called me shortly after the incident. I told her to get over to my place right away. Her vehicle is out of sight in my garage."

"Have you called the cops yet?"

"Yes. They were here already and took down a full account of the incident. They've assigned a police unit to do frequent checks on us for the next twenty-four hours," Marsala replies.

"I'm coming over now," Maggie declares.

"No!" Marsala replies quickly. "I want you to get out of town tonight for a few days . . . a week, maybe."

"What! Why?"

"I am concerned about your safety, Maggie."

She pauses. "Not fully understanding. Exactly what are you not telling me?"

This time, Marsala hesitates.

"Mr. Marsala! James! What are you not telling me?"

"Damn reporter's instinct in you! The man also mentioned you when he approached Emily in the garage," he concedes. "That's why I need you out of town for a while. Pack your stuff. Don't tell me where you're going. Reach out to me via burner phone. I'll update you when I hear from you. Do you understand?"

"Mr. Marsala, am I in danger?"

"I really don't know," he replies. "He had a knife, so I'm concerned about both your safety and Emily's."

"You left that part out. That changes a lot of things."

"What do you mean?"

She pauses again, rubbing her cheek. "This whole Larry Evans story is affecting a lot of powerful people. In the beginning, I thought it was just an innocent news story, but it's ballooned into something that's getting out of control. I was a little concerned about it before. But with the attack on Emily, I'm downright scared shitless."

"I hear you; I understand, Maggie," Marsala responds.

"James. I mean Mr. Marsala. I'm leaving town, but I don't think I'll be back. I don't think you'll be hearing from me again."

"What! You can't be serious?" James asks.

"I am," Maggie replies. Her voice is calm, like she's taken a huge load off her back. "I am still young—youngish," she chuckles. "I can easily find another gig as a reporter, or better yet, maybe as a researcher where my name won't appear on the byline. I have a decent savings account, so I'll be able to weather the lack of paycheque for a while. Don't worry about me."

"I hear you and yes, you can call me James. I'll miss you, Maggie, big time. You and Emily made a hell of a team."

"And a lot of money for the paper."

"Yes, a lot of money." James laughs.

"Be safe, James. Thank Emily for everything. I'll miss you both. Bye."

"Bye, Maggie."

The line goes dead, and Maggie shuts off her phone. She opens the back of it and pulls out the battery pack. Taking all necessary precautions to minimize her online footprint. She walks over to her closet, pulls out her suitcase, and lies it down on her bed. She turns back to face the closet and sighs.

What the hell is going on in this world?

DAY THIRTY-SIX —
SURPRISING NEWS

———

That night, after sitting with the president to review the issues of the day and the strategy on defending the video scandal, the vice president retreats to his office. He's reviewing documentation when he gets pinged with a new email notification.

He glances at the sender's address, and it states, "DOJ Office." He clicks open the email and reads it through. "Oh my God!" comes out of his mouth. He presses the intercom button on his office phone console. "Helen, track down the attorney general right away. I need to talk to her," he barks into the phone.

"Yes, sir! Right away!"

"Fuck!" he yells.

DAY THIRTY-SIX —
BE PREPARED

––––

The evening is a quiet one. President Campbell sits on the couch in his study with a few papers in one hand and a glass of red wine in the other. The day has been uneventful as he has gotten back up to speed. With the help of the Secret Service and a couple of senior IT technicians, his executive secretary has relocated to just outside his private study so she can filter in the information slowly. The president has asked to be reached by telephone only. No personal visits until he is back in the Oval Office, working behind the Resolute desk.

His cell phone rings on his side table. It rings again. Noticing the name on the caller ID, he picks it up and answers it. "Hello."

He listens attentively to the person on the other line. "Yes, everything is in order," he says in a calm voice. "Thanks." Hesitating in wanting to say more at first, he finally hangs up the phone and places it back on the side table. He takes another sip from his wine glass and places it on the side table next to the phone. *It's going to be a big day tomorrow!* He stands up from the couch, walks into his room, and gets into bed.

DAY THIRTY-SEVEN
— COMMITTEE
MEETING SURPRISE

—

Vice President Randolph Chamberland, President Campbell, and the members of the Executive Committee all sit around the conference table in the Situation Room. Outside, a small contingent of marines are on full alert, standard operating procedure.

It has been a tense week of bad press for the president. Initially, he claimed the audio recording was fake news put together by a dark conspiracy trying to kick him out of office, but a newspaper who hired specialists to validate the file quickly rebutted this. Furthermore, the audio recording was turned over to the FBI, who also authenticated them.

His approval rating has taken a double-digit tumble into the low teens. The positive numbers represent only the die-hard loyalists now—people who see Campbell as a man who can do no wrong.

Today has brought more devastating news, the subject of the executive meeting.

"Gentlemen," the Chamberland says (there are no women), "this meeting will come to order. We have two items on the agenda. This will be short and quick."

"What are the items?" Campbell demands. "Why has the agenda not been published ahead of time?"

Chamberland ignores him. "These are extraordinary times. The presidency is in a bad state. We need to address certain issues that have arisen in the past week and as recent as yesterday evening."

"Yesterday evening?"

"Yes, Mr. President," Chamberland responds smugly. "We have received confirmation that Jason Stands, one of your senior advisers, along with close to a dozen other individuals, have been arrested in Canada—Montreal, to be specific—on multiple weapons-related charges. Additionally, authorities found documents, laptops, and other surveillance and communication devices detailing a plan to acquire or terminate Larry Evans."

The president remained stone-faced at first after hearing the remarks from the Vice President but then slowly turns away, avoiding any eye contact with other members of the Executive Committee. As for them, their focus oscillates between the president and the vice-president, hoping to extract more from their facial expressions.

Chamberland continues to read from the document in front of him. "All members of this party are American by birth. All members, except Mr. Stands, have previous military training in the Marines, Special Forces, or Rangers. The seized military equipment included SIG Sauer P226 semi-automatic pistols, Mossberg 500A2 shotguns, fully automatic HK416 assault rifles, two CheyTac M200 Intervention sniper rifles, stun grenades, combat knives, numerous boxes of various ammunition, and the list goes on. The authorities have documented 54 violations of illegal arms under the Canadian Firearms Act. Each violation in itself carries a minimum sentence of three years' incarceration. Comparing these violations against the American prohibited weapons list, which is a little more liberal, they would still be facing over two dozen charges."

"Just get them back," Campbell says. "Demand that they be returned to American soil! Goddammit, I will if you are too weak."

"There have already been backroom discussions about this scenario, and the Canadian government's, the RCMP's, and CSIS's answer is an unequivocal *no*," Chamberland says. "The charges are too severe for the operatives and Jason Stands to simply be released into our custody, where the Canadians believe they will be freed without a slap on their wrists."

"These are our boys!" Campbell continues. "I'll give the prime minister a call tomorrow morning and straighten everything out. I'll remind him who he's dealing with."

"I don't think that will do any good, Mr. President. Need I remind you that they are not above the law—our laws or foreign laws, for that matter?" Chamberland pauses, shaking his head in frustration.

The group around the table is at a loss for words.

Campbell remains silent and emotionless.

"Now, I could go on, but you can all read it in the documentation provided in front of you, and I want to jump to the juicy part. During the interrogation, naturally, these military personnel were not very cooperative with the RCMP and CSIS investigators. Their steadfast refusal to answer any questions about their presence in Montreal or their intentions in the city did not go over well with RCMP. Nothing of value was garnered from them. Our senior adviser, Jason Stands, on the other hand, did not have a spine of courage and sang like a canary."

Campbell looks over but remains silent.

"Mr. President, according to Jason Stands, you authorized the mission to dispose of Larry Evans during a meeting with your advisers about a week ago. It was a near-unanimous consensus, except for Henry Mood, who advised against the operation. Henry Mood, to my knowledge, is no longer your adviser. Is that correct?"

"Are you taking the word of a low-level adviser against me, the president of the United States?" Campbell asks.

Chamberland puts down the document and makes eye contact with his boss. "No, I am not. I am taking the word of a senior member of your advisory group who was arrested in a foreign country—our closest ally and long-lasting partner. He was arrested with nearly a dozen other military operatives in the possession of over $3 million worth of military weapons and ammunition, communication gear, and surveillance equipment, all delivered in a Bombardier C-143 jet that in itself is valued at over $40 million. We are still researching the ownership of that private hangar in Montreal where the jet is currently parked in, but I'm pretty sure it is off the books. I don't think he's some low-level adviser, Mr. President."

Chamberland pauses to catch his breath. "Oh, and by the way, I'm not taking the word of Mr. Stands only. I also have confirmation from three other people present at the meeting when the marching orders were given to Jason Stands: Dr. Phil Norton, Daniel Esposito, and Mark Deerson. All of these senior members of your advisory group have admitted to being present when you gave the order. Jason Stands, while under interrogation by RCMP, provided their names. The information was then sent to the justice department under high-level clearance. They were picked up late yesterday evening, and they confessed to being complicit in the illegal mission you authorized. All of their careers are over, and they will spend a good part of their remaining lives behind bars. I sit here utterly stunned by the whole event. Your blatant disregard of the law. What do you have to say for yourself, Mr. President?"

Campbell stands and stares at his vice president, who was once a trusted friend of many years. Today, he is a sworn enemy at the gates of power. He points his finger at Chamberland. "I am the president; you are not. I make the decisions to protect this country. I have more political experience than most of you in this room. I know how to play the game better than any of you. I have more courage than all of you put together to make the hard decisions." Campbell waves his finger around the table and returns to look at Chamberland. "You, more than anybody else in this room, cannot go high and mighty on me. You are equally guilty."

Chamberland stands and yells, "Are you delusional? What are you talking about?"

"Like it or not, you were also a part of the operation to take down Evans. You all have your dirty hands in this plot," Campbell proclaims, smugness in his tone.

"What the fuck are you talking about?" Chamberland barks.

"You were involved!" Campbell repeats with an icy stare.

"I knew nothing about this operation," Chamberland says. "I would have never sanctioned it. The only reason you put this operation in place is because you couldn't keep your fucking fingers off your Twitter account or keep your fucking mouth shut in front of the camera when you were asked to comment about Larry Evans."

Campbell steps forward slightly. "Randolph, do you seriously think that this mission would be sanctioned and authorized by me without any support from my vice president or any other members of the Executive Office? I would give the go ahead without the by in from members of this group around this table? You are sadly mistaken." Campbell smiles at him. "Do you think I will go down for this without taking a few of you along with me on this ride to hell? You're all a bunch of fucking amateurs. That is why you will always be a vice president and never a president."

"Again, what are you talking about?" demands Chamberland.

The secretary of defence stands up and declares, "That is enough. Now, what is going on here, Mr. President?"

Campbell looks around the room, soaking in the anticipation of what he is going to say next. "OK, let's go through the numbers. Let's start with transportation. That's an easy one to detail. The Bombardier C-143 jet," he declares.

"What about the plane?" asks the secretary of defence

"That particular jet is out of Little Rock Air Force Base in Arkansas. It is one of many C-143s that are part of the 19th Airlift Wing, among other Air Wings. Did you know that Mr. Vice-President?" asks Campbell.

"No, I did not. I don't see the point to knowing this."

"What does that have to do with anything?" The Secretary of Defense asks.

"This base is in your district, Mr. Secretary of Defence. The authorization for re-tasking this particular plane to Canada came out of your office," Campbell adds.

"You are lying! That's impossible!"

"Not at all. Everything is documented and signed off by your office."

The secretary of defence slams his fists down on the table. "You bastard!"

"I am not finished. All the operatives were based out of Little Rock before retiring—although for some, they were forced to retire after some questionable behaviour unbecoming of US military personnel. It seems they all found quick and more financially rewarding employment in black-ops assignments. Let's go on. The equipment was staged and loaded along with operatives, all from Little Rock; after all, it is the home of four Airlift Wings specializing in transportation of men and material."

The Secretary of Defense, Matt Devlin, barks out his protest, "That is a lie! This is all a damn lie!"

"Is it? Is it really?" Campbell responds. "You approved the paperwork. It's dated and stamped with your official seal. Your assistant handed you the paperwork, and you approved it. You are so lazy that you didn't even bother reading what was put in front of you. If you care to see it, I have a copy of all the documentation. If you let this go by, imagine all the other shit that you've signed off on. I think I should launch an investigation into your incompetence."

Campbell turns to Chamberland. "As for you, Mr. Vice-President, the weapons and ammunition were signed out of the Redstone Arsenal facility in Alabama and then transported to Little Rock. All paperwork, again, went through your office. All $3 million worth of weapons and ammunition you listed before came from there. I have copies of those also. Your signature appears clearly on the paperwork. You are as dumb as a doorknob. Again, do you even bother checking what paperwork is put in front of you?" He turns his attention back to the group. "I review everything that is put in front of me."

An expression of disbelief crosses Chamberland's face. He steps back in silence to reflect.

Campbell turns to Treasury Secretary Sidney Casper. "Flight and landing permits, fuel charges for the jet, they were all approved by your department. Again, signed by you personally. As this was all non-scheduled work, it fell under your department for approval. Again, does nobody actually read what their assistants put in front of them? You bunch of dummies."

"You fucker! You set us up!" screams Casper.

Campbell steps away from the table. "So, you see; if I go down, you all go down. You all get the picture now. You are equally guilty in this scandal. Like the British are keen to say, 'in for a penny, in for a pound.' You guys are in for the whole way."

Devlin yells, "You bastard!"

"Relax, Devlin, you piece of shit. I should have fired you last year," Campbell says. "Now that everything is out in the open, let's agree to put all of this behind us. It will be our dirty little secret, one that we won't dredge up again. Let's move forward with running this country again. I, for one, am very hungry. Let's say we wrap this up now and sit down for a nice steak dinner with all the trimmings." Campbell walks toward the door.

"Where are you going, Mr. President?" The secretary of the Interior asks.

"Excuse me?"

"I asked where you were going. This meeting is not over."

Campbell gazes at him, taken aback by his bluntness, speaks out. "Who do you think you are? Do you know whom you are talking to? I am still the president of the United States."

"Not for long!" The Secretary of the Interior announces. "I figure both you and the vice president will be resigning after this admission of wrong doing and with the secretary of defence and the treasury secretary implicated in this scandal as well, unbeknownst to them, it falls on me and the remaining executive members present in this room to decide on the future of this government. I will be invoking the Twenty-Fifth Amendment. I am sure you are aware of what this is, Mr. President?"

Chamberland calls out, "This is outrageous. You cannot do this!"

"Mr. Vice-President, Mr. President, with the information that has just been presented to this committee, it is only logical that you all excuse yourselves from this meeting. This also goes for the treasury secretary and the secretary of defence. Your input on all further government matters is null and void. Based on these revelations, the integrity of this presidency has been seriously comprised. I am initiating Continuity of Operations protocols for continuance of government. It gives me no great pleasure to do this, but you four will now be escorted out of the Situation Room.

I will immediately be advising the attorney general on this situation. The situation you have put us and this country in."

Three other members of the committee stand up at first and then the remaining members.

"You can't do this, Maxwell!" The president blurts out in anger.

"To respect the Executive Office of the President, I ask you to remain silent until the attorney general is fully up to speed," Maxwell pushes back with determination. "I will not ask you again, Mr. President. That also goes for your group of accomplices." Maxwell glances over to the vice-president, the secretary of defence, and the treasury secretary.

Maxwell pushes the intercom button on the table.

A voice comes over the intercom quickly. "Yes, sir?"

"This is Chris Maxwell speaking. We have a situation. Please open the doors and call in the White House Police Force to escort and place the president, the vice president, the secretary of defence, and the treasury secretary in individually secured rooms. I want armed guards posted. Advise the Secret Service to assist. Do not allow any of these individuals to communicate among themselves. Strip all communication devices from of them. Do not allow them any outside contact except if pre-approved by me, and only me, until further notice. This goes for staff as well as family members. Do you understand?"

The response over the intercom is quick and without hesitation. Professional. "Yes, sir."

Within seconds, the door opens, and eight marines enter the room, taking positions beside the four men, two apiece. Additional marines stand by the door.

"You will pay for this, Maxwell. You will pay dearly with your career," Chamberland yells as he starts walking towards the exit of the Situation room with a marine escort.

President Campbell remains quiet. His face shows signs of defeat. Glancing over at Maxwell as he strides towards the exit. "Beware the quiet ones. I should have known." *Damn! He always towed the party line and protected it, but he was always inconspicuous. He foiled a plan I thought was foolproof.*

The vice president and president depart first, followed by the treasury secretary and the secretary of defence.

The doors close.

Chris Maxwell turns to the remaining members of the Executive Committee. "We have a lot of work to do now—first of all, establishing the continued leadership of this government." He presses the intercom button again. "Please get in touch with the both president pro tempore and the attorney general through whatever means possible and tell them that their presence is urgently needed in the Situation Room. Thank you."

"Yes, sir. Will that be all?" the voice asks.

Maxwell surveys the room and then checks his watch. "It's going to be a long night; can you please arrange for food and drinks to be brought into the Situation Room? We will be here for a while."

"Yes, sir." The intercom switches off.

DAY THIRTY-EIGHT —
THE BIG ANNOUNCEMENT

"Breaking news. This just in: absolutely shocking news from the White House this morning. President Campbell's widely speculated future has been confirmed this morning. The White House has announced that Franklin Campbell has stepped down as the president of the United States, effective immediately. The president's office has not scheduled a news conference, and none will be, according to the White House. The White House and West Wing offices have been cleared of all media personnel, and a news embargo has been imposed until further notice.

"Now, what is more stunning is the following announcement. Vice President Randolph Chamberland along with Secretary of Defence Matt Devlin and Treasury Secretary Sidney 'Sid' Casper have also resigned. Information has come out that these three men are accomplices to a failed mission undertaken by Senior Adviser Jason Stands and unnamed ex-military personnel into Canada in order to retrieve Larry Evans. If this is indeed true, the ramifications will be immense and damaging for the relationship between the United States and Canada, its most important ally in world affairs and second-biggest trading partner.

"As mentioned, the details are sparse, but we will hopefully have more to report as the White House updates news networks.

"The question on the lips of many Americans is, 'Who is in charge now?' Well, let's break it down. If the president cannot fulfill his duties, then these duties fall on the vice president. But since the vice president is out of the picture, they fall on the speaker of the House of Representatives. We have been told that the speaker, due to health reasons, has turned down the position. Next person in line of succession is the president pro tempore of the senate. This position is presently held by Senator Alexander Gains, a veteran of the political scene and who just recently announced that he will not be seeking office in the next midterm elections but will be stepping down. So, on we go. Next on the list is the Secretary of State. That position is currently vacant due to the recent departure of Jane Philips. Next comes the Treasury Secretary, Sidney Casper. Well, he has been implicated in the Jason Stands scandal as well and has resigned. So, we move down the line. Secretary of Defence Max Devlin has also been implicated in the scandal and has resigned.

"Now we come to the attorney general, Chloe Williams; she has not been implicated in the Larry Evans failed abduction or other scandals. So, according to the laws of succession, Chloe Williams will be sworn in this afternoon as the next president of the United States. Not only the first woman to hold this post, but also the first African American woman in this post. We here at NNC congratulate Chloe Williams on her new role."

DAY FORTY-FIVE —
CLEANUP DAY — ACT I

———

Within the RCMP walls in Montreal, Chief Superintendent Boucher is in the regional office. The phone rings, and he picks up the receiver. "Chief Superintendent Boucher, here."

"This is Leo Caldwell, senior adviser to President Williams."

"Yes, Mr. Caldwell, what can I do for you?"

"This is a courtesy call on the behalf of the president."

"Go ahead, I'm listening."

"This concerns Jason Stands and his operatives. We have concluded that we will not be pursuing any attempts to request their return to the USA. I—"

"Please, Mr. Caldwell," Boucher interrupts. "First, thank you for your courtesy call; it's nice of you to reach out and introduce yourself. I'm sure we'll have an excellent relationship like we've had with representatives from previous administrations."

"Thanks, I hope to have a constructive relationship with you too," Caldwell responds.

"Next, you seem to be mistaken that you and the president's administration have any say on the status and prosecution of Jason Stands and his operatives. You don't, you never did, and you never will."

"But he is an American citizen—"

"And they broke numerous laws in our country. Laws that carry serious criminal penalties. They will never step foot on American soil in their remaining natural lives. For you to think otherwise shows your inexperience in foreign affairs. This is something you will need to get up to speed on quickly, or you and your administration will be left behind, and the influence that your country has on the world stage will quickly disappear. I would be glad to advise you in the future on any other topic that might involve our two departments again, but at this moment, that is all I have to say. I wish you a good day." Boucher replaces the receiver and sits back in his chair.

DAY FORTY-FIVE —
CLEANUP DAY — ACT II

—

The Old Port, Montreal

Benjamin Dowds and Larry Evans sit outside a restaurant under a veranda in Place Jacques Cartier. It's a nice spring day, and a small celebration lunch is in order. To avoid the noon tourist rush, they decided to meet at three in the afternoon.

Carson, Randall, Patrick, and Arthur, a small part of Dowds's security group, are positioned strategically at separate tables around them.

Larry admires the open-air terrace. Several other tables are occupied but none of them are adjacent to them. He gives Carson and Arthur a nod. They in turn smile back. He wonders how many more of Dowds' crew are within the square.

Well, since Larry first met Dowds over forty days ago, his conviction that Dowds is more than a humble lawyer has not wavered. His connections and resources have been nothing short of impressive.

Both Larry and Dowds people-watch while sipping their Canadian beers and wait for their orders to arrive, a large bucket of mussels in vodka sauce with a side order of fries. The restaurant is well known for their mussels and assortments of sauces. The large plate of fries is just a delightful bonus.

"The final payment from Campbell's accountant has cleared," Dowds says. "He's paid up in full, which is kind of surprising, given that he lost his job."

"I wasn't too concern about that. I'm pretty sure you were several steps ahead with Plan B, C and D on the remote possibility he would renege on the settlement. " Larry says.

"Only B and C. and 'Yes', it was in his best interest to pay," Dowds says with a grin. "Don't you worry; he's far from broke. Remember, he made his money in the aerospace business when he was in his mid-twenties, and it just grew from there. Probably still worth north of $1 billion."

"Good. I'm glad. I wouldn't want to lose sleep over the fact that he's broke," Larry states. "On a more serious note, I need to thank you again for everything. You've outdone yourself. So much so that I want to change the terms of our contract."

"Hmm," Dowds says with a tinge of concern.

Larry waves his hand. "No, nothing like that. I want to add another 20 percent of the settlement as payment to you and your guys. I'll leave it in your trusting hands to split up. God knows, I have more money than I'll ever need."

"That is most generous of you, Larry. Can I call you Larry? It seems we have been through some tough times in these last few weeks and we have connected in bringing the bad guys to justice. Wouldn't you agree?" Dowds jokes.

"You're funny . . ." Larry pauses when Arthur and Carson quickly walk over to the table, and without waiting for an answer, grab Dowds and Larry under their arms and lift them out of their chairs.

"We need to move, now," is all Carson says.

The four of them rush into the restaurant toward the back exit. Randall stays back and calls over the waiter to settle the bill. Patrick waits for them at the rear door.

Outside, two other beefy men are dressed casually in light jackets to shield prying eyes from their concealed weapons. Carson crosses through the door first, followed by Arthur, Dowds, and Larry with Randall pulling up the rear.

Together, the five men form a pentagon around Dowds and Larry as they pace down the street to waiting Black SUVs with dark tinted glass.

Drivers are behind both steering wheels. Engines are on. In a precision manoeuvre, Dowds and Larry are quickly steered into the back seat of the second car, followed by Carson. Arthur takes the passenger seat up front. Randall, Patrick, and the remaining two men jump into the first car. The two cars accelerate up the street and take a sharp right at the first intersection. Two blocks later, they pull over to the curb.

Nobody talks as the security team does what they're supposed to do, and they do it efficiently.

Carson finally breaks the silence. "Unknown parties broke the perimeter. They've been neutralized. We're going there now for identification."

"How many?" asks Dowds.

"Three men," Carson responds in a serious tone, clearly not happy with whoever is sending him information.

The two vehicles pull away from the curb and drive down the cobblestone streets of Old Montreal. Everybody in the vehicles is silently grateful that the vehicles have excellent suspension; the history of the city is amazing but driving on the cobblestone roads can do a number on your neck muscles and leave you with a headache.

After a few more turns down narrow streets, the vehicles stop in front of an old stone building. The security team jumps out of the car, and they position themselves between the entrance of the building and the passenger door of the SUV.

Arthur gives a signal, the passenger door opens, and Carson, Dowds, and Larry rush into the building. Patrick and Randall follow. The remaining members of the team stay outside, watching the vehicles and the surrounding area.

Inside the building, two other casually dressed guards carrying assault rifles on shoulder straps stand at the bottom of the stairs.

"Where are they?" Carson demands to the two guards.

"Fourth floor, sir," responds the guard closest to Carson. "Kyle and his men have the whole floor sealed. I've got additional men patrolling the other floors."

"Thanks," Carson responds. He heads up the stairs, followed by Patrick.

Larry pulls Dowds aside. "More men? Kyle and his men? How many people work for you?"

Dowds looks at him seriously. "You really don't want to know." Dowds turns and races up the stairs.

Larry and Randall follow. Arriving on the fourth floor, Dowds and Larry where several more men with automatic rifles and wearing ammunition vests are guarding the doorway.

Dowds spies Carson across the floor near a set of windows. The whole floor is one big room. Construction material is scattered about, giving the impression that some kind of renovation is in the works.

Dowds and Larry walk over to Carson. He and five more men, all heavily armed, gather around three bodies on the ground. Several more armed men look out the windows overlooking Place Jacques Cartier, their weapons hidden from anyone who might look into the building.

The bodies have bullet wounds in their chests. Blood pools under their bodies.

Dowds looks at Carson. "You know them?"

Carson nods. "I know of them. Not personally, but they're Americans, all of them—government black ops. That one there is serious business." He points to the body that looks a little older than the two others. "One of their best, Marshall Potts. If he's involved, there are some serious people backing this operation. He doesn't come cheap. This whole operation probably set somebody back $10 million."

Dowds glances over at Kyle and says, "Walk me through it."

"Our spotter was stationed in that building." Kyle points to a five-storey building on the opposite side of the plaza. "He called me in with the details. We were parked down the street, so we rushed in and surprised them. One of them raised his rifle at us. We took them down. Our estimate is that they would have been ready to carry out their mission in about thirty more seconds if we hadn't stopped them—end of story."

Larry steps forward and stares down at the three bodies before him, shaking his head. "This isn't good. This isn't good at all. Carson, are you sure about their backgrounds?"

"Yes, I have an eidetic memory; I remember faces and names pretty well. All three are active government operatives," Carson replies confidently.

"OK, call in a crew to clean up this mess," Dowds says. "I want nothing to indicate that three men have just been gunned down here. Can you do that?"

"No problem, boss," replies Carson.

Dowds glances over to Larry, his eyes tight and worried. "Evans, is there something you want to tell me?"

Larry stands there silently, shifting his attention from the three bodies on the ground to Dowds.

"Evans! What is going on here?" Dowds repeats.

"We need to talk—not here," Larry responds. "In private."

DAY FORTY-FIVE —
CLEANUP DAY — ACT III

―

Interrogation Room, Springvale Police Station

Two casually dressed men sit on one side of a table in a small room with no windows. Neither of them is clean-shaven; both have several days' worth of hair growth on their faces.

A police officer quickly enters the room and sits in the empty chair across the plain metal table. He lays down a file folder. "I will get straight to the point, as I don't have all day," he says. "The first person who confesses gets a reduced sentence. The other will serve the maximum time. Any questions?"

"Who the hell are you?" blurts one of the men.

The officer gives him a quick glance before he opens the file folder and scans the first page. "Officer Scarborough, my name is Captain Paul Henderson from the New Jersey State Police. I have been reassigned to Springvale as the interim police commissioner due to the dismissal of Police Commissioner Maco. Does that answer your question?"

"Why are we here?" Officer Scarborough asks.

"You gentlemen have been detained for attacking an inmate who was held in this police station about one month ago."

"Are you kidding me? What evidence do you have?" demands the other man.

Captain Henderson glances at his file again before turning his attention to the second man. "Officer Batista, we have video surveillance footage of two masked men entering the cell of one Eddie Mitchell. The two men then proceeded to hit Eddie an estimated twenty times, based on the medical exam performed on him, before departing."

"What does that have to do with us?" Officer Batista asks.

"Well, the two masked men were recorded entering the police station at exactly one in the morning. The front desk was surprisingly vacant at the time. This is something we'll need to review in the near future. Other police personnel may be involved, here." He pauses. "The two men beat the inmate, exited the holding area, and left the station at 1:04 a.m. From there, we picked them up walking around the side of the station toward the parking lot, still masked. They got into a dark four-door sedan and exited the parking lot. A traffic camera picked up the vehicle at the traffic lights about one hundred yards down the street. At this point, the masked gentlemen removed their masks, therefore enabling us to establish their identities."

Captain Henderson pulls an eight-by-ten blown-up picture of two men in a car. The timestamp is 1:08 a.m. The men in the front seats are Officer Batista and Officer Scarborough. Their masks are off.

The two officers silently look at the picture.

"So, who's talking first?" Captain Henderson asks.

DAY FORTY-FIVE —
CLEANUP DAY — ACT IV

Having been the mayor of Springvale for close to two decades, Jason Frakes has developed a lifestyle that places him in the higher end of social circles. After settling his lawsuit with Larry Evans's attorney, he has been able to hold on to his principal residence and some small assets through the liquidation of some overvalued real estate.

His house is a two-storey Georgian style house with cream-colored bricks all around it, four bedrooms, three bathrooms, and an in-ground pool in the back. The double garage with a paved driveway can easily accommodate the four full-sized police cars that pull in.

A police sergeant and four officers approach the front door. More officers remain by their cars. He rings the doorbell. "You two," the sergeant says, pointing to two of the closest officers. "Go around the back to make sure nobody decides to leave."

They nod and set off. The sergeant faces the front door. There's no answer, so he presses the doorbell again. After several more moments, he spots movement through the glass door behind the lace curtains.

The former mayor of Springvale, dressed in dark blue shorts and a baggy white t-shirt, opens the door. The fifteen-hundred-dollar custom made suits a thing of the past. "What's going on here?" he asks in an elevated, agitated tone.

"Mr. Mayor, we're here to take you into custody for aiding and abetting first-degree assault against Eddie Mitchell."

"Who the hell is Eddie Mitchell? I don't know what you're talking about. This is ridiculous."

"Mr. Mayor, Eddie Mitchell was the man that Officers Batista and Scarborough attacked under your and Police Commissioner Maco's orders," the sergeant responds.

"That is bullshit!" Mayor Frakes pushes back.

"Well, bullshit or not, we have sworn written testimonies from both Officers Batista and Scarborough, along with Police Commissioner Maco, that you ordered them to intimidate Larry Evans to drop his lawsuit against the city, the police force, and the Springvale Starline Hotel's staff. The three of them were taken into custody this afternoon. You are the last clog in the insane plan to mess with an innocent man," the sergeant responds.

"Maco!" Frakes shouts, snapping out of a momentary trance.

"Police Commissioner Maco acknowledged that you commanded him to 'take care of' Mr. Evans."

"That fucking spineless weasel!"

The sergeant nods to two officers. They step forward.

"Mr. Mayor," the sergeant says, "I am placing you under arrest for aiding and abetting first-degree assault against Eddie Mitchell. At this point in time, I will read you the Miranda rights. You have the right to remain silent. Anything you say can and will be used against you in a court of law. You have the right to an attorney. If you cannot afford an attorney, one will be provided for you."

The two police officers pull the ex-mayor's arms behind his back and handcuff him. The ex-mayor lowers his head, and the two police officers escort him to one of the waiting police vehicles.

The police sergeant follows.

DAY ONE HUNDRED

———

Two months later

The idyllic resort island of Saint Lucia in the Caribbean, with its abundance of palm trees in full bloom and wild vegetation every-where, is a great place to relax with no worries from the outside world. Five-star resorts dot the white sandy coastline. The hot sun beats down on tourists and locals alike, and there's not a cloud in the sky. Umbrellas are everywhere for people seeking shelter.

Jalousie Plantation Beach, snuggled between the twin volcanic peaks south of the Soufrière, is the place to be. Open-air bars every hundred metres satisfy the thirst of vacationers.

A man wearing a weathered Panama hat, Ray-Bans, and a colourful shirt draping over the top of his shorts stands peacefully at an outdoor bar at the edge of the beach.

He watches as the waiter is busy putting together an order and placing drinks on an oversized silver platter.

Just behind the bartender, a television playing a local new channel hangs from an overhead metal beam that stretches across the length of the bar. A message suddenly flashes across the screen: "BREAKING NEWS ALERT." The reporter stops his story mid-sentence and pauses to listen to his earpiece.

The bartender stops what he's doing.

"This just in: the former president of the United States was discovered unconscious this morning on his bedroom floor at his private residence. The Secret Service agent on duty discovered him, from what reports are telling us, around six this morning. As the former president was an early riser, it was not uncommon for him to be up and about, attending to his daily affairs while the sun rose. Attempts to revive him were unsuccessful. The cause of death, at this moment, is unknown. We will have further details as they are made available from the White House." The anchorman pauses in disbelief before he continues. "Once again, the former president, President Campbell, has passed away this morning from reasons unknown. He was sixty years old."

The bartender, not a big fan of the former president, shrugs and returns to his large drink order. He places the last two drinks on the tray and arranges them for balance. "Here we go sir. All done," he exclaims proudly to the Panama hat man.

"Thanks."

"Are you sure I can't carry the drinks over to your friends?"

"That's all right. I've got it under control. I used to be a bartender in university back in the States," the man lies, but nobody will ever know, certainly not the bartender. Not that the bartender would care anyway, his end goal being a nice tip. The Panama hat man places five $100 bills on the counter.

The waiter looks down and acknowledges the generous tip with a big smile. It's more money than he will make in a regular week, and the Panama hat man knows this. "Thank you very much, sir. You are very generous!" He bows his head in appreciation.

"You're welcome," the Panama hat man replies, also smiling. He expertly picks up the tray of drinks. He turns toward the beach where an assortment of men and women sit on a dozen lawn chairs arranged in a circle.

He stops at the first chair to his left; he leans over and hands the first drink over to a woman lying comfortably on the chair. Her body and legs are tanned, not burnt, expertly managed by sunscreen.

She pulls up her designer sunglasses and smiles as she accepts it. "Why, aren't you the gentleman, bringing me a drink?" she exclaims. "And my favourite one, at that! How did you know?"

"I do my homework," he responds.

Amanda Chase flattens the crinkles on her long dark blue dress and adjusts her stance beside a familiar bar counter. Standing an arm's length from her is a casually dressed man. She swings her hand up toward the man's face and connects with his left cheek.

He stumbles back and loses his balance for a split second but is able to recover. He collects himself, sensing the slight sting on his cheek. "Not bad! But you need to cut your swing short and bring your arm up more from the waist, rather than from over your shoulder and back. He'll have less of a chance to react. It should seem more impulsive than planned."

"What about the head injury?"

"We'll practice that tomorrow."

"The symptoms?"

"The drug will manifest indications of a concussion for several days. The symptoms will fade over a short period of time, so whatever tests the hospital does, they need to be done rather quickly. The drug is completely harmless. No side effects."

Amanda nods.

"Anything else?"

"Nope."

"Good. I need to ice my cheek tonight." He rubs his cheek with the tips of his fingers, flinching.

Amanda gives him a devilish smile.

$$\oplus$$

"So, how's your head injury? Any more lingering symptoms?" the Panama hat man asks, trying to keep his focus on her eyes and nowhere else.

"Completely healed after a couple of days," she chuckles.

He pulls away and steps over to the person to the right lying quietly on the extended beach chair. A baseball cap with the New Jersey Devils logo covers his face from the sun.

"It is my time to serve you today!" the Panama hat man announces.

The man pulls off his cap, and the Panama hat man hands him a drink.

"Thank you." He grasps the drink, exposing an elaborate tattoo on the man's arm.

$$\oplus$$

Barney the bartender pulls out his cell phone from his back pocket to answer a call. "Go ahead."

"The meeting is set for ten tonight," the voice on the other end says.

"Everything is in place," Barney responds and hangs up. Cocking his head slightly, he peers over to the couple sitting at the end of the bar. He nods his head toward them. They do the same.

He turns to the attractive woman in a blue dress and gives her the same nod.

"We are a go."

She pushes away the drink she has been nursing, gets up, and walks around the corner out of sight.

The martini I'm going to serve is spiked with a concentrated dose of alcohol, Barney told Amanda during rehearsal. *Whatever you do, do not drink it. Evans won't be able to talk himself out of the smell on his clothes.*

Finally, the bartender grabs the attention of the front desk manager by arching his arm over his head, stretching. The desk manager spots the pre-planned gesture. No words are spoken, but the message is received. *No more rehearsals. This is for real!*

"Sorry, buddy, but I don't have any cash on me to tip you. Can I catch you later?" the tattooed man says.

"Don't worry. I'm good," proclaims the Panama hat man. He pulls away, still expertly balancing the tray of drinks, and slides over to the right to a couple sitting on a beach chair built for two.

The Panama hat man hands each of them a glass of champagne. The woman smiles. "You are such a gentleman."

"You're not the first to tell me that today. I can't let it go to my head."

The couple smiles.

"Officer, my husband and I were having a nice, quiet drink at the bar, minding our own business, when we heard voices behind us in an elevated manner," the woman says.

"An elevated manner?" the police officer asks.

"What my wife is trying to say is that the man and woman on the other side of the bar started yelling at each other. My wife is just being polite," the man clarifies.

"Yes, yelling," she confirms.

"So, what did you observe next?"

"Well," the woman pauses for a moment, catching her breath in all the excitement, "the man must have said something that she didn't particularly like, because all of a sudden, she slapped him straight across the face. It must have been a hard slap, because he stumbled back a few steps."

The man grins. "Oh, yeah! It looked like a hard one."

"Thank you for adjusting the bill," the man responds to Howard, the front desk manager.

"Have a pleasant trip home. We hope we'll see you back in our city soon," he responds.

The couple pick up their bags and head out of the hotel. The man points to the maintenance area to the far-right of the building. They walk over, pop open several of the garbage and recycle bins, and empty in the contents of their suitcases.

The man takes the empty suitcases, pulls out a folding pocket-knife and goes to work on disassembling the suitcases; shredding the top covers off, twisting off the plastic handles and ripping the inter lining out of each case.. He hands the suitcases to the woman, who expertly flips them into separate garbage bins.

The man flips the lids back over. Closed. He gives her a satisfied smile.

The Panama hat man offers the next drink to another man who sits up from his beach chair. He accepts the drink, a pint of Molson Canadian beer.

"I've been waiting for days to have this drink!" Howard exclaims. "I hate that watered-down American stuff."

$$\oplus$$

"It's a go. Start the security footage re-route." Howard types his text message and hits Send.

$$\oplus$$

Pablo Sanchez, sitting in front of his security monitors in his office at the hotel, receives the message and immediately re-routes the hotel security footage to a hidden directory.

$$\oplus$$

Howard smiles as Agent Shearing and Agent Sutcliff depart the hotel after their unsuccessful bid to acquire the hotel videos or to speak to Pablo Sanchez. He picks up his cell phone and texts a message: *Feds are gone. Video files have been picked up.*

$$\oplus$$

The Panama hat man crosses the path to another group of occupied beach chairs. The next person to receive a drink is a woman. She smiles as she accepts the drink.

"Your performance was Oscar worthy, my dear," the Panama hat man says.

"I want Angelina Jolie to play me in the movie version."

"Really? I've got nothing against Angelina, but I was thinking more along the lines of Rosamund Pike. Great actress!"

"Yeah, but she's British."

"She does a flawless American accent. You have to see her in *Gone Girl*. Amazing performance."

"Yeah, yeah! You've got a thing with women with sexy, scratchy voices. Demi and Rosamund to name a few!" she says with a chuckle.

"I will not argue with you!"

Susan Sanders, human resources manager for Commlink Services, walks into a small room with nothing but a square desk and two chairs. Howard sits in one of them.

"You ready to go through the conversation?" Howard asks.

Hesitantly, Susan responds, "Let's do it. I've memorized my talking points."

"And the recording device?"

"I'm impressed by the work that our people have done. It's totally embedded in the lining of my briefcase."

"Six different microphones so you don't need to worry how you position it," he responds.

"I'll activate the recording when I reach in to get a pen."

Susan sputters but responds nonetheless. "Yes, sir. I will notify you when everything is done and notify your assistant when I am done clearing out my office. I assume I will not need to apprise you on the second task?"

"You are correct on that account." He pauses and then waves his hands in dismissal.

Susan exits the board room, walks past the executive secretary, and rounds the corner, and heads to the bank of elevators, smiling.

⊕

Susan looks at her watch. One hour of playing solitaire on her laptop has passed.

"OK. Enough negotiating," she says to herself. "You drive a hard bargain, Mr. Dowds. Here is my final offer ... What! Too much, you say? I disagree. You deserve every penny that our company is willing to pay."

She pauses, pretending to listen to the imaginary Dowds. "OK, OK. I'll toss in another $5 million, but that's as high as I can go." She pauses again and then smiles. "You are welcome, Mr. Dowds."

Susan shuts the laptop, picks it up, and tosses it across her office. It hits the opposite wall and crashes to the ground in pieces.

"Settlement negotiations are complete." She leans back in her comfortable leather chair. She rubs the hand rests. "I'm going to miss you, comfy chair. You've been good to me."

⊕

The Panama hat man steps over to a man lying on the beach chair. With a hat shading his face, he doesn't see the Panama hat man standing over him.

A kick on the side of his chair startles him, and he sits up to get a view of man blocking him from the sun. "Hey!" he states, coming out of his afternoon nap.

"Drinks are served," the Panama hat man says as he hands Dowds a drink. "I'm glad you stuck around after the Old Port incident with the shooters."

"Well, that little talk afterwards put everything in perspective and answered some questions that Susan didn't want to fill me in on."

"Still, I saw your talents first-hand in the courtroom and boardrooms. I was aware of your sources, but you and your group have impressed me every step of the way."

"Thank you. By the way, Susan is amazing."

"That, she is!"

"Officer Belker, I am concerned about the safety of Mr. Evans," Dowds says. "Can you do something for me?"

"What exactly do you have in mind, Mr. Dowds?" Carl Belker asks.

Dowds hands him a large manila envelope from his briefcase. "All the instructions are in the envelope, along with compensation for all parties involved. You will understand once you read the note in the envelope. A package via courier will arrive addressed to you with the remaining materials."

"What exactly are you getting me into?"

"I would never jeopardize your career. I'm strictly looking after my client to make sure he gets to the courtroom in time. Please read the note and contact me if you have any further questions."

"OK. I am only doing this because I like Mr. Evans. There is something fishy about this whole case."

"There is something very fishy, but I believe that the truth will always set you free. Thanks again." Dowds turns away, walking out of the police station.

Carl heads back to his desk and sits down to read the instructions in the envelope.

Along with the instructions, Carl pulls out two bound packs of $100 bills.

He makes the changes to the prison cell chart. Carl then explains the plan to Eddie Mitchell, who will be in Larry's place. He hands over a protective vest to the inmate in case he is attacked. "The vest is designed and made of some sci-fi material that apparently will absorb 95 percent of a human punch. If it comes down to body blows, you should be good."

The inmate agrees to the deal and the compensation.

The door opens to a small room occupied by Benjamin Dowds. Susan Sanders walks in.

"Benjamin Dowds, nice to meet you," she states.

They shake hands.

"Now, Benjamin, we have studied your file and your work for the last while, both in the UK and back home in North America, and we think you are the perfect fit for our project. Your skills and resources fit in perfectly with our little project."

"I didn't know I had a file," he states, a little perplexed.

"My dear, everybody has a file," she says. "Now, the project is not short in duration. We forecast that it will take more than sixteen months to complete, and during this time, we will need your full dedication."

"That's a long period for a single client. You'd need to really open up your wallet for me to clear out my schedule for the next year and half, roughly."

"Mr. Dowds, upon this project's completion, there will be handsome payouts for all participants. You would never have to work another day in your life."

Dowds eyes widen at this statement. "OK, you've got my attention."

"Trust me when I say I had your attention and your answer even before you showed up at this meeting. I do my homework on the people I pick, and I do it very well. This meeting is just a formality." She smiles.

"You are very sure of yourself, Ms. Sanders."

"I am. I love my job, I do it very well, and I am compensated very well for the work I do. I can't complain."

"Good to know," Dowds replies.

"This project's success rests on protecting our people from any legal issues that might befall them," Sanders points out.

"Even if they are guilty?"

"Trust me, they won't be guilty."

"Are you sure about that?"

"We've done our homework. Many months of work. Our playbook is solid and covers all scenarios. We will even send you cases during dry spells to keep you focused on the endgame."

"Well, then, it seems you have everything covered," he says. "One more question: will I know which are the filler cases and which cases are related to the project?"

"Nope. I expect you to dedicate your energy equally to everything I or my associates send you. Are you comfortable with that?"

"I'm good."

"There's one more item I need to tell you before this is finalized."

"What is it?" he asks.

"The project comes with a certain level of risk that we have identified and accounted for, but I must warn you nonetheless."

"What type of risk, exactly?" he asks, concerned.

"Oh, the usual stuff. Kidnapping, murder, possibly hired assassins."

"Oh! OK. I'm in. I'm tired of my regular white-collar crime cases."

"Mr. Dowds, when I said I do my homework, I said I do my homework. Your legal abilities, as outstanding as they are, are not the only reason we want you on this project. My staff has documented your other skills, and I must say, they will complement the work we need you for."

"I see! Then I look forward to being part of the team," Dowds responds.

"Good. In the meantime, we'll provide you with whatever financing you need to keep your operations going as we gear up our operations. We'll also give you enough to wind down your current cases."

"That would require a substantial amount of funds."

She smiles. "We are well financed. Did I not mention that?"

"Good. Let's get started." Dowds smiles back.

The Panama hat man walks over to the next person. He is a little scruffy looking, his belly sticking out of the waist strap of his shorts. He's middle-aged with grey in his beard.

Chuck, the technical wizard of the group.

"Your brains and gadgets always amaze me," the Panama hat man says. "Thanks for a job well done." He hands him a pint of beer.

"Always glad to work with you," the man responds.

"It's time to send the audio files to the vice president," Susan announces over the phone to James.

"Will do, Susan," Chuck replies. "Shit is going to hit the fan when Chamberland calls an executive meeting."

"That's the plan."

"I'd love to be a fly in wall in that room."

"Yep."

Chuck pulls a small, metallic rectangular box from his desk drawer. He hands it over to Susan. "This will self-activate at the sound of the first voice and will continue recording for the next four straight hours. It's coded to not upload to a secure server until it's out of range of the White House perimeter in case surveillance is active. It's my finest work."

"Good, I'll give it to my contact," Susan says. "When the recording is done, I'll reach out to you to get the recording prepped for the next step. Thanks, James."

He raises his hand toward her. "Hand me your cell phone."

"Why?"

"Hand me your phone first!" he says.

Susan pulls it out from her back pocket and gives it to him.

He quickly and expertly taps away at the touch screen. "I'm installing a special program I wrote."

"What does it do?"

"First, you'll have to pass this on to the rest of the group. If any of you are compromised, the program will wipe any contact information and history pertaining to this operation."

Impressed, she asks, "How does the device go about doing this? How will it know if I'm compromised?"

"Well, that's a trade secret, but in a nutshell, it is a combination of biometrics, facial recognition, and typing patterns. Your cell phone will have foolproof protection against snooping eyes."

"Nice touch, Chuck!" she exclaims.

He pulls a sheet from his desk and hands it over to Susan. "Those are the instructions for the software. Get it done, and quickly."

"Thanks." She accepts the document, folds it in quarters, and pockets it.

Chuck, still sitting in his chair, looks up and smiles. "It's my pleasure, working for you guys again."

"Yeah, right. You just like the money. The job pays well."

"The job pays extremely well. I'll be able to retire after this."

"Retire! You're only, like, thirty-five!"

"Yeah, but it's a constant battle, keeping up with the latest tech and code. Too much out there to absorb. Too much happening too fast."

"OK, I hear you, but I bet if the big guy comes calling for another job, you won't say no."

"Hell, no. If the boss calls, I'll be there." He laughs.

She, in turn, starts to chuckle.

Bernie Andrews, White House aide to the president, walks to the opposite side of the Oval Office, his right hand in his side jacket pocket. He cradles a small metallic box with a glowing green LED light on the top side of the box and lets it go, focusing on President Campbell.

"And honestly, the American public will eat it up. They're a bunch of sheep. They need to be led. They need to be defended from the outside world and it is a cruel world. I am their shepherd. A shepherd to three hundred million dumbass, idiotic creatures who can't either think or protect themselves I'll guide them to prosperity. Just look at the economic numbers, employment numbers. It has never been this good."

In unison, the other attendees start clapping.

Bernie Andrews accepts a drink from the Panama hat man.

"Thanks, Bernie, for your dedication to this job. I'm pretty sure that with the former president out of the picture, people will lose interest in who recorded his demise. Unless the lunatic conspiracy-theory knuckle heads never give up."

"Yeah. You're right. Can't count them out." Bernie states. "But in the end, I'm out and comfortably retired, thanks to you."

The Panama hat man hands the last drink on the tray to Alexandra, the special-ops team leader. She reaches up and accepts a drink. Her tanned muscular legs and arms are evidence of years of training and combat missions.

"Thank you for your dedication and for being the only person to take a bullet for the team—even though it was a rubber bullet," he declares.

"It stung for about week and left a nice welt. It's still noticeable," she states.

Alexandra walks toward the Bombardier C-143 jet parked in the enclosed hangar. A dark green duffle is slung over her shoulder.

She punches a memorized number into her cell phone. "Dowds, we're a go for the extraction mission. Arriving in Saint-Hubert International Airport just outside of Montreal tomorrow. I'll text you all the details on a secured link. Make sure to use only rubber bullets, as none my people coming off the plane will be locked and loaded with live ammo."

"No worries, I'll reach out to my contacts at the RCMP and get the ball rolling," states Dowds.

Having handed out all the drinks, the Panama hat man steps aside while a waiter carries a silver tray full of envelopes to every individual in the group.

"Enjoy the compensation in the envelopes," the Panama hat man says. "Instructions to retrieve the monies are enclosed. You all deserve this. You can quietly disappear into the night and never look back." He raises his glass and toasts them. "Thank you all. Job well done."

In return, they all smile and acknowledge each other on their work.

The Panama hat man removes his shades and smiles.

Late summer evening in Miami, Larry Evans sits at the edge of a bar at the Cape restaurant, one of many such establishments near Miami Beach. The restaurant offers a rooftop terrace for its clientele to relax and enjoy the cool breeze and active night-time scene that Miami has to offer. A quick rain shower had forced the rooftop patrons to quickly gather their drinks and hustle down into the main floor where they easily resumed their socializing without so much as missing a beat. The dimmed lighting overhead offered little help in making out any distinguishing features of the people around him but this doesn't bother him too much. His contact would find him.

Larry reached over on to the bar surface to pull back his Panama hat closer to him as the empty spaces around him were quickly filling up.

He continues to pull on a gold band on his right ringer finger while nursing his drink to idle away the time when a man wearing a dark blue raincoat with a matching fedora approaches him. He carries a rolled-up umbrella.

Larry looks down at his watch. *Just in time.*

Larry turns to face him and smiles. "Has it stopped raining outside?"

"The rain has let up, but it won't for long."

Correct answer.

"I have a job for you. My sources say you're the best man for the job. I represent someone who would very much like to meet you."

DAY ONE HUNDRED — GOODBYE, EMILY LEWIS

———

Emily Lewis walks back to her desk with a bottle of Pepsi from the soda machine, placing it beside an empty one and her laptop. Alt-Ctrl-Del, and her computer is unlocked.

An email notification appears on the ribbon bar. She double-clicks it, and the email browser blows up to full screen. Emily eyes widen with excitement when she notices the name of the sender: Maggie Summers. Without hesitation, she opens the email, spots the attachment and clicks on.

Dear Emily,

I hope you're doing well and in good health. It's been almost three months since I last saw your contagious smile. It was a hard decision, but it was the right one to leave Springvale. The thought of what you went through that night knocked me out of my senses, and I panicked for my safety. I've kept track of your news articles for the last few months. Keep rocking it sister!

I know James promised both of us raises and paid vacations a while ago, but in case he reneged on the promise, I have included a link to an electronic transfer that should take care of all your future raises. I came into some money recently, and I wanted to share a part of it with you. I learned a lot from you and consider you a friend. What better way to show my appreciation for you, then for you to have a drink on me on a sandy beach under an umbrella in the tropical islands? Enjoy.

Miss you dreadfully,
Maggie

Emily wipes away a tear before clicking on the attachment. The electronic transfer pops open to reveal an official page from the Bank of America. On the bottom, $750,000 is displayed.

Her eyes expand. "Are you kidding me?" she whispers and starts giggling. She pauses and raises her head over the top of her screen to scan the office floor; nobody heard her.

She relaxes back into her chair. Clicking on the confirmation button, she completes the transfer. Within seconds, a text notification appears on her phone. She picks it up; the $750,000 appears. Emily giggles again. "Thanks, buddy," she whispers.

DAY ONE HUNDRED — GOODBYE, CARL BELKER, AND THANKS

———

The Purolator truck pulls in front of a small cottage with a sloped roof. The courier gets out of the truck on the passenger side, walks up the stone walkway, and rings the bell.

Within seconds, a face peeks through the curtains. Carl Belker looks at the courier. The courier raises a package. With his other hand, he asks for a signature.

Carl pulls back from the window and unlocks the door.

"Mr. Belker, can you please sign for this letter?" The courier hands him the electronic pad, and Carl does his best signature with the stylus. The courier hands over the package. "Thank you, sir, and have a good day."

Carl closes the door behind him and walks into his living room. He scrutinizes the package and notices the label. It's from Dowds and Associates in Montreal. A look of bewilderment crosses his face. He doesn't recall knowing anybody from Montreal.

Carl tears open the package and pulls out a letter. He peals back the envelope flap carefully and pulls out a folded letter. He unfolds it and starts reading.

Notification of settlement:

Carl Belker versus Horizon Garden State Health Services.

Notification of settlement in the sum of $7,750,000 to be paid to Carl Belker for the wrongful diagnosis leading to the death of Julia Belker.

Dowds and Associates, attorneys representing Carl Belker. Services retained by Larry Evans, Montreal, Canada.

Carl is speechless upon seeing Larry's name at the bottom. He looks around his room, in the dark on how to react, what to do or say. There is nobody to see him react. Nobody to talk to. He rereads the letter to make sure it isn't a joke. He turns over the letter to find the attached certified check.

"Fuck, Larry, what did you go and do?" Carl starts laughing.

DAY ONE HUNDRED —
GOODBYE, RONALD SLATER

—

Ronald Slater returns to his hotel room after a busy day of chasing down more leads on the missing eyewitnesses. Like Amanda Chase, they are the key to shedding some much-needed light on the case that has claimed many people's careers and livelihoods.

The mayor of Springvale is now in jail, along with Police Commissioner Maco and several of his police officers who partook in a late-night misinformed attack on a person in the Springvale jail.

Additionally, multiple administrators at different levels of the municipal hierarchy have lost their jobs for attacking Larry Evans on social media.

At the hotel where the event took place, the front desk manager and bartender were similarly dismissed after the surveillance tape surfaced, clearly contradicting their accounts of the assault. The regional directors cleaned out the hotel management for failing to handle the incident and letting it spiral into a social media circus.

Larry Evans's former employer lost a wrongful-dismissal case that, according to some circles, is estimated to have cost them $60 million.

The final blow has been the fall of the president of the United States along with the second, third, and fourth in the line of succession, leaving the first African American woman as the president.

What a wicked chain of events this has evolved into, Slater thinks. *All these separate pieces in a giant jigsaw puzzle.* He thought they were unrelated at first, but after many hours of reviewing the pieces, he isn't so sure anymore. His unkempt hair, several days of facial-hair growth, and the pizza stains on his worn-out T-shirt indicate many hours of focused determination, hours leading to a conclusion that's starting to scare him. His outings from his hotel room in the last few days have been few and far between.

The first knock at the door goes unnoticed as Slater hunches in his chair, staring at his laptop screen; he's turned down numerous offers from the hotel cleaning staff to provide him with clean sheets and fresh towels.

The second knock startles him. He glances over to the door, waiting to see if it continues. It does. Slater pushes back his chair, walks to the door, and peers through the peephole: a hotel staff member standing at the door with a large package. Slater opens the door.

"Sir, package for you," the hotel staff explains.

Slater accepts the package. "Thanks." The staffer nods, turns away and heads down the corridor to the elevator.

Slater closes the door behind him. He rips open the package, pulling out what seems like a nice but worn leather-bound agenda. He turns it over and notices the writing on the front cover: "Yearbook 1991, Lester B. Pearson High School."

Slater smiles and walks over to the desk, pushes his laptop aside, and opens the yearbook. He flips through a dozen pages, back and forth, searching. He stops at a page with four class pictures, two on each page. Examines the first, disregards it. Scans the one below it and smiles.

He scans the list of students underneath. Finds Larry Evans. Row one, fourth person from the left. He's obviously much younger, but he's definitely the forty-six-year-old Larry Evans of today.

Slater grins at his discovery and returns to the list of students in Larry's class picture. No name stands out in the first row. He starts with the second row. Nothing. Third and final row. Amanda Cummings, nope. Walter Abrams, nope. Joe Calcio, nope. Bernie Andrews, nope.

Wait. That name rings a bell. Isn't that one of the ex-president's senior aides? He finds Bernie Andrews's class picture. Slater's grin falls, and he turns pale with shock and disbelief.

He leans over to his laptop and types Bernie Andrews's name into a search engine. A dozens of hits, in order of importance, quickly flood his screen. Slater searches for images instead. He scrolls through in search of a younger version of Bernie. He passes easily forty pictures before he comes to a stop. In front of him is the same class picture of Bernie and Larry.

"Fuck m—"

Two high-calibre bullets pierce two small holes in the window.

They're much bigger in Slater. The first one hits the target head on—literally.

"Target is down. Move," a sniper says from two hundred metres away, several floors up in an adjacent tower. He places his rifle down and picks up a cell phone. "Target is down. Cleanup crews are entering the room now. He found the connection, from what I see on his laptop and yearbook."

"Good; report back when the scene has been sanitized."

Back in the hotel room, four people stream inside, pushing laundry baskets on wheels. All are dressed in hotel uniforms. They quickly gather Ronald Slater's personal items and toss them into the laundry baskets.

Behind them, four more members dressed as utility personnel walk in. Two carry a window panel to replace the damaged one. The other two roll out a large plastic drop sheet and place the body onto it. The well-orchestrated cleanup is done in under ten minutes, removing all evidence.

"Team is out," the sniper says to the man at the other end of the line. A man in a Panama hat who stands on warm sand with clear blue skies overhead. In front of him, his party exchanges salutations to a job well done.

"Thank you for the update," he says. "Now, get your ass down here. The champagne won't stay cold all day. Be on the first flight out. Be here tonight."

"Bye." The sniper hangs up, flips the phone over, pries open the back cover and pulls out the battery. He then proceeds to smash the phone into multiple pieces.

The man on the beach opens up another screen to a video call with President Chloe Williams. "You heard the conversation?"

"I did," she replies.

"All loose ends are tied."

"How about your people?"

"They came through this spectacularly. After almost two years of planning down to the last details . . . mission accomplished. I hope you are happy with the results?"

She smiles. "Extremely, Mr. Evans. Extremely."

"Yes, Mr. Vice-President, what can I do for you?"

"Do you know what that fucking idiot did?"

"Calm down, Randolph, and start from the beginning," Chloe Williams states.

"Campbell sent a hit squad, led by Jason Stands, into Canada to eliminate Larry Evans about a month ago. Problem is, they were all arrested for possessing major illegal weapons and are facing life sentences. The RCMP has them all locked up. They'll never step foot in the USA again. Do you believe this shit?" Chamberland states.

"Randolph, get a grip on yourself. This has gone too far. You need to put an end to this, and you need to do it right away. Call a meeting of the Executive Committee tomorrow morning to iron this out. Campbell is done. The presidency cannot survive this. Make the call, Randolph. I will be waiting for the news."

"Thank you, Ms. Williams." He hangs up.

Chloe Williams picks up her phone and dials a number that few people have access to.

The phone rings twice before the person on the other line picks up.

"Sir," Chloe says, "the vice president is aware of the Jason Stands disaster and will be coming for you with guns blazing tomorrow. Do you have everything in order?"

"Yes, everything is in order," he says. "Thanks." He hangs up.

"By the way, that little stunt in Montreal has your fingerprints all over it," Larry says.

"Mr. Evans, it's only business," President Williams responds. *Damn! I lost my best operative in Potts on that mission.* "I needed to make sure all my bases were covered. That's all."

"By trying to eliminate me!" Larry responds. "That wasn't cool! That's not going to work for me, and it won't work for you either. Do you know why?"

"Why is that, Mr. Evans?" she replies in a calm manner.

"I have your playbook. I have your notes. Our meetings and conversations have been recorded even if your scanners haven't pick up my equipment. I would highly recommend you not pull that stunt on me again. The fallback would be immense and quick. Not just for you, but your backers also. That impressive group of yours that meets at the Fairmont in New York on the first Tuesday of every month? They go down also. You see, Madame President, I have two years' worth of recordings of their group meetings, agendas, actions taken and the names all the associates that your group has been involved with. That is all in my playbook. All that information would be released. So if we are taking about play-books, mine's is ready, and it won't take two years to execute. I'm just saying."

President Williams pauses. "Mr. Evans. I will update the group on your proposal and will abide by your statement going forward," she responds, her voice cracking in surprise.

"I am not finished. Your little stunt, even though it failed, can't be brushed aside without any consequences on your end."

"Do tell, Mr. Evans. What do you have planned for me?"

"Not specifically you, but one of the members of that secret society of yours will need to take the fall," Larry says, his demeanor taking on a dark and serious tone. "I won't tell you who or when, but suffice to say, it will be career-ending, and depending on how he or she handles it, life-ending."

"Before you go making statements like that, Mr. Evans, consider who you are dealing with. Do not underestimate our resources and resolve."

"I think the question is better directed at you and your band of eleven co-conspirators," Larry states. "You see, I have intimate knowledge of every single one of them. I know what makes them tick. Their personal history, their detailed financial status, and for some of them, what gets them off. I've got to admit, some of your partners are into some pretty kinky, fucked-up stuff."

"So, what do want from me?" President Williams asks, retreating.

"Simple. Just pass on the message to your group at your next meeting. I think it will be in their best interest to put this whole episode behind us. Do you not agree?"

President Williams pauses again. "Yes. Let's do that."

"Well, if that is all, it was nice knowing you, but we will never talk again after I hang up. You won't find me or any member of my team in the future."

"You are funny, Mr. Evans. I have the NSA and the CIA at my disposal. I'm pretty sure they'll be able to find you. Remember, the eyes in the sky are everywhere. Especially when they're staring down at a house in the Upper East Side of New York City. That's where you are right now, isn't it?"

Larry looks around the beach with the white sands, lawn chairs, and tropical trees. "Yes. You got me. You got me good. Your guys are good. I guess you've been tracing this call from the get-go."

"Like I said, I have the NSA and CIA at my disposal along with a few others that can trace the location of anybody I want," President Williams states.

"Never be too confident. It could be your undoing. It was for your predecessors! As for your intel agencies, they are amateurs. My people and resources are much better." Larry laughs.

"Do you want to wager on that?" Williams responds, grinning at the potential challenge.

"OK, if my team and I avoid your one-hundred-thousand-plus agents, drones, and satellites for the next ten days, then you pay us double the amount you paid us for this job," Larry announces.

"Hmmm. A billion dollars. I can do that. If I win and I track either you or even one member of your group, then you come to work on another deal that is a little more time sensitive."

"How about this? If you don't find me within the next forty-eight hours, you dish out another billion dollars. I'll take your job, but the price will be double the current one. Don't worry; I know you're good for it. Just a drop in the bucket of your black-ops program budget. Nobody will notice. Actually, if I understand it correctly, the Defence Appropriation committees only sees the total budget amount. No line item amounts, so basically you can easily hide these payouts without anybody questioning it. Your predecessor spent a lot more on bad decisions from my data. By the way, say hi to Jack for me," Larry states.

"It's a deal. The clock starts—"

Larry disconnects before she can conclude her statement. He pulls out the backing on the phone and pulls out the battery. Pulls out the SIM card. Cracks them in pieces and deposits them in trash bins on the way back to the beach to join the festivities.

In the president's residence, Chloe Williams picks up another cell phone on the glass table in front of her and presses an icon on the main screen.

Within seconds, the sound of a man's voice comes on.

"Did the trace complete?" she asks. "Where is he?"

The voice responds, "The trace is completed, but I don't think he's there."

"What do you mean? Who lives there?"

"The head of the DSNY."

"DSNY?"

"The Department of Sanitation for New York," he responds.

President Chloe Williams contemplates this for a moment. She shakes her head in disappointment. "The trace was garbage. That's what he was trying to tell us. He knew the call was being tracked. Damn," she exclaims in frustration. She hangs up the call without saying anything further.

Damn! This did not go as I planned! Clearly, she is a little shaken, clenching here palms. She has always prided herself on being ahead of the game.

Larry Evans knows so much about the Fairmont meetings. This is not good news. I'll need to make the group aware that he knows about their existence. She is a little nervous about their reaction; being the president of the most powerful country in the world is secondary to responding to them.

She breaks out of her mini-trance and looks at the cell phone. There's nothing she can do at the moment, so she pulls out the battery from the back of the phone. With a manicured nail, she pries open the SIM card slot, pops out the SIM card, and places it on the coffee table in front of her.

A man walks in from the adjacent room. He strides over to Chloe, who is still sitting on the leather couch. He leans over and kisses her on the lips. They both smile.

"So! Is it over?" Jack Sully asks.

"It is. All done."

He looks over to the coffee table with the phone and its parts. "Do you want me to destroy that one also?" he asks.

"Yes, please, honey, and then meet me in bed." She smiles seductively.

Jack pulls back, grabs the phone and its disassembled parts, and hurries over to the kitchen's industrial strength garburator. Within seconds, the crunching sound of hard plastic and thin metal being chewed up echoes into the living room section of the White House residence.

Chloe smiles as she gets up from the couch and walks to the bedroom.

THREE YEARS AGO —
BACK WHERE WE STARTED

———

Larry Evans sits at a small table across from Chloe Williams, MaryAnn Lewis, Maggie Summers, and Susan Sanders. The corner area of the warehouse, just outside several windowless offices was designed as a common area for the staff eating area. A wooden counter against the wall held several microwave ovens, a sink, dishwasher on one end and a double door fridge on the opposite side.

Chloe addresses the group, "Thank you, everybody, for this meeting." She turns to face Larry. "Mr. Evans, you and your group come highly recommended from my associates. I assume you have read over the high-level plan that we presented to you," she says, referencing the document on the table. "Do you have any questions for us?"

"Yeah, my team and I have spent the last few weeks digesting the material. Your work is pretty thorough, and I'm pretty sure you know what the first one will be," he says.

"Yes, once this job is over, and it comes to its intended conclusion, you'll be the most famous person to go up against a sitting president and bring him down," Chloe says. "You might even say infamous, as this will probably be your last job. The payout will be substantial enough for you to live on very comfortably for the rest of your life."

"There is no probably about this. It is a definite that it will be our swan song, for both myself *and* my team, three of which are sitting at this table tonight," Larry says. "We've done a lot of work together, and I trust them with my life."

"Our trust in you and your team is of paramount importance to us," Chloe says, "as I re-iterate that my associates have very deep pockets. The financing of the project is the least of my worries."

"Are we ever going to meet your associates, Ms. Williams?" Larry asks.

Without batting an eye, she responds, "No, but rest assured that all communications I have with you and your group will be relayed back to them, and we are aligned on all the aspects of the project."

"Good. The timeline of this project will not be short, so I hope you and your associates have the patience to see it through," Larry states.

"Mr. Evans, as you get to know me better, you'll find I do my homework very thoroughly before I proceed with anything. As for our joint venture, I don't see it being completed any time short of sixteen to twenty months after its kick-off date. What I've given you in this document is the canvas and the paints; you have the brushes and the palette. Mix everything together and make a masterpiece out of it." Chloe smiles.

"That's all fine, as long as you don't touch the canvas and don't play with my brushes."

"Don't worry. I have full confidence in you, Mr. Evans."

"Thanks. And by the way, this is the last time we will ever see you. Have a good day, Ms. Williams."

On cue, Chloe stands, smiles at the four of them, leaves the table, and proceeds out the door.

Larry waits until Chloe is gone before he speaks. "Howard, Pablo, Bernie, you can come in now."

The door to the adjacent room opens, and three men step into the room.

They all assemble around Larry. "This is the big one. You've all been asking when the time is to pack it in. Well, after this one, we'll be done."

The group claps in delight.

"Thanks, but that date is a little far into the future, and we have a lot to do."

Susan is the first to speak. "Where is the kick-off place?"

"Springvale, New Jersey. Howard, Bernie, Pablo, you guys are at the Springvale Starline Hotel.

The three guys nod their heads.

Susan, I need you for your HR set-up at a company called Commlink Services in Montreal. I'll be applying for a position there in a few months as a salesperson. I'll build up a list of fake clients to build up my creds."

"Maggie, you have the media side. Manage the *Springvale Journal*; feed the media frenzy to get gossip engines going. I have a list of people you want to entice. MaryAnn, you get the fun job— you're now Detective Lewis."

MaryAnn smiles.

"Reach out to your support groups, and let's nail down the details in the next month," Larry says. "We need full, detailed bios for everybody that will pass the harshest NSA scrutiny. Everybody," Larry says, surveying the group, "needs to be fully invested in their identities. No mistakes!"

"Understood," MaryAnn responds.

"How about the attorney?" Larry asks. "We need a good one. Any ideas?"

"Yeah, I have just the person," MaryAnn says. "Benjamin Dowds. Solid, smart, very resourceful, both legally and otherwise.

I've been tracking him for the last six months along with several others just in case we ever needed this type of asset."

"OK, put him on the review board along with Amanda and Arnold," Larry states.

"Do we fold him into the 'know?'" Maggie asks.

Larry contemplates this. "We will need to figure that out. The tighter the circle of knowledge, the better." Larry looks over the group. "I consider you all to be part of my family. We've done a lot of work together. Some of it has even been good."

The group chuckles.

"But this one will be our defining moment." Larry picks up a glass from the table, and they follow suit. "To family," he proclaims.

They all raise their glasses and salute him.

DAY ONE HUNDRED AND ONE — THE FAIRMONT GROUP MEETING

———

President Chloe Williams calls an emergency meeting at the Waldorf-Astoria hotel in Chicago. Since it has been used for previous presidential meetings, security protocols are quick to put in place.

By arriving at Chicago's O'Hare Airport in a smaller aircraft than the traditional Air Force One plane, it's easier for her to avoid any curious onlookers. The early morning departure from the White House and the arrival in Chicago is off the books. She travels with a fraction of the substantial Secret Service detail that usually accompanies a president. The motorcade itself is scaled back to four large SUVs with darkened windows and high-grade bulletproof armoured plating.

The government aircraft arrives just after eight in the morning and taxies into a hangar on one end of the airport. The plane enters the hangar and comes to a full stop. The large hangar doors close, and the security detail pulls back slowly into the inside of the hangar.

With the area secured, the lead Secret Service agent relays the information to his counterpart in the plane. "POTUS is cleared to exit Air Force One."

Seconds later, the main airplane door opens, and several members of the president's travelling detail exit the plane. The SUV engines turn on in unison. The president follows her security detail out of the plane, down the stairs, and into an armoured vehicle.

On cue, the hangar doors open, and the SUV motorcade accelerates out of the hangar.

The ride to the Waldorf-Astoria is quick and uneventful. The underground commercial garage doors behind the hotel are open when the motorcade pulls in, not missing a beat.

Several police officers and Secret Service agents patrol the outside area. Other security officials patrol the underground parking lot.

The elevator delivers the president, along with her immediate security detail, to the fourth floor with a conference room. Two well-dressed men stand in front of the double wood-panelled doors with communication earpieces in place, pistols concealed within their jackets. They open the doors when the president is within a dozen feet.

The president walks through the entrance without slowing down.

The room is simple in design and furnishings, a contradiction to the elegance of the rest of the historic hotel. Twelve chairs, eleven of which are occupied by men, surround a circular table.

President Williams walks to the unoccupied chair, pulls it back, and collapses into it. No member stands to acknowledge her—a sign of disrespect for the presidency or a sign of her minor position within of the group.

"You're late, Chloe!" declares an older man directly across the table. He is well dressed in a suit that matches the grey in his short-trimmed hair.

"Traffic was a bitch. Sue me!" President Williams shoots back, not in a good mood.

"You called this meeting. An emergency meeting, something we've never had to do in all the years that this group has existed," the man says. "You broke protocol. You've put the security of this group in danger."

"This couldn't wait for our next scheduled meeting. I couldn't send what I have through our communication network, as I believe it's been compromised."

"Bullshit! Our communications, security procedures, and protocols are the best in the world, and they're what have kept this group's presence unknown to everybody outside this room. Our influence on this country's and the world's future has never been greater. We can't let our feet off the gas pedal now. Acquiring the presidency was just the first stage in our plan."

"Mr. Chairman, I fully understand the end goal," the president announces. "Unfortunately, we have an urgent issue that is more pressing and needs our immediate attention. Everything must stop until this issue is resolved."

"What do you mean, everything? We can't do that. What is the problem?" the member to the left of the chairman says.

"Mr. Chairman, Mr. Vice-Chairman, Larry Evans is aware our group's existence. He knows everything about this group. He is an immediate threat to our agenda."

"Chloe, you have at your disposal the full resources of the NSA, CIA, FBI, and half a dozen other intelligence agencies that can find him and make him disappear. If you can't, then I'll call my boys to take care of it," the chairman responds in a condescending tone.

"It's not that easy."

"Explain yourself, Chloe," the chairman says. "It sounds like you're not telling us everything."

Agitated by his tone, President Williams stands up and points her finger at him. "You will show me some respect. I am the president of the United States. You will address me as Madame President."

"Sit down and shut up, Chloe," states the chairman. "I will address you as I see fit. Do not question me! Do you hear me?"

President Williams pauses, slowly looks around the table. Quiet, emotionless faces stare back at her. She sits down and remains quiet.

"Now, Ms. Williams, please explain why it isn't easy to dispose of Mr. Evans."

"As I mentioned before, Mr. Evans knows everything about us. He has managed to make or obtain recordings of all our meetings going back several years—almost back to when we made our first contact with him. He has our playbook. He claims that any attempt against him or any member of his team will lead to the immediate exposure of our group."

The chairman shakes his head, his hands clenched. "Impossible! It can't be. I don't believe you. I just don't believe it."

"Those are the facts, and we can't change them. We have underestimated his determination to stay one step ahead of us."

"Do you believe him? Do you think he would expose us, knowing full well that he would be a dead man regardless of the outcome?"

President Williams clears her throat. "Larry Evans has proven himself to be very resourceful. More than I originally gave him credit for. He came highly recommended." She pauses. "Maybe I should have vetted the people who recommended him." She glances around the table at the solemn faces staring back at her. "This one's on me. I own that. Nevertheless, the threat is real."

"I ask again, Ms. Williams, do you think he would expose us?" the chairman asks.

"I do. He's made it abundantly clear that his continued silence is contingent on his continued heartbeat."

"Well, you know what they say. If you can't beat them, join them. Is he willing to come aboard?" the chairman asks in a reserved manner, his face flushed, frustration setting in slowly.

"Larry Evans be a part of this group?" she asks, taken aback.

"Why not!" the chairman responds. "He's a team player, at least with his group. Why can't he also be a member of our team?"

"That will never happen," President Williams responds with confidence.

"Why?"

"He doesn't trust me."

"Why is that Ms. Williams?" the vice-chairman asks. "What gives you that indication?"

"Well, about two months ago, while the operation was winding down and all loose ends were being cleared up—"

"You tried to dispose of him!" the chairman interrupts.

She hesitates. "Yes. It went badly. Very badly."

"How badly?"

"We lost Marshall Potts in that operation. That's how badly. So, like I said, we cannot underestimate Mr. Evans's resolve if we go after him."

"And his group?" the vice-chairman asks.

"Yes, he seems to be very attached to them."

"How about Dowds?" the chairman asks.

"Yes, I would include him in his band of merry men and women."

The chairman slowly gauges the pulse of the group around the table. Dejected looks all around. But there are still glimmers of hope for the final battle.

"We will need to review this Evans affair further," the chairman advises the group. "In the meantime, we'll cease all activities for the next seventy-two hours until Ms. Williams has further conversations with Mr. Evans about his career path."

"Yeah, that's going to be a problem," she states.

"Why, Ms. Williams?" the chairman asks.

"We lost track of where he is. My boys can't find him anywhere."

"What the fuck! Are you kidding me?" the chairman yells. "You have a $200 billion annual budget for surveillance, and you can't track down one man?"

"That is correct."

"You have seventy-two hours to find him, Ms. Williams. This is definitely on you. You own this!"

"Yes, Mr. Chairman," she murmurs nervously.

"Are we done, Ms. Williams?" the chairman asks.

"There is one more matter I need to bring up to the council today."

"Go on," the chairman responds.

"Mr. Evans wasn't too pleased with my attempt to terminate him."

"Continue."

"He stated that in no uncertain terms that because of my failed attempt on his life, somebody here has to take the fall."

"Who?" asks the chairman.

"He didn't say which one of us he'll be targeting, nor did he say when this will happen."

"How serious is the threat, Ms. Williams?" one of the silent members to the right of the chairman asks.

"Based on what he said about some of our members' unusual habits, I consider it very serious. In his words, 'somebody, soon, will need to take the fall.'"

"I suggest all members beef up their security and go into lockdown for the next little while," the chairman says. "No further communications of any sort until I allow it. Is that understood?" The chairman surveys the members again. They all nod in agreement.

"Meeting adjourned," the chairman states as he pushes his chair back, stands up, and walks to the doors.

The remaining members of the group follow his lead, keeping a healthy distance from the chairman, who might explode at them also.

Back on Saint Lucia, Larry Evans turns off his live video feed from the completed meeting. He smiles. "Let the chase begin."

The End

CHARACTERS

Alexandra — a black-ops leader

Amanda Chase — the woman in the blue dress

Arthur MacEvoy — a security man under Benjamin Dowds

Arthur Randle — the lead attorney for Commlink Services

Assistant Commissioner Albert Burrows — the Springvale Police assistant commissioner

Barney — the bartender at the Springvale Starline Hotel

Benjamin Dowds — a lawyer at Dowds and Associates

Bernie Andrews — a White House aide after Henry Mood quits

Captain Paul Henderson — an New Jersey State Police officer

Carl Belker — a duty officer at the Springvale Police Station

Carla Di Rienzo — the managing editor of the *Newark Journal*

Carson Days — a security man for Benjamin Dowds

Chief Superintendent André Boucher — RCMP officer

Chloe Williams — the attorney general

Chris Maxwell — the secretary of the Interior

Daniel Esposito — a senior adviser to the president

Detective MaryAnn Lewis — a police detective in New Jersey

Dolores Walker — Benjamin Dowds's secretary

Donald — one of Mayor Frakes's assistants

Dr. Phil Norton — a senior adviser to the president

Emily Lewis — a *Springvale Journal* reporter

Hendrik Vinke — a Dutch businessperson Benjamin Dowds represents

Henry Mood — a senior adviser to the president

Holly Waldon — the Springvale Starline Hotel's regional director

Howard Johnson — the evening front desk manager at the Springvale Starline Hotel

Jack Sully — the chief of staff under President Williams

James Marsala — the managing editor of the *Springvale Journal*

Jane Philips — the secretary of state

Janice Connors — Susan Sanders's assistant

Jason Stands — a senior adviser to the president

Jerry Garcia — the senior Secret Service agent in charge of White House security

Joanna Strauss — a guardian to the executives at Commlink Services

Judge Clarence Lerno — a judge in Springvale

Larry Evans — a sales rep for Commlink Services

Leo Caldwell — a senior adviser to the president

Maggie Summers — a *Springvale Journal* reporter

Mark Deerson — a senior adviser to the president

Marshall Potts — a black-ops agent

Matt Devlin — the secretary of defence

Mayor Jonas Frakes — the mayor of Springvale

Mr. Arnold — a senior official of the city of Springvale

Mr. and Mrs. Jeffrey — a couple staying at the Springvale Starline Hotel

Nurse Pearson — a nurse at Summit Oaks Hospital

Officer Batista — a police officer reporting to Police Commissioner Maco

Officer Michael Winters — a police officer at the Springvale Police Department

Officer Scarborough — a police officer reporting to Police Commissioner Maco

Pablo Sanchez — the security manager of the Springvale Starline Hotel

Patrick Malone — a security man under Benjamin Dowds

Police Commissioner Maco — a Springvale Police commissioner

President Franklin Campbell

Randall McGregor — a former SAS of the British Army

Reid Beckett — a security guard at the Springvale Starline Hotel

Robert Decker — the head of security at the Springvale Starline Hotel

Robert Vines — the night duty officer at the Springvale Police Station

Ronald Slater — a reporter for the *Newark Sentinel*

Sidney "Sid" Casper — the treasury secretary

Special Agent Anthony Sutcliff — an FBI agent

Special Agent Marco Shearing — an FBI agent

Susan Sanders — the human resources manager at Commlink Services

Thomas Albert Jr. — the lead prosecuting attorney on the case against Larry Evans

Thomas Roundtree — an accountant at Commlink Services

Vice-President Randolph Chamberland

Walter M. Redman — the chairman of the Commlink Services Executive Board

ACKNOWLEDGEMENTS

—

First, I want to acknowledge and thank my wife and partner, Monica, for supporting and encouraging me from day one to follow my dreams of writing this novel. Her enthusiasm gave me the courage and confidence to complete this work. Her numerous reviews of the material and late-night discussions helped me shape the end product.

Next, thanks to my daughter, Caitlind, who took the first deep dive into the manuscript, provided me with some medical pointers, and helped me cleanup of some of my long-winded sentences. Her encouragement and thumbs-up on the final result was a great vote of confidence.

Special thanks to all my siblings (Giannina, Tiziano, Daniel and Eros) for providing feedback during the edit reviews and never-ending encouragement to completing this project.

Additionally, thanks to my wife's uncle Dave McMechan for spotting some continuity issues during his read-through and to Francis Springer, a long-time friend and co-worker whom I reached out to for his opinion.

Finally, thanks to the team at Friesen Press for the great work in helping put together my novel. I learnt a lot and it will only make me a better writer.

CPSIA information can be obtained
at www.ICGtesting.com
Printed in the USA
LVHW052154150921
697902LV00001B/6